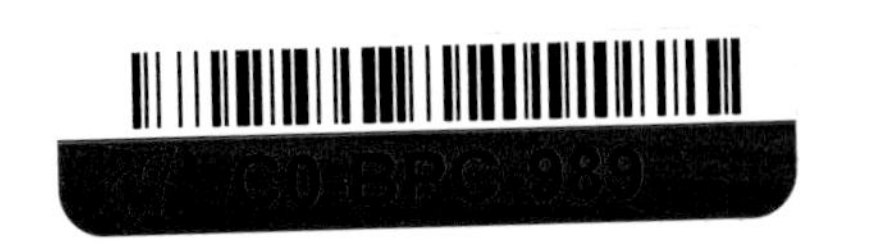

# QUANTUM TIMES

First Edition Design Publishing

**Quantum Times**



ISBN 978-1622-879-74-8 PRINT
ISBN 978-1622-879-75-5 EBOOK

LCCN 2015946447

July 2015

Published and Distributed by
First Edition Design Publishing, Inc.
P.O. Box 20217, Sarasota, FL 34276-3217
www.firsteditiondesignpublishing.com

*This Book is dedicated to Sarah*
*For so many reasons!*

"Quantum mechanics is stunningly successful. Not a single prediction of the theory has ever been wrong....However, quantum mechanics also displays an enigma. It tells us that physical reality is created by observation, and it has 'spooky actions' instantaneously influencing events far from each other - without any physical force involved. Seen from a human perspective, quantum mechanics has physics encountering consciousness." *

*From Quantum Enigma by Bruce Rosenblum and Fred Kuttner (Physics professors at the University of California)

# QUANTUM TIMES

Written By
Bill Diffenderffer

# PART ONE

## Time: Soon

# PROLOGUE

All of a sudden, there it was. Huge and gleaming in the sky. The size of a twelve story Manhattan office building. But a building that seemed to have no straight lines anywhere in its design; it was all flowing curves. And it shone, particularly in the night sky, as if its surface was all metallic and rigorously polished.

It was high up, about 20,000 feet higher than the usual airline traffic, and could be seen in the daytime without a telescope and at night it could be tracked by anyone looking up at the sky on a clear night. One had to believe it wanted to be seen for rather than some standard orbit it followed a meandering path that ensured at some point each day it was overhead all the population centers of the Earth.

Its path was unusual for another reason. When the technologically advanced countries of the world trained their earthbound and satellite based sensor arrays upon it, as they did almost instantly, they could detect no apparent thrust engines or the use of energy of any sort for the many course adjustments and its occasional acceleration and deceleration. It quietly, for it was quiet too, travelled about ignoring the laws of physics.

Perhaps in less trying times the wiser advisors to the Heads of State of the world's powers would have successfully advised their leaders to stay calm and just observe this strange new thing that had just appeared in the sky overhead. But these were not normal times. Based on the event that had just transpired a few days earlier, the militaries of all the major powers were on full Red Alert, all at battle stations, all with weapons at the ready, fingers on triggers, nerves frayed, fear and anxiety paramount. Days earlier millions of people had been incinerated and it still wasn't clear why or what had happened there. Though that event was clearly the result of earthbound actions, nothing seemed certain. So these were very trying times.

Nothing at all happened during the first twenty four hours following its arrival. It just meandered over the population centers silently, threatening only by virtue of its sudden existence, communicating nothing. Yet this silence was more unnerving than if it had screamed hostile intent.

So as it approached for a second time the western border of China, while it was still over Russian airspace, the Chinese leaders watched it intently, watched it with eyes that hadn't slept since it first appeared in the sky and had had very little sleep in the week before. Watched it with minds dulled and frayed by recent disaster. And at that moment in time, that huge unidentifiable object did suddenly increase its speed and drop down in altitude. So the Chinese reacted. The missiles armed with nuclear warheads that they had kept lined up on The Object (as everyone was calling it) since they had first observed it, were fired. And as they streaked to their target, the Russians who had prepared for just such a potential action, fired their missiles at it as well. The Americans, armed and ready of course, did not react. They had computed the trajectories and knew they were not then at risk. They just watched. But their protocols had all been raced through and their fingers were poised over the proverbial buttons.

Radar systems belonging to all the advanced countries all over the world tracked the flight of the two sets of missiles. Seconds passed like hours. The destruction of The Object seemed certain. Huge in the sky though it was, it was just office building size – no match for multiple nuclear warheads. The missiles inexorably closed in on their target, visible on the radar screens and their contrails visible to the naked eye to those near enough and looking skyward.

As they approached to the last mile of separation, the blips that were the missiles on the radar screens disappeared. The contrails that were visible suddenly ceased. More seconds passed and nothing happened. Minutes passed and the silence continued. No explosions occurred. The Object maintained its charted course as if oblivious to the danger it had been in. It passed over Beijing and then veered northward on its way to passing over Tokyo. It took no other action. It completely seemed to be ignoring the destruction that it had been threatened with.

But after a couple of hours, electronic devices all over the world had their screens commandeered. Whether the devices were huge Pentagon computers, office desktops or the billions of smartphones belonging to ordinary people, they all showed the same message. It began with visual images of the missiles fired at the object and the missiles were tracked in their course and as they neared their target they were all shown to just disappear – to just pop out of existence. And those images were then followed by a single line of text – text that was in whatever language that the particular device on which it was appearing favored.

The text was in all caps: DO NOT DO THAT AGAIN. PLEASE!

*****

FIVE DAYS EARLIER

Experts believed it began with a purge by the Supreme Leader of several of his most senior advisors and military leaders in the now non-existent country of North Korea. The ones purged were deemed by outsiders to be more conservative and experienced and reasonable than the Supreme Leader was himself – that is to say they weren't irrational and egomaniacal. The purge itself was dramatic, irreversible and undeniable: the six purgees were executed by firing squad on national television. In that ill-fated country senior leadership positions carried certain risks; risks that increased geometrically with any disagreeing with the will of the Supreme Leader who was obviously all-knowing and all-powerful, at least in his own mind.

Then things happened quickly. North Korea fired three missiles at a South Korean military installation on an offshore island that was the subject of a territorial dispute. The North Koreans had done this before and had been warned not to repeat that behavior. They had chosen to disregard that warning and this time the South Koreans fired back, aiming at the launch site of the missiles. The South Korean missiles hit their target and destroyed it.

In moments, North Korea launched more rockets, this time targeting military bases in South Korea. South Korea retaliated. The Supreme Leader did not hesitate. To his mind, what was the point of having nuclear weapons if you never used them? He was all powerful! Glorious victory over the hated mercantilists of South Korea would be his. He would be respected and revered by all! The South Koreans had tied themselves to the weak-minded and impotent Western Powers. They would respond with economic sanctions – so what! He ordered the use of nuclear weapons against Seoul. He smiled as he witnessed on his monitors the mushroom shaped cloud over that despised metropolis.

Unfortunately for the Supreme Leader he saw no more after that. A similar mushroom shaped cloud now hovered over Pyongyang, his capital city where he and many millions of his citizens instantly perished. North Korea and South Korea now no longer existed for all practical purposes.

The people of the two Koreas were not the only ones to die of course. Unlucky people from all the countries in the world who happened to be there suffered the same fate. More importantly from a geopolitical standpoint, soldiers and statesmen from China and the United States were also lost. For many tense hours following the nuclear holocaust, they glared menacingly at each other since China had been allied with the North and the US was allied with the South. But wise enough leaders did control things at the two superpowers and neither exacerbated the situation. Both were scared and in shock. Both had their military poised and ready but no aggressive orders were issued. But it was a near thing.

Over the next few days all the world leaders communicated with each other. All claimed to be horrified and that this sort of thing must never happen again. All claimed to have had nothing to do with the events that had just occurred. All were innocent and none had any culpability. All claimed to be equally shocked and appalled. All promised their deep and lasting commitment to world peace. All volunteered to help the survivors and deal with the fall-out: the economic fall-out, the political fall-out, and, of course, the radioactive fall-out. But all the communications were just words words and more words. Truth and lies blended together so seamlessly that lines of delineation disappeared, just as the two Koreas had. For in truth, for all the world's leaders, the unthinkable had happened. Over twenty million people had just been killed in a nuclear war that had lasted less than an hour.

This would soon prove to be only the beginning of the UNTHINKABLE.

# CHAPTER ONE

*"I think I can safely say that nobody understands quantum mechanics." Quantum Mechanics "describes nature as absurd from the point of view of common sense. And it fully agrees with experiment. So I hope you can accept nature as she is – absurd."*

Richard Feynman,
*Nobel Prize winning Physicist*

At the small Deli/grocery store on Lexington Avenue on the Upper East Side David Randall found a prepared lasagna that he and Gabriela could have that night for dinner and their favorite bottled water, so as he left the store he was cheered that maybe things were getting back to normal. The hoarding that had emptied the food store shelves in the three weeks since the arrival of The Object seemed to have abated. Walking down Lexington toward his apartment on 73rd Street carrying his packages he wanted to believe that things were getting back to normal, but he couldn't convince himself. Eerily, little things were off. Like the street traffic. There were fewer cars in the streets; even taxis seemed to be missing. And drivers were using their horns less but when they did use them, they laid on the blasts longer than they used to. Just eerie.

As he walked, he passed several bars and was tempted to go in one and have a beer. The five o'clock crowd was gathered in the bars though 5 PM was still two hours away. In passing up the temptation David felt no more virtuous than those in the bars. With the world as weird as it was now, having a drink in the afternoon at one's favorite bar seemed to be a pretty rational act. In the last two weeks he had spent several afternoons at Clancy's.

With his usual monitoring antenna extended to the conversations of people on barstools within earshot, he had come to identify the three current barroom discussions: First there was the 'we are all doomed and the world is going to hell.' Then there was 'I always knew aliens from outer space were coming.' And some of those people claimed that they had seen aliens before – only now those same people were listened to where before they were dismissed as nut jobs. The third popular discussion was David's favorite: Was the coming of the aliens related to the nuclear destruction of North and South Korea? The timing of the two events could not be ignored.

As he kept walking David noticed there were more 'Going out of Business' signs in the windows. Several of those stores were neighborhood stores that David had shopped at over the years and knew to have good businesses. Thinking there might be a story there, earlier in the week David had gone into a couple of the stores to ask why they were closing. Several of the owners had been quite candid. They wanted to get out of the city fast and move out to the country where they felt they would be safe. Or at least safer. New York City was too much of a target. They feared Armageddon. David knew they weren't the only ones, but he didn't want to write that story.

Interestingly to David, though everyone seemed afraid, there was no unanimity about what they were afraid of. Some feared The Object but many could put no name on what they feared. They just knew things were bad and these times were dangerous. David got that; he had that same sense of unease and disquiet. The combination of nuclear warfare and aliens from outer space could spook people. David shrugged, thinking it was just an internal shrug, but he actually shrugged. It was the story line of a bad horror film for teenage boys – or a good spoof of one. Truth really is stranger than fiction – at least stranger than serious fiction.

As he neared his apartment building, he almost turned around to go have a beer at Clancy's. He probably would have except he was expecting a phone call based on a text he had received. It wouldn't be such a good idea to take that call at Clancy's.

When he finished the call with the editor from The Washington Post, David Randall smiled and put his feet up on the side of his desk. He looked out the small window of his home office (which also happened to be his living room) and thought about how the arrival of The Object in the skies above the Earth three weeks ago could be very good for his career. All of a sudden people everywhere, people who had last thought about reading anything that even bordered on "Science" when they were in college or high school, now wanted to read about interplanetary travel and astrophysics. The call from The Washington Post's editor was proof that things had changed. Rather than David calling the editor to pitch some science based story, the editor had called him and practically begged for David to give him anything and everything David could come up with that was at all about The Object and how it had suddenly appeared out of nowhere.

Better yet, the science that had to matter here was Physics. And David had written a lot about Physics. True that since he had dropped out of Columbia University's Physics doctoral program ten years ago he didn't actually have a PhD, but he had co-written a best-selling book by Janis Wheeling who had recently won the Nobel Prize in Physics. Also, articles he had written had been published in all the major newspapers across the country and his series of articles on CERN's proof of the existence of the Higgs Boson had won him a Pulitzer. That definitely counted! So he had the background, the sources and the ability to write real science that ordinary people could read and understand. And now he had a blank check from The Post to write whatever he could come up with. Sweet!

Thinking about that blank check made him smile again. Maybe at last he could actually put some money into investments. He had some banker and lawyer friends who were always talking about putting money into this and that – real Wall Street kind of conversations – and he just had to keep his mouth shut. He knew he was smarter than they were but they were the ones living on Park Avenue in multi-million dollar apartments with doormen.

But the stock market was bouncing all over the place. One day it was up hundreds of points and the next day crashing downward. It was the optimists against the pessimists and neither side had any real idea what was going to happen with the world. David thought it had always been that way but now it was more obvious. Still he wasn't sure which side of the argument he would bet his money on. Gold hidden in the mattress had its allure.

With his feet up on his desk, trying to come up with deep thoughts about the mysterious Object, he realized he didn't yet have anything to write. At least not anything that represented a new and fresh angle on it. Of course no one had really approached it scientifically yet. Its mere existence had been mind boggling, especially as it showed up so quickly after the annihilation of North and South Korea. Connected or not, that was bizarre! And also of course, the appearance of The Object had caused the whole planet to be shaky, confused, scared, buzzed, distracted, disoriented and a whole lot of other adjectives he could come up with and that was just describing the more sane people of the world! The extremists, the borderline crazies and the real lunatics had gone way over the bend into favorite fantasylands and religious epiphanies and excesses over the idea of extra-terrestrials.

But overall, he mused, he had to give people credit. After the first few days of emptying out of supermarkets, the Home Depots and Lowes, the gun and ammo shops, and anywhere else survivalist gear could be found, goods and services had again become available. Store inventories had been replenished and he could again find what he needed to eat at the same little groceries he had always shopped at. The lasagna he had just put in his refrigerator was proof of that.

In fact, life had resumed its normalcy remarkably quickly. At least superficially. Perhaps that was because after its single communication to practically everyone in the world about not firing any more missiles at it, The Object had remained completely silent. It just meandered its way across the skies as predictable now as the Sun or the Moon in their daily paths. The fact that there was no indication at all whether it had arrived with good or evil intent did not seem to matter. People had returned to their day to day existence. Well at least most people. Not all.

It then occurred to David that perhaps that was not true. Perhaps it was communicating with the Government or several governments? He needed to try to look into that. As he considered that possibility, he rejected it. First because so far everything it had done seemed to maximize its exposure. Secondly, if the government was communicating with The Object, they wouldn't be able to keep it a secret.

Right then he heard the sound of a key opening the lock of his front door and as he turned to it, it opened and Gabriela came into the room. Looking a little disheveled as she usually did when returning from Columbia where she was a professor in the Physics Department but still looking great with her jet black hair, tall, trim figure, olive complexion and general Spanish gypsy looks, she tossed her knapsack on the couch and plunked herself down next to it.

With her typical lack of preamble, she looked at him and said, "It's making me crazy!"

"It being The Object, I presume." David responded.

"Of course! What else is there now in the world of Physics? "

David knew what she meant. Physicists were really not happy about The Object. For weeks they had been trying without success to determine how it had arrived undetected by any of the thousands of telescopes that routinely observe all that occurs out in space, telescopes that map star positions, planet orbits or even potential killer asteroids. In the time before the arrival of The Object not one telescope anywhere had picked up anything that could have been The Object traversing the heavens. It just suddenly appeared. The physicists just hated that!

And right after they finished hating that, they hated that The Object seemed to move all over the place without the apparent exertion of any energy - even when traveling through atmosphere. Laws of Physics were not supposed to be so easily circumvented! Einstein would have hated it too.

David smiled and said, "I love The Object!"

Gabriela was not amused, "And why is that?" David's sense of humor was usually wasted on Gabriela, and frankly on most people. It was usually somewhat self-involved and often more than a little esoteric; still he was popular with people because he was non-judgmental and invariably good humored. And he rarely felt threatened or insecure. Physically and intellectually he could always hold his own. His years of playing Lacrosse could be traced on his lean and athletic frame along with a scattering of scars including a ten stitches scar on his chin. Also with longish sandy hair and wired rim glasses he still looked like the good looking boy next door that mothers wanted to introduce to their unmarried daughters.

"Because The Washington Post called me today and basically put me on retainer to write whatever I come up with on The Object. This is the best assignment I ever had!"

Gabriela regarded her boyfriend of many years with knowing eyes. "What about the story you were working on about the ability of quadriplegics to manipulate controls of their wheelchairs through a mental interface with a computer? I thought you were really excited about that – the whole mind over matter thing."

David grimaced. "Yea, that is pretty cool. First you insert a small chip studded with wires no thicker than a strand of hair into the part of the brain's neocortex that controls movement. Then the motor signals are transmitted to an external computer which decodes them and transfers them on to robotic devices. The ability to use their thoughts, though actually it is electrical current, to activate the controls of the wheelchair is amazing – and I've seen it work....But forget about all that! It will have to wait. I can get back to that. The Object is front and center for now."

Gabriela leaned back on the sofa as she kicked off her shoes and then tucked her legs under her. It didn't surprise her that David would jump from one story that just a few days ago he was very excited about to something new. His focus on something could be deep and intense, but rarely lasted for long. He would think of something new then switch to that. Still she was glad that he was not that way about women, just ideas. That trait though served him well as a writer about scientific breakthroughs. "So what are you going to write?"

"I don't know yet. I hoped you could help me. What are the brainiacs in your department saying about it?"

Gabriela shrugged, "Lots of theories but no data. Half of them really don't want to admit that it is there. But they are all Superstring theorists, so of course they are thinking in terms of higher dimensions. "

"That could be interesting."

Gabriela shook her head, "I think they are all missing the key point. This thing could be dangerous! We all seem to be forgetting what it did to those nuclear missiles that the Chinese and the Russians fired at it. Where did they go? How come they didn't blow The Object to smithereens?"

"Smithereens? Is that a technical term you Physicists use?"

"Don't laugh! This isn't funny! What do you think happened to those missiles? Those missiles were the best weapons we have! Don't you realize that we are probably defenseless against that thing! Doesn't that scare you?"

He knew Gabriela was right. Though she had a tendency to dark forebodings which she claimed was a family trait borne out of generations of oppression for being Eastern European Jews, this was more than that. They really did have no idea about the true intentions of The Object. Why had it appeared? And where did it come from?

"So what do you think we should do?" he asked her.

"How should I know? But I hope our generals in the Pentagon are thinking about this!"

"Gabriela – that is a great point! And guess what? I actually know one of those generals. My Dad's younger brother, my Uncle Mark, is a general at The Pentagon. I saw him a lot when I was growing up. He's the one who first got me interested in science. He gave me a pretty good telescope for my twelfth birthday. Of course they have hundreds of generals there but I wouldn't be surprised if he's caught up in this. Maybe they all are! He does some sort of advanced weapons development thing. I'm going to call him!"

*****

Brigadier General Mark Randall was right then sitting in his office at his desk with Colonel Jake Schneider sitting across from him. Mark and Jake had been friends ever since they had met at a Seminar at MIT on nuclear engineering. Since the seminar was about the use of tactical nuclear weapons, one had to have special clearance to even know the seminar existed. That had been ten years earlier and they had worked together ever since and had become godfathers for each other's kids and that sort of thing.

They had just come out of a briefing where most of the officers there had more stars on their uniforms than Mark did. Mark and

Jake had already attended several meetings just like it in the few weeks since The Object had arrived so dramatically overhead. Each meeting started with a discussion about whether there were any new developments. Several of the generals would then voice guesses about what was going on but then admit they did not have anything new to add. The second item invariably would be about the timing of the arrival of The Object and the destruction of North and South Korea. It rankled everyone that the timing was so close together.

Then one or another of the brighter generals would remind everyone that the timing had to be coincidental if The Object really was from "Outer Space" since distances just across our Solar System were so vast let alone from anywhere more remote in the galaxy. Then as that realization sank in there would be stunned silence until one general or another would plaintively say, "Are we sure that The Object is actually from Outer Space"? Could Russia or China have put it up there? Then another round of silence until another general would say convincingly that there was no way that the United States could do it and if we couldn't do it then no other country for damn sure could do it! And that would for a moment make everyone there feel a little better until they realized it actually made everything worse.

So then the meeting would come to a very desultory close but before it ended the generals would come up with a wish list of what they would really like to know and then Mark and Jake and a few other lower level officers like them would be given an even longer "To Do" list than the one they had from the previous meeting. But when it came right down to it though their instruction was easy – FIGURE OUT WHAT THE OBJECT IS AND HOW TO DESTROY IT!

Mark Randall had spent his career in the Army figuring out how to destroy things and he was very good at it. In truth though, he had rarely seen any of his plans actually put into effect. He had done a tour in Iraq during the first Gulf War but that was the only action he'd seen and even there the really clever things he had prepared were never needed. He knew he had received his last promotion and with his thirty years in, he realized this assignment was probably going to be his last. The worry was that it might be everyone's last assignment.

Jake Schneider was in many ways Mark's alter ego. Where Mark was creative and theoretical, Jake was practical and disciplined. Mark determined what should be done and Jake made sure it got done. They looked enough alike to be brothers, both were a little above average height, fit and trim with straightforward features that didn't reveal much and had enough creases in their face and tightness in their jaws to suggest they took things seriously.

"So where do we start today?" Jake asked Mark.

"I guess we start with what we know, but that sure as hell won't take long."

"We don't know shit!" Jake responded.

"True but let's go through it. We know The Object is about the size of our average aircraft carrier. We know we can't penetrate what is inside it, if anything. We know its dimensions but we don't know its mass or actual composition."

"But it could have a large fighting force in there with weaponry we can't even imagine," Jake added.

Mark continued, "We know that it apparently arrived here completely undetected."

"Yea... like a frigging Klingon Bird of Prey out of Star Trek using a cloaking device!"

"Exactly. So we should assume it has the ability to reflect radar and perhaps even deflect light itself. Which means that were we to attack it, it might be able to just disappear on us. It would be there somewhere but we wouldn't know where."

Jake just shook his head, "We will have to shoot at something we can't see with missiles that just disappear before they hit the target."

Mark went on, "That's the next thing we know: The Object can somehow eliminate our missiles with no apparent leftovers – no explosion, no fragments, no nothing. No energy signs. If they can do that to missiles streaking at them, what else can they do that to?"

Jake held up his hand to stop Mark. "They? Who's 'they'? Is there a 'they'?"

"Something or somebody sent the video and the text message about not shooting anymore missiles at it. This is something else we know. And I'm going to keep saying they until I know better.

They somehow know how to speak English...and damn near every other language in the world. And beyond that, they somehow could hack into every computer and smart phone in the world at the same time and deliver the same message. We can't do that. Google can't do that. And our friends at the NSA can't do that."

"I sure hope these guys are friendly!" Jake muttered.

Mark's cell phone rang and he checked the caller ID and saw it was his nephew. He was about to push the call to voicemail but frustrated with the direction of his conversation with Jake, he took the call. "What's up David? I'm sort of busy right now."

"Hi Uncle Mark. Sorry to disturb you but I've been assigned to write about The Object for The Washington Post and I wondered if The Object was communicating with the Government in any way? Are you caught up in any activity related to The Object?"

"You know if I am, I couldn't tell you. Everything about The Object is classified right now."

"I thought that would probably be true. But I had to ask. And we hadn't talked for a while, so I just thought I'd call."

Mark was about to end the call, when he thought of something. "David, what exactly does The Post want you to do?"

"The editor knows I have a lot of contacts in the physics community. He wants me to write about The Object from the standpoint of the science involved. There seems to be a lot about The Object that doesn't seem to make any sense to us. What we have already seen from it we would have said was impossible."

Mark realized that he needed to reach out to the science community more than he had been doing. "Yea, I know. Are you going to speak to that Nobel Prize winning Physics professor you wrote the book with – Dr. Wheeling?"

"He's next on my list."

"Perhaps you could do something for me. If he has any ideas about The Object – no matter how farfetched, could you call me and tell me about them?"

David thought for a second, "Sure, I'll do that. But I have to ask you a question first. And I realize you can't tell me anything you know. But it would be very helpful in my conversation with Janis Wheeling if I can tell him what the Government doesn't know."

"You want to know what I don't know?" Mark asked.

"That's it. I want to know if the Government knows any more than what the public seems to know. Has there been any communication with it"

Mark paused again. He understood that he probably shouldn't say anything. But he thought David's help might be useful. "Sorry David, I can't tell you anything. There is...nothing, I repeat nothing ...I can tell you. You got that."

On the other end of the line, David smiled. "Yes Uncle Mark, I got that.

Mark said again, "You come up with anything, you call me!"

"I got that too....Say hello to my favorite aunt."

"I will. Come see us soon."

Jake looked back at Mark when Mark ended the call. "What was that all about?"

"That was my nephew. He writes science based stories for newspapers, including The Washington Post. He's been assigned to write about The Object. Normally I wouldn't have said anything to him, but David is a brilliant kid – I guess he's not a kid any more, I think he's about 33. Anyway, although he dropped out of his doctoral program in Physics from Columbia, it wasn't because he wasn't smart enough. I think he was just too ADD. He was the kind of kid whose teachers were always writing on his report cards that he should be doing better. He likes bouncing around, chasing whatever he finds interesting at the moment. But he is tightly connected to the physics community including a recent Nobel winner who he co-wrote a book with. David has the ability to not only understand theoretical physics but he can explain it so that ordinary people can understand it. My guess is before we're done with The Object we are going to be exploring a whole new world of physics – and I want all the help I can get!"

Jake just shook his ahead again, "This is not good! This is not good at all!"

*****

The Alien looked up at the sign that was obviously meant to be a location identifier. "Times Square" it read. It had taken a little while for him to realize that signs like that one were location aids. It was so primitive yet apparently necessary even in this city that he had been briefed was one of the great cities of this world. Once again he was surprised at how greatly the technology at use on this planet varied. Some of the technology here was quite advanced, especially in certain nations; while in other nations people lived as they would have a thousand years earlier.

Without question he thought that to understand the civilization and culture of any new world one had to commingle with the people, walk the ground they walked, watch their daily habits. In no other way could one truly assess the dangers and recognize the opportunities. It was one thing to observe and study from their low space orbit, quite another to mingle among them. This was why he was now out walking the streets of New York City while others like him were in other major cities around the world.

Though he had worried that his costume and cosmetic adaptations might be inadequate, now he no longer worried. Just here on this busy corner he observed humans looking far more diverse to each other than his deviation to their norm. As he became more comfortable in his surroundings he found he liked the frenetic busyness of it all. The noise and clamor, the roaring traffic, the frantic racing about of all the yellow vehicles, and the pedestrians hurrying around to fulfill personal missions, all left him with a sense of visiting back in the history of his own home planet. It must have once been like this, he thought.

As he walked he noticed the sky darken and the city transform to a blaze of lights but there was no loss of energy or dynamism. The mood of the humans he watched had changed slightly from the daytime but whether they were happier or not, he could not tell. He wondered if these "New Yorkers" were any different from the people in smaller American cities or towns. Would people in Beijing or Moscow be the same? There was so much they needed to learn for their mission to be successful.

He came upon a vast open parkland with people sitting on benches or strolling or running down a myriad of pathways. He kept walking and observed as full darkness fell that the crowd of people had vanished. He kept walking northward. Out of the park, he approached a neighborhood where people seemed to live in high rise buildings showing wear and tear that the buildings he had passed earlier did not reflect. The stores on the street also shared in the general disrepair.

As he passed along a particularly shabby and ill-kept alleyway, he noticed that three young men seemed focused on him as he approached where they were leaning against the side of a building. "A long way from home, aren't you?" the tallest of the three spoke up as the three of them stepped in front of him to block his passage.

Quickly the alien looked them over to determine their probable intention. On other worlds he had seen their kind before. Their facial expression and unkempt appearance communicated to him all he needed to know. With them there were no smiles of fellowship or offers of assistance. Further, they believed themselves to be menacing and took satisfaction from that. They believed themselves to have power over him. These three sought to victimize him in some manner.

His instructions were clear about such encounters: be friendly, say as little as possible and go on about his way as quickly as possible. He did not think that approach would work with these three, but he would attempt to do so. So he answered in a respectful manner, "Yes...actually. My home is far away. Thank you for asking. Have a good evening," he said and then tried to walk around them. The three seemed to have anticipated his movement and once again they moved to block his path.

"Not so fast big man, first give us your wallet and that nice coat you're wearing," the one who had first spoken said.

The alien then realized that now he was being directly threatened; the demeanor of the three young men had become more bellicose. He thought about his instructions but they had not covered this point, and besides he knew he was not going to surrender his coat and he had no wallet. "I'm sorry but that cannot happen," he said.

"What you mean 'cannot happen'? And where you from anyway, your accent is strange as hell!" This speaker was the shortest of the three. His facial features were not at all attractive, the alien thought. His nose looked broken and his skin was splotchy. The alien was surprised that someone would allow himself to have such a deficient appearance.

The alien was disappointed to hear that his accent seemed strange to their ears. He thought he had pronounced his English appropriately. But he had to admit that their pronunciation did seem different from his. "I think you should let me pass now – it would be better," the alien responded. He regarded the three young men with what he thought was a benevolent and friendly gaze. He observed however that it seemed to have no effect. In fact their look at him seemed to harden and take on a feral anticipation.

It was then that things went badly. One of the young men, the tall one who had first confronted the alien reached into a pocket and pulled out what the alien recognized as a dangerous projectile weapon and pointed it at him while the other two tried to grab hold of his arms. The alien came from a warrior culture where such actions were intolerable and the insult unforgivable. So his response was immediate and severe. Though he had been issued none of his usual advanced weaponry for what was supposed to be an unprovocative excursion, he had of course carried within the sleeve of his right arm what in English he thought would be called a 'slicer', the electromagnetic blade of which could instantly cut through the hardest of materials.

It sprang into his hand and in the next instant it was slicing through the wrist of the young man who had held the gun which then fell to the ground. The next flashes of the alien's arm brought the slicer through the throats of the young man who had held the gun and the other man who had been standing next to him. The third man who had been further way from the alien did not move as he watched the alien slice into his comrades. The alien paused and regarded the man – letting the man decide what next to do. The man looked down at his two friends who were now bleeding and dying on the sidewalk.

This one remaining was the short one with the broken nose who had questioned the alien's accent. His eyes were wide and unbelieving but his muscles seemed paralyzed. He was confounded by a turn of events that was both unexpected and fatal for his friends. He could see his own future in their dead eyes.

The alien saw that the man no longer mattered. "Go away!" The young man turned and ran off.

The alien looked around to see if there were any other threats to him. He saw someone across the street look his way then turn and walk quickly down the street. He looked back at the two young men now lying on the pavement.

"Regrettable," the alien said to himself as he walked away. He would have to report the incident to his commanders though his actions had been irreproachable. As he continued walking, he considered the objectives of the mission to this Earth in light of what he was learning about its people. He knew that the three young humans would not be the last ones to die. He also knew that a microcosm of experience often is a true reflection of a macro environment. As he had already observed, humans were by nature predatory and dangerous.

# CHAPTER TWO

*"Science cannot solve the ultimate mystery of Nature. And it is because in the last analysis we ourselves are part of the mystery we are trying to solve."*

Max Planck

David Randall's day began with a blast; a blast that hit everyone in the world who was linked to an electronic communication device. As David did most mornings, just before getting up out of bed he reached for his smartphone lying on his bedside table and scanned it for messages that might have come in overnight. And there on the screen as soon as he turned the phone on, ignoring the phone's message protocols was The Object's email blast. Once again in every favored language of the device owner, a simple text message was displayed. It read:

> **"We would like to communicate with Benjamin Planck. He will know how to reach us."**

David called out to Gabriela who he could hear stirring in the kitchen, "Gabby, check your phone! The Object is speaking again!"

Gabriela still clad in the running shorts and tee shirt she usually slept in came into the bedroom carrying a cup of coffee, "What are you saying?"

David handed her his phone and showed her the message. She read it and with her natural skepticism said, "How do you know it's The Object?"

"I'm sure it is but you check your phone and see." She picked up her phone from her bedside table and checked for the message. She nodded when it was there too.

She added, "Who's Benjamin Planck? I've never heard of him."

"Let's google him." They both entered the name and scanned the entries. There weren't that many and nothing stood out. No Benjamin Planck seemed to have ever done anything notable let alone done anything that would get the attention of beings from a different world. Lots of entries for Max Planck, not so much for Benjamin.

"This just gets more bizarre," David said. "The Object arrives and then except for the message about the missiles the Chinese and Russians fired at it, it goes radio silent for 4 weeks and then says it wants to talk to someone that nobody has ever heard of!"

"And even more strange," Gabriela pointed out, "it said that the now mysterious Benjamin Planck will know how to communicate with The Object. Tell me David, would you know how to communicate with The Object?"

"Good question."

As Gabriela headed back to the kitchen, she asked, "What are you up to today?"

As David headed to the bathroom to take a shower he said, "I'm meeting with Dr. Wheeling and then I guess I'm going to try and figure out who Benjamin Planck is....you know that name sort of rings a bell in my brain. I think I've heard it before. "

"Well if he's not in Google he doesn't exist."

"That's not entirely true."

As she drank her coffee she thought about how good it was to see her longtime boyfriend excited about a project. Too often he was in between projects and not really doing anything. He didn't have steady income and though he was a brilliant writer, he didn't get paid much for what he wrote – not living in New York City kind of income. She had to admit he wasn't good marriage material. At least according to her mother. Her mother had really been getting on her lately about that. Her parents wanted grandchildren. She was starting to want a baby too and that definitely meant getting married first. Her old world parents would kill her if she wasn't married.

David was the problem. The very thing she loved about him, his easy way about doing things and that he never got mad at her – unlike her strict parents when she was growing up – was the flip side of his lack of drive and ambition. And he loved her, she knew that – even though she was quite hard on him at times – and usually she regretted it afterwards. Still she still had hopes for him. If he ever found something to really sink his teeth into, he could be as big a success as anyone in the big competitive city they lived in. She was sure of that – well mostly sure.

*****

When David entered Dr. Wheeling's office at Columbia, the Nobel winner was frowning at an equation he had written on the large whiteboard hanging on the side wall. The physicist was tall and thin and slump shouldered. His dark hair was sprinkled with gray and pulled back in a short ponytail. His eyes were almost crystal blue and wide spaced. Though approaching 60 years old, he radiated an intensity and energy that was off-putting to anyone who wasn't used to being around him. He had won his Nobel Prize for work he had done years earlier that had led to the reduction of the amount of heat generated by electronic devices – work that he now casually dismissed as 'practically engineering.' Like many others in the field he was enthralled with chasing the holy grail of the "T. O. E.": the Theory of Everything that would unite the world of physics.

Without turning away from his work on the whiteboard, Wheeling said to David, "Have you decided to come back to physics yet and leave your stupid writing business? Such a waste of a good mind!"

"Still writing Professor -- which is why I'm here. I'm writing about The Object – specifically about the science of it. I hoped you might have some ideas." As he spoke David sat down on a chair across from where Dr. Wheeling was standing. From past experience he knew the professor liked to stand or sit on his desk while having David sit on that particular chair – hopefully raptly attentive to the professor's every word. David didn't mind – most of what Wheeling had to say was well worth listening to.

Wheeling wrote a few notations on the whiteboard, then stared at the work and nodded his head up and down a few times. With his skinny frame, long neck and thin face he looked a bit like a crane bobbing for a fish. Then he turned to face David and nodded his head a few times more and said, "The science of The Object .... By which of course you mean the physics .... In such a situation it is of course about the physics!" As he spoke, he sat down on the edge of his desk.

"You know I have been thinking about The Object – and some people from the government have asked me about it ... what I think. I don't think the government people know anything."

David agreed, "I don't think they know anything more than we do."

"I'm sure they know much less!"

"So what do we know?" David asked.

"I will tell you but first let me ask you a question. Is there anything, any data, anything at all to contradict what we think we saw when it first arrived... that is....anything to suggest that it did not just pop into existence into our sky?"

David shook his head, "So far no one anywhere has claimed to have detected it on its way to Earth. Far as we know it just all of a sudden was there."

"Exactly!" Wheeling emphasized with his long index finger stabbing at David who had taken a seat across from the desk. "So let us assume that is what occurred. Now how did it get here? That is the question. To my mind there are only two possibilities. One is that it arrived travelling faster than the speed of light. If that were true, no one would see or detect The Object until after it had arrived. Unfortunately, Einstein told us that is not possible. Einstein's reasoning is very compelling and no one has been able to prove differently in the last hundred years. In fact according to all that we know, travelling faster than the speed of light is impossible!"

This was precisely the kind of conversation David had come to meet with the brilliant professor hoping to have. So to keep it going, David asked, "So what is the second possibility?"

Wheeling wagged his finger at David, "Well, let's see if you remember ANYTHING from your studies of physics. We believe there is something that pops in and out of existence. So David my lapsed physicist friend, do you remember what it is?"

David started to shake his head and make the excuse that it had been awhile, but then he thought he knew the answer – even though it could not apply because it related to actions occurring at the smaller than atoms level. "Well, quantum mechanics argues that particles can pop in and out of existence but that is at the subatomic level. The probability that anything with any real mass could pop in and out is so highly unlikely that it borders on impossible."

"Very good David, you do remember some first semester physics....Now note that you said it was highly improbable but NOT IMPOSSIBLE! That is correct! Traveling faster than light is impossible but popping in and out of existence at the quantum level is not impossible and only approaches impossibility though it never gets there as the mass of the object increases. "

"So what is the point as it applies to The Object?"

Dr. Wheeling gave David a grin that David had come to recognize as usually preceding a smug but enlightening observation. "As Sherlock Holmes said, "When you have eliminated the impossible, whatever remains, however improbable, must be the truth."

"I don't believe Sir Arthur Conan Doyle wrote that with Physics in mind.

"That is irrelevant!"

"So you are saying that to understand The Object we have to look at Quantum Physics to explain its behavior?"

"Indeed. That is correct."

"That would be so bizarre!" David exclaimed.

Dr. Wheeling rather resignedly nodded, "The behavior of particles at the quantum level is very bizarre. As our friend Einstein said, 'it is spooky!' But it is all we have for now."

David thought about what he remembered about quantum mechanics and shuddered at the thought of going down that rat hole. Then he said, "We also have the new communication from The Object about wanting to talk to someone named Benjamin Planck."

The professor spread his hands out with his palms up. "I know nothing about a Benjamin Planck. I asked about him. No one seems to know him."

"The funny thing is Professor I recognize the name. It sounds familiar."

"Of course it sounds familiar David! Max Planck...one of the most famous names in physics. Of course Planck sounds familiar."

And that's when David remembered. Benjamin Planck! All of the physics students at Columbia just called him 'Planck.' How could they not? When he had Max Planck's last name....and David then remembered that Planck had said Max Planck was his like great great great uncle. But when Planck introduced himself he said his name was Ben.

"Professor, I remember now! About ten years ago, the same time I was there, Ben Planck was a doctoral candidate in Physics at Columbia. We were sort of friendly competitors. But honestly, he was way smarter than I was. He was smarter than the professors!"

"But I have never heard of him. Did he not move forward in a career in Physics?"

"It was ten years ago ... but as I remember it....His doctoral degree advisors didn't like what he wanted to do his thesis on. They pushed him to do something related to Super String Theory. He considered that a fun mathematical puzzle but not what he was interested in. So he did what they said, he got his degree and then dropped out of sight. I never heard from him or of him again."

Professor Wheeling was intrigued. "Do you remember what it was he wanted to pursue – what was the core idea?"

David leaned back in his chair and tried to remember back ten years earlier. He knew he would remember...he always remembered things. All he had to do was get his mind back into that frame of reference. He stared up at the ceiling and then as if it was written on the ceiling of Dr. Wheeling's office he recalled a discussion Planck and he had had over beers at Planck's apartment one night. Planck had just been told he couldn't do his thesis on what he wanted. The powers that be thought it too insignificant and silly – they had actually used the word 'silly'.

David nodded to himself and then said, "He wanted to explore the issue of the need for an observer in quantum physics. He could never choose to ignore that the famous double slit experiment produced different results if the passage of the electrons through the slits were observed versus not observed. He thought that the classic Schrödinger's Cat thought problem was actually true at a deeper level of existence. I recall he used to take the philosophical question of 'if a tree falls in the forest and no one is around, does it make a sound?' and add to it. Planck would ask: if there is no one ever to observe the fallen tree, does it even fall? Or is its falling suspended until an observer finally arrives. Then he would ramble a little about 'consciousness' and some equation that he had envisioned. "

"So what else?" Dr. Wheeling asked.

David thought a moment longer, "He thought the universe was a vast sea of potentiality and it was consciousness that gave it form."

Dr. Wheeling's focus was full on David, with all its intensity boring into him. "And what else?"

"There is no 'what else?' The Ben Planck I knew was not much of a talker. That conversation was the longest I ever had with him. We were in his apartment because he almost never left it and talking to him was usually like talking to the wall. He was very shy and usually monosyllabic."

"But you say he was brilliant. How would you know?"

"It was just obvious. The papers he wrote... his comments on anyone else's work. He'd say something you first thought was ridiculous and then he would say just a little more and then you'd realize he saw connections that everyone else was blind to."

Dr. Wheeling was back to nodding his head like a crane going after a fish. "We have to find him! It is so obvious!"

"What's obvious?"

"David, think about it... we were just saying that to explain the behavior of The Object we had to examine it in terms of quantum physics. Then we discover that of all the 6 billion people on this planet The Object wants to communicate with a young physicist who had a strange idea in the field of quantum physics – though perhaps not just at the quantum level -- that was not mainstream and so was rejected. Obviously he was on to something and somehow The Object knows it! Now that is another question for us! So how does The Object know of him? And WHY do they want him"

"OK, I get it! So we have to find him. But how do we do that? I'm sure the government with all their resources is already looking for him. People all over the world are now looking for him."

"The governments are looking for someone with the name Benjamin Planck. But we know who he is. And it would not surprise me that perhaps he will not want to be found."

"But we can tell our government who he is."

"No David -- that we cannot do! If the government finds him first they will hide him away and keep him from us! He is too important to trust to any government. Too much is at risk!"

"You don't trust the U.S. Government?" I was a little shocked that he had said it.

Dr. Wheeling just shook his head. "The fate of our world may depend on this! Would I trust any government with that? Look what just happened in Korea! There is no Korea now! Millions of people are dead because our governments did not know what to do about one crazy leader who was allowed to keep nuclear weapons as his personal toys!"

I couldn't argue the point. "I've got to find Ben Planck."

*****

The Alien was dazzled by the lights of downtown Tokyo. The crowds of humans pulsed with a frenetic energy that this Alien found distasteful. He had requested to come to observe Japan in the hope that he would find something different. But this seemed much like what his cohort had observed upon his visit to New York. He realized he had been hoping for something that could not be.

Before disembarking from what Humans now called The Object, he had learned about Japan's history and culture. He had been shocked to see Japan's cultural history was so similar to his own. But Japan had drifted away from the cultural underpinnings they shared whereas his whole planet had fully embraced them. Although the terms were different and the actual histories evolved differently, the similarities were astounding. What here was called Zen Buddhism and truly practiced now by only a few, on his planet it was practiced by the majority. And the warrior code that evolved out of Zen Buddhism that was here called 'the Samurai Code', on his planet was embraced by all - in fact growing up outside The Code was unthinkable and dangerous. How could one not put honor and wisdom foremost? And how could one not approach life fearlessly? Warriors needed such a Code!

He was also learning how few people here engaged in deep meditation. How was it that though it had been practiced here for centuries, it had not spread and evolved to its higher manifestations? On his planet it was a guided daily ritual for the multitudes! The power of his world depended on it!

Curious about its historical antecedents, while walking through the busy shopping district, he accessed the encyclopedic data compiler his cohorts were building and submitted a query about how the Samurai Code had developed here and why it had not spread across the planet. Similar to his own planet's history, it had evolved in earlier centuries when Zen Buddhist monks who had come to Japan from China interacted with warring clans in the age of territorial acquisition. The fighters had found that Zen mindfulness could prepare them to enter battle fearlessly and more strategically. Again his planet shared a similar history. "A Zen warrior was a victorious warrior!" was a rough translation of his planet's most quoted saying.

But as he accessed the data compiler further, the similarities disappeared. Here Japan discarded its cultural ties to a warrior code and lost confidence in the benefits of meditation. It seemed to become a copycat culture with a diminished sense of itself. The Alien was coming to believe that he had less to learn on the streets of Tokyo than he had hoped. And what he was observing was not redemptive.

The Alien realized he was hungry and selected a busy restaurant where he could blend in easily. He ordered by pointing at menu items while saying little and he was unsure what food would be served. When it came he was happily surprised - much superior to their shipboard fare. He also found it amusing to figure out how to use the wooden sticks he was provided as eating utensils. He observed the other diners using them and found he could get most of the food to his mouth.

In the bustle and din of the restaurant he overheard snatches of conversation and watched the animated expressions on the faces. Watching people eat communally was very informative he believed. So much of cultural values and social customs were on casual unprompted display. He found he felt good sitting amongst these people. Interestingly, they seemed happy and involved in their own personal affairs. He sensed no general awareness of the risks and dangers that existed on their planet. He remembered a quote from this planet's great playwright, "Where ignorance is bliss, tis folly to be wise."

It became clearer to him why this planet might be doomed.

*****

Back at his apartment, David started his search for Ben Planck. He began by trying to remember every detail he had ever known about the young man that David and his friends had just called Planck. Then he Googled every data base he thought at all possible. He checked for civil and criminal actions, financial records, obituaries, and social networks and even dating sites. He used all the skills he had acquired while hunting down facts for his writings. He did find some Benjamin Plancks but they just turned out to be clearly not the one he was looking for – but he realized they were already being harassed by virtue of their names – David was clearly not the only one now looking for someone named Benjamin Planck.

Hours went by. Somewhere in the middle of his search he recalled that Planck had loved to watch baseball and always seemed to be wearing a Yankees baseball cap – But he never attended a game at the stadium, only watched on the TV in his small apartment. And he never went to sport bars to watch – in fact he never went to bars at all.

And Planck knew every baseball statistic! Planck loved to present before any action occurred the statistical probabilities of a hitter advancing a runner or a pitcher getting a batter to ground out as opposed to striking out. So David searched baseball references to find a Planck somewhere mentioned. Nothing.

Then he remembered something else about Planck, he loved weather forecasts! He would track the statistical probabilities associated with the weather. He was fascinated with the popular example of Chaos Theory where the butterfly flaps its wings in Brazil and storms develop in Florida - or some such thing! Twenty minutes chasing down that rabbit hole got nothing too.

David's head hurt and his back hurt. Gabriela had arrived home and had gone about making dinner; that is calling for take-out which tonight was to be Italian. She called out to him from the kitchen whether he wanted a drink? Definitely!

When she brought him his usual gin and tonic she asked how his search was going.

"I got nothing!"

"How long have you been looking?"

"Forever!" David went on to describe in detail about the trails he'd tried in his search. He told her about the baseball connection and Planck's fascination with the weather. He wanted sympathy.

But rather than stirring her maternal instincts, Gabriela's penchant for scientific inquiry was roused. She pursed her lips and tugged on her longish straight black hair and stared out the window while she thought. Not for the first time, looking at her David thought about how her intellectual intensity cast a mask over her really lovely features. Only after a couple of drinks in the evening did the hidden flirtatious woman in her ever show herself. Gabriela continued in silent thought for a few moments and then said what David should have thought of. "He does not want to be found but somehow The Object knows about him. So we have to assume he is somewhere here and he has done something that captured their attention."

"But he keeps a very low profile," David added.

Gabriela nodded her beautiful head, "So let's start with where he is hiding. Where would someone like him hide? Did he ever talk about somewhere he always wanted to go to?"

"I remember telling him where I always wanted to go. We were watching a baseball game and I had just come back from a spring break trip to Nassau in the Bahamas. I told him what a great time I had had at Paradise Island. I had walked away a small winner from the Blackjack tables....he was interested because of his usual fascination with probabilities." David then smiled as he remembered something else.

"And you know what... he said he loved islands. He loved going to a remote beach that no one ever went to. He said he envied Robinson Caruso. He said he had read that book about ten times."

Gabriela interrupted with, "Really? You remember all this?"

"What can I tell you...I have a great memory – and the more I remember the more other memories come back to me! Memory works that way you know."

Gabriela held up her hand to stop David. "You know what I know," she said. "I know that The Bahamas has like 700 islands and that a lot of them are remote and have very few people on them and would be a perfect place to hide if you wanted to be like Robinson Caruso!"

David reluctantly went back to his desk with his laptop thinking about all the islands in The Bahamas where Planck could be hiding and then if not there, all the other islands in the Caribbean or anywhere else for that matter. But he was on the hunt and he emphatically did not want to go back to Dr. Wheeling without having found Ben Planck. And he agreed with Gabriela: Planck had done something that brought him to the attention of The Object – so there was something to be found. So he resumed his search focusing first on The Bahamas and then crossed that looking for baseball and weather notations.

An hour later he hit pay dirt. In an article in The Nassau Tribune from six months ago there was a story about a little island southwest of Nassau that had somewhat miraculously been spared from a hurricane that should have blown right over it but which had instead at the last minute detoured right around it. That season there had been a number of hurricanes. And the reason the story received the attention of the newspaper was that not just that time but a year earlier too the little island had been detoured at the last minute though reliable local forecasters had been certain that the island was in the middle of the projected hurricane paths. Given how close the hurricanes had come before the last minute detours, the probability that the island would twice be spared seemed highly unlikely.

And further down in the story, there it was. A local resident of the small island, the Director of a religious order there, was quoted as saying it was just God's will that they had been spared destruction by the hurricanes. And that man's name was Planck.

Triumphantly David shared the story with Gabriela. She too instantly believed this religious leader would prove to be the right Benjamin Planck. But her reason took David's thinking to a whole other level.

"It fits," she said. "Do you know why The Object wants to meet with your old friend Planck?"

David shook his head, "How would I know that?"

Gabriela smiled and gave him her 'she was smarter than he was' kind of look. "Because he moved those hurricanes around his island!"

Mostly because of the look she had given him, David argued "How could he have done that? It's a hurricane ... it goes where it wants to go!"

"Go and meet him and you'll find out how he did it. But he did it!"

"I guess I'm going to The Bahamas. You want to come?"

"Let's see ... it is summer and I have no class to teach and we're talking about a trip to The Bahamas to meet with probably the most sought after person in the world right now. What do you think?" Gabriela smiled and nodded.

*****

Sitting at his usual seat on Air Force One Hank Scarpetti, the Chief of Staff to the President of the United States, found himself looking out the window when he should have been working at returning emails with these few minutes of alone time. He was too tired to work and too amped to sleep. And he had eaten too much too quickly at the $5000 a plate dinner – and the food had been cold and tasteless. He had fallen off his diet for nothing; his good intentions to lose some of the extra twenty-five pounds he was carrying around had failed him again. And the fundraiser in Miami the President and he had just left hadn't gone all that well. Sure they had raised some dollars for the campaign war chest, but the heavy hitter donors and packagers who had been in attendance had obviously left disappointed with how little the President had told them about what was REALLY going on with

The Object. The President didn't want to admit that he didn't know any more than they did so he bluffed them with a national security excuse.

Once the fundraiser was over and they were back on Air Force One heading back to D.C., the President had roasted his Chief of Staff for not having anything that the President could say. Scarpetti really couldn't blame the President – it was his job to know the important things that were going on. He was supposed to make the President look good and in control. The sad truth was that they didn't know anything about The Object. Like everyone else, all they could do was guess.

Guessing wasn't much of a basis for action or policy making. The President desperately wanted to appear to be doing something. The media was hounding The White House for answers to questions about The Object. And they had an endless stream of questions. Unfortunately, The White House had no answers – lots of experts with lots of what they claimed were educated guesses, but to Scarpetti they didn't seem any better than what his golf buddies came up with. Though he shouldn't disparage his golf buddies – they were pretty big players in Washington in their own right.

In fact he realized he should call one of them. General Carl Greene had been put in charge of the military's response to all things related to The Object. Maybe Greene had come up with something he could feed to the President.

Thinking about what the military might know led him to thinking about what had happened in Korea. As cynical as he had become – and the Chief of Staff to the President of the United States had to be extremely cynical just to survive in D.C., and he had now served two Presidents in that position – he still was amazed at how quickly the nuclear holocaust that had destroyed North and South Korea had faded from the nation's consciousness. Once The Object had showed up, the Korea story disappeared in the media. It was like the media couldn't concentrate on more than one thing at a time. A visitor from outer space was a bigger story than nuclear destruction with twenty million killed. Now there were just routine follow up stories about Korea much like the stories that followed the cleanup after a Category Five hurricane destroyed an island country like Haiti.

The American people didn't like the Korea story to begin with. They wanted to forget all the Americans – soldiers and civilians -- who had died there. They wanted to forget that it had been American nuclear weapons that had been used to respond to the North Korea nukes. Scarpetti knew that all the protocols had been followed and the United States had to do what it did, no one argued otherwise; both parties were in in true bi-partisan lock step on that, still the result was horrific. It gave him nightmares and he knew the President was suffering too.

Scarpetti liked the President. He liked that the President was a genuinely nice man. A little too sure of himself and too concerned with his own destiny but Scarpetti had seen worse among the political leaders who commingled in Washington like prideful roosters. He had been brought in just a year ago as the savvy political pro that would help rescue this administration's agenda from the quagmire it had settled into. At sixty years old it was to be his final hurrah; a proof point that he had a made a difference with his life. He thought he had been making some progress before Korea happened and then The Object showed up. Now he knew he had just been moving the furniture around.

The thing about Washington he had learned was that most of the time just moving the furniture around was enough to get by. The country was pretty indestructible; at its core it had an ambitious and inexorable spirit that pushed it forward and it was big hearted too in a way that made him proud to be an American. The President's job – and his by extension -- was just to ensure that the country remained strong and that all the people benefitted. Most of the time, that was it. Just do that. Not that doing that was so easy, but it was clear to him what was called for.

But now was one of those times which occurred only once or twice a century when the world shifted. New major forces came into play and real existential risk surfaced. Now the political leaders in Washington had to be good at something more than just winning elections. Maybe once upon a time Washington had been about more than just elections, but probably that was all it had ever been about. If so, then during those prior existential risk moments, the country had been lucky. The leaders could do more than just win elections. With the challenges now facing the country and the political leaders running the country now, it was going to take a lot of luck. Scarpetti wanted to believe that he could help the President make the right decisions so that luck was less of a factor. Sitting there at 35,000 feet onboard Air Force One he wasn't at all confident. The country needed to be lucky.

He took another sip of the scotch and water he'd been working on for the last thirty minutes. He wanted to gulp it down and get another but he knew he'd had enough. He couldn't afford a hangover tomorrow: there was just too much to do. Being a good drinker was a real political asset in Washington circles but at sixty he couldn't drink like he used to. The hangovers came quicker and lasted longer. He took another sip.

Looking out the window at thirty five thousand feet he saw the continuous blaze of city and suburban lights below that more than anything showed the population density of America's East Coast. All the people down there were looking to the President – and by extension, looking to him – to get them safely through the geopolitical unrest caused by the nuclear devastation in Korea and the risks and uncertainty of newly discovered alien life that now hovered threateningly above their heads. Until just a few weeks ago he believed ardently that the U.S. government could protect and serve the people, could guide and deliver them to a safe and prosperous future. Now, sitting quietly and alone in the sky over Washington, numbed a little by the good scotch whiskey, he felt no such certainty. And he wasn't the only one feeling the stress and anxiety. He'd been around the White House of too many administrations not to be able to sense the collective mood. The people that worked there, from the President on down, all felt it. They were the true insiders and knew the detail of things. And like him, they were worried and unsure of what was happening. Unsure of what was going to happen. They were scared. And so was he.

*****

As the pilot of the small chartered airplane circled the little island sitting like a beach encircled jewel in the quiet turquoise waters of the Caribbean, David spotted the small landing strip and then alongside that a row of two story buildings that he had been told was the remnant of an exclusive resort hotel that had gone bankrupt twenty years earlier. Gabriela sitting next to him was also craning her neck to look out the window and in the window seat in front was Dr. Wheeling doing the same thing.

Seeing the island somehow made this hastily set up trip seem real whereas before it still had seemed dream-like. With his eyes still on the island, David thought about the sequence of events over the last 48 hours that led him to an encounter with no predictable outcome. Once he had verified that Ben Planck was still on the out of the way island with the foreboding name of Pirate's Cay, getting a phone number for him was easy. But before attempting to call Planck he had informed Dr. Wheeling of how and where he had found Planck and the professor had immediately told David he too wanted to go with David to meet Planck. As it turned out that was a good thing because when he finally succeeded in talking to Planck, Planck was not at all eager to meet with David.

The call had started with a brief recollection of their days as doctoral students at Columbia and then quickly Planck stated that he was not the Benjamin Planck everyone was looking for. He had already been emphatic about this to the local Bahamian Police who had come to check and then to agents from the FBI who said they were running down everyone with the name Benjamin Planck. Planck then told David what he had told everyone else: in fact Benjamin was his middle name. He had actually been named after his great great great uncle and his first name was indeed Max. Then he said that his little island community was a Zen Buddhist retreat and nothing he had done or had been doing could possibly be of interest to The Object or anyone else for that matter. Even this brief exchange had taken slow minutes as Planck's reticence to talk had not changed.

David heard him out but kept prodding. He brought up the matter of the hurricanes and Plank's attachment to physics. Planck just remained silent to that line of approach. Then David mentioned that Dr. Wheeling also wanted to come meet him. After confirming that indeed it was_the Dr. Janus Wheeling, winner of the Nobel Prize, Planck's attitude changed. He had read Wheeling's major papers and books and yes he did know that David had co-authored the recent bestseller – for a book on theoretical physics. On the proviso that Dr. Wheeling came too, Planck invited them to come see him.

The small plane landed and taxied over to a hut with an extended roofline where waiting and disembarking passengers could gather in the event of rain. As the three of them exited the aircraft, David saw a lean suntanned young man wearing khaki cargo shorts and a white tee shirt standing next to the hut waiting for them. It took a moment before David recognized him as Planck. Planck looked younger than David would have thought and more like a California surfer than the bookish pale skinned nerdy student he had known ten years earlier.

As they approached him, he came forward too and everyone said hello and David introduced Dr. Wheeling and Gabriela, who David said was his girlfriend. Gabriela was quick to add that she too was a physicist and for a rare moment David wanted to be able to say that he was too.

In the next moment Planck stated without preamble that he was sorry to disappoint them but as he had said to David on the phone call, he was not the one everyone was looking for. Then he just looked back at each of them. For the moment David was at a loss as to how to respond.

Clad in white slacks and a multi-colored, floral patterned Hawaiian shirt, looking not at all like a famous physicist, Dr. Wheeling smiled back at Planck and nodded his head several times. "Planck ... may I call you Planck? For that is how David always has referred to you."

Planck nodded.

Dr. Wheeling went on, "Well Planck, if I were in your circumstances I would say exactly that. Good for you to be wise enough to want to stay anonymous – to hide away in fact. But I'm sure you are the one and more importantly I know why you are." The professor held up his hand when Planck started his denial. "Planck, once David told me about you, I did a little research on your work while you were a doctoral candidate at Columbia. I ignored your actual work that earned you your PhD but looked at what you had originally submitted – that which your advisors were foolish enough to discard. With the benefit of hindsight and the knowledge that The Object's appearance substantiates.... And then what appeared to happen with respect to the course changes of the hurricanes ....well, obviously, you are not only the one everyone is looking for but quite possibly you might be the only one who understands how it is that The Object is here now."

Planck looked past the three of them for a long moment and then turned back to face Dr. Wheeling. The seriousness of his expression put the lie to his tanned beach boy looks. Then with his mind apparently made up, he said, "Dr. Wheeling, I am on the frontier of the most important physics discovery since Einstein. Honestly, I could use some help."

Wheeling just nodded as if he had known that all along. "That is why I am here," he said.

The three of them gathered up their bags and squeezed into a jeep that Planck had parked nearby. He drove them a few hundred yards to what once had been a 50 room resort hotel sitting almost in the sand of a white sand, coconut tree enclosed beach. To their surprise it did not look run down and it was not deserted. There were a number of people around looking very much like they had been there awhile. No one had funny drinks with umbrellas stuck in them, no one was sunburned, and no one was sitting with their legs in the pool, though the pool looked great. Rather they all looked like they had a purpose for being there. There were several small study groups meeting under the roofed porch or where there were clumps of shade. These people tended to be in shorts and a tee shirt. But there were more sitting alone or in quiet conversation with one or two others who had shaved heads and were attired in monkish robes, robes that had to be hot in the summer heat.

To their questions Planck explained that his island really was a Zen Buddhist retreat where a very deep meditation was practiced and he looked forward to introducing them to the Zen Master who led the group. But there were also some physicists who had been invited to come once sworn to secrecy. And some of the physicists had crossed over, as Planck himself had done, and now mixed with both groups. In fact, Planck explained, that joinder of the two disciplines was essential to the work that was done there on the island.

When asked, he said he had acquired the island 4 years earlier and the number of residents had grown slowly to its current population of 29. The people who were there had been carefully selected though word of mouth alone had identified them. When Wheeling asked how all this was funded, Planck cryptically replied, "The Universe provides."

Planck settled the three of them into a room for the professor and a room for Gabriela and David. The rooms both had beachside views but the furnishings were spare. Also Planck apologized that though it still looked like a resort, it functioned like a home: a home without servants or cooks. Planck shared that their Buddhist master insisted on that.

They agreed to meet late that afternoon after everyone had settled in.

*****

The Alien walking down the Champs Elysees felt disoriented. Paris was not what she had expected. She had thought she was prepared and would know the streets; but much was different. The beauty of the city was there; but the look and feel was wrong. She had been led to expect it would look more like Berlin or Munich.

The city was more beautiful than she had imagined. This Paris was different than the Paris she had thought she would see. She had not expected to see The Louvre in its stately majesty or the triumphant symbol of the Eiffel Tower. She liked best the brasseries and bistros with the customers sitting outside in the summer sun arguing art and politics or more prosaically just sharing their day's events. She had sat at one and had a vin blanc and imagined herself a Parisian. With her cosmetic changes she thought she not only fit in but that the males passing her by found her attractive. She rather liked that.

She liked the clothing that the females in Paris were wearing. The flow of the soft fabrics and the bare arms and legs combined in a tantalizing fashion; very different from the skin tight militaristic tunics of her planet. The skirt she had on was knee length and when she had been sitting at the little table on the street and sipping her wine she had crossed her legs and felt a delightful flirtatious naughtiness that would have earned her a reprimand at home.

She was thrilled that she had been selected to be one of the planet visitors. Though most of the cadre wanted to go down planet side, only a few were selected. This was only her second mission but her scholastic diligence had been rewarded. But perhaps because she was so inexperienced she could not see what made this planet such a danger to so many. She hated that it might soon suffer extinction. She knew it could happen.

# CHAPTER THREE

*"Consciousness determines existence." It "was not possible to formulate the laws of quantum mechanics in a fully consistent way without reference to the consciousness [of the observer] ...the very study of the external world led to the conclusion that the content of the consciousness is the ultimate reality."*

Eugene Wigner
*Nobel Prize winning Physicist*

Planck had asked them to meet him in what used to be the lobby of the resort hotel at 4PM. At the appointed time David and Gabriela and the professor walked from their rooms to the central building which housed the lobby. The lobby had large hurricane shutters at the front and the back which were fully opened and gave the appearance of always being in that open position. A breeze drifted through the room and the sibilant sounds of the waves cascading to the shore were a quiet reminder of the resort that this building once was. Planck was there to greet them but to their surprise the lobby which had no furniture was filled with the twenty or so island residents all seated on the floor, many in the lotus position.

As David approached Planck he was struck by the incongruity of it all. He had come with a Nobel Prize winning physicist to talk to a grad school friend of his on a tropical island where religious zealots were apparently meditating. They were there because some extra-terrestrials wanted to meet his friend too. And somehow in the ten years since he last saw his friend, Planck was looking better than ever – and part of that look was of a man who knew things that no one else knew. Like the secrets of the universe.

"Just go with it," he thought to himself.

Planck met them at the entrance and put his finger to his lips to suggest they be silent. They noticed he had a small grocery bag in his hand. He led them a few feet away from the lobby where he felt more free to talk.

"I believed our discussion would go better if we started with a little demonstration. But there needs to be a slight alteration in my plans because we must address a more serious, but purely internal, matter." As Planck spoke he looked mostly at Dr. Wheeling but Gabriela and David were given brief glances too.

Planck went on when they all nodded. He then opened the grocery bag he was holding and showed that it contained four bananas bound together just as one would purchase them at the grocery store. They were six or seven inches long but were not nearly ripe, in fact they were green. "Quite green aren't they?" He said as he put them back in the bag and curled the edges of the bag so that it was closed and handed the bag to Dr. Wheeling.

Planck then said, "I would like the three of you to join us in a meditation exercise for a few minutes – just sit quietly and try to quiet your mind. Try not to think of anything. When thoughts do pop up, just push them to the side. Let your mind be quiet and still. You needn't close your eyes, feel free to observe. See without thinking about it. Professor...I would like you to keep the bag with you and do not open it until you leave the meditation. Keep it with you in such a way that no one could interfere with it without your knowing. David and Gabriela feel free to watch the bag if you like. You will understand later why I ask that. Fifteen minutes will be enough, and then the three of you should get up and leave.

"I will need to stay in the meditation for a while longer. One of our members has just learned that he has a brain tumor and we need to address that. I suggest that when you do get up and leave the meditation you might gather together outside and discuss....discuss instances of mind over matter. "

Dr. Wheeling with no hint of bemusement repeated, "Mind over matter." Then he nodded his head several times as if he had known that was to be discussed.

Planck then brought them into the lobby and showed where they should sit on the floor near the back. The people in the room were silent and sat motionless. No one looked up at them. Planck moved to the front of the room and sat down there. Gabriela sat in a pretty good semblance of the lotus position and David and the professor did the best they could. The professor placed the bag down on his lap with his hand firmly clasping it. David looked at his watch to check the time.

First the time seemed to turtle by for David but once he stopped watching the minute hand of his watch and instead just tried to see the room without looking, his watch soon showed the fifteen minutes was up. He stood up and went outside and Dr. Wheeling and Gabriela joined him. They walked out on the patio and sat at a round table for four with a beach umbrella in the middle of it.

Without saying a word, Dr. Wheeling opened the grocery bag and took out of it four beautifully ripe yellow bananas. The three of them stayed silent moments longer and stared at the bananas. Then calmly the professor took one of the bananas and as he unpeeled it he said, "Reality is different than I had supposed."

"Could it be a trick of some kind?" David asked but he didn't know how it could have been.

Dr. Wheeling shook his head. "The Object is real. Moving the hurricanes was real. These bananas were green and now they are ripe and these bananas are very real." In emphasis of his last statement he ate the top third of the banana. Then he said, "This is not the time of tricks and magic. This is the time to re-think what is real."

"I think we should do what Planck asked us to do. Let's talk about mind over matter." Gabriela said. Then she went on, "As physicists we try very hard to ignore certain things we know are true. We know the need for an "Observer" in quantum physics exists, but we try to ignore why or what that means. The role of The Observer is to turn potentialities into actualities, but why that is so we try not to ask. But it is predictable and experiments like the classic double slit experiments substantiate it. And in fact we have many instances where 'mind' affects 'matter'."

David agreed, "This issue has bothered me for a while. It is why I was writing the article on how quadriplegics were interfacing with computers through mental exertions to move their wheelchairs. But similarly, we know that what we think affects the molecules in our bodies: we routinely think ourselves sick through stress. We also know that we can think ourselves healthy too – the placebo effect shows that...and that prayer can help as well. People with positive attitudes are much more likely to recover from serious illness than people with negative attitudes."

Gabriela added, "I know as a physicist I'm supposed to reject that work by Emoto where he shows the effects of human consciousness on water molecules but I don't think his work has been proven to be a sham."

Dr. Wheeling had finished his banana. "I believe that the issue is now decided—the mind can rule matter – though I did just eat the evidence," he said with a smirk. "We are not here to debate that issue. We are here to understand the physics of it and perhaps to use that understanding to save our planet from The Object – if in fact our planet does need saving from The Object."

As if on cue, they saw Planck leave the lobby and come their way. He pulled a chair from a nearby table and sat down with them. He gave the group a boyish smile but said nothing. Then he raised his index finger and pointed at the bananas.

Dr. Wheeling nodded his head up and down, up and down, then gave Planck a bemused smile, "The banana was delicious. Never before have I observed a physics experiment that was both edifying and edible."

Planck grinned, "It wasn't magic, you know. It is both predictable and repeatable. It is just not particularly believable. That is why I thought it best to just show you."

"How do you do it?" Gabriela asked.

"I did not do it – all of us together did it. During the first fifteen minutes while you were there all of us, all 29 of us, meditated on the ripening of those bananas. I had set that up with the team earlier today. I apologized to them for the parlor trick nature of it but felt it was necessary. Then we had more serious work to do."

Dr. Wheeling seemed already to understand. "Your colleague with the brain tumor. Would I be correct in supposing that your group meditated on its disappearing? Is he now going to be all right?"

Planck nodded, "We think he'll be fine. How did you know?"

"You mentioned earlier that you needed to address that. And I have noticed that all of the residents here – yourself included – look remarkably fit and healthy. So is it the power of meditation by a large trained group with everyone focused on a single thought?"

Planck nodded and smiled again. "That is partly right. But it really helps if you have one of these." He put his hand to his right ear and pulled out a little device that resembled a hearing aid. "This little amplifier helps a lot. It broadcasts my thoughts to the Universe. Once I figured out the right frequency the Universe became much more attentive."

Dr. Wheeling, Gabriela and David all stared at the tiny electronic device. Planck said nothing.

"An amplifier," David said, not a question just a simple statement while his mind was considering the implications.

Planck then added, "We think it might work better if it was implanted inside the skull but we are not sure yet."

Dr. Wheeling started nodding his head as he did whenever his thoughts were crystalizing, "I suppose the challenge was in tuning it – both to receive and send...finding the right frequency."

Planck nodded, "More trial and error than theory. And it doesn't receive, only send. We may be talking to the universe, but it is not talking to us."

Nodding again the professor said, "Of course. I meant it receives your thoughts – not those of the universe. The electronics themselves I'm sure are quite simple."

Planck smiled, "Perhaps not that simple for me. Getting it calibrated to read very faint electromagnetic waves took some doing."

"Yes but the theory is not new."

"Agreed."

David interjected, "In doing the trial and error...what was the experiment?"

Planck smiled again, "Not very original, I'm afraid. We moved pennies with our minds."

"You can move pennies with your minds repeatedly and under observation?"

"Yes," Planck replied, and then added, "But we found that moving objects through space takes a lot of mental effort. It really is not something the universe wants to do. It prefers to change the state of things. That is easier. Like turning off cancerous cells in the body... or making green bananas ripen."

Almost concurrently Gabriela asked, "You can cure cancer?" and David asked, "You can manipulate matter at the molecular level?"

"Yes and yes. But we are still learning. We are at the very beginning of the journey."

Gabriela's eyes were wide with excitement, "But why are you keeping this a secret? You should be publishing your work, get the peer review, and wait for the Nobel Prize!"

Planck just shook his head, "It scares me to death." The three of them just looked at him, not understanding. Planck went on, "If it weren't for the appearance of The Object we would not now be talking about this."

Then Dr. Wheeling started nodding his head again. Whereas just a few moments earlier his eyes had been bright with excitement and a smile had danced on his lips, now his expression had turned somber and his eyes had narrowed with apprehension. "I think I now understand what the scientists working on The Manhattan Project felt as they designed the first nuclear bombs," he said. "The social and political implications of Planck's work are staggering!"

"One more question Planck before I must go and just think about things. Am I correct in surmising that the distance between the participant or participants who are engaging in the mental exertions and the object that is the subject of those exertions -- that distance between them is largely irrelevant? The trick...no not trick...the change you just effected to our bananas, you could have done that with us in the room or the bananas could have been 5 miles away or five hundred miles away or even five million miles away?"

Planck regarded the professor with a look of grateful appreciation. Dr. Wheeling's mind could advance with his own down the dark hidden pathways of a reality that glimmered tantalizingly close.

"Yes professor that is correct. The challenge is to locate the object in the mind. Where it is physically doesn't seem to matter. But you need to have a very precise vision of where it is exactly. You can't just give GPS coordinates."

Dr. Wheeling's expression turned gloomier, "Oh my God. Mankind is not ready for this."

When Dr. Wheeling walked away wanting some time to think, Planck too said he had some things he had to do. All agreed to meet in three hours for dinner and to resume the conversation. Gabriela and David went back to their room and decided to take a walk along the beach. They changed into shorts and tee-shirts and walked out of their room and soon had the sand underfoot and the cool ebb and flow of the sea nuzzling their ankles. The sun was nearing the horizon and a breeze lightly drifted over them dissipating the lingering heat of the day. Though they walked holding hands their thoughts were far from any notions of romance.

The writer in him led David to composing paragraphs in his mind that he was afraid he might never see published. "We are now among the very few people in the world who know that the laws of physics ... the laws of the Universe ...allow a man with just his mind –"

"Women too!" Gabriela interjected.

"Yes. Allow a person with just his or her mind to alter the molecular structure of matter and to move that matter through space. Moreover we know that this power of mental manipulation can be enhanced with a simple electronic device that broadcasts electromagnetic waves to an accommodating Universe that is apparently open to suggestions. So, you want to change the weather? Move a hurricane from here to there? No problem. You want to cure your friend or colleague of a brain tumor? No problem! Your fruit isn't ripe yet? No problem! Who knew?"

Gabriela kicked some of the surf at David. "That's why you are a writer and not a physicist! Think about what we are learning! Is everything we thought we knew about physics wrong or does this fit somewhere in it or on top of it? Planck several times mentioned 'The Universe' as if it is a partner in this. I can't wait to find out what the frequency is of Planck's little device. Is the

Universe really listening to it? I think we are going to have to redefine what we mean by 'the Universe'."

David kicked some water back at Gabriela. In doing so he took note of how great she looked in the little cropped off tee and running shorts she had on. Looking at her, people would have guessed swimsuit model long before they would have considered astrophysicist. As he was thinking about what they might do back in their room before dinner, Gabriela said, "You never told me how good looking Planck was."

"Ten years ago he wasn't. It's not that he looks so different – but now he just looks better. I guess he works out now but not then. He looked more sickly and neurotic then....Why? Do you find him attractive?" David had always been good enough looking in the sandy haired boy next door way to not have to think about how he looked. Now however, comparing himself to Planck, he felt like he might be losing out. Planck he was sure would fine Gabriela beautiful – and he didn't seem to have anyone.

"Let's see... he sort of looks like Brad Pitt and his IQ is probably around 200 and maybe his work will rewrite the laws of physics. And he doesn't feel the need to talk all the time. Sounds to me like he's every brainy girl's dream!"

David started to think about whether he should be worried. He didn't normally think in those terms. Actually it had never occurred to him before, but he had to admit, Gabriela could easily find Planck very attractive. He found he didn't like that thought at all. He tried to not think about it, and yet there it was in his mind again.

Gabriela had a delighted little smile which she hid from him when she saw the effects of her words about Planck. She took his hand and said they should go back to their room. She seemed to have the same idea in her mind that David had a few moments earlier. Apparently all the talk about physics was a turn on. Or maybe it was just the island palms swaying, the setting sun and the warm ocean breeze on their bare skin. The laws of chemistry, if not physics, seemed to be working as usual.

Later when David and Gabriela went to rejoin the professor and Planck, they found them already in spirited conversation sitting at a table on the outdoor patio. "David, Gabriela, I'm glad to see you. Planck and I have been having a wonderful conversation.

My recent work and his actually coincide....He has just been much bolder than I have in pursuing the logical extensions of what our studies and theories have been telling us. Once again it is the young minds who lead the old in Physics."

Planck looked up at them with a smile and waved them to take a seat. "Dr. Wheeling is too modest. I am already sitting at his feet and learning. I was right in sharing my secret with him... and you too."

"So where are we?" David asked as he and Gabriela took seats around the table.

The professor took the lead. "Basically we have three challenges to overcome and all three need to be addressed quickly. The first is what to do about The Object wanting to communicate with Planck? I think we know why it wants him and perhaps even how it found out about him.

"The second challenge is in advancing the understanding of the Physics involved in his work. In dealing with The Object, whether it is friendly or hostile, we may need to use what Planck has been discovering.

"The third challenge is in determining what to do about releasing to the world generally and other physicists specifically the results of Planck's work. We must do so for two reasons: one because others are probably working on it already – rarely are even the most brilliant breakthroughs not being worked concurrently by one or two others and their purposes may be less benign than Planck's. Second, the existence of The Object and the challenges it presents us may require full exposure."

"Wow," David uttered.

Then Gabriela interjected, "Since we are physicists I think we should start with the second challenge. The better we understand the actual physics involved the better we should be able to address the other two challenges."

Dr. Wheeling and Planck both agreed. As it was Planck's nature to talk little and the professor's nature to lead any intellectual conversation, he spoke first.

"My new friend Planck and I have been talking for over two hours and in those two hours my thinking has crystallized more than in the last twenty years. The foundation for all physicists' dream of a Theory of Everything is found in Planck's work. Not surprising to me is that it is rooted in extending quantum physics to the Einstein world of large masses. What happens at the absolutely tiny quantum level sets the rules for the universe itself.

"As we all know, it has been well accepted for years that an "observer" is necessary at the quantum level to turn potential mass into real mass. Without an Observer the world – the universe itself – is just a wave function of probabilities. Until the Observer shows up, nothing actually happens. Without an Observer, the universe, as it was at the time of The Big Bang, is almost without mass but it has almost limitless potentiality.

"The Universe then consists basically of the laws of physics spoken in the beautiful language of mathematics. The laws of physics and our mathematics are the Universe. But there is something else lurking out in the universe –something that changes everything – literally changes everything. It is the Observer. Or as it is better described, it is "Consciousness!" Dr. Wheeling paused and took a sip of the ice tea he had placed on the table.

Planck at this point spoke up, "The issue of consciousness is what has absorbed me from my first studies in Physics. My intuition from the first day was that rather than being a by-product of the universe, it was the universe itself. Consciousness is The Observer required by quantum physics—and it is in everything! A man's consciousness is just a piece of it. Moreover, the universal consciousness that exists – and always existed – has two imperatives of its own, for reasons I have no idea, but it is observable. The first imperative is to expand! It has a deep hunger for expansion. That is why the universe itself is expanding. And the second imperative is complexity. The more complex the universe is, the more interesting it becomes. A man's brain –or a woman's brain," Planck added with a glance to Gabriela, "is perhaps the most complex structure in the universe – at least it is so far of everything we have discovered."

"So much for Occam's razor!" David interjected. "You know I never did like the idea that a simple theory is better than a complex one. That to me seemed just a contrivance to make Physicists' work easier."

The professor chimed in here, "And this is where Planck made his breakthrough! He theorized that the Universe –

'consciousness' – needs instruction. It wants to be told what to do. It has been waiting patiently for us to develop enough to replace the burden of potentiality it has borne with our own wants and requirements – something that we have probably been doing since our earliest days as microbes without really knowing that we were now dictating to the universe what we needed and wanted."

David added, "So this universe/consciousness 'encouraged' the development of increasingly complex biological entities which ultimately became us and now it is willing to do what we want it to do? Isn't that a lot like the doctrine of Intelligent Design which all serious scientists hate the idea of?"

Dr. Wheeling shook his head, "What we are saying is not Intelligent Design. But we know simple organisms evolved to greater and greater complexity. Most of the organisms' efforts failed biologically but some succeeded by virtue of Darwinian selection. And we know that at some point in the chain of evolution that consciousness evolved to the individual level. Besides most scientists – physicists especially—prefer to ignore the consciousness issue altogether. It is the elephant in the kitchen that is so inconvenient. We know it exists but why and how?

Planck shook his head. "I think, David, consciousness is not just a property of higher forms of being, just in us. I think it is meaningless to think of it as separate from all matter, organic or inorganic. But we have become self-aware and now our will is stronger within its massive vastness. But the point is yes, the universe will within some as yet unknown limits do what we want."

David said, "You know what's funny? My sister receives a blog every day from quote the Universe close quote that gives very positive advice about how the universe wants her to get everything she wishes. And in fact there are lots of people who just generally believe that if you work hard at something the universe will aid and support –help you get what you want, that it is on our side. I've talked to a lot of people that believe that – not in a scientific kind of way but just a casual but real belief. I've heard business leaders say that if the team all will work in the same direction that the universe will support their clear intentions. I'm just saying, a lot of people believe that."

The physicist in Gabriela was fully engaged, "So where is the energy output for all this? Energy has to be involved to perform these changes of state at the massive level we are talking about."

"Precisely!" Dr. Wheeling exclaimed. "And the answer lies in something we have only recently come to believe in. An energy so vast that it moves galaxies with hundreds of billions of stars –"

"Dark Energy!" Gabriela said, "It must be Dark Energy."

Planck nodded, "That's what I think. We theorize that all of the matter and energy that we can observe is but 4% of the universe and that 96% is Dark Energy and Dark Matter – most of that Dark Energy. Imagine if that can be put to our use!"

For all four of them the potential change in the world they knew was overwhelming. They sat silently pondering this strange new view of their universe.

"So as to The Object wanting to communicate with Planck," Dr. Wheeling stated, "I think we now know 'why Benjamin Planck' and how they came to know of him. I think they somehow know how to trace unusual displays of Dark Energy – just as we know how to spot unusual electromagnetic displays. And they traced that Dark Energy back to Planck."

David's mind was now in overdrive, "So what should worry us is that what we are just figuring out, The Object has already mastered. If so, they are so much more powerful than we are that they could annihilate us – our whole planet – the way North and South Korea just annihilated themselves!"

David thought about it some more and then said, "Planck, if The Object wants to talk to you, I think you better give them a call."

*****

The leader of the Alien Earth Expedition stood on the grounds of Lafayette Park in Washington D.C. looking at the home of the man who was the most powerful human on this planet. In the weeks since the Expedition had arrived, he in particular had been responsible for understanding the leadership and government structure of this particular country – the country which from a militaristic standpoint was most clearly capable of global domination. His seconds in command were even now visiting the countries here called China and Russia and some political combination called Europe, but those countries were both less powerful militarily and less of a cultural leader.

The Alien Leader had admired the architectural beauty of the structures he had seen as he walked through this city. They spoke of grand vision and humanistic pride; they promised foundational strength for future generations. From what he had been learning, their leaders and legislators did not measure up to the architectural promise. Small minded partisanship ruled over wisdom and balance. The fateful signs of economic stagnation and political decoherence were everywhere visible to his experienced eye. And if it was so visible here then it would be worse in the other leading nations whose histories he had now accessed. This world was ripe for destruction.

The population's inclinations seemed guided toward their lowest common denominators. Leaders were chosen based on charisma and patently unredeemable promises rather than experience and judgment. Empty ideology was communicated as if bearing great truths. The galvanizing strength of Balance was nowhere understood.

In all the media he had been observing it also was clear that the virtues of respect and politeness, honesty and self-discipline were ignored. Vacuous celebrity ruled. He had seen countless proofs that the destinies of civilizations were cast by the values evident in those civilizations. This was a civilization in decay. Now its true mettle would be tested and he doubted it would pass the test – a test that was rigorous and demanding, brutal and without conscience.

He was not unsympathetic to the people or dismissive of the government's good intentions. The problem here he believed was that the political leaders had no true understanding of the challenges posed by accelerating technological development. Predisposed to solving future problems with solutions from the past, these leaders offered no new visions and would be blindsided by unanticipated challenges. Enormous challenges lurking twenty to thirty years in the future were either unknown or disregarded, yet these challenges would be upon them in a mere blink of civilization time.

The Alien leader had seen the consequences of civilization decay on other worlds - and always the political leaders had failed to recognize the early signs. Instead, in their ignorance and egotism, they pranced about in their robes of self-importance giving meaningless speeches and posing and basking in media's glare. The people they served said nothing, though they knew better. No child stepped forth and asked why their emperors wore no clothes.

*****

After hours of debate it was decided by Planck, Dr. Wheeling, Gabriela and David that Planck could not just privately reach out to The Object. The objectives of The Object were too much unknown; whether friend or foe too many unanticipatable consequences were possible. They came up with a multi-tiered approach that would precede direct contact, but first they had to be sure that Planck was the one The Object wanted. So their task began with sending out a message and seeking confirmation.

Planck organized his full meditation group and had them focus on a simple message. If The Object responded to this form of approach, they would learn more than just that Planck was indeed the one sought.

With their minds they focused on "Am I the one you seek? If I am, please say 'yes' through your usual communication."

In just moments, "Yes" appeared on their smart phone screens and on electronic screens everywhere else.

Dr. Wheeling spoke for all of them when he said, "That settles it." Then they started implementing the plan they had developed.

# CHAPTER FOUR

*"I do not know any sense in which I could claim that the universe is here in the absence of observers. We are together, the universe and us....I cannot imagine a consistent theory of everything that ignores consciousness."*

Andrei Linde
*Stanford University Professor of Physics*

Their plan started with David's writing a limited version of the story for publication in The Washington Post that would hopefully be picked up by other newspapers. It would report that it was believed that the Benjamin Planck that The Object was looking for was a young physicist who had been doing work in quantum physics based on the role of the Observer. It would hint at a new understanding of how consciousness had evolved, but it would stress that Planck's work was preliminary and theoretical. Nothing would be said of the ability to manipulate matter with one's mind and definitely nothing would be written about his little electronic amplifier!

David himself would provide a few modest quotes but claim to be as mystified as anyone about why The Object was interested in him. However David would admit that he had reached out to The Object in an unspecified way and that the "Yes" that had appeared on all the electronic screens worldwide had been in response to a query he had put to The Object.

David did stipulate that Planck did not want to be interviewed by anyone other than David and that Planck would not appear publicly. He insisted on staying out of the public glare and his whereabouts were to remain unknown.

In the article Dr. Wheeling's role was to be identified and Wheeling would confirm that David's work was interesting but still untestable. He was to downplay its importance.

And that was all that was to be written.

David wrote the story just that way and all four suggested edits and deletions and argued that too much was said and too little. They wrangled over details until David took the lead and just said they were done. That afternoon David submitted what he had written to his Editor at The Post and resisted the ranting and raving of the editor who sensed that David was holding back on more of the story. Still with David not conceding anything more, the Editor said the story would run the next morning.

At the same time that David was writing the story, Dr. Wheeling reached out to several other leading physicists who Wheeling admitted were "almost as highly regarded in the theoretical physics community" as he was. Planck had agreed that too much was at stake to work through the customary protocol of releasing a paper and then having it peer reviewed. Dr. Wheeling had convinced Planck to present his work with a demonstration to the select few he would contact and that they would all be sworn to secrecy. A meeting in New York would be set up for a few days later.

They all had also agreed that a meeting with the Government of the United States would also have to be set up immediately after The Washington Post had published the story. As it turned out, David was the only one with a contact, his uncle, Brigadier General Mark Randall, that seemed at all the right starting point. Dr. Wheeling said he had met the President's science advisor but was not impressed and it was only a casual acquaintance anyway. They figured David's uncle was as good a way to start as any. Planck himself knew no one.

In fact, Planck's participation in all these discussions was limited. The more they considered the likely events that would follow the story's publication in The Post, the more he withdrew from the discussion. The withdrawn and uncommunicative Planck that David had known at Columbia was reappearing. Planck made Wheeling and David promise that they would take the lead on moving forward and that he could remain closeted away in the background. Only in the discussions with other physicists did Planck want to play a central and vocal part.

Though they discussed how The Object might react to what they were doing, none actually had any particular insight. Too much was unknown.

With no part to play, Gabriela listened to the discussion and said little. Only at the end when all was set to role forward did she speak up. Cassandra like, she voiced her concern that they were opening a Pandora's Box. Things would not go well. David dismissed her concerns to himself and the others as just her usual dark personality. They all went to bed that night on Pirates Cay thinking the morrow would be an interesting day.

*****

The next day's Washington Post had the front page headline and story:

> **Benjamin Planck Found! Aliens confirm he's the one they want**
> Story by David Randall
>
> *The worldwide manhunt for Benjamin Planck is over. The man the aliens of The Object told us they wanted to meet has been identified as Benjamin M. Planck, a young physicist with a PhD from Columbia University who has been residing at a Zen Buddhist retreat on a remote island in The Bahamas. While at the retreat he has been doing research in the field of advanced theoretical physics focusing on the need for an Observer in Quantum Mechanics. Although very reluctant to come forward into the public glare, Mr. Planck has agreed to share with this newspaper the nature of his work and why it appears to have gained the attention of The Object.*
>
> *That Planck is indeed the man The Object was seeking was confirmed by a message sent by Planck to The Object. The manner with which Planck communicated with The Object is still undisclosed*

*but it was the reason for yesterday's cryptic "YES" message sent out by The Object worldwide. Planck did confirm to this newspaper that the form of his message was only possible as a result of the research work he has been involved with over the last five years. Planck described that work as "demonstrating that the fundamental nature of the universe is a construct of consciousness." He emphasized however that his work is still very preliminary and theoretical. If not for the enormous amount of attention flowing from The Object's seeking him out, Planck emphasized that he would not be going public with his theories at this time.*

*Planck has shared the basics of his work with the Nobel Prize winning physicist, Dr. Janus Wheeling. Dr. Wheeling describes Planck's work as brilliant and transformative but hastened to add that "It is not ready for Prime Time. It needs much further thought and experiment before it could be published for peer review." Although it should be noted that as Dr. Wheeling observed, "The Object seems to think that Dr. Planck's work has merit. They aren't asking to communicate with me or anyone else."*

*As made available thus far, the implications of Planck's work would not just cause a dramatic new understanding of the laws of physics, but could also raise far reaching issues in the fields of philosophy and religion. If consciousness is indeed a fundamental attribute of existence as Planck's work appears to indicate, man's role in the universe would take on a potentially much more involved prominence. This view would be at odds with the understanding and theories of a majority of theoretical physicists today.*

*Planck's theory positions consciousness not as a result of formative drivers of the Universe but instead as the principal causation factor. Planck says, "It is consciousness that drives the universe to*

> *evolve from an infinite state of potentiality into specific states of existence." Moreover he asserts, that consciousness "has the power to change any particular state of existence into a different state of existence." In other words, according to Planck, even after matter has coalesced into a particular form, that particular matter can be changed into a different molecular structure through the application of the force of consciousness.*
>
> *Planck acknowledges that his work borrows from views of physicists like John Wheeler who have long wondered about the role of consciousness in the formation of the universe. He believes he is merely moving their ideas forward into a more structured and empirically provable theory. He also insists that his work is very preliminary.*
>
> *This of course leaves us with the question, "Why does The Object want to communicate with Dr. Planck?"*

*****

As the leader of the team watched the sun rise he uttered a curse in Russian then switched to English to tell the boat captain to take the boat in a little closer to the island but to stay out of sight of the buildings near the shore. He had hoped that he could have made the pickup while it was still dark but the instructions had come too late and there had been too much to do. Still the instructions were clear. Regardless of what might be involved, he was to complete his mission.

He knew why it had to be done. The intelligence service for which he had been working for the last ten years had been looking for a week for any signs of the person they needed to extract and then suddenly the pieces of information they had meticulously gathered all came together and they knew they had the right person – or at least they could not afford to pass up the chance. It turned out that he was closest to the target and could put together the team in the time available. He also knew that time was precious. Others would come to the same conclusion. He had been a little lucky to be able to move so fast, but others might be lucky too.

He decided the big fishing boat was close enough and he motioned to the three others of his team to get in the smaller boat with the little outboard engine. He joined them and they shoved off toward the deserted piece of shore they had chosen as their point of entry. The four of them all wore shorts and loose fitting un-tucked-in Tommy Bahama shirts and might resemble any group of guys out for a day of fishing except none had much of a tan and there wasn't an extra ten pounds of fat on the four of them combined. Like the team leader they were very fit and very sure in all of their actions. Each also had a pistol tucked into their waistband though make and model differed based on personal preference.

As they neared the mangrove lined shore they jumped out of the small boat and pulled it up on the sand where it was relatively hidden. If things went to plan they would be back to it in minutes. They left at a trot toward the resort buildings that were only a few hundred yards away.

Their problem was they did not know much about the layout of the property nor exactly where their target would be. It had been agreed that once they were within sight of the buildings, the others would get as close as possible while staying out of sight while the leader would simply walk in from the beach and ask for the person they were looking for. He would claim that his boat had broken down on the other side of the small island. From what they had seen there was little likelihood of real resistance and the leader believed that keeping things simple was often best.

As he approached the main building he was surprised to see how many people were about despite that it was only a few minutes after sunrise. But as he got closer he saw they were all in a main room sitting monk like in prayer. Most of them never looked up at him even though he was now only fifty feet away. But one who had looked up rose from where he was sitting in a lotus position and came over to talk to the leader.

The leader smiled. The man he had come to take was the man who was approaching him.

Planck came within a few feet and asked, "Can I help you?"

The team leader's response came quickly. "Yes, you can come with me."

Planck was surprised. "Who are you and why would I do that?"

The leader motioned to his men to show themselves and he took out his gun and pointed it at Planck, "You will come with me because I have this gun and because they also have guns."

Planck looked at the three other men. Then he looked back at where the prayer meeting had been taking place. Everyone there was now looking at him. Though they saw the men with the guns, only one of them reacted. David stood up from where he had been sitting in the back of the room and looked at the man with Planck. Planck raised his hands to them all, including David, to remain calm. As Planck lowered his hands, David saw him press his index finger into his ear. He's pressing his amplifier deeper to ensure it doesn't slip out, David thought when he saw Planck's gesture.

Planck saw that David noticed and subtly nodded. "Let's go then," Planck said and went with the leader and his men back to where they had left their boat.

David watched the men lead Planck away and then followed them. He stayed back what he hoped was a safe distance. He saw them pull the little boat back into the water and put Planck in it and climb in after him. He saw them start the engine and take it out to the bigger fishing boat. Then he watched that boat head off away from the island. It was too far away for him to read a name. He watched it a while longer until it was almost out of sight but then he noticed it didn't actually go out of sight. He could not see any detail, it was too far out, but he could see that something was still there. It seemed stopped in the water. He wasn't sure but it occurred to him that Planck might have something to do with that.

Staring at the boat, he thought about what he had to do next. Then he took out his smart phone and he called his uncle, the general.

General Mark Randall was in a hastily called emergency meeting with about twenty other senior officers tasked with dealing with the threat posed by The Object. The meeting had been called as soon as The Washington Post had come out that morning with his nephew's article emblazoned on the front page. It also had an old picture of Ben Planck. The three star general leading the meeting was passing downstream the shit he had just been getting from his boss for not knowing sooner than The Washington Post anything about Benjamin Planck. Mark Randall had already had to confess that it was his nephew who had written the story.

Then his cell phone started vibrating and he checked it and learned that David was calling him. He just shook his head resignedly. He knew he had to take the call and he knew he first had to interrupt the general who was then speaking and then tell everyone who was on his line.

Then he answered David's call with everyone in the meeting watching him.

Without preamble Mark Randall asked, "Is the story in The Washington Post true?"

"Yes,'" David replied.

"David, right this minute I'm in a meeting at the Pentagon with some of the highest ranking officers in our military. Now is not the time to play games. Before you called we were speculating that there is more to your story than appeared in The Post. Do you know more than you wrote in your article?"

With the abduction of Planck David knew that their previous limited disclosure plan was out the window. After a moment's pause, he said, "Yes – actually there is a lot more. But before I say anything more, I have to ask you a question. Because I think we have an emergency to deal with."

"Hold on David, I'm going to put my phone on speaker. Is there any reason I shouldn't do that?"

After another pause, David said, "No I guess not."

"Alright. You're on the speaker now. What's your question and what is the possible emergency?"

"My question is, did anyone in the U.S. government just send a team of men to kidnap Benjamin Planck off the beach here in Pirate's Cay in The Bahamas? ....Because if you didn't, someone else sure did!"

Looking around the room of men, all Mark Randall saw were faces bearing the same shocked expression that he felt his own face probably showed.

"David, give me a minute. I need to put you on hold." Mark pressed the mute button. Looking once more around the room, he asked, "Does anyone know anything about this?"

Everyone there looked at each other. Each of them knew it was possible that someone else was doing something. In the room were senior leaders not just of the branches of the military but also of DoD, CIA, DIA, Homeland Security and The White House. All shook their heads. Mark Randall knew that mere denial by them did not mean for certain that no one was doing anything but from the way their conversations had been going he believed they all were equally in the dark about who Benjamin Planck was and why The Object was interested in him.

Before switching off the mute button Mark said to the men and women in the room, "If it wasn't us, then there are a whole lot of things we have to do immediately. Everyone nodded their assent. Mark hit the mute button.

"David, it wasn't us. Please tell us what you know."

Feeling more awed and intimidated than he would have thought by people he figured were now listening to him on the other end of the call, David recounted how Planck had just been kidnapped off the beach and then taken away by the men in the fishing boat. Then he described how the fishing boat seemed to have stalled just at the visible edge of the horizon.

General Mark Randall told David to hold on again and switched him back to mute. To the people in the meeting room he said, "Obviously we have to get a team out there immediately." A Navy Admiral and a man in civilian dress rose out of their chairs, nodded their heads to the people in the room and left the meeting.

At that point the Army General who had been leading the meeting came over to the table in front of Mark Randall where his cell phone was resting and motioned to Mark that he wanted to speak to David as well.

"David, this is General Carl Greene. I'm the one in charge on this –at least for the moment. You mentioned that you knew more about this Benjamin Planck thing than was in the paper. Could you tell us what you know please? We are all very eager to hear but take your time and please be complete."

On the other end, still standing on the beach in front of the resort buildings, with the view of the fishing boat still barely in sight, with a somewhat stunned sense of weird reality settling in on him, David locked his mind in on just telling what he knew. All of it. Once he had met Planck on the island he had known that events could get very big very fast, but it had all seemed so theoretical, just discussions on advanced Physics, Planck playing the role of the brilliant young Einstein and Dr. Wheeling playing the role of the dubious but equally brilliant older scientist. David and Gabriela were the privileged audience. The role playing was over.

"Sir, I'm not really sure where to begin...Perhaps I should start with how I found Planck – and by the way, he did not want to be found, and that was before The Object said it wanted to meet him! After that started, he really did not want to be found! He is somewhat reclusive ... which is why it has taken this long." David went on with how he had remembered Ben Planck from his days at Columbia and thought that he might be the right Benjamin Planck. Then David told them he had spent many hours hunting Planck through the internet and how he had come up with the story about the two hurricanes that against all-weather tracking odds seemed to go around Pirate's Cay where David had set up a religious retreat.

Then David described how he had enlisted Dr. Janus Wheeling to go with him to meet with Planck and that once there they learned that Planck had moved theoretical physics to a new frontier.

General Greene interrupted, "Wait a minute...let me digest what you just said. You said that this Benjamin Planck had the power to move not one but two hurricanes so that they wouldn't hit his island. And then you said that you and Dr. Janus Wheeling –the Nobel Prize winning Dr. Wheeling no less, went down to this tiny Bahamian island where Planck had a sort of meditation slash theoretical physics group. And that then you and Dr. Wheeling and Planck discussed theoretical physics. Do I have that more or less right?"

"Yes sir...I know it sounds pretty bizarre."

General Greene cut in again, "Son, everything about The Object is pretty bizarre. It's because your story is bizarre that I tend to believe you. I also have read your science writings in the past. I loved your series about finding the Higgs Boson. So I have a simple question for you. Do you believe ....and does Dr. Wheeling believe that Planck moved those hurricanes away from his island?"

"Yes sir, I do. And so does Dr. Wheeling."

Greene continued, "I have a feeling I'm not going to like the answer to my next question. How did he move those hurricanes?"

David's response came quickly, "With his mind, Sir."

"With his mind?"

"Yes sir. Actually with his mind and with the minds of other people here on the island. About thirty other people."

Then David heard the General say, "This is going to be a nightmare."

There was total quiet in the meeting room. Then General Greene finished shaking his head and asserted control. "David, is Dr. Wheeling there with you on the island?"

"Yes sir."

"Well I think it is too dangerous for you to stay there. I don't want anything more said on your cell phone. I'm going to send a plane to go pick you up ...you and Dr. Wheeling. I want to bring you here to the Pentagon. And then I'm going to want to hear everything. We happen to have an Air Force base at Homestead in Florida. My guess is a plane will be there in not much more than an hour. Is this all right with you?"

"Do Dr. Wheeling and I actually have a say in this?"

"It is better if you say yes. But yes you will be picked up there."

"Then I better go find Dr. Wheeling."

David found Dr. Wheeling in the lobby area. He had heard the bare details of the kidnapping of Planck. David filled him in on what he had seen and on the conversation he just had. He agreed that Planck's kidnapping changed everything. He went back to his room to gather his things. David went back to his room and found Gabriela and caught her up too. She wanted to go to the Pentagon with him but since they didn't know how that would work out and no one knew anything about her yet she ultimately agreed to find her way back to New York. Both Dr. Wheeling and David thought it would be best if she could share what they now knew with a couple of Wheeling's peers and she was the best one to do that.

Neither Dr. Wheeling nor David were really comfortable with submitting themselves to thecare and control of the generals in the Pentagon, so they thought the more people that knew they were there the better. David then called the Editor at the Washington Post and just told him that there were new developments that he could not yet talk about but that if he didn't hear anything from him in two days to start asking questions at the Pentagon. David wasn't sure if he was being paranoid or smart... or dangerously naïve.

But before the military came to get him there was one other person David wanted to talk to there on the island. He went in search of Catherine Ozawa; the Zen Master Planck had brought to the island. Planck had introduced them the first afternoon.

With his usual almost total recall, David remembered the brief bio Planck had told him about Ozawa. She had been born in San Francisco to parents who had emigrated from Japan prior to World War Two. As an adult she had returned to Japan and studied at a Zen Buddhist monastery there for ten years. As a woman that had been difficult but she had adjusted to what could be done. In her bio she had written, "On the path to Enlightenment there aren't separate restrooms for men and women." David had liked that when he read it.

Then she had returned to the Bay area where she founded her own retreat. Along the way she had also studied advanced physics and had a Doctorate from Stanford to show for it. She found no incongruity between Zen Buddhism and theoretical physics. She thought the doctrine of Karma was just another way that the Observer functioned in the universe. She also had worked at some early Silicon Valley start-ups that were now worth billions of dollars. Planck sought her out and convinced her to come join him on Pirate's Cay.

David found her in conversation with two of her students in the lobby. When she saw David wanted to speak to her she left the two monks and came over to where David was standing under a palm tree.

Catherine Ozawa was in her late sixties. Somehow she looked like age was not relevant to her. Her face was lined with a few wrinkles that seemed to be in the right places, laugh lines stood out around her eyes. Her body was lean and her posture straight. Her hair was mostly white and short. Her eyes were somehow old and her expression calm but careworn.

David stared awkwardly for a moment; he had never talked to a Zen Master before. "I'm sorry; I don't really know what to call you. Should I call you Master?"

"Just call me Catherine."

"OK Catherine... I guess you pretty much know about everything that goes on here..." Ozawa nodded and David continued, "Well, whoever it was that just abducted Planck, it seems it was not the US government. I just was talking to a bunch of generals and they claim ignorance. But within the next two hours I'm betting this island will be swarming with soldiers. And Dr. Wheeling and I are going to be picked up and taken to the Pentagon."

Ozawa considered the implications, "I had better go and tell everyone."

"Before you do there are some questions I'd like to ask you."

"I'm sure you have many."

David smiled, "Yea. Too many for the time we probably have. But my first one is, how powerful is this mind over matter capability that you and Planck and the others here are working on?"

Ozawa held out her hands with the palms open to the sky. "How powerful is the universe?"

"Is that a koan? Like what is the sound of one hand clapping? I think I need to talk to the person with the Doctorate in Physics not the Zen Master."

Ozawa laughed, "No that was not a koan. That was my physics answer. What we are learning here is that consciousness gives form to everything. So the power is almost infinite. However, if the question you really are asking is how much can Planck and those of us here actually manipulate so far, well the answer to that is not all that much. We are just beginning to learn."

"Moving hurricanes is not such a little thing."

"That depends on the point of comparison. Let me answer your question this way – with what we know how to do already we can change weather patterns all over the world. We can solve the global energy problem. We can do things that would seem like miracles. But...and this is a big but, we have no solution yet for the law of unintended consequences. We are not wise enough to use the power – and mankind is definitely not wise enough."

David paused then and looked at the little wizard of a woman who was telling him that the world was about to change. "You know that there is now no way to hold this back – your secret will not be a secret much longer."

Catherine nodded. "I told Planck that. The coming of The Object hastened everything... but the future can never be held back. The ocean's tides cannot be resisted."

"Was that the physicist or the Zen Master?"

Ozawa laughed again, "That was the Zen Master."

David nodded, "Then let me ask the Zen Master a question. I've been beating my head against the wall on this. What does this new understanding of physical reality actually mean for us as people? Is this a good thing or a bad thing?"

Ozawa held her hands out with palms up again, "It won't change the fundamental nature of man or of life. Life is change. Karma will still exist. A man will still be judged by the good and bad he does. The cycle of life won't change. Actually for me it solves a puzzle that has confounded me since I was a young woman. You see, in Zen Buddhism we believe that Karma is real, reincarnation is real. But we do not believe in a god. Buddha was godly but not a god. So the puzzle for me was, 'how is Karma determined? Who or what is the judge? There is cause and effect, but as seen through what lens or set of factors? But now the answer is less cloudy. Karma is administered through Consciousness. So now I have a new puzzle. What is consciousness?"

"You got me! But I have another question: what is the role of meditation in this?"

"It is pivotal! Only through meditation can one truly learn how to focus the mind with such clarity that the universe can pick out the individual message from the sea of chaotic mental states produced by the billions of people just on this planet. Meditation provides the clearest link –the link without static –to the universal mind. In fact, new studies show that the physical mind, the brain, actually changes at the neuron level in those people who engage in significant meditation. There are physical and functional changes to the brain that improve a person's ability to perceive reality."

David interrupted, "What you are saying is that meditation will not only allow you to better perceive reality – it can also allow you to change reality. And that, Zen Master is a whole other thing!"

Ozawa just held her hands open again.

David just shook his head. "In a few hours I am going to have to explain that to a roomful of military bigwigs who are just going to hate all this. And then they are going to want to know how to weaponize it."

As if on cue they heard what turned out to be two Gulfstream executive jets coming in to land on Pirate Cay's landing strip. David said goodbye to Catherine Ozawa and wished her luck and went to find Dr. Wheeling.

It took only a few minutes for the team of ten men coming off the Gulfstream jets to approach David and Dr. Wheeling as they waited at the front of the retreat's main building. Though clad in polo shirts and either jeans or khakis, the team made no attempt to hide their weaponry. The one in charge walked right up to them and introduced himself as Captain Donald Deutsch.

He said, "Dr. Wheeling, David, as I think you know, I'm here to take you to a meeting at the Pentagon. But first if you don't mind, I'd like my men to look around the island and make sure that everything is OK." David noticed that his men were already moving, doing exactly that.

David then introduced him to Catherine Ozawa who he described as the leader of the Retreat that accounted for the people and the buildings on the island. Turning to Ozawa Captain Deutsch informed her that he had orders to leave most of his men on the island to ensure that whoever had abducted Benjamin Planck did not return to take anyone else. Both Dr. Wheeling and David looked at each other with quick glances that suggested they did not quite believe that was the real reason but said nothing.

Ozawa smiled and said that she and her people would welcome their presence.

Captain Deutsch turned back to David and the professor. "For your information, we sent a team out to find the fishing boat."

David interrupted and pointed out at the tiny blur of a boat that could still be seen on the water's horizon. "You mean that one?"

"Yes sir, that one."

"Well that's great! Is Planck OK? Was there any trouble getting him?"

The Captain's response was a negative. "We didn't get him because he wasn't on the boat. The boat was deserted."

David was incredulous, "There was no one on it?"

Captain Deutsch looked back impassively and gave a minimal shake of his head. "The boat was just floating there. No one was on it. Strangely when we tried to start it up again, we couldn't. The engine seemed frozen."

David thought about that and then asked, "What about a little dingy with an outboard? Was it there?"

"Yes, it was there. It wasn't used to take anyone off the boat. We couldn't get it to work either."

Dr. Wheeling spoke up for the first time, "It seems our problems are getting bigger. I presume you are still looking for him."

"Yes sir, we are. But frankly we have no idea what happened on that boat."

"I guess some other boat must have met them and picked them up. Is there no sign of any other boat?" David asked.

"No sign at all."

"Poor Planck," was all David could think to say.

Captain Deutsch gestured to one of the unmarked Gulfstream exec jets. "I'm to get you to Washington as fast as possible. So we need to leave now. My men are going to stay and ask questions about the abduction this morning and they'll be able to follow up if anything new happens here. Shall we go?"

A little more than four hours later, accompanied by David's uncle who had met them at an entrance to the Pentagon, and after walking down more hallways than David had ever known to exist in a single building, they entered a meeting room and were introduced to General Carl Greene. The General then introduced the other officers in the room and the lone civilian sitting at the table. Counting Wheeling and David there were a total of eight to sit at the meeting room table. Dr. Wheeling did not need the last introduction to the man in the grey suit.

"Andrei! How nice to see you again. How are my friends at MIT? Are you here perhaps to help our military friends with a little physics?"

Dr. Kasinsky rose out of his chair to shake Wheeling's hand, "It is a pleasure to see you again, Janus. I'm very much looking forward to hearing about the 'little physics' that we might discuss. From time to time I do some consulting with our friends here but I think this might be especially interesting."

David looked at Kasinsky with surprise. He hadn't expected another physicist to accompany the generals, but he realized he should have. Kasinsky was average height, middle aged and balding but his round face was enlivened with large round eyes that seemed to actively regard everything around him.

With everyone seated General Greene spoke first and had everyone introduce themselves. Then immediately he switched to the core topic. Greene had the look of a man who would always be focused on the core issues with no tolerance for perambulations. Certainly now, with the seriousness of the issues they all confronted, whatever casualness and humor might sometimes be revealed on his face were nowhere to be seen. His close cropped dark hair had grey mixed in and his square brow and cheekbones and strong jawline all showed a weather beaten tenacity that would yield to nothing. Yet his blue eyes betrayed his stern countenance, they suggested a warm and engaging intelligence. If he was the man in charge at the Pentagon for all things alien, David thought that an open mind was going to be needed.

"As I understand things," Greene began, "we have two distinct challenges that seem to have occurred concurrently but perhaps deliberately so. And at the core of both of those challenges there seems to be scientific issues that go to the heart of theoretical physics. The first challenge is presented to us by The Object and its apparent ability to move in defiance of physical laws – and its ability to simply disappear multiple missiles. The second challenge comes from the discoveries of Benjamin Planck that seem to suggest that mind over matter should not be just relegated to some sort of metaphysical daydream. Somehow the human mind can manipulate matter. And this capability is no longer theoretical it is actual and replicable."

The General paused and looked around the room. Then he added, "And it also appears that these two challenges come together because The Object has asked to communicate with only one individual out of all the billions of people on this planet and that individual is Dr. Planck. And to make matters even more challenging, Dr. Planck now seems to have been abducted by parties unknown off of his small island in The Bahamas where he was doing reality changing physics unknown to all of the rest of us."

The General paused again and looked around the room. "Now do I have that about right?"

No one said anything. His two staff officers and David's uncle, General Randall, all looked down at the table.

Greene looked at Dr. Wheeling. "Could you at least summarize what new physics we have here? Now it was a long time ago but I had Physics at West Point and I have followed it as an interesting hobby. But please feel free to dummy it down somewhat."

Dr. Wheeling responded by standing up and addressing the group as if he was speaking to a class back at Columbia. "Let me explain. For the last 100 years, theoretical physics has had a huge problem right at its heart. We knew how matter behaved at the large mass level. Classic physics as explained by Einstein. And we knew how matter behaved at the particle level. Neils Bohr, Max Planck and many others showed us quantum mechanics. All of our electronic devices work because of what we know about quantum physics. However our problem is that those theories don't work together. Though Einstein and Bohr were friends, their theories do not get along with each other. They are ultimately incompatible. Hence for a 100 years we have been looking for a theory that ties them together –what we call The Theory of Everything.

"What our friend Benjamin Planck has shown us is that what we know about quantum mechanics can in fact also apply to the everyday world of large mass. But the quantum world is a very strange world filled with spooky and bizarre results. It is a world of potentiality where a particle could be here or it could be there. Particles can pop in and out of existence. Where particles that are entangled can influence each other instantly regardless of distance and ignore the speed of light barrier. And worst of all, and we have many experiments that show this, it is a world where nothing becomes real until an Observer is there to see it. Particles remain in an opportunistic state. And when they did resolve themselves to a particular result because of the Observer, we did not know why it picked the result it did from what could have been many possible results –although we knew that some results were more likely than others."

Dr. Wheeling looked to Dr. Kasinsky, "You would agree?"

Kasinsky nodded, "All of that is well understood."

Dr. Wheeling continued, "What Planck figured out was that the Observer is really what we call consciousness and that consciousness can dictate quantum level results and then he figured out how to instruct that consciousness to produce a particular result and then to his great surprise he discovered that what could be done at the particle level could be done at any level of mass."

Dr. Kasinsky interrupted, "This makes me think of John Wheeler's famous statement of 'it from bit'. That is that at the core of reality is information. Quantum Information. Matter evolves from information. And consciousness is the user of that information. Or perhaps it is better to say that Consciousness is the construct of that information."

Dr. Wheeling approved. "Perhaps that is correct. But let me continue. Because the next thing that Planck discovered was how to issue instructions using meditation powers aided by an electronic amplifier to literally change the state of matter."

General Greene interrupted here, "Not just changed particles ...he changed the weather – he moved hurricanes around. Is that right?"

The Professor nodded his head, "Yes that is correct. But we are at only the beginning. The limits of what can be done are as yet untested."

General Greene was shaking his finger to get back to a prior point. "Dr. Wheeling, you just mentioned something I had not heard before. Did I hear you say that Dr. Planck invented an electronic amplifier that somehow enhances the ability to change matter? Really, an amplifier?"

"Yes an amplifier that fits in the ear that essentially makes it easier for the Universe to understand what it is being asked to do. Think of it as a reverse hearing aid."

"How is that even possible?" The General was clearly dismayed.

The Professor was in his best classroom mode. "Conceptually it is quite simple. The brain is essentially an electronic device that emits electromagnetic waves. The amplifier essentially increases the volume of the waves. And then when you give such a device to a group of people all of whom together focus on the same action, the volume and the clarity of the message is increased proportionately."

David spoke up then, "General, perhaps an analogy will help. Imagine you are standing at the entrance to a very large and very busy restaurant. You would hear a loud buzz of conversation but you couldn't pick out the words of any one person at one of the tables. But if now that person and the others at his table had bullhorns and all shouted the same message, even over all the cacophony of the people in the restaurant you would still hear the message shouted by that table. We think that is how this works. Normally, the universe just hears the cacophony of individual minds so it goes about doing what it does, but whenever one message starts dominating, then the universe moves in that direction."

The General looked back at Wheeling. "Would you agree with that?"

The Professor smiled. "David has a wonderful ability to simplify very complicated matters. But essentially, yes, what he said is what we think happens."

"And Dr. Kasinsky what do you think of this? Is it possible?" The General asked.

Dr. Kasinsky looked left and right and then left and right, obviously considering how to respond. Finally he said, "Before The Object came and then asked for Planck, before I heard that he moved hurricanes around, I would have laughed and said it was nonsense. But The Object is here and it did ask for Dr. Planck and my colleague Dr. Wheeling assures me that the hurricanes did change their path, so with all that, the explanation that what we see is quantum mechanical applications subsuming Einstein's universe. Well, I guess so."

The General nodded, "I'm taking that as a yes." He turned to his fellow officers at the table. "Do you guys have anything you want to ask?" No one spoke up.

"All right then," General Greene continued. "I'm going to put the physics of all this aside. That's not my day job. My day job is keeping this country safe. And what I have been learning today scares me very badly. So my next question is, is it possible that anyone else here on Earth, not counting The Object, may have figured out the same things that our now missing Dr. Planck figured out?"

Dr. Kasinsky responded, "In science it is rare that just one scientist figures out the breakthrough thinking. Usually more than one researcher is on a concurrent path, even though neither one knows anything of the other."

"I agree," said Dr. Wheeling.

General Greene just shook his head. "Then let me imagine something really horrible and then you tell me whether it is possible. If someone in say China figured out how to do what Planck figured out – only he was working for the Chinese government – and they asked him to move a hurricane, or a typhoon in this example, so as it would not move away from a city but rather move to hit a city or say the nuclear plants in northern Japan, would that be possible?"

At this point one of the General's officers sitting at the table spoke up, "In other words, could the typhoon that devastated the Japanese economy and re-invigorated their anti-nuclear policy a couple of years ago been the result of 'weaponizing' the weather?"

Dr. Wheeling said what everyone had already concluded, "A hurricane or typhoon, same thing, would go where directed."

"And no one could ever prove anything," the General added. "What a strange new world we are about to live in." He looked back at his fellow officers. Their expressions told the same story; the implications were mind-numbing.

"But one thing is very clear – we have to find Dr. Planck and get him back!" He stood up from his chair. "One more thing, Dr. Wheeling, David, I think we had better go meet with the President. I think he will want to hear this directly from you."

# CHAPTER FIVE

*"Before an observation is made, an object exists in all possible states simultaneously. To determine which state the object is in, we have to make an observation, which 'collapses' the wave function, and the object goes into a definite state. The act of observation destroys the wave function, and the object now assumes a definite reality."*

Michio Kaku
*Professor of Theoretical Physics at the Graduate Center of the City University of New York*

The number two in command of the alien expedition stood at the edge of the giant square in the heart of the old city in Beijing. He marveled at its ancient beauty, its feeling of timeless and indefatigable power. He had now spent weeks learning all he could about China's culture and history and he was stunned how this huge country could have had its billion people dominated by so few for so long. And the power of those few was staggering. Whether it was the Emperor and his senior advisors during earlier centuries or the Head of the Party and the small number of senior Party leaders, who were running the country now, control over the hundreds of millions of people was almost absolute.

And to the Alien's mind, the history of this wonderful land and its hard working people did not do much to recommend that leadership. Life seemed to come very cheap here. Millions of people could be lost and no one might notice. This was a country where secrets stayed secret. The men in power faced no internal challenges. And their global intentions were obscure and undisclosed.

It was ironic that like Benjamin Planck in the United States that they too were keeping secret that they had discovered the ability to manipulate matter through meditation. They too kept secret that they had invented an amplifier to better accomplish their purposes. But unlike Benjamin Planck their reason for keeping it secret was not out of fear of its use. They had every intention of using it. Their early trials they viewed as astoundingly effective. The Aliens had traced these attempts and well understood what had occurred.

It was not in the Alien's mind to judge how the Chinese had used this new capability against their old enemy Japan. Japan's treatment of the Chinese during and preceding what here was called World War II was horrific. And memories of devastation and butchery could be generations long. The Alien's culture included such memories. And revenge, even long later, could be noble. War was a natural event, and not just for humans. But war had consequences that could last forever. The Alien knew that his opinion about what to do about China was still unformed. As everything about China, on its surface it seemed simple to understand; but complexity always hid underneath.

What most intrigued the Alien about China was its difference in historical perspective compared to the industrialized western countries. This led to a vast difference in the perception of time. Particularly compared to the ever impatient and immediate United States, China's thoughts were long term; its strategies would be unhurried. Also importantly, it had no moral or political construct that limited its dreams of empire. Empire was its natural destiny, China believed. Whether it would take twenty years or a hundred years, no matter; the desired result was unchanging and the means would be adapted to the times. Any relationship with China that did not address that understanding would fail.

The Alien had seen other nations on other worlds with the worldview of China. Their drive for empire was always inexorable and indefatigable. And it was always a challenge for their neighboring countries. Wars were inevitable.

*****

Gabriela knew she had to get off the island. As beautiful as it was, the ocean at its edges was a prospective prison wall. As she watched the executive jet bearing David and Dr. Wheeling take off, she knew she shouldn't be far behind. She didn't trust the situation to stay stable. The forces that were coming into play were much too big and the collateral damage to those who were just casual observers could be substantial – even fatal she feared. And that wasn't just her eastern European ancestors talking to her, as David would have claimed.

Just then she spotted Catherine Ozawa walking across the grounds. She called and walked over to her. As usual, she went right to her concern. "I have a problem."

Catherine smiled, "You want to get off the island. Very wise."

Gabriela nodded, not surprised at all that this wise woman knew immediately what her problem was. "Yes exactly! And quickly!"

"I think that if you do not leave quickly you will soon not be able to go at all."

"You think that too?"

"I'm surprised they haven't already locked down the island. I think that is only because they have not figured it out yet. But they will."

"By 'they' we mean our government, right?" Gabriela did not find Ozawa's agreement comforting.

Ozawa nodded, "Yes of course. They will do what government's do. When they don't know what to do, they increase their control over everything. The people on this island know too much."

"So are you going to leave now?" Gabriela hoped she would say yes and that she could go with her.

"No I'm going to stay." When Gabriela showed her surprise at her answer, she continued. "This is my island. Actually it belongs to Planck and me, but he is not here so I should watch over it. But even if that were not the case, I would stay. The work will go on here. Most of my students and fellow physicists have all decided to stay. This is a good place to ride out the coming storm."

"If no one is leaving, how can I leave?" Gabriela asked.

"Actually, one of our number is about to leave. Apparently he is not eager for a close examination of his past. So two of our team are going to take him to Nassau on one of our faster fishing boats – there on the dock you can see they are about to leave." She pointed down the beach about a hundred yards away to the small jetty where a fishing boat was rocking and several men were tending to it.

Gabriela looked over at them. They looked about to cast off. 'Can I go with them?"

"I think you should. But go right now. They will not wait." She waved at the men at the boat and one of them saw her. She held up her hand for them to see and pointed at Gabriela. They nodded.

Gabriela realized there was no time to go back to her room to pick up her things, she turned back to Catherine Ozawa.

"Good luck, Gabriela, I look forward to seeing you again!"

"You too!" said Gabriela as she turned to hurry to the boat.

*****

Their meeting with The President of the United States was set for 10AM the next morning. Dr. Wheeling made dinner plans with a friend from Georgetown University and David went off to stay the night with his uncle Mark. He assumed that once at Mark's house they would talk about The Object, about Physics and all the rest of it. But he was proved wrong. His uncle informed him that General Greene had ordered him to not talk to David about any of it. They had to keep it to family matters.

In the morning Mark Randall drove David to pick up Dr. Wheeling from his hotel and took them both to The White House. He helped usher them through the process but then handed the two of them over to General Greene who led them into a meeting room. Neither David nor Dr. Wheeling had ever been in the White House before so they both walked through it somewhat star-struck. Neither of them knew one room from the next. David decided to act cool and didn't ask and Dr. Wheeling seemed preoccupied with other thoughts – not unusual for him.

When they entered the meeting room in the West Wing adjacent to the Oval Office, it was clear that the meeting had been going on for a while already. David had prepared for the meeting by convincing himself that he would not be overwhelmed. But as the President came over to shake his hand, he felt that resolve slip away. It wasn't just the presence of the President but there in the room as well was his Chief of Staff Hank Scarpetti, the President's chief political advisor, Barbara Wilcox, the Secretary of Defense, Joe Anderson and someone who he thought was the Chairman of the Joint Chiefs – whose name he couldn't remember. No introductions were made and Dr. Wheeling and David took the two empty seats they were directed to.

The President retook his seat at the head of the table on a chair that had a higher back than everyone else's. David had heard of the man's charismatic warmth but had doubted he would succumb to it, yet as he saw the man from just a few feet away and as that man smiled at him, he wasn't so sure he could resist. President Roger Morningstar was about six feet tall and rugged looking – like he really had worked on the ranch his family had owned in Colorado. He had dark wavy hair streaked with serious looking grey, a strong chin and well-spaced brown eyes. His family had settled in Colorado just after the Civil War and raised cattle, took trail drives, fought Indians, outlaws, rustlers, droughts and blizzards – at least they had if you believed the President's oft told tales. And his stories were probably mostly true. He claimed his black hair was a genetic trait inherited from his great great grandmother who was some relation to the famous Sioux Indian chief Sitting Bull.

He was in his sixth year as President and his tenure as the head of the country was remarkable, as most pundits had often observed, for its lack of remarkableness. He had so far passed no significant legislation, formulated no meaningful foreign policy doctrine and marshalled no productive economic programs. The country was wallowing and just going about its business while losing its sense of purpose. The President's poll numbers held remarkably steady right around the 50% range. Mostly people thought he was 'good enough'. And it had to be admitted, the country's expectations of its political leaders weren't very high.

President Morningstar had come into office with great fanfare and promises. He promised all the right things. Somehow regardless of the group he was talking to on his campaign, he always managed to say or at least imply what they most wanted to hear. He was for bi-partisanship and open government, he would rebuild schools and take care of the elderly; he would guarantee the return of manufacturing jobs and strengthen the capital markets. Life would be good again. The fact that there was nothing in his prior life's experience to suggest that he had ever done any of these things was dismissed as being small minded. After all, he had an undergraduate degree from Harvard and a law degree from Stanford – so he must be brilliant. In fact some pundits gushed that he might be the smartest US President ever! So much for Jefferson and Lincoln.

As his staffers discovered, he did have a wonderful, broadly curious mind. And in discussions he was always respectful of others' opinions. He wanted everyone to end up agreeing. As he argued with people he would shift his position closer to theirs until everyone walked away thinking that everything had been agreed upon. Then an opposing group would meet with him and they would have the same sort of meeting – but walk away with a different agreement. The result with this President was that there seemed to be lots of agreement but things never got done.

The truth as the President saw it was that he was elected to run things – and he liked the position of power. He had been treated all his life as the center of everyone's attention – and in his mind he deserved that. In return he had learned, it worked even better if everyone agreed with him. He had found that was the best way to win elections. And he was very good at winning elections. Going all the way back to running for Class President in the sixth grade, he had never lost one.

"Well gentlemen," the President started while looking at David and Dr. Wheeling, "My advisors here have been bringing me up to date on what you two and the missing Dr. Planck have been up to and though my understanding of the Physics might be a little light, I think I get the gist of it all. All quite brilliant actually. I look forward to getting deeper into it. But I wanted to talk to you two because I need to hear about this as directly and unfiltered as possible. Now for the moment let's put the theoretical physics aside, tell me why I should believe this whole mind over matter thing. Frankly it sounds pretty far-fetched."

Dr. Wheeling, as was his want, took the lead. "Mr. President...without getting too deep into the theory, you should believe it because it is the natural extension of what we have discovered to occur at the quantum level of existence. We knew of the importance of the Observer in quantum mechanics. And we knew of the mysterious properties of consciousness. Yet we were hesitant as physicists to link the two. Dr. Planck was bold enough to do so..."

The President held up his hand, "Please one moment Dr. Wheeling. When you start putting words like quantum mechanics into your sentences my friends here in the room start staring blankly at me."

"Perhaps I should try to explain," David said. "What troubles everyone here is the idea of mind over matter...the idea that one can change the physical world we are used to living in just by the application of mental processes. I have a new word for you - let's call it 'mentalization.' But in fact, this is not a new idea. The central idea has been around for centuries and many people believe in it. Prayer is one of the examples. Many people believe that their prayers are answered - that physical realities occur because of their prayers. They attribute that to God. Now whether you believe in God or not, many doctors will tell you that prayer helps some people get well - that is 'thoughts' effect physical changes in the body."

The President held up his hand, "Are you saying that this is somehow about the nature of God?"

"No I'm not, but I expect that many of your constituents will link the idea of a universal consciousness as a proof of God's existence."

The President nodded, "I can see that - in fact I might be able to use that if I ever have to explain this to a national audience. What do you think Barbara?"

Everyone looked at the hawk-faced woman to the President's left. "I'll have to do some polling but that might be a good approach."

"This is helpful," the President said to David, "Keep going."

David saw all eyes were on him. "So my point is that the idea of mind over matter is not so foreign to mankind. There have been all the claims that people could bend spoons with their mind or move things around – I'm not saying those claims were true, only that many people believed they could be. The fact is, that if Dr. Planck tried to bend a spoon with his mind ...well I think that spoon bends – particularly if he has his team with him and his amplifier in his ear."

"Have you actually seen that happen?" the Secretary of Defense asked.

"Not that, no" David replied, "But Dr. Wheeling and I did see Planck turn unripe green bananas into ripe yellow ones. Hard to believe I know – and it may sound like a parlor trick, but it wasn't. Planck handed Dr. Wheeling a grocery bag that had green bananas in it then he and his team did a little meditation or mentalization about those bananas turning yellow. Then we opened the bag and the bananas were now ripe."

The Secretary of Defense looked at Dr. Wheeling. "You saw it – no tricks, no optical illusions, no magician's magic or prestidigitation?"

Dr. Wheeling smiled at the group. "All he did was change the state of certain of the molecules in the bananas. Just the application of our new understanding of physics."

The President's Chief of Staff, Hank Scarpetti, spoke up, "I think we have to accept that this new Physics is real – that mind over matter is real. The Object wants Dr. Planck. Dr. Planck has been kidnapped. The Object did not ask for some hack magician and we have no reports of missing magicians. Also, we have a very distinguished Nobel Prize winning Physicist sitting in front of us telling us this is all true; so let's start accepting that this new understanding of reality is for real and let's start deciding what in hell we are going to do about it!"

David regarded Scarpetti closely. He had heard that Scarpetti was the one who made things happen. But Scarpetti didn't look like it; he had none of the President's imposing physical presence. At average height and twenty pounds overweight and thinning hair cut short, he was easy to overlook. Only his unwavering gaze above his sagging jowls suggested there might be something to him. But David thought he could also see hiding under Scarpetti's very ordinary appearance a fearless resolve to push himself and his ideas to the forefront of any debate. He was a man who liked being the power hiding behind the curtains.

"I agree with Hank," the President said. "So what do we do about it? Barbara what do you think? What do you think the polling will tell us? What will the people want us to do?"

"I'll get right on that, Mr. President." She replied.

"Hold on, let's think about this," the Secretary of Defense, Joe Anderson interrupted. "Is this even something we want the people to know about? I think before we do anything we need to throw a big blanket of national security over the top of this until we understand the ramifications much more than we do."

"I think Joe is right," the President agreed. "This could be huge! This is important! ... You know what I think? I think we need the equivalent of The Manhattan Project. And it needs to be as secret as that was all during World War II. This is like discovering nuclear energy – like creating the atom bomb! We need to be in complete control of how this is disseminated. The people need to be protected from this – it could cause panic."

Hank Scarpetti agreed, "We need to know a lot more about this. We need to see it – understand how it works. Something as revolutionary technologically as this looks like it will be will change how our society works. We can't just let that run its course without any oversight by us. We have to manage how this unfolds."

As the President looked around at his team for agreement, David looked at Dr. Wheeling. As they exchanged a glance they shared the same thought – they both wished they were somewhere else.

Right then the President remembered they were in the room. He looked back at them. "I hope you two want to be part of the project. What do you think we should call it?"

Though the President was smiling at them, David didn't like the smile at all. He was afraid that if he and the professor didn't want to be part of the project they would be hustled off to some place like Guantanamo before they could even make a phone call.

Fortunately Dr. Wheeling spoke up for them, "Of course! We consider it our duty as Americans to do what's best for our country."

"Splendid," said the President as David admired the subtlety of the professor's remark. Later, if there was a later, he would have to ask Dr. Wheeling what he really thought.

*****

Dr. Janus Wheeling didn't really appreciate that he was being detained somewhere in the bowels of the Pentagon until the soldiers, who he now thought of as guards, led him into what looked like a hotel room and then walked out of the room and closed the door behind them – a door he then noticed could only be opened from the outside. He had wondered why earlier they had told David to follow two of them in a different direction, now he knew. As an eminent professor and Nobel Prize winning physicist, he found it hard to believe that they would detain him against his will. He had never thought it possible that anyone could fear that he was a threat to national security.

He then realized that fear was the key to it. When governments were afraid, their actions could be extreme. When fear takes hold in a government, their need to tighten control was inevitable. So he found himself standing in the middle of what was a well-appointed cell. He then caught a glimpse of himself in a mirror: a tall, thin man with black hair streaked with grey and just long enough for a little ponytail, wearing the blue pinstripe suit and dark tie he had picked for his meeting at The White House. Even with the suit he still looked like a college professor. He took the jacket off and wrapped it around a desk chair and then loosened his tie. He sat on the side of the bed.

One hour went by and then another as he continued to sit on the side of the bed. At first he was impatient and angry; then he found the quiet and solitude of the room was inducive to thinking through his situation. He found that he was not concerned. He expected that someone would come soon with an agreement for him to sign. They would want him to work for them and in return, after he signed a non-disclosure agreement that if violated would constitute a breach of national security, they would release him. And then they would send him somewhere to work on their hush hush project to learn the New Physics Planck had discovered and then hopefully to weaponize them.

To his surprise he found that he had no intention of signing anything or going off to the current equivalent of Los Alamos and engaging in their Manhattan Project. He found he was eager to meet again with Planck and David and hopefully with whoever or whatever ran The Object. There was going to be a need to explain these New Physics and their implications to the general public – to the peoples of the world. He found he wanted to be part of that – to even be a leader of it. He realized he had grown too detached, too willing to rest on his laurels. The coming times would be challenging and new leaders needed to emerge. He would refuse to sign anything that would limit his role.

Then he surprised himself again as he found himself thinking about Dr. Mary Grasso, a professor of Biochemistry who recently he had met at a dinner put together by mutual friends who were trying to set them up. Mary and he had followed that with a dinner at an Italian restaurant that they both knew. But that had been four nights ago and he had not called her afterward. He regretted that now and was annoyed that he could not call her. They had taken his smart phone and no phone was in the room.

Though only a few years younger than his just about to be sixty years, he found her attractive and fun to talk to; and not at all alike his quiet ex-wife. Mary said she liked going to the movies and the symphony. Then they had talked about running in the park, spurred on in part by his overstating his level of cardio vascular conditioning. But he would get in condition. As soon as he escaped the clasp of the government, he would call her.

As he sat there on the bed in some high security area in the Pentagon, he smiled to himself. He remembered a favorite time in his life when he was hard at work on solving the problem that had led to his winning the Nobel Prize. His commitment and focus was so total – nothing else mattered. Yet it was a great time. A lot of years ago, he conceded, but not too many. He had simply grown a little complacent. Time to throw that off! Though brilliant physics insights tended to come before one was thirty years old, what the situation now called for was something he could well accomplish. Now was not the time to yield to age ...or to a government that thought it knew best what was needed.

*****

Later that evening, Hank Scarpetti took a sip of his single malt scotch as he sat in the kitchen of his longtime friend General Carl Greene who also had a glass of scotch in his hand. The two of them had agreed they needed to meet as soon as possible when they had walked out of the meeting with the President that followed the meeting with Dr. Wheeling and David Randall. They had been friends long enough and good enough that they trusted to talk frankly with each other. In D.C. that was rare in normal circumstances and these circumstances were the antitheses of normal.

At sixty years old and having spent twenty five years in Washington including ten years as a Congressman from his home state of Illinois and then four years as Chief of Staff of a former President, Scarpetti thought he had seen it all. Then six months earlier he had reluctantly agreed to take another stint as Chief of Staff because the current President's term and a half in office was a widening sinkhole for their Party. He thought he had just started to make some progress when The Object had shown up on the horizon. Its arrival he at first had thought, like any good politician, might be a great opportunity – if it didn't destroy the planet – but now he wasn't so sure. Between dealing with The Object and dealing with the implications of the New Physics – the term now used around the White House because they couldn't really describe what Planck had come up with, real leadership was going to be required of the President. And no amount of issue polling could fill that need.

Scarpetti looked over at his friend and was struck how strong and fit Greene looked – not just physically strong, but intellectually and emotionally too, yet they were both about the same age. Greene looked ready to face these new challenges. But Scarpetti couldn't say the same about himself. It wasn't just that he was twenty five pounds overweight, balding and a little jowly, he was tired too. But he knew he had to rise up and find his A game again. He just had to!

"So Carl, you've been working on this New Physics thing for a couple of days now – what does your gut tell you?"

"I think it all is for real."

"If it is – then everything is going to change."

"Maybe...but maybe not as much as you think." The general said as he sipped his drink.

Scarpetti sipped his as well and then said, "You want to hear something funny? You know Jill and I have been married now for about eight years. A second marriage for both of us... and we both had been single for a while before we met. Well about a year before we met Jill wrote down on a piece of paper a list of all the characteristics that she wanted in a man. And some of the things she listed were pretty darn specific. At the time I was still living in Chicago. She put that list in a drawer and forgot about it. But then I moved here to D.C. and we were set up on a blind date and from the first day we met we started being together – like we were made for each other. A couple of months later she found the list – and I pretty much was everything she had listed. We joked and said it was that list that brought me back to D.C. That it was the Universe bringing to her what she asked for."

"The Universe?"

"Yea, the Universe. Of course that was just a way of putting a name on how our individual personal realities come together. Who knew it might have been the actual force?" Scarpetti took another sip. "Pretty ironic, don't you think?"

"If Dr. Planck is to be believed, apparently Jill's list was received loud and clear."

"Yea... of course now Jill says after having been married for a while she'd like to add a few things to that list."

"My wife would like a list like that too."

They both just sat in silence for a moment and then each knew it was time to talk about what they really needed to talk about.

"So what do you think of the President's idea to start up some kind of Manhattan Project to deal with the situation?" Scarpetti asked Greene. Scarpetti had long ago learned that starting conversations with questions was a great way to ensure that he didn't say something stupid by talking before he had been thinking.

"I don't know that it is even possible in this age of the Internet – information flows too freely."

Scarpetti shrugged, "Perhaps...but I think we have to try. We can't afford to lose control of this. People would start looking to the Universe for assistance and stop looking to government. We could lose our hold on them. And the people aren't ready to deal with mind over matter. That would put too much power in their hands."

Greene was not surprised by his friend's answer, though he didn't agree with it. With all that had happened in the last couple of days he'd been forced to accept that major changes were looming. As intelligent as he knew he was, he knew there was no way he could anticipate all that was ahead. He had decided the best he could do was to help steer its military implications. "You think the government is ready for this new power?"

"Absolutely! We are the only one's who'll know what to do. We have the smartest people in the world within our government - we have the academic community to draw on. Who else could do it? You know you can't put this kind of control in the hands of the people. Forget what we say on the campaign trail - this is the biggest thing to hit mankind in a thousand years! Situations like the one that faces us now are what governments are supposed to manage."

"You think the government can manage this? This President's administration isn't exactly known for management competency."

"That's why I'm here now. I know how to manage this!"

General Greene had learned to be more cautious in the use of power - like most senior military officers. "So the answer for now is to throw a shroud of 'national security' over it all?"

"Yes! Damn right."

"And that's why we just took a writer from The Washington Post and a Nobel Prize winning physicist and put them in isolated detention, shut off from communication with anyone."

"That's what the President wanted - and I agreed. We didn't want to do it, but national security required it. Otherwise David Randall could write all about this at a much deeper level than he already has and it would go on the front page of The Washington Post. And even if we could strong arm The Post into not printing it, David could post it on the internet and the world would see it."

Scarpetti paused but only for a moment, "And if Dr. Wheeling started writing his views, it would be even worse - now you have a Nobel Prize winning physicist saying it. We can't unwind that sort of thing. We either control it now or we lose it forever."

Greene took another sip of his scotch as he thought about what Scarpetti had said. "You know I think the people will adapt to this pretty well. At the individual level, it will take years before they learn how to do what Planck says is necessary. Meditation isn't that easy. You ever meditate?"

"Hell, I don't have the time."

"And there's the matter of the amplifier," the General added.

"The amplifier, yes. Do you think we can put out some kind of electromagnetic wave that would block its transmissions? You know – jam its frequency. Could we do that?"

"I don't know. We'll have to see."

"Well get your smart scientists to look into that."

General Greene tried a different approach. "In talking with Dr. Wheeling several other thoughts came up. He thinks that with the New Physics we can solve the energy problem. And we can grow more food – enough so no one anywhere goes hungry."

"Forget all that! Not our problem. That doesn't help our government. In the land of milk and honey no one needs big government – or a military for that matter. Let's stick with what we know!"

"So how long are we going to keep Wheeling and Randle under wraps?"

"Until we are sure they'll see things our way!"

"That's what the President wants?"

"Are you kidding? I had to talk him out of dumping them in some landfill in Maryland. He's a whole lot harder and tougher than people think."

*****

It took Gabriela a whole day to get back to New York from Pirate's Cay. The boat ride to Nassau took hours and then getting to the airport and waiting for her flight took hours more and then she faced the 3 hour flight and taxi ride back to the apartment in the upper eastside she shared with David. But she had put her time to good use thanks to her cell phone. Dr. Wheeling had asked her to enlist if possible but at least inform other physicists of the results of Planck's work. The physicists she contacted were eager to meet and a time and place were set. He had said when two nights ago she had told him about the meeting that he would try and call in. She knew that yesterday the professor and David were supposed to have had a meeting at The White House, but she hadn't heard from him since. She had been trying to call David too but his phone just went to voicemail. She had just gotten the same result now when she tried to call Dr. Wheeling.

So she resolved to just carry on without their input. She knew what she needed to do. As she stood at a whiteboard in the empty classroom at Columbia she had just started on that.

It would be better to say that the classroom was empty of students. In front of her lounging on desktops or seated were four of the most distinguished physicists then teaching or researching in the New York area. The classroom was chosen because it had whiteboards; the idea of talking physics without whiteboards would have been just crazy.

Gabriela had secretly been thrilled when Dr. Wheeling had asked for her help. She knew that Planck's work would ripple out in the physics world like the ripples caused by a fat man doing a cannonball into the middle of a backyard swimming pool. She wanted to be in the center of that! It could make her career. And now there to meet with her were physicists whose work she had admired since she was a young doctoral student.

The two physicists who were there from Princeton – the two with the most credentials – were there because they had received a message from Dr. Wheeling a couple of days ago that their coming to the meeting was essential and vitally important. Of the other two, one was Gabriela's mentor at Columbia and the other was the latest brilliant young physicist who was then at NYU and who happened to be Gabriela's friend.

Gabriela had just finished detailing Planck's work and the events of the last few days. They had recognized Planck's name as the person The Object was seeking. They had already asked a few clarifying questions about how the group meditation took place and about the engineering of the ear plug amplifier.

The older of the two Princeton physicists, Dr. Craig Smolin, one of the early disciples of John Wheeler, then asked, "So what exactly does Dr. Wheeling wish us to do? Where is he in this?"

Gabriela looked at all of them as she said, "First he apologizes for not being here. He is in Washington now as we speak. Yesterday he took the President through all this and he is still caught up with The White House and the Pentagon—I think. His anticipation of that is why he asked me to coordinate this meeting. I think he is concerned that our Government will try to control how this develops – sort of a new Manhattan Project. Dr. Wheeling does not believe that would work in the current environment or be a good idea."

"I see." The others in the room all seemed to agree.

Gabriela continued, "Dr. Wheeling is also hopeful that you might explore the theory of what Planck is proposing and help iron out its wrinkles. As this goes public he feels it would be very helpful if distinguished and influential physicists such as yourselves could speak up for it. Otherwise misinformation and disinformation could create more confusion and dismay than it already will."

"It's already going to create bedlam!" replied Andrew Susskind, Gabriela's young physicist friend.

"And there is still The Object out there, intentions unknown. We may need these new physics!" added Jennifer Davies, Gabriela's original faculty advisor and mentor.

Dr. Smolin said, "So let's get back to the physics – too bad my departed friend John Wheeler isn't around for this. He would have loved it! And it is not far from what he was thinking. He thought information might be at the core of reality – his 'it from bit'. He even had a name for it: he called it 'Participatory Physics.' Of course Hawking will hate it!"

Jennifer Davies then spoke up. "It seems to argue in favor of the Strong Anthropic Principal. The idea that the universe is the way it is so as to give rise to life and mind. Planck just goes one step further and says at its most fundamental level the universe is the Observer or Mind or consciousness, take your pick. The laws of physics are its creative tools and mathematics is its form of communication."

Gabriela joined in, "And that explains the 'Goldilocks conundrum' – why the universe is so uncannily perfect for the creation of intelligent life. Why the force of gravity is exactly what it is, and the same for the strong and weak nuclear forces, and that electromagnetism works just the way it does. All of which are so delicately calibrated, change the force of any one of them even a little, and the universe never forms or at least not in a way that sustains life."

The second professor from Princeton, Chandler Freeman added, "Speaking for Super String theorists. We are not going to like this. It suggests 'intelligent design'."

Dr. Davies argued back, "No one is suggesting intelligent design at the biological level. But Super String theorists admit that explaining why the laws of physics and mathematics work so well for the development and existence of life presents a problem – you try and solve that problem with the concept of the multiverse but that just seems to be borrowing a Darwinian model with none of Darwin's painstakingly developed biological and fossil history."

"Well I like putting consciousness at the center of it all." Andrew Susskind replied. "Super String has major problems. First, in order to explain how our universe can be so perfect for intelligent life it posits that our universe, a universe so vast and old with trillions of stars in it, is just one of ten to the 500th power of potential universes – essentially an infinite number of other universes. Of course they have no proof whatsoever of the existence of any other universe – but they believe that they do exist. Sounds like 'faith' to me – a word of course they reject. Then Super String needs eleven dimensions, not just three or four counting time, to make the mathematics work. Can't get the math to work? No problem – just add a new dimension to space/time....Then it just ignores the implications of the need for an Observer at the quantum level and how consciousness came into existence."

Chandler Freeman shook his head, "It is true it is not fully worked out; but you have to agree that it does explain much of what we know. It is not out of faith that most of the theoretical physicists on this planet believe in some form of Super String theory."

Andrew wouldn't back off, "Well then, I eagerly await their explanation for how Ben Planck moved the hurricanes with his mind and the minds of his fellows on the island. Or just ask them to explain how Planck turned green bananas yellow in just minutes."

Freeman held his hand up, "For now I accept that was done. But we need much more experimental data to confirm Planck's work."

Gabriela felt she needed to get the group back on point. "Let's not just focus on Planck. Let's remember that there is The Object up in our sky and all of us can see that. And all of us have observed that it just showed up out of nothing – like a quantum particle popping into existence. And all of us saw those missiles just disappear in front of us. Like a quantum particle popping out of existence. Our current understanding of physics doesn't allow for any of that given the masses involved! I think we will discover that Planck's physics does. And I think we should try to figure out how The Object does what it does. And we don't have a lot of time because I don't know what The Object is waiting for, but I for one don't think it is going to stay quiet for much longer!"

Dr. Smolin stood up from where he was sitting, not to leave but to get their attention. "I think we have only scratched the surface of what we are confronting. Let's put the issue of the role of consciousness aside for the moment. Gabriela's point is a good one. How did The Object arrive here? I hear people talking about a wormhole or some such nonsense. And some talk about traveling faster than the speed of light. I think more nonsense. Einstein isn't wrong there. But The Object is proof that something else is at work. And I believe that there will be more changes to our understanding of physics than just those associated thus far with Dr. Planck. We are at the beginning of a new frontier."

"But why isn't it doing something? It's just up there doing nothing!" Andrew said.

Dr. Smolin shook his head, "Oh I don't think it is doing nothing. We know it has no language problem with us. And we know it understands our electronic devices better than we even do -- it uses them in a way we can't duplicate. No it is not doing nothing. I'm certain it is studying us -- studying us in great detail. But why is it studying us and what will it do when it is finished its study?"

Jennifer Davies then spoke up, "One thought occurs to me. I start by choosing to believe that most of what we know about physics is in fact true. It also seems that most of what we have been talking about is best explained by what we know of how particles behave at the quantum level. I plan to go back and think about what if one could apply consciousness to alter matter in ways consistent with quantum behavior with the one exception that added mass is not a constraint."

As often was the case, Gabriela was on the same wavelength as her mentor Jennifer, "That would bring into the discussion quantum entanglement and other strange particle behavior."

"Yes, it would. And we know that entangled particles can instantly affect each other regardless of the distance separating the two particles. The limitation of the speed of light does not apply to them." Jennifer Davies assented.

"Very interesting. I think we all should get to work," Responded Dr. Smolin.

That evening Gabriela returned home eager to share her day's events with David. She had held her own with some of the best minds in the world of physics. David would downplay it; not to belittle it but because he believed of course she could do it! She still hadn't heard from him but felt sure he'd call if he wasn't home already. But when she arrived home he wasn't there and she could see he had not been there earlier. She realized she hadn't heard from him in two days – the last time they had talked was the evening before his morning meeting in The White House. It had been bothering her all day that she couldn't reach either David or Dr. Wheeling but now it really hit her. Where was David?

She needed someone to talk to but now realized how much she depended on David to be that person. She didn't really do the girlfriend thing. Most of the people she worked with were men and the few women friends she had had no clue about the work she did – and frankly that never bothered her much. Her relationship with David filled that void. At the end of the day they would usually go out to one of several restaurants they frequented and they'd talk. David understood what she did and she loved hearing about the research he would do as he wrote about some new scientific development.

They talked about getting married but so far David hadn't showed up with a ring and she didn't bring it up. They both said they couldn't imagine taking time out for children but that wasn't as true for her now as it had been. They were happy together, and had enough friends who weren't happy in their relationships, that they told each other that they didn't want to change anything.

She loved that David was so even tempered but could get all excited about some new scientific development. At heart he was a jack of all trades kind of guy – no one thing could hold his attention for long. And he was so smart that he could learn the basics of anything regardless of complexity and then be able to communicate the core ideas so that anyone could understand them. That was his real gift.

Now she really wanted to talk to him and she didn't know where he was. And the hours were just creeping by. She tried to catch up on her emails but couldn't stay focused on them. She realized she should eat something though she wasn't hungry. She microwaved a Boston Market dinner which she ate while watching an old movie on television and then went to bed and slept badly.

By late afternoon the next day she still hadn't heard from David. Now she knew she had to do something; but what do you do when your boyfriend goes off to meet with the President of the United States and then you don't hear from him again? She tried Dr. Wheeling's number again and just got voicemail again. She realized that whatever had happened to David had probably also happened to Dr. Wheeling. And she also realized that filing a missing person's report or checking for unidentified males at local hospitals wouldn't be much use.

Then she thought about reaching out to David's uncle, General Mark Randall. She knew David had been in contact with him. It took her some time but finally she found the general's contact information. But before she tried to call, her phone beeped with a text message.

The text read, "Don't worry about David we'll take care of it" and it was signed Planck.

Gabriela's relief was immediate – David was all right! And so apparently was Planck! Then her curiosity hit her. Where was Planck? And how did he know David was OK? And who was the 'we' he referred to?

# CHAPTER SIX

*"The universe does not exist 'out there', independent of us. We are inescapably involved in bringing about that which is happening. We are not observers. We are participators. In some strange sense, this is a participatory universe....Today we demand of physics some understanding of existence itself."*

John Wheeler
*Princeton Professor of Physics*
*and one of the most highly regarded*
*physicists of the 20th Century*

Hank Scarpetti walked in to see his boss, "Mr. President we have a problem."

The President looked up from his desk in the Oval Office. "What's happened?"

"The Object just told us to return Dr. Wheeling and David Randall to Planck's island in The Bahamas unharmed and immediately."

Annoyance plain on his face, the President shook his head, "Is it another worldwide blast?"

Scarpetti could see the President's stubborn streak setting in. "It appears not. But the message is on my smartphone and on my laptop. Why don't you check yours – almost no one has access to that."

The President opened a drawer and pulled out his phone. For security reasons he rarely used it. He turned it on and looked at it. The message was there too. He nodded to his Chief of Staff. "How would it know we have Wheeling and Randall? No one was supposed to know!"

"I don't know sir."

"This doesn't make any sense to me. Why would it care? And why does it think it can just order us around?"

Scarpetti refrained from saying the obvious. "I think The Object could have put the message out worldwide which would have been much worse for us politically. I think it's trying to work with us on this."

"What the hell is The Object anyway? How in hell does it even know who Wheeling and Randall are – and I repeat, why does it care? .....So you think we have to do it?" The President pulled on his right earlobe, a gesture Scarpetti had seen many times when the President seemed confused about an action to take. "Can't we just hide them away somewhere and claim to know nothing about them?"

"Mr. President this isn't some newspaper with a story. Or some accusation by a Senate subcommittee. Those we can ignore. We can tell them whatever we wish. We don't know what the consequences could be here. At a minimum The Object could communicate it worldwide – that would not be good for us."

"So I have to do it? ...I'm tired of the goddamned Object just orbiting around over my head, over my country, and then sending out cryptic text messages worldwide. Why won't it communicate with me? First it cares about this damn Benjamin Planck. Then it cares about a damn physics professor and a newspaper writer! But the President of the United States it doesn't care to talk to. What sense does that make?"

"Maybe it makes sense where they come from."

"And where is that?"

"I don't know sir."

"Admit it. You don't know shit!"

Scarpetti remained silent.

The President continued tugging on his earlobe. "We've got to find a way to talk to these aliens. Things always go better once people start talking. Hank, do whatever it takes, but we have to meet with The Object."

Scarpetti nodded, "I understand, sir. But right now we have to do something about Randall and Wheeling."

"All right. Take them back to the island. We have a Seal team there now, didn't you tell me that?"

"Yes sir, we do."

"Well when you drop Wheeling and Randall off, let's leave the Seal team there. Let's see what happens. Maybe there's a reason that The Object wants them there."

*****

When they came to get David he was relieved to see that Dr. Wheeling was with them too. When the meeting with the President was over, General Greene had them taken back to The Pentagon for more discussion but instead they had been ushered somewhere down in the bowels of that massive building and David had been put in a room that resembled a hotel room complete with the little toiletry bottles in the bath and a white cotton robe in the closet. Except there were no windows and the walls were concrete. Not until they closed the door behind them did David realize he had just been imprisoned.

In the room was a TV with Basic Cable but no phone and they had taken his mobile. Food was brought into him and a change of clothes complete with socks and underwear - somehow they knew he wore boxers. Two days went by with no visitors and his guards not saying anything. Where he was could not be permanent and he feared what might come next. He thought they probably hadn't figured out the next step.

What really irritated him and he kept coming back to it was that he had known that it was possible that the government would try to restrain Dr. Wheeling and himself from speaking out. Yet he had done almost nothing to protect himself from it. Sure he had half-jokingly told the Washington Post Editor to look for him if he didn't get back to him in a couple of days - but what good was that really? This was the President of the United States behind this, not just some local politician! And in truth, what they were dealing with could easily be viewed as national security. Until now, David had never truly considered how broad a net could be thrown under the guise of 'national security'. Somehow he, a writer who covered new developments in science and technology, could be deemed a threat to the national security of the United States.

He had never taken seriously Gabriela's dark distrust of government; he considered it just a residue of her family's bad experiences in post WWII Eastern Europe. She thought he was naïve. Government everywhere and throughout history was the same. It was a beast that always hungered to get bigger and stronger. Whether it considered itself benign or recognized itself as tyrannical, it wanted the same things. 'Power corrupts and absolute power corrupts absolutely'. David had known that quote since he'd been in college and knew it to be true but never acted as if it meant anything.

Over the slow moving hours David thought about The Object, about Plank's physics, about the interaction of the two and about how best to go forward. It was all so fascinating to him. His instincts told him he was at the center of the biggest story in the world. And he felt he understood it better than anyone. This was his chance to finally do something. He had to stay with it and not get distracted. If he could just keep from screwing up, this could give him the opportunity to show everyone that he had real ability. He could prove to Gabriela that he was worth it. This time he'd give it everything he had, no quitting on it! Now he just had to get out of the dungeons of the Pentagon!

When they came in the morning to take him and Dr. Wheeling elsewhere, the guards gave no hint of what was coming next. Looking at Dr. Wheeling it was clear he did not know either. They exchanged weak smiles and followed their captors. As they passed down a long hallway and through a guarded doorway they were stopped at a desk where they were given a form to look over. David read that it was an agreement that they would not divulge publicly that they had been held for two days against their will. It had them agreeing that the national interest was at stake. The professor who was reading an identical document nodded. David and Dr. Wheeling signed it without saying anything. What would have been the point; they just wanted to be released.

Then they were led into a passageway with a few more people in it including an officer who approached them with a smile. His manner was so casual it was as if he had run into them in the lobby of a hotel. "Dr. Wheeling, Mr. Randall, I'm here to return you to Pirate's Cay, which I believe is where we first picked you up from. Once there we will leave you on your own."

David looked at Dr. Wheeling who seemed to share David's puzzlement. David said, "Pirate's Cay? Why don't you just drop us off in downtown D.C.? We'll be fine there."

The young officer shook his head. "My orders are to take you to Pirate's Cay. Travel arrangements have been made. You needn't be alarmed."

When David and Dr. Wheeling boarded the executive jet that was to take them to the island they were surprised to find General Greene already on board. The general rose out of his seat to greet them. The general was not in uniform. He had on a sport coat and slacks but somehow looked just as much a three star general. His expression was formal, that of a man determined to do what he knew to be an unpleasant duty. Before they could say anything, Greene said, "I want to apologize for the treatment you have received the last couple of days. All I can say is that these are extraordinary times."

"On whose behalf are you apologizing?" asked Dr. Wheeling. The prize winning physicist's tone was arch and severe. David had never seen him so quietly fierce. David shared his anger at their incarceration but knew he couldn't match Wheeling's proud disdain.

General Greene looked back at them with sorrow but without wilting under Dr. Wheeling's glare, "Perhaps only for me. One of the reasons I'm here is because I deeply regret what happened to you."

"Someone above you ordered it," David said.

"I've said all I will say."

Dr. Wheeling then responded, "You said one of the reasons. What are the other reasons?"

"You don't know why you were released, do you?" When neither responded, the general added, "Apparently you have a new friend. A very high up friend."

"Who is higher up than the President – because I presume it was he who ordered us to be held in custody." Dr. Wheeling replied.

The General's eyes held a tint of humor when he responded, "Well high up in the sense of 'high in the sky.' It was The Object. Frankly The Object seemed to know about you two. It said we should release you and take you back to Pirate's Cay."

"The Object did that?" David asked.

"So I was told. That's one of the other reasons I'm on this plane. I want to see why The Object wanted you there."

While on the flight down to the small Bahamian island, Dr. Wheeling and David confirmed that each was all right and had in fact experienced the same treatment. David tried to get General Greene to explain the government's perspective on The Object and what exactly were the national security concerns that had required the imprisoning of David and the professor. The general's answers were non-committal. Most of the flight was passed with little conversation; each man busy with his own thoughts.

When they exited the airplane on Pirate's Cay one of Zen Master Ozawa's monks picked them up in a Jeep Cherokee and took them to the lobby of the main Retreat building. Though they had no clue how it came to pass yet, they then understood why they were back at Pirate's Cay. There coming forward to greet them with a big smile was Ben Planck.

"Planck! How in hell are you here?" David exclaimed with a wide smile on his own face. Planck shook the professor's and David's hand and then turned to Greene and said, "General, I'm glad you've come. We know you at least are a friend."

General Greene shook the proffered hand with a look on his face that was only rarely there, a look of very real puzzlement. "You are the missing Dr. Planck, I presume?"

Planck just smiled and then turned and waved forward a very tall man with long blond hair and a short cropped beard. His facial features all seemed perfectly proportioned and his skin was clear and without lines or blemishes, yet he did not look young. His eyes could have been a hundred years old.

"I'd like to introduce to you guys the man who rescued me from the Russians that took me off the island and who just a few minutes ago returned me here to my island."

The tall blond man stepped forward. "No need for introductions. My name would translate in English as Plato –the name of one of your most famous philosophers, is it not? And as to you gentlemen, I already know who you are. Dr. Wheeling I am honored to meet you. General Greene, I respect your leadership.

And David, I believe your skill and talents are going to be very useful to us all in the coming battle."

General Greene recovered from this surprising turn of events fastest. "Mr. Plato..."

The tall blond man held up his hand, "Just Plato."

The general continued, "Plato it is. Well sir, you know who we are, but we don't know you. How is it you came to rescue Planck?"

Plato smiled, "Let me answer the first question – then I think you will have many more questions than those concerning my new friend Planck."

Dr. Wheeling, the general and David regarded Plato with an equal sense of expectation. Plato's physical presence was so dominating and his manner was so supremely self-assured that if he had opened the buttons of his shirt to reveal a Superman insignia on his chest, none would have doubted he came from the Planet Krypton. His answer was yet more surprising.

Actually it was Planck, unable to suppress his excitement, who answered for Plato. "Plato is the leader of an expedition to Earth. He's the one who is in charge of what we call The Object!"

"Well well well," exclaimed Dr. Wheeling. "Curiouser and curiouser!"

David's astonishment was phrased differently, "This just gets better and better!"

General Greene's response was of a different order. At last he could get an answer to a question that had been front and center in his mind for weeks. "If you are indeed from The Object, why are you here and what do you want?"

Plato returned General Greene's steadfast gaze. "Admirably direct, General. Where I come from, directness is respected – though that is not true everywhere else. The answer to your question is simple, though you may not understand it at first. The answer is that The Object, as you call us, is here to save your planet from destruction."

The military man stood up even straighter and more combatively. "And who is it that threatens our destruction?"

Plato looked back at General Greene with the eyes of a man who had seen everything there ever was to see. "I believe you already know the answer to that question. So I will answer it with a question. A few weeks ago, just before our arrival, over twenty million people perished in a brief but horrific exchange of nuclear weapons. Who was responsible for that, General?"

Greene knew he was trapped before he started. "Well there were complex political issues dividing North and South Korea and the leadership of North Korea was very unstable..."

Plato held up his hand to keep Greene from continuing. "General, you know better. Do not treat me like an uninformed electorate. The leaders of this world allowed nuclear weapons to be used as toys by a homicidal megalomaniac who was just a child. And that was obvious to everyone here, but no one did anything! And more than twenty million people died - and that is just the beginning. Your world teeters on the edge of one disaster after another. And the consequences of those disasters each day become greater and greater. So I ask you again, who threatens the destruction of your planet?"

General Greene just looked away.

Plato then continued. "We have been observing your planet closely for a while now. Our statistical models show a 34% likelihood of a human caused global mega disaster occurring here within the next twenty years and a 63% likelihood of one occurring within the next 35 years. Within that time period there is a 17% likelihood that the disaster will be so great that civilization on this planet will perish and archeologists from other planets ten thousand years in the future will be finding your ruins under the shifting sands of deserts."

After stunned silence lasting what felt to them like hours, David replied, "I hope you are here to change those odds."

Plato nodded.

General Greene was still combative. "Plato...you look like us - you look human. Yet you say that you are from The Object -which we believe is not from Earth. How do I know you actually are from The Object?"

"Yes I see that you need proof. Not unreasonable. What would you like me to do?"

The General thought for a moment. "If you are from The Object, how about showing me how you got down here? That would be a start."

"I like it," said Plato. "One moment, my 'ride' as you would call it, is just on the other side of the beach. I'm instructing it to come here now. As a military man you should appreciate this."

Planck looked at David, "This is very cool. I've ridden in it."

As he finished speaking, a dark ovoid object the size of a city transit bus approached them from behind the mangroves on the beach to their west. Silently it came to hover over them twenty feet above their heads, then it shot skyward soundlessly and was out of sight in seconds then just as quickly it returned to hover above them, then it somehow changed the colors of its skin so that it was almost impossible to see even though it was mere yards away.

"General, if you had been trying to track it with radar or any other sensing device, your screens would show nothing. Are you satisfied?"

Greene studied the vehicle silently hovering over them. He looked for a propulsion system and saw nothing, nor did its shape look particularly aerodynamic. What he had just seen did not seem possible and the acceleration and deceleration he had witnessed would have produced G forces that no human could endure. "Our military has nothing that could do that. We have some jets that can approximate it but not soundlessly and not move at such extreme speeds in both directions and come so immediately to a complete stop above our heads."

"So, General, go ahead and ask your next question?"

"You're right, I have another. How is it that you appear human?"

Plato smiled, "Of course, that is the question. The answer is that I appear human because my DNA is essentially identical to yours. My ancestors too were homo sapiens."

Dr. Wheeling and David shared looks of amazement with the General. "Are you somehow from our future?" David asked.

"Time travel is still beyond us," replied Plato.

"But you are from Earth?" David followed up.

"No, not the way you think. I am not from this Earth."

Dr. Wheeling started nodding his head up and down. David knew the head movement as the indicator that Wheeling now understood. "So you are from 'an' Earth but not this Earth. And let me guess, your Earth has developed technologically faster than ours. I guess that makes us the dumb kids."

"There are many Earths, Dr. Wheeling. Some less advanced than yours, some more advanced than mine."

"How many is many?" David wanted to know.

"We don't know. We know once there was just one Earth and then it cloned itself and then the clones cloned themselves. I use the word 'clone' because it is a word you are familiar with. What occurs is not actually cloning. We think of it as an original parent Earth and it had daughters and then the daughters had daughters and so on."

David saw how it might be. "On each of these Earths, are there people? Homo sapiens?"

Plato nodded, "Yes, on most of them. But on a number of them, people are no longer on them. Mankind on those planets destroyed themselves, leaving just barren husks of once thriving planets."

"Now I get it," said General Greene.

"I feel like Charlton Heston at the end of the original Planet of the Apes movie when he sees the broken down Statue of Liberty rising out of the sands on the beach in the Forbidden Zone." David said.

*****

Plato suggested that he and General Greene should go and meet separately.

Planck was eager to share his experience and new insights with Dr. Wheeling and David. So they split into two meetings, each going off to a meeting room in the Retreat building.

As they walked away, Plato towered over the shorter General Greene like a basketball center towers over a six foot guard. But there was nothing in the general's demeanor that suggested a lack of physical presence, even when in the company of the towering Plato. Greene had an inner force that reduced any physical shortfall to meaninglessness. They entered a meeting room and chose to sit across from each other at a table.

Plato spoke first, "General Greene I view it as quite fortuitous that you happened to come with Dr. Wheeling and Mr. Randall. I think you are an ideal emissary from your government. You have a very distinguished record of accomplishments – from a Silver Star for heroism in battle to a Master's Degree in Electrical Engineering and another Master's Degree in Weapons Technology. Very impressive."

"If you know all that about me you probably also know that I am not here in an official capacity – I am not an emissary of my government. And how do you know what is in my record?"

"We have access to any computer files we are interested in. As to your being an emissary, well, you are here as am I. You would be lacking in initiative if you did not take advantage of the circumstances and nothing in your record suggests that you lack initiative."

"Fair enough, let's talk... Perhaps we can begin by your explaining a little further your statement that there are many Earths?"

"That is a good starting point. General are you familiar with the quantum physics thought exercise called 'Schrodinger's Cat?' "

The General nodded, "In the thought experiment, a cat is put in a box with a poison that has a 50% chance of killing the cat. Until the box is opened, the cat is presumed to be neither dead nor alive. It is a probability function. Only by opening the box and observing the cat is one of those outcomes determined."

"Very good. Then you probably also know that some quantum theorists suggest that the universe could divide itself at the moment of the determination event such that in one universe the cat lives and in an otherwise identical sister universe the cat dies. Quantum physics theory allows for all possible outcomes."

"Yes but that is just a thought experiment," the General insisted.

"The rational mind suggests that, of course. How could a universe instantly duplicate itself? But your problem here is that you think of the universe as being made up of things .... Of matter and of energy. That it is a material universe. But actually, contrary to what common sense would tell you, it is not a universe of matter. In its raw state it is made up of information. Information that interfaces with what you call Dark Energy and Dark Matter. It is framed by the laws of physics. Its language is mathematics. And the boss of it all is 'consciousness.' "

"So how does that produce many Earths?"

Plato regarded the General for a long moment. "I cannot tell why it works but I can tell you how. It seems that whenever on any Earth there is a major event where one multitude of people opposes another multitude of people, each group crying out for a victory of their own, the universe provides each of them what it wants. For example, one of my crew members is from an Earth where the Germans won what you call here World War I. On that planet there was no subsequent World War II. Their history from the early 20th Century to the Present is quite different from yours. My Earth's departure from your Earth came more than two thousand years earlier. In my Earth, Alexander the Great died before he moved his army into Asia. His successors kept Greece strong through the build-up of Rome. So Greek thought and culture prevailed into the historical period you call the Middle Ages – where frankly your Earth stayed rooted in ignorance for a thousand years."

The General thought he understood even as it occurred to him that he should think he was listening to a lunatic. "So we all have Earth in common, but our histories are different – the difference starting whenever one of these cloning –like events occurs?"

"That is correct. But we have more than just our Earth in common. We have our ancestors in common as well. Neither one of us is more or less human than the other."

"And what about the people alive at the moment of the splitting? Are they alive on both Earths?"

"Yes .They would have to be, don't you see?"

"The ramifications of that are going to make my head spin. But putting all that aside, earlier during your introduction to David, you said he would be useful 'in the coming battle.' What coming battle are you referring to?" The General leaned forward in his chair and his hands on the table curled into fists.

"And this is why I wanted to talk to you – a leader of your country's military. Regardless of which Earth one is on, as I said earlier, mankind is the same. Our species seeks dominance and competitive advantage wherever it is and wherever it goes. We are capable of great brutality. We destroy whole cultures without even a qualm of conscience. We of what you call The Object may be the first to arrive but we will not be the last. What brought us here will bring others – others who have far more dangerous intentions than we do for your Earth."

"Why now? What has changed from before when we were left alone?"

"Actually the beacon you sent out to the other Earths technologically advanced enough to assess it is a combination of several factors. One is the growth of your population into billions of people – Your Earth's consciousness factor increased, also Planck's manipulation of matter with his mentalization as he calls it, registered on our sensors, and lastly the sudden extinction of the consciousness of twenty million people left a dark hole noticeable for what was no longer there."

"So the battle you refer to is coming to us from these other Earths?"

"The battle – which may come in many forms – is more a result of your geopolitical forces...however visitors from other earths will come here to take advantage of your Earth's instabilities and vulnerabilities. They will aid and abet animosities, they will instigate violent confrontations. They will do what men do to take advantage of weaker players. If it were not for the present conditions already here, there would be no battle."

General Greene knew he needed to stop and think about things. He had outdistanced his protective cover. He should pull back and await further orders. Much as he hated it, he had to get the elected officials involved. Still he had to ask one more question.

"And what about you, Plato? Are you here to attack us too? What do you want from us?"

Plato did not respond immediately. He wondered how much he should say. He and his team had been monitoring all of Earth's communications for weeks and he himself had specialized in learning the power structure of the superpower countries. He had not yet resolved a communication strategy that would optimize his objectives. This Earth's governmental practices were partisan and divisive on even relatively unimportant matters. They continually sought tiny tactical political victories at the expense of dealing with larger truths.

Finally he said, "We can each help the other. The scale and consequences of the battle that exists are much greater than you imagine. No one of the many Earths can avoid involvement -your Earth is involved already - you just don't yet know it."

"At least tell me what the battle is about?" The General demanded.

"The war is about what all of man's wars are about. On every Earth - and now in alliances of Earths - men fight over power and control. Man fights to control the resources that produce wealth and influence. When was it ever different?"

*****

Planck and Dr. Wheeling and David chose to sit around one of the outside tables covered by an umbrella. An ocean breeze was cooling off the worst of the late afternoon heat and each of them welcomed the island beauty. Each of them had spent the last couple of days confined in a small space: David and Dr. Wheeling at the Pentagon and Planck onboard The Object.

"So Planck...last time I saw you, you were being kidnapped. How is it that you are here now?" David asked.

Planck grinned, his boyish beach boy good looks at odds with the serious theoretical physicist he was. "Bizarre right! So I was taken by sort of a Russian equivalent of a Navy Seal team. They get me on their fishing boat and we start heading out to sea. I'm trying to figure out if I can do anything. There are about six of them and they all have guns. I've got my amplifier in my ear but I was scared and couldn't really focus on what I should do. I didn't know what I could do. Basically all I did was stare at them and stare out the boat at the waves.

"So I don't know what I should do.... But then their boat's engine dies and they can't get it started again. One of them tries the dinghy's outboard and that won't start either. And I wondered if I had done that somehow - but I didn't think I had - though then it seemed like I should have thought of that. Then from out of nowhere The Object's shuttle appears and it is hovering right next to the fishing boat. Then there is this huge booming sound and a super bright flash which they told me later knocks us all out. Next thing I know I am up on The Object and I never see the Russians again though I'm told they were dropped off unharmed back in Russia somewhere."

"So you were up in The Object all that time? More than two days?" David asked.

"That's right! I've been talking to Plato and his crew. They are from a number of different worlds, but all are simply different historical versions of Earth, some are almost identical and others totally different. And the people can look just like us or some interesting variations – though I was told those were culturally selected, not biologically. Like some of them are this very pretty light shade of green – but that is by choice. The universe is so different than what I had envisioned."

Dr. Wheeling had listened quietly but intently, now he had to ask, "So how does the universe work? What is different from what we thought we knew?"

"The key difference is that the universe is in a continuous state of 'potentiality'. What becomes material is what the Observer wants to arise out of the flux of possibilities. Matter is just the Observer's preferred state. But the Observer is not a defined consciousness, it is an aggregate consciousness. As an aggregate it has no single orientation. But at any moment in time as it relates to any particular space-time location, its aggregate mind leads to one result, but that result can arbitrarily be influenced if that particular space-time is a matter of specific and exceptional focus from within the overall consciousness."

The professor nodded his head, "I see. So all of humanity is just a part of the universal consciousness but with Planck's group mentalization aided by his amplifier he can influence local space-time by virtue of an exceptional focus directed there – potentiality is instructed to take a particular form or result. To the universe as a whole, that local space-time is an infinitesimally small fraction of all space-time."

Planck agreed, "I think that is how it works."

"So why did The Object, I guess I should say Plato and his team, want to communicate with you?" David asked.

Planck's expression changed then to a much more serious demeanor. "First, let me tell you, you can't always tell what these guys are thinking. And since they come from a mix of Earths, some of which have very different histories and cultures than our own, you shouldn't assume that they all think alike. Plato in particular thinks with a very different perspective than you or I do.

"Also, they seem to have instant access to vast data files as if their brains have a computer chip inside them, so sometimes talking to them seems like you are talking to a computer."

"So why you?" David repeated.

"Yea, why me? Well what Plato said is that in their experience once an Earth has developed the ability to manipulate matter with my so called 'mentalization' that the cultural and scientific changes at that Earth are so dramatic that the Earth enters a whole new historical cycle. Those changes can be transformative in very positive ways or very destructive ways. Some Earths become visions of prosperity and wisdom while others literally destroy themselves. Plato says there are not a lot of in-betweens – the Earth goes one way or the other."

"And what drives that? Why does one Earth become great and another Earth become a huge dust ball?"

"Plato says it is driven by the wisdom of its political leadership."

David just shrugged his shoulders, "Then we're toast!"

Dr. Wheeling, who had been listening and considering the new information from Planck now bobbed his head up and down several times, and then said, "Actually what faces our Earth now, we have faced before. Planck's mentalization should be viewed as no different than any previous major technological advance. At numerous times in our history major new technologies changed cultures and created both opportunity and danger.

"Whether you consider the changes driven by the invention of the wheel or of nuclear power, both opportunity and destruction followed. The recent invention and development of the Internet has wrought enormous cultural changes. Some good some not so good. Setting Planck's work to the side, scientists all over the world are working on tremendous new technologies that will radically alter cultures and societies. Geopolitical structures will have to change.

"Also," Dr. Wheeling continued, "With each new technological change, man's ability to destroy the Planet seems to increase. Before gun powder was discovered, killing people in war had to be done one person at a time and from very close range. Gun powder led to more and more powerful explosives. Bigger and bigger bombs were developed until whole cities could be destroyed like the fire-bombing of Dresden during World War II. Then we came up with the atomic bomb and its ever more powerful progeny. And then of course we started on potentially even more dangerous biological weapons. However that same growth in understanding chemical and biological reactions is leading to the eradication of diseases and the lengthening of the lifetime of mankind." The professor paused as if to stop, then had one more thought.

"Benefit and destruction are the constant yin and yang of scientific advance. And the stakes keep getting higher!"

Now David really understood what the Alien leader had said earlier, "So when Plato told us that their statistical models show us with a 17% chance of turning our Earth into barren desert within the not so distant future, he was just forecasting the likelihood of our governments screwing up so badly that we off our own planet.... I guess I'm surprised the probability isn't higher!"

# CHAPTER SEVEN

*"There is a universe where Elvis is still alive."*

Alan Guth
*Massachusetts Institute of Technology*
*Professor of Physics*

Hank Scarpetti hung up his phone and considered what the Chairman of the Joint Chiefs had just told him. Human beings from other Earths with different histories. But more technologically advanced though not from the future. He would never have guessed that!

He hated that the military was ahead of him on this. He should have thought of having one of his people go with the professor and Randall back to the island. Instead the damn military could claim first contact. What a political coup if he could have had the President there! Instead it was General Carl Greene and Scarpetti wasn't at all sure that he could trust his friend Greene on this. Even though he and Greene had been friends for years, he really didn't know what Greene's political views were. Too often in Scarpetti's experience military leaders wanted to act like they had no political views, but then WHAM as soon as they retired they wrote books that made civilian leaders look like idiots.

Scarpetti had to figure out how to play it all. He knew the President would want to meet this Plato guy immediately. But something like that couldn't be scripted and this President didn't do so well without a script in front of him. The President was smart enough, you'd think, since he could remember all sorts of facts and figures, but he seemed to have no idea how issues would play over the long term. And the one thing Scarpetti knew about life in politics – sooner or later the long term would arrive and bite you in the ass! He had the scars to prove it.

He thought then about pushing General Greene to the side on issues relating to The Object. But then the Chairman of the Joint Chiefs would just appoint someone else to be the liaison – or worse do it himself! Scarpetti figured he'd be better off with Greene, they were friends after all. And better the devil you know than the one you don't!

He realized he'd gotten used to The Object just floating by overhead and not really doing anything. Amazing how fast you could get used to something like that! But now this guy Plato had arrived and worse yet, he was talking about involving Earth in some kind of cosmic war. Of course as soon as the military heard that they figured this put them right in the center of everything! The President was not going to like that! He hated sharing power with anyone!

Then Scarpetti thought of one thing the President would want to set up immediately, He'd want a new Cabinet level Secretary – Secretary of All Things Weird and Alien, Scarpetti mused. Actually he knew he had to start thinking about that. Who would the President want to appoint to take lead within the White House? Of course, the Secretary of State would argue he should be in charge and The Secretary of Homeland Security would argue for herself. Scarpetti shuddered and thought no way! He'd been brought in by the President to keep that sort of thing from happening. Those Departments were so cumbersome and overstaffed that it would take a year for them to figure out The Object had landed.

Scarpetti knew he had to come up with someone quickly or the President would pick one of his old political cronies. As cynical as Scarpetti was, he knew he couldn't let that happen. This issue was just too big. The future of Planet Earth was at stake. Scarpetti sat at his desk and thought about all the political leaders he knew. Who would he trust to be the Government's interface or Ambassador to The Object? Who should the President appoint to work with Plato and Plato's team?

Scarpetti started thumbing through his contact list. He thought about Congressional leaders and political supporters. He thought about current and past leaders of his Party. He thought about state governors. Who was savvy enough, wise enough, that he or she could be trusted on this? This would require real wisdom. A real understanding of how things could turn out over the long term. Sitting at his desk, Scarpetti leaned back, defeated. He could not think of anyone. Never before had he actually had to think of who was wise. Wisdom wasn't a requirement for political leadership. It would just get in the way of how politics really needed to be played. And those few who were wise also tended to be honorable – and that really didn't work!

Scarpetti leaned back in his chair and clasped his hands over his protruding stomach. Over the last thirty years he had worked tirelessly and he thought brilliantly to get himself to where he was the Chief of Staff to the most powerful person in the world. He himself thereby became one of the most powerful. That was a long way to come for the son of an airline mechanic who had worked his way through the University of Illinois. He'd always been underestimated by the people around him and he turned that into an asset. He had hid his ambition and worked closely with people whose personalities were shinier and more charismatic than his. Then when they failed, as they inevitably did, he was there to save the day.

Now he had a front row seat at the table of one of history's turning points. A moment where the life of the planet was at stake! And he realized he was not prepared for it – not at all prepared. He had scoffed at grand strategies and lofty visions. Get the tactics right and chalk up the election victories! But he knew this new challenge would take more than great tactics. It would require vision and an understanding of long term consequences – something he had never been good at. And he had spent his whole life around people who he knew were equally unsuited, most of them woefully so, though some in their arrogance would never admit it or even know it. And he knew the President was one of those.

With all that in mind, he walked into the Oval Office to tell the President about General Greene's conversation with Plato.

*****

Plato left General Greene to communicate with other generals at the Pentagon and found Dr. Wheeling, David and Planck in animated discussion. He joined them and took a seat where the sun's rays could find his face.

"Across all the Earths that I have seen so far, we all share a love of the sun," he said.

"So all the Earths share the same position in our Solar System?" David asked.

Plato nodded. "Otherwise they would not be Earth. However the stars are different."

"If the stars are different then these Earth's must be very far apart," Dr. Wheeling observed.

Plato nodded again, "Yes Professor. So far apart that we are not sure they are even in the same universe – as you think of it. But rather than thinking in terms of distance, you should think in terms of dimensions. We have gotten away from thinking of a universe or multiple universes. We just call it The Existence."

"So if it is so vast, how do you move about from one Earth to the next?" David asked.

"In your quantum physics you call it 'entanglement.' All of the Earths are essentially entangled with each other. It is as if each occupies the same space-time but different frames of reference. Yet the physical existence history of each overlies the others. As the moment of dis-entanglement recedes historically the two worlds drift further and further away and the bridge between them becomes more difficult to cross.

"Between 'entangled' worlds, the usual limitations in Physics, such as the speed of light, do not apply. But there are still limits none the less. For example, for I know this will occur to you to ask, we cannot move whole armies of men and materiel from one Earth to the next. Though of course, man being man, that was tried. Above certain low limits, either nothing would happen or worse some subset of the men and their weapons would simply disappear. Where they ended up no one knew."

David had been thinking along a different track. "So if there are many Earths and many different histories, there must be many different cultures as well."

Plato shook his head and held up his hand, "Less than you would think. As the Earths' civilizations mature the most powerful countries in each tend to evolve culturally into just a few successful models. Those Earths that do not have civilizations that take on the culture of one of those successful models tend to not survive what we call Stage III – which happens to be the technological age your Earth is just entering. "

"Now I am afraid to ask. Is our Earth mapping to one of those successful models?"

Plato looked back at David. "There are three basic cultures that survive. One is a culture of brutal and repressive tyranny where a tiny few dominate the many. The more absolute the tyranny, the more survivable it is. The second culture that survives is what you would call extreme libertarianism. There is virtually no government but resources must be plentiful. The third culture is actually the one where I come from. It is a culture that marries two conflicting ideals. It is based on the pursuit of wisdom while maintaining military dominance. Its closest comparison on Earth is the Zen ideal of the Samurai Philosophy. But it is approached through the rigor of pursuing the perfect rendition of Wisdom and Martial Arts. One without the other fails to last."

"So is yours a warrior culture?" David asked.

"Not so much as it is a culture that understands that one must always be willing to fight for one's beliefs – and if you fight you must win. One of your Presidents said it well, 'Speak softly and carry a big stick.' "

David then repeated the question, "So how is our Earth doing?"

Plato paused again. Then replied, "Your world is just at the beginning of Stage III – the stage where technology capability increases geometrically and resource abundance truly becomes possible. Will your leaders possess the wisdom to master those challenges?"

The four of them sat silently. Plato leaned back in his chair and let his face feel the warmth of the sun. He felt the soft brush on his skin of the slight breeze and heard the whispering of the lovely turquois Bahamian waters ebbing and flowing at the shore. He had learned to take advantage of the quiet moments in the long war he was fighting.

Dr. Wheeling was the one who interrupted. "So what happens next?"

Plato looked once more out to sea and then returned his gaze to the professor. "I suspect that our General Greene after conferring with his leaders in Washington will request that I go and meet with your President. And I will do so." He paused then for a moment before continuing, "But there are some things I would like you to do. Very important things!"

Later Plato excused himself from the others. He had been shipboard for weeks and the opportunity to be out in the sun and feel an ocean breeze blowing over him was not to be missed. He found it a wonderful surprise that Planck lived on this rather deserted tropical island. It had been a long time since Plato could walk along such a beach and he took off his shoes and rolled up his pant legs. He set off walking and tried to set his mind at ease – to just walk and not think. After a few minutes he saw a woman walking toward him from the other direction. When they came up to each other, she paused to say hello.

Plato accessed his internal data file and said, "Catherine Ozawa my name is Plato."

The woman smiled, "Welcome to our island. Thank you for returning Planck to us. I was worried for him. I talked with him for a few minutes earlier and he shared with me his recent experience. The universe is infinitely surprising."

"I understand you are both a physicist and a Zen Master – a combination that is unusual on your world but not so much on mine."

Catherine smiled again, something that Plato noticed seem to come very easily to her. "I claim neither distinction; I am a physicist only insofar as I have studied physics. And as to being a Zen Master, I only claim to be on the path. But tell me about your Earth. I am curious about a world where Zen and physics come easily together."

Until she had approached he was happy to be alone, but something about this woman he found embracing. She radiated a calm energy and clarity of being. The marks of age on her, the lines in her face and her short white hair, he barely noticed and knew them to be both irrelevant and reversible. "If you will walk along this beautiful beach with me, I will enlighten you as to my Earth."

Catherine nodded as she turned around, "Come then let's walk."

After walking a little while in an easy silence, Plato found himself telling her about his Earth, an Earth very different than the one whose sandy beach was now underfoot. The dominant culture on his Earth had grown out of a Greek civilization torn asunder by centuries of strife between the philosophically opposed Sparta and Athens. Over the centuries Sparta had gained control of what were here the Americas, North and South. Athens had triumphed over Europa and Africa. Asia had mostly been a neutral land.

Sparta had retained a rigorous military tradition and held to Plato's philosophy of Ideals. Athens had taken on an Aristotelian society with its democratic energy and scientific emphasis. Though geographically born right next to each other, it took them a thousand years, countless wars and near mutual-extinction for them to finally learn to co-exist. Once they did evolve to welcome mutual co-existence, their Earth flourished. They had no stagnant Middle Ages filled with bloody territorial struggles. Every couple of hundred years or so, their political leaders would forget and a war would pop up, but it would be quickly ended. The people knew better and would refuse to fight. Let the politicians kill each other, they would say. Their last war was quite a time ago.

"How long ago was that?" Catherine asked.

"Over three hundred years ago."

"So where does all our human competitiveness and aggression go?"

"We are an old civilization. Our population is in the millions not the billions. We have no scarcity of resources. We are a world of warriors who don't fight and philosophers who think they know all the answers – and maybe they do. Our scientists are the only ones actively engaged. Our science is well advanced ahead of yours. They have the universe itself against which to fight their war of wits. The universe surrenders its secrets sparingly."

Catherine Ozawa listened to Plato tell of a world she could not imagine. "So do you leave it often?"

"For a long time now I have been constantly traveling. I rarely go back for long. I return frequently but still love leaving it more. I still love venturing out. I have traveled across both light-years and across dimensions. And I have found a mission that suits me."

"And what is that mission?"

Plato refrained from saying the first answer that came to his lips. He found he had already talked to her more than he had intended. It had been a long time since he had talked so freely – and here he was talking unreservedly to a woman he had just met on a beach.

"I think it too soon for me to tell you all. I need to maintain some mystery or you will think too little of me. Let's just say that like Odysseus I like voyaging under the stars."

Catherine regarded this tall strong golden haired man with the ancient eyes. "So tell me this. Have you been voyaging long?"

"For some time yes...about 60 years."

"That is a while. You don't look old enough for that to be true. How old are you?"

As if consulting an internal clock, he paused then said, "One hundred sixty-three years, eight months and seven days and twelve minutes."

"Remarkable. You must share with me your secrets to aging gracefully."

Plato realized it had been a long time since he had felt attracted to a woman; yet here it was. He wondered if he had been seeking it. "Actually, I would like to do that. I'm sure you could, not that you should."

"We'll see. But tell me, where were you before you came here?"

Plato stopped walking then, looked at her and then looked out to sea. "Before here I was on a different Earth. An Earth similar to this one – at the same stage of development. I was there for over ten years."

Catherine could see that Plato's demeanor had changed – a deep sadness was etched clearly in his face. "Why did you leave?"

"I left because I failed in my mission." He paused again and continued looking away from her and toward the horizon. "I left because there was no longer a world there. The warring countries blew their world up. Now it will be a centuries-long reclamation project. My heart is too broken to be a part of that."

Catherine looked closely at Plato and saw past the handsome face to the pain the man carried inside. "I apologize. I have asked too many questions. Let's just walk." Without thinking, she took his hand and they walked together. Plato could not remember when last he had walked a beach with a woman hand in hand. He now remembered that he liked it. He was not so old after all.

*****

When later Plato pulled David aside he told him it was important that David be the first one to write what was to appear in the world's newspapers. He advised David to write up everything he knew immediately. David put his smart phone to record and started asking Plato questions. Plato made no attempt to evade any question or direct how David was to write the article.

When David's article appeared on the front page of the next day's Washington Post, it was immediately reprinted across the worldwide news media. The newspapers reprinted his story word for word, but as was the practice, they wrote their own headlines. The Washington Post went for directness.

*****

**Other Earths Exist!**
By David Randall

*[This article is based on an exclusive interview with the Leader of The Object]*

*The Object is from Earth – just not this one – so says the Leader of The Object. In fact, he says there are many Earths scattered amongst the cosmos. The Leader, who calls himself Plato, says that The Object has come to our Earth on a goodwill and fact finding mission and means us no harm. In fact, Plato says he has come to share with us cultural and technological knowledge that will help us in the future as we learn about and experience a universe that is much more complex and interconnected than our science had led us to believe. We are not only not alone, but we Homo sapiens are spread out into the universe. Our Earth is but one of many Earths which are identical in origin but different in historical development.*

*After months of silently hovering in the skies of Earth while observing the goings on below, the Leader of The Object came down to the island retreat of Benjamin Planck, the young physicist who previously as reported in this newspaper had been the subject of a worldwide manhunt based on the message from The Object stating it wanted to meet with him. Plato just showed up to meet with Planck and Planck's guest, Dr. Janus Wheeling, the noted Nobel Prize winning physicist.*

*When asked why Plato went first to meet with Benjamin Plank and not the leaders of the world's government, Plato replied, "I will meet with them soon. I wished to first meet with Dr. Planck because it is his work here that led us to this Earth. Plato confirmed that Planck's work is directionally correct though still rudimentary. Through his work, Planck sent out a 'calling card' – so it seemed polite for us to visit him first." (When asked, Planck stated he had no idea that his work could have such an effect.)*

*According to Plato, he is from an Earth that developed on a historical timeline that is significantly different from this Earth's development. Plato's Earth is no older than our own but its technological and cultural development occurred at a faster pace than that of this world. He pointed out as an example, that on his Earth there was no 'middle ages' period where there was almost no technological development for a thousand years. He hastened to add that our Earth is more advanced than some other Earths and that there are other Earths more advanced than his home Earth.*

*He describes his Earth as one whose historical development was influenced much more by the ancient Greeks of the fourth and fifth Centuries BCE. The cultures of Athens and Sparta thrived far longer on his Earth than on our own. Plato also informed us that the name of the spaceship we call The Object is actually The Bucephalus – named after the horse that carried Alexander the Great to so many victories.*

*He has come to this Earth, he says, in order to help us get through an era that on other earths has shown to be a particularly deadly period when the destruction of the planet itself is a possibility and the deaths of billions of people a real probability. He points at the recent catastrophic nuclear war in the Koreas as a proof.*

*He is also here to help us with the myriad challenges imposed by what we will learn to be a very interactive universe. What has thus far seemed to us to be a vast and disinterested universe where we are but a tiny blip of existence, we will learn is actually a universe that invites interconnectedness. Plato says the universe is actually an infinite provider of resources that can empower the growth and prosperity of civilizations. He says Planck's work is in fact opening the gateway to all that the universe offers.*

*Plato went on to say that we should expect for representatives of other Earths to soon come calling*

*[story continues on page A6]*

*****

Back aboard The Bucephalus before his trip to Washington, Plato conferred with Liu Bei, his second in command who had been meeting with China's senior leaders. The report made by Liu Bei was not heartening though not unexpected. China was the most important of the superpower's to Plato's long term strategy but was also thought to be the most intractable. Plato would have liked to take the lead with China himself but reluctantly had agreed that Liu Bei was a better choice because of his common ethnicity. Liu Bei had come from an Earth where their historical line differed from this Earth's from around the year 1100. In his world China had become transcendent and was the leading geopolitical unit of a model successful Planet.

This China's historical line was different in significant ways. This China had yet to fulfill what it regarded as its destiny as a nation. For over two thousand years it had out endured all its invaders and learned that its peasant populations would survive any new incursions. The people's ability to suffer and survive through any chaos was its ineluctable strength. Where its western competitors thought in terms of months and years, China thought in terms of decades and centuries. It had always been patient and now it was confident too.

But the recent annihilation of the two Koreas was very alarming to China's leaders. Korea was a constant adjunct to all of China's history and now it was no more. And China knew that it itself had miscalculated and it was bearing the bitter fruits of that miscalculation. Many Chinese had died and more would die from the radioactive fallout. Economic interests were liquidated. The Party itself was in massive reorientation as it dealt with the disaster. The quiet millions of its people were stirring discontentedly.

Liu Bei had selected his name from early Chinese history with the hope that these current Chinese leaders would embrace the subtle compliment, yet it arose no reaction. The Chinese leaders' focus was so internal and insecure that Liu Bei's arrival seemed more an inconvenience than an important augury of things to come. He was treated as an unwanted interloper not an ambassador from distant worlds. All of the attention of The Party leaders was on the mighty ocean that was the Chinese People; that ocean was roiled and angry and uncertain. How could the Koreas be gone? What would come next? What new tragedy?

Liu Bei had to report to Plato that he had not succeeded in his mission. He had not even been able to get them to admit that they had discovered the same mentalization as Planck. Worse yet, he reported that in a coming battle, China might well favor the opposing forces. Where they had once thought that China might be their greatest ally, now the opposite might be true. The events that led to the destruction of the Koreas would have societal consequences.

*****

Plato was ushered into the Oval Office by Hank Scarpetti to meet President Morningstar who came out from behind his desk to meet him. In person Plato found the President to be more careworn than what showed in the data library Plato accessed. His posture was not quite as straight and his jet black hair had more than a mere touch of grey. But his smile was warm and engaging even as his eyes seemed restless and uncertain.

The two shook hands and then Plato turned to the other two men in the room, men he recognized as he accessed his data network as the Secretary of Defense and the Chairman of the Joint Chiefs. Then he also saw that General Greene who had brought Plato in to meet Scarpetti had followed him into the office. All the men sat around the small table in front of the large fireplace.

The President spoke first, "I understand that you refer to yourself as Plato. I hope that I may refer to you that way as well. But I'm curious, is that your real name or one you chose for us?"

In the President's tone as he formed the question Plato saw that it had been rehearsed. It was like moving the king's pawn in a chess match, a good way to open up the game.

"On my Earth the culture of ancient Greece was far more enduring and admired. Its philosophers are our heroes. My choice of name reflects that. I always find it somewhat disheartening when I find worlds that dismiss philosophy as a mere academic pursuit."

"And do you find that so on our world?" President Morningstar asked.

Plato demurred, "I am still just learning about your world – and your world has more than one culture. But in your country it does seem to me that your citizens look for self-help in psychology when they would be better served by reexamining their philosophy."

"I will keep that in mind. And have you been to many Earths, Plato?"

"Yes I have been to many Earths."

The President paused to reflect on that, then looked at Scarpetti – who nodded. Then he asked, "So why have you come to ours?"

And so it began.

"Mr. President, I presume you have already heard all that I have told General Greene about the risks your world now faces – existential risk."

The President held up his hand as if talking to one of his staff members. "Yes, I have heard all that you have told General Greene about various probabilities of our Earth's demise or destruction. With all due respect, I don't really know how you can determine such things. Yes I know our world is a dangerous place. Even more than my predecessors in this office, I view myself as a caretaker for the world. I do not think it to be in such peril as you do – at least not in so far as the risks originate on this planet. I cannot know as yet what new perils will come to us from other worlds."

Plato's voice softened as he assumed his most benign manner. "Mr. President, what comes from other Earths can be far more helpful than harmful. But much of that depends on you. Your existential threats do not originate off of this planet. They will grow out of the seeds you have been sowing for centuries. But in our analysis, it is in your twentieth century that the beginnings of potential destruction are found. And this twenty-first century shows no course corrections but rather an exacerbation of dangerous trends."

"Oh I believe I fully understand our history. I have always had good history books on my bedside table – I understand the trends that matter. My administration has the most brilliant minds of academia represented and I consult them. We engage in truly enlightened conversations. I would love to invite you to join in them...Would you join us?"

"I would welcome such conversations. I share your love for history – but given all that I have seen across many Earths, I have found history to be a much more complicated predictor of events than most people believe. But importantly, the collective histories do create a body of data from which precise calculations of probabilities can be made."

The President smiled, "I look forward to our future conversations. There is much we can both learn, I'm sure. But please let me get to a matter of more concern to me. You have told General Greene that we should expect other visitors from other Earths – visitors that would be more dangerous to us than yourselves. You tell us that we have nothing to fear from you but we should be wary of them. Is that correct?"

Plato nodded, "Yes that is so."

At this point, the Secretary of Defense interrupted. He was a large beefy man with short red hair and small, round eyes, "Well, Plato, if they were here in this room, would they be saying the same thing about you? Would they tell us that we should trust them and not trust you?"

Plato nodded again as he looked closely at the powerful head of the Defense Department. He saw the man shared little of the President's charm. Instead he saw a man who gloried in the power he wielded and wanted to exert his authority. "I'm sure they would."

"So there you have it!" said the Secretary of Defense.

"And what is it you think you have?" Plato responded.

The people in the room fell silent. That question hung in their minds. The President looked to Hank Scarpetti, who merely looked away.

General Greene spoke then; he had been silent until then knowing that he was there only because he alone had thus far met Plato. "Perhaps Plato if you could tell us of the nature of the threat we would be better able to assess friend from foes?"

Plato looked around the room before he spoke. Greene he knew as a serious thinker, combative but not quick to judgment. The Chief of Staff he knew only from what he had seen in his file: that he was a true strategist in thought and deed. The Secretary of Defense had been a US Senator for many years and would think in political terms – as he expected Scarpetti to do. President Morningstar was still a puzzle to him.

"Before I can describe the threats, I need to tell you what draws other Earths here. It is not your planet itself or its physical resources. There is no desire for any of the militaries of any Earth to come here to conquer or control territory as you think it. That is so not because they would not like to, but because physically they cannot. We know of no way to bring armies here. The universe that separates us by unimaginable light-years and across dimensions makes such invasions impossible. The physical interaction between Earths is only possible on a very limited basis.

"But not all interactions are physical. As you are discovering – as Benjamin Planck is proving – the universe –what we call The Existence – is mostly Dark Energy and Dark Matter, not the physical matter you think of as the stuff of reality. And Dark Matter and Dark Energy are the foundational forces of 'Consciousness'. And Consciousness is what your Earth has that the rest of the Earths that have reached the necessary stage of development will want to come here to affect and to interact with. For the consciousness that is here has its emanations at all the other Earths --- just as theirs have emanations here – emanations that you do not yet appreciate or understand. For all Earths are entangled by it. And the ability to affect that consciousness is what every Earth comes to seek. They will want to meld your consciousness into theirs – which will make them stronger."

President Morningstar nodded as if he understood. "What I am hearing is that the threat to us is not a military one. Rather you want to control our minds, is that it?"

"No sir, it is not possible to control minds – one can only influence them – or destroy them...as you just did in the Koreas. But the mental state of humanity in the aggregate matters a great deal – both in how mankind deals with the problems and opportunities of its own creation and how it interfaces to the consciousness of the aggregate of Earths."

"So no invading armies or lasers shot from space?" the Secretary of Defense emphasized.

"No invading armies from space, Mr. Secretary. However, there are already plenty of armies here for them to use. The next wave of Earths coming here will bring new technologies and advanced knowledge to seduce less ambitious countries and extremist groups. You will find their gifts have many strings tied to them – strings that may bind the arms of some and strengthen the arms of other. The new technologies they bring will be both dangerous and destabilizing and the promises they make are yet more seductive and more dangerous."

The Secretary of Defense continued, "So it will be another arms war. Well we know how to win that kind of war."

The President shook him off, "No it's not about that." Then turning back to Plato he said, "I'm sure there's a lot that I don't understand yet, but my government will work with you on this. I'm sure we can do the right things here. But you need to work with us too. Do things our way. Let us manage what gets communicated to the people. They aren't ready to hear all this. I'll appoint a team to work with you and we both will work with each other through the team – that's how I like to do things here. I have to control the message. I don't want to scare our people with things they will never understand. Trust me to make this all work out."

Plato listened and was not surprised by what he heard. He had come to expect it. "Unfortunately Mr. President, in my experience that approach does not work."

"Well Plato, that might be your experience on other Earths with other leaders, but here I think I know best. You can trust me on this."

Plato returned the President's confident gaze. "Sir, all that I would point out is that I believe you will find that there will be no way to contain this story. Events will occur that make that impossible. Ultimately, what will matter will be the actions you take, not how well messages are communicated."

The President held firmly to his view, "Don't worry Plato, when action is required, we'll take it. But for now, let us handle the communications."

# CHAPTER EIGHT

*"To the mind that is still, the whole universe surrenders"*

Lao Tzu

General Greene escorted Plato out of The White House. He wanted to explain why the meeting with the President had gone as badly as it did, but he knew it wasn't his place. The President perceived Plato as a threat and wanted to show strength in return. Greene would have recommended a less testosterone driven encounter. But instead he just said, "Where would you like me to take you?"

"General if you could help me get back to Planck's island in The Bahamas that would be appreciated."

"Of course, how about if I drive you to Andrews Air Force Base and set up transport from there?"

"Excellent."

As they drove to Andrews in the general's staff car, General Greene raised the issue that seemed to have been too casually dismissed during the meeting with the President. "Plato, I believe you are here to help us, but every time I hear you talk, you seem to mention more threats to us."

"The threats are not of my making. To use one of your expressions – don't shoot the messenger."

"If I heard you correctly, others are going to come who will try to create disorder and chaos here on this planet for reasons of their own."

"Yes."

"Well our planet has enough chaos and disorder. Particularly as a result of the nuclear weapons destroying North and South Korea, our world is a box of explosives waiting to go off. Old hostilities between Pakistan and India, both of which have nuclear weapons, are surfacing again. Iran with its new nuclear weapons is threatening Israel. The whole Middle East is smoldering with daily suicide bombings occurring somewhere in the region and al Qaida growing more active. Africa is ubiquitous tribal warfare. While China is demanding more control and influence in Asia to the disquiet of its regional neighbors."

Plato folded his arms across his chest, "Your President seemed to think he had all that under control."

"We both know that none of that is under control....but you are saying that visitors coming from other Earths will go to those countries and religious fanatics and political extremists and offer them new dangerous technologies and make promises of support that will encourage all of them to more aggressive actions. That is what you are saying will happen, correct?"

"Unfortunately yes, they will go to them. And they will go to them speaking in their own language, in their own dialects, dressed like them and even looking like them. For each Earth has races and ethnicities just like this one. It makes them extremely persuasive."

"And why would they do this to us?" the General asked.

Plato was sympathetic but had no comfort to offer yet. "Do not think of the other Earths as monolithic. Some that will come will be helpful and unthreatening. Their intentions will be good. Some are neither good nor bad, just curious. But others are rapacious. They are bottom feeders who have learned how to benefit from the chaos and destruction of others. Though the rewards have changed with the times, there will always be those who want more than they have. There are always those who have no empathy for those who are not like them. All Earths share the most horrible examples of people in the millions dying for the territorial ambitions of kings and emperors and modern political leaders like Hitler and Stalin and Mao."

"It sounds like we don't have a chance," the General said.

"It is the same struggle every Earth must survive in order to reach the next stage of development. Some Earths have survived it. My Earth did. There is hope for yours."

"So what do we have to do?"

Plato smiled, "I was hoping someone would ask me that. Before a problem can be solved, the problem must first be recognized to exist."

"You don't think we know there's a problem?"

"I don't think your government wants to admit to how great the problem is. I think your people take too much for granted and take too little responsibility. Your country has no view of long term consequences and chooses leaders with no experience, no wisdom and no true judgment. A 51% majority is treated as a political mandate to impose poorly developed programs on the other 49% and then all lament the partisanship and lack of support. In my world, the great sin in all things personal and political is to be out of balance. Balance based on mutual respect and an appreciation of all things shared in common is the basis for survival. Balance is no virtue here – it is all teetering from one extreme to the next. Leaders are applauded who can inflame the minds of twenty percent of the people. In my world such leaders are shunned as selfish and reckless. In an increasingly dangerous world, the loss of balance invites destruction."

General Greene listened to Plato with mounting desolation. He did not respond. As the car neared Andrews, he then asked, "So what are you going to do?"

"I'm going to make sure that everyone sees the problem."

*****

As David opened the door to his New York City apartment, Gabriela bounded off the couch where she had been working on her laptop and jumped into his arms. Joyfully he held tight to this beautiful dark haired woman who miraculously loved him. And she too thought his love was a miracle. Though just a few days had passed since they were together on Pirate's Cay, those days had been scary and eventful and their world had changed. Suddenly they were involved at the heart of revolutionary times, not political revolution so much as cultural and technological. And each had so much to tell the other.

Each of them had also dearly felt the absence of the other in the recent days. Locked away in the Pentagon, David had yearned for Gabriela. He had so much to share with her and then his bed seemed so empty. For Gabriela too his absence had been hard. But all of that was washed away in the flood of new experiences they saw in their future as soon as they stopped hugging each other. The new experiences had to wait a while as they laughed and hugged and talked over each other and then as they started kissing and tossing off clothes and then as they used the couch in ways it hadn't been used for lately.

Afterward they threw on some clothes and tucked into the corners of their couch to talk, with so much to talk about. But David felt he needed to start with something else first. He went down on one knee in front of her and took Gabriela's hand and said, "I don't have a ring yet – but I'll get one. I just don't want to wait another moment. I want us to get married. Will you marry me?"

The breadth of Gabriela's smile was answer enough but her "Yes yes yes" sounded wonderful to his ears. Then after a little more hugging and kissing, Gabriela's usual manner resurfaced. "So what brought that on?"

"I knew I needed to do it when I was locked away at the Pentagon. I wasn't scared as much as aware that the future was far more uncertain than I had truly appreciated. Before The Object arrived, it was so easy to just stick to my routines day after day. And you were part of those routines. Now I know that nothing is certain and lives can change, the whole world can change from one day to the next. If those kinds of changes are out there, I want to be sure you are with me."

"I know what you mean. That's what I've been feeling." Gabriela leaned forward just to take David's hand. They exchanged a long loving gaze. Then Gabriela said, "Ok. So what is happening? Tell me about Plato!"

Later after each had talked and talked and talked and both were all caught up with the goings on of the last few days, they returned to what would happen next.

"I think it depends," David said. "Right before Plato left Pirate's Cay to go to meet with the President, he told Dr. Wheeling, Planck and me that he wanted us to do some things – things that he thought were very important. It was like all of a sudden we were on the same team – his team. Planck, who had spent a couple of days on The Object, was clearly already on Plato's team."

"What does he want you to do?"

"Well first, he wants me and Dr. Wheeling to return as soon as possible to Planck's island. Plato is planning on making that his base of operations. In fact, he is going to bring his crew members down to the island. He says they are all bored up on The Object and want a little R & R on the beach."

Gabriela laughed, "I guess that means they really are just like us. We all love the beach!"

"He wants me to do a full interview with Planck and he wants me to learn all about The Object so that I can write about it. But the next thing he wants from me is the strange one. He wouldn't tell me why, but he wants a list of the most influential people in the United States. He wants everybody from the CEO's of the TV networks and Cable companies to the most popular actors and athletes to the bloggers who have a million followers."

"Why do you think he wants that list?"

"I can only guess that he wants it because he wants to influence them.... Anyway, my point is that Plato wants me to do these things to serve some purpose of Plato's and The Object's. But what do they really want? Are they good guys or bad guys?"

"I think you should do what you do best. Write the story. Follow it step by step. That's what you do."

"That's what I want to do. So I guess I'm going back to the island."

"And you said he wants Dr. Wheeling to come to the island as well?"

"Yes – I think because he wants him to be a spokesperson – about what exactly I'm not sure."

"Well that settles one thing," Gabriela said adamantly. "If you're going back and Dr. Wheeling is going, then I'm going too!"

*****

After several days at home, Dr. Wheeling returned to Pirate's Cay to find it more resort like and less like a monastic retreat. People he didn't recognize were out by the pool and others were sunning themselves on the beach. Then he looked closer and saw that the appearance of some of the newcomers to the pool and beach area was markedly different than what he had thought previously was a human norm. Skin colors varied from the white to black he was familiar with but included yellows and greens and blues he had never seen before. Hair colors and styles varied with new creativity that would be the envy of avant garde hairstylists everywhere. Then he noticed ear shapes varied too. Almost all the crew, male and female, stood well over six feet tall and looked like they spent all day in the gym and had never tasted junk food.

As he approached the lobby he saw monks meditating there led by Master Ozawa and then he saw Planck rising from where he had been sitting to come over to him.

"Dr. Wheeling! I'm glad you returned."

"Planck I'm glad to see you too. What is going on around here?"

Planck seemed like a little boy at his own birthday party, "My island seems to have become an interstellar rest spot. We've been joined by some of Plato's cohorts off The Object. As you see, physical appearance seems to be more a matter of choice with them. By the way, we don't call it The Object anymore. It actually has a name. It's called The Bucephalus, after Alexander the Great's horse."

"I'm surprised you are not besieged by the media."

"Yesterday was the first day, right after the Navy Seals left. We are keeping it secret. I think Plato wants to use this as some kind of base of operations – although to do what I'm not sure. I told him to make himself and his team at home. I did have to send a boat to Nassau to get more supplies. But I figure I owe him since he rescued me from the Russians. So what brings you here?"

"He said I should come back. He says he has a role for me but I am not sure exactly what it is he wants me to do."

"You should go find David, he's here too. Gabriela as well. He spent a lot of time with Plato this morning. I think he knows what's up."

Dr. Wheeling found David sitting by the pool writing on his laptop. He noticed Gabriela in a light blue bikini floating on an air mattress in the pool. She looked lovely. His eyes lingered on Gabriela; she saw him looking and waved at him and gave a smile. He waved back and then smiled to himself as he remembered his previous evening in the city with Dr. Mary Grasso, a lovely woman in her own right, he thought.

"Professor, good to see you here. I'm a little surprised but Plato told me he thought you would come back."

"I surprise myself too. Planck tells me perhaps you know why I'm here."

"I think I am beginning to know. Or at least I know what Plato wants me to know. What he tells me makes sense. Frankly it is stuff I never wanted to hear but can't ignore once I did. And it is stuff you always sort of knew anyway, you just didn't want to look at it straight on. Plato makes you take the rose colored glasses off."

"So tell me."

When David finished, Dr. Wheeling nodded several times. "Yes that is what I expected. What he told us when we first met him. He wants us to help lead the world away from insanity. And what exactly is it that Plato wants?"

David shook his head, "I'm still working on that. But I'm pretty sure we're on the side of the angels."

"So how do we do this?"

"Wait until you hear." And David told him how it would start.

Later that day as Dr. Wheeling returned to the open air lobby from his room, he found the grounds of the retreat deserted. No one was lying on the beach or lounging around the poolside. But for the sounds of the waves and the chirping of birds, the sound of his steps on the gravel path was all he heard. As he neared the lobby he saw why. The lobby was full with the silent crowd of Planck's original group and crew members down from The Bucephalus all sitting on floor mats while meditating. He saw there too at the back were David and Gabriela. In the front of the room were Planck and Ozawa and Plato.

Dr. Wheeling took a seat at one of the umbrella-covered tables just outside the lobby. He enjoyed the peacefulness of the setting. After 10 minutes, while all the others remained where they were meditating, Catherine Ozawa rose up and came to join him.

"Dr. Wheeling, I am so glad to have a chance to talk to you."

Until she came over it hadn't occurred to the professor to seek her out, but now that she was there, he was glad. Looking at her was like looking at a beautiful hand carved piece of antique furniture. Form and function blended together timelessly. Her gaze rested on him and it was as if she saw him just the way he would want to be seen – though he really didn't know what that would even mean.

"I feel the same way. I see you have expanded your practitioners...is that the right word?"

Ozawa smiled, "As good as any. Perhaps next time you'll join us."

"I don't know that I understand...why are Plato's people meditating with you here?"

"Meditation is very common with them. It is part of their culture. When I talked to Plato about it, I felt like the student talking to the Master. He says the mind is the doorway to existence...a quiet mind. A quiet mind welcomes stillness. There is no balance without stillness. Existence without balance invites chaos. Chaos breeds destruction.

"What is fascinating," Catherine Ozawa continued, "Is how that links to understanding the physics of the universe – of the many worlds. The universe starts in balance with empty Potentiality. Then a quantum anomaly, a singularity, occurs and we have the Big Bang when everything is chaotic and then the hyper expansion in the early moments when that chaos is spread. Then the laws of physics get to work, the force of gravity forms stars, stars go nova and more and more fundamental elements are formed – and somewhere within all of that is consciousness arising, consciousness with its own imperative to expand. Its own imperative to encompass existence which leads to intelligence -- then mind gets to work and order comes out of chaos. Balance is restored and the cycle is complete"

"It is that last part that an old physicist like myself has trouble with." Dr. Wheeling responded.

"For this I find it better to think like a Zen Buddhist and not a physicist." Catherine laughed. "The idea that the universe seeks balance is like saying that the ocean seeks to be wet. There is no seeking. Whether a universe or a man, balance is the natural state – it is all the same."

"But man doesn't seek balance, rather the opposite it seems."

"An enlightened man is in balance."

Dr. Wheeling pointed at the group meditating in the lobby, "Is that what they are doing there – seeking enlightenment?"

Ozawa shook her head, "No not now. Plato is leading them to focus on an event he seeks to cause. They are working."

Dr. Wheeling looked over at the group where all was quiet. Everyone there was perfectly still. The only sense of movement came from a soft breeze coming in off the ocean with a delicate salty edge.

Ozawa looked at them as well then turned back to the professor. "Dr. Wheeling, how would you like to join me on a walk? There is a path bordering the shore that is quite beautiful as it wraps around the island. There is a form of meditation in Zen Buddhism known as *kinhin*. There is a certain rigor to it, but let's put that aside. Just walk with me and do not think of anything. Just see. See the island, see the sand, feel the sand, see the water and walk. And be aware of your breath as you walk. When we finish the walk I think you will feel very refreshed. And your steps on this walk may lead you on your own path to enlightenment."

Dr. Wheeling smiled, "Sure, it will be good to stretch my legs."

"Yes, it will do that at least."

*****

The next global communication from The Object was not a short text message as had been the two previous ones. This one was long and detailed and described where The Object had come from, how this Earth was just one of many, and that soon there would be others coming to investigate this Earth. It also presented the risks in horrifying exactitude to this planet's survival: risks from further nuclear war, risks from terrorist use of biologicals, risks from environmental and economic degradation. And each risk was accompanied by statistical evaluations based on twenty-five year and fifty year models. And on such time scales, the risks were not low, rather they approached certainties.

And it showed how each risk could act in conjunction with other risks so that something that might seem minor could swell to major catastrophe. World economies were far more fragile as they grew more interconnected. Butterflies flapping their wings had grown to monstrous proportions and chaos loomed just out of sight.

As a last visual, it showed aerial photography of what the Koreas now looked like.

Plato's transmission in all the world's languages to all electronic devices was bleak and terrifying to see and to read.

It was accompanied by a stellar light show that was equally horrifying; the Earth's sky seemed all aflame for a two minute period that seemed to last forever. Over all the major continents and over the oceans of the world, the horizon seemed on fire. No movie's special effects of an Armageddon was ever more realistic – though what was seen left no mark anywhere afterwards – that is no physical mark. The emotional after image was scarring. No movie screening held such long term impact. The movie screen had been the Earth itself, the audience was everyone and only afterwards was it known to be a hellish mirage.

It was quite an attention getter. Plato hoped that everyone now understood the problem.

Plato had put David to work as well. David wrote a full account of all that he had witnessed. He wrote an interview with Planck and he wrote up an interview he had with Plato. In each the same themes were repeated. The world faced grave dangers that needed to be confronted. Changes in philosophy, in governance, in cultures and in societies needed to occur. People needed to take responsibility. Things would not just stay the same as they had always been. It was an illusion not to see that huge changes had already occurred. It was a delusion not to see that larger changes were coming. Technology change was accelerating and putting ever more dangerous capabilities in the hands of both unstable countries and unstable and extremist religious and political factions. His articles were published in media worldwide.

The results of Plato's actions were as varied as the people who observed them.

Stunned silence, crying and screaming, prayer gatherings, binge drinking, pagan rituals, star gazing, families gathered, suicides, lonely wanderings, rioting in the streets. Churches were jammed as were the bars. People looked for guidance from pastors and rabbis and mullahs and bartenders and actors and reality TV stars and talk show hosts and parents and grandparents and business leaders and NFL quarterbacks and talking parrots. As fears subsided, people calmed down and

Plato's message was considered, discussed, argued, confirmed and rejected, and all of the above all at the same time.

Plato knew that whether it would make a difference, time would tell.

*****

"This all makes us look like idiots," the President said to Hank Scarpetti and Barbara Wilcox, his chief political advisor, as they sat facing him at his desk in the Oval Office. "We had rioting in Los Angeles and Chicago with mobs looting stores. We've got our churches filled with crowds claiming 'the end is near, repent!' Parents pulled so many kids from schools yesterday that the schools all closed down. Businesses shut their doors."

Barbara held up her hands, palms out to him, "When you go on TV tonight you'll calm things down. This could be a great moment for you to demonstrate your leadership. The people want to hear that there is nothing to fear. You have things under control."

"But we don't have things under control. Those things that Plato is saying, they are true. I can't just go on national television and tell them don't worry, no big deal! And you're telling me the ratings are going to go through the roof – everyone in the country is going to be watching me. And I have nothing to tell them!" His usual strong clear baritone voice was sounding more like a shaky tenor.

Barbara Wilcox was steady as always. Despite almost no sleep in the past two days her short brown hair was meticulously in place and her make-up looked like it had just been put on at a movie set. Her blouse and skirt were unwrinkled. She prided herself in always maintaining a calm and wise persona. Her detractors called her the ice queen and made no mention of any wisdom, though her political smarts were not in doubt. "You tell them they have nothing to fear but fear itself. You go all Churchill on them. This is your stage, your moment to show them your greatness."

The President shook his head in denial. "Forget about greatness! I just want to calm everyone down! Life is no different today than it was last week before this started. Plato is exaggerating everything. The world has always been a dangerous place. But we are doing the right things. My policies are working and making the world safer!"

Hank Scarpetti had been listening quietly. He knew that in other rooms staffers were already at work writing the speech. He had talked to Barbara earlier and knew she had instructed them to write a 'Churchillian' speech about not giving in to fear....typical of her she was confusing what Roosevelt had said with Churchill, but the point was the same. As soon as she had told him that she was going to so advise the President, he knew that any chance of a really substantive speech was lost. If he argued with Barbara in front of the President for a speech that really addressed the issues head on, he knew he'd lose.

And if he did somehow win the argument with Barbara, the President would ask him what the substance of the speech should be. The trouble with that was that Hank knew he didn't know what to say. And perhaps that was the real point of what Plato was doing. He hadn't suggested answers yet either. What the President needed to do was go on national television tonight and both admit that the problems were real and that he would lead the people as they solved the problems. Roosevelt didn't tell the people not to worry about Hitler; he assured America that it would prevail regardless of the strength of the enemy.

Scarpetti knew the President would not see it that way. The President could not admit that after six years in office, the world was now in such a mess. His policies had not made the world safer – in fact, the world was less safe. The Arab nations were at war with each other and with themselves, terrorists were everywhere. Religious leaders there were screaming louder and louder for the destruction of Israel. The example of North Korea somehow seemed to encourage extreme action, not discourage it. Crowds were gathering in the world's capitals and were milling about with only random destruction as a plan and, like mobs everywhere, were not rational. And fear only made everything worse.

*****

**Illusions or reality**
By David Randall

*This is my first blog post of what I hope will become a series. Let me start by saying that in this blog, I am not writing on behalf of any newspaper or media institution. When writing there my reportage will be as unbiased and fact based as possible. Here I intend to express my personal observations and viewpoints – hopefully the two will overlap!*

*Plato showed us our world on the precipice of destruction and doom. Even as we knew the fires in the skies were an illusion, we feared it as a coming reality – at least I did. In fact I find myself increasingly confused by what is real and what is an illusion. I know that there is war and destruction occurring somewhere on this Earth even as I write this, but here in New York City as I look out the window at Lexington Avenue all I see are people walking the streets going about their business and cars rushing past. I see Lexington Avenue; I don't see the wars and the death. I also don't see children starving in the Sudan or rebel forces killing and maiming and raping in Central Africa. But just because I see Lexington Avenue and I don't see the wars and the terror and the other atrocities of the world, that doesn't mean my only reality is Lexington Avenue. I know better than that. And so do you.*

*Now Plato wants us to see the reality of our future as driven by present events. Seeing that reality is harder than seeing realities of events that are separated from us just by geography. We know that what goes on in Africa and the Middle East are real – we can see it on the news on our TV's.(Though judging reality by virtue of seeing it on TV must be discounted by all else that shows up as 'reality TV. ) No, Plato wants us to see a reality that we are separated from only by TIME. Can something be real if it hasn't happened yet?*

*Here is where things get tricky. Einstein has taught us that time and space are inter-related. His theory of relativity is based on that interrelationship. So I think we should listen to Einstein when we think about the future Plato has presented to us. It is as real as a child walking up to a classroom blackboard and writing in chalk that two plus two is five. Sure it is a mistake, but the child really wrote it. But another child could follow that child and erase the five and write a four. Only what Plato is showing us won't be so easy to erase. And if we don't treat what he shows us as real, then we won't start trying to change it now – and maybe there won't be any children then.*

*****

When David finished his blog's first piece he hoped over time his audience would grow. At first only a few people would find his blog online, but perhaps over the months to come his following would grow to hundreds – maybe even thousands of readers. Plato had other ideas. Plato sent out a note to all computer and smartphone devices worldwide that David's blog was worth following. Within hours of his posting it, David's blog was accessed by millions of people. And that was just the first few hours.

# CHAPTER NINE

*"There are more things in heaven and Earth, Horatio, than are dreamt of in your philosophy."*

William Shakespeare
*Hamlet,* Act I Scene V

On Sunday morning in front of his two thousand strong congregation of the Church of Universal Blessings in Houston Texas, with his cable TV channel viewers watching from their homes in the suburbs and countryside around the fifty states, the Reverend Teddy Wentworth focused his sermon on Plato's miraculous arrival in The Object and on the message Plato had just delivered to the peoples of the world. When the reverend focused on a subject people listened. A former University of Houston offensive lineman, he was a big man with a deep base voice and a powerful presence. At a little over fifty years old with a shock of silver hair down to his collar and a face with craggy features and glistening blue 'born again' eyes, his fervor and faith and his caring for his flock of church-goers radiated out of him.

For months now his sermons had stressed his concern for the dark and dangerous path he thought the world was on. He had found biblical parallels that worried him and caused him to fear God's wrath as the peoples of the world seemed to be getting further and further away from doing God's will. Then there was the horror of nuclear devastation in North and South Korea followed by the arrival of The Object. All his fears were being confirmed. His most recent sermons had been dark and foreboding.

Then Plato came out of The Object and beamed out his message of looming and predictable mass deaths and planetary destruction, followed by the optical illusion of the heavens on fire. But Plato had offered up hope too. The future was not written. Man could save himself. Reverend Teddy Wentworth found in Plato's message both a confirmation of his beliefs that the people of the world were heading toward doom and damnation and a pathway for salvation if mankind would return to a righteous path.

Moreover, as it happened, he had a parishioner who taught Physics at the University of Houston who had two days earlier sought to explain to him the basis of Planck's work. Reverend Teddy, as everyone called him, was fascinated by the relationship of consciousness to the workings of the universe. During that hour with his physicist parishioner, Reverend Teddy had a flash of insight he believed came straight from God that consciousness was God's great gift to the universe.

That Sunday morning as he gave his sermon the passion of his beliefs welled up in him and he departed, as he sometimes did, from his prepared text. In his text he had planned to say how interesting he found the timing of Plato's arrival. He found it interesting because it came at the same time as he, Reverend Teddy Wentworth, had been declaiming in his sermons in recent months how dangerous the world was becoming and how much we needed our savior Jesus Christ to send us guidance from above. And he had planned to say how interesting he found the work being done by Benjamin Planck with its emphasis on consciousness. That was really all he had intended to say.

He had started his sermon as planned by talking about how mysteriously The Object had arrived. And then he quoted from Plato's message to the world about the dangerous state the world was in. Then he switched to how Plato had come looking for Benjamin Planck and confirmed that Planck's theory was true. And he presented what his parishioner physicist had told him about how Planck's theory had consciousness as the foundational force of the universe.

Experienced public speaker that he was, he could see that his audience was following his words with rapt attention. Two thousand pairs of eyes, not counting the many more watching on their televisions, were focused on him; no one was walking to the restroom or whispering to people next to them or coughing or even moving restlessly in the wooden pews. They were fully caught up in what he was saying. And it was at this point that his insight and his passion took over. Here he departed from his text.

"My fellow believers in the power of God, we are indeed at a time of miracles! We have prayed for guidance from our savior Jesus Christ in these perilous and confusing times and he has answered our prayers. I know that Plato's coming here at this time is no accident. It is no accident that he comes with great powers and a warning of things to come – terrible things to come. And when he spoke to us, you knew as I knew that he was telling us the truth. He was telling us God's truth – just as God told Noah of the coming of the flood!"

Reverend Teddy paused there to catch a breath. In that moment he saw his audience had ramped up its attention even further. They wanted him to keep going.

"It is no accident that Plato has come among us. It is no accident that he is giving us God's message and God's warning. Did not God send us his only son, Jesus Christ, when we were in need of a savior? Was that an accident? I ask you was that an accident?" Reverend Teddy's voice rose as he demanded an answer from the crowd. "Was that an accident or just a random event? Was the arrival of Jesus Christ at a time of dark days, was that an accident?" Then he shouted at them, "Tell me that was no accident!"

And the crowd responded as he knew it would, "No accident! No accident! No accident! No accident!" And "Praise God" was shouted and repeated by others. Then Reverend Teddy held his hands up to quiet his crowd even as the passion and energy of the two thousand people in front of him flowed back to him.

"So I say it is no accident that Plato is here now bringing us God's message. He has been sent to us by God to deliver us from the evils we are facing. We must listen to him, be guided by him, we must embrace him." The reverend paused then. He looked deeply into the hearts of his audience and they felt his eyes upon each of them, for he truly cared for them and believed his own words – and they knew that he cared for each of them. Reverend Teddy, they knew, was a good and godly man who lived humbly and did good deeds for the poor and the afflicted. And he was a wise and intelligent man. And it didn't hurt that he was a natural orator and charismatic leader.

"And I will tell you another thing!" Reverend Teddy continued, still speaking spontaneously, his prepared text no longer in his mind as he moved about the front of the stage to stand closer to his people. "It is no accident that Plato has sought out Benjamin Planck to share with us Planck's wondrous theory of consciousness. Planck's theory will give us the tools to lift ourselves up again and restore us in God's bounty. We must heed Plato's warnings and embrace Planck's theory. Did not God give Noah the tools to build his ark? He didn't just warn Noah of the coming of the flood! We must accept the rightness of Planck's theory of consciousness. It is God's mind we will be tapping into." Reverend Teddy paused again and when he resumed his voice was quiet and soft. The audience held its breath and not so much as sighed.

"God wants us to know his presence through consciousness. It is God's great gift to us! Now is the time for us to learn how to use it. It is the wonderful tool that God has given us to defeat the darkness."

Reverend Teddy was finished. He knew he had said more than he had ever intended. But it had felt right. The audience was stunned he could tell. But his instincts told him they needed one more thing.

"Come, pray with me. Our father who art in heaven, hallowed be thy name...." The crowd prayed with him. And his viewers watching the telecast across the country on that Sunday morning followed along.

That is how the fastest growing religious movement of the century began.

*****

The second stage of Plato's plan began when the first of many private jets landed at Pirate's Cay. Several days earlier, David had completed the task he had been assigned by Plato of identifying the most influential people in the United States. He had given the list to Plato and then Plato had taken it from there. Plato had sent out invitations. And he had modestly admitted to David that the

RSVP's had come back almost without exception positively. When the Leader of The Object invites you to come meet with him, it's a hard invitation to refuse – especially given the egos of most of the attendees.

So coming to Pirate's Cay in waves would be tech company Founders, Media company CEOs, Global bank CEOs, million-follower bloggers and tweeters, famous actors and athletes, political pundits, self-help gurus, religious leaders, billionaire hedge fund managers and a few thoughtful people who when they discovered who else was invited, thought they had been invited by accident, not knowing how influential they actually were. They were chosen regardless of political or social ideology. In fact their diversity was intentional. The date and time of their invites were staggered so that no more than twenty were on the island at any one time, so meetings with Plato could be small.

The meetings would be held in the lobby of the retreat with chairs positioned in a U formation with a seat for Plato at the front of the U. The meetings started with Plato introducing himself briefly and then introducing Dr. Benjamin Planck. Planck with the help of Ozawa and several other meditation practitioners demonstrated 'mentalization' by first ripening a banana before their eyes. Then Planck asked anyone in the meeting to stand up and then they made the chair that person had been sitting upon disappear and then reappear. Planck then introduced Dr. Wheeling who gave a ten minute discourse on the fundamentals of what they were now calling 'Participatory Physics' while highlighting the primacy of consciousness. Dr. Wheeling then took the group through the history of physicists' views of the 'Many World's Theory' first proposed by Hugh Everett III, a student of the great John Wheeler.

Then Plato reasserted himself. He did so by first screening a silent documentary of a world looking like Earth but subtly different. The cities had similar names but the skylines were different, people looked the same but their clothes were different. This planet which Plato labeled Earth #278 looked modern and prosperous and healthy in the early pictures but with a time stamp that marched forward in years it could be seen to first lose its look of prosperity and then all the pictures showed a sickening people and planet until the whole of the planet looked desolate and empty.

At the conclusion of the screening, Plato said only that the people of that Earth #278 evolved cultures that were constantly at war with ever increasing deadliness. No one country was strong enough to prevail militarily and no culture prevailed ideologically. But the countries stayed separated from each other with rigid boundaries so no integration took place. Then one culture attacked its neighbor with advanced biologicals that poisoned water reserves. That action was duplicated elsewhere and soon water shortages existed where none had before. Then the wars for water began and lasted for years as the world became a dry and barren place.

Then Plato ran another screening. This silent documentary showed two countries with thriving cities with millions of people and beautiful countryside. Then with a time stamp that rolled forward in minutes not years, the cities and countryside were obliterated and covered with mushroom shaped clouds. The world travelers in the audience had recognized their own Seoul and Pyongyang.

After the second screening, Plato turned to the meeting attendees and looked to them one after the other while saying nothing. When he had finished looking at each individually, he started to speak.

"Earth #278 was lost because the prevailing cultures never sought integration among themselves. They each thought they were superior to the others, they never sought their commonality. Leaders gained political strength by emphasizing their differences and denigrating those who were not like them. They deliberately brought out the tribal instincts in their followers, instincts developed over mankind's million years of evolution. Tribalism – that most destructive of man's sociological tendencies. When one tribe attacks another tribe all of man's worst attributes come to the fore. Murder, rape, cannibalism and torture are all aspects of tribal warfare.

"Tribalism exists in many forms and in all cultures, both primitive and advanced. It shows itself in social, political and even athletic alliances. As cultures decay it is the lowest common denominator and its most dangerous. Tribalism is what tore Earth #278 apart."

That was the blueprint for what would be many meetings. Then Plato would take questions and interact with the actual participants.

So it was at the first meeting, which went much as planned up to the point when things changed.

Plato paused and asked, "Are there any questions?"

Plato looked around the room at faces that were too stunned to speak.

"All right then," he continued. "Let's talk about the second set of pictures. Would someone please identify them?"

After a few moments where no one spoke up, the CEO of a global bank stated they were pictures of what had been North and South Korea.

Plato searched out each of the faces in the room and then returned his gaze to the bank CEO. "Thank you. Now since you were bold enough to speak up, would you please tell me who is responsible for this tragedy? Note I am not asking you about Earth #278, you weren't there. But you were here for the destruction of Korea."

The bank CEO refrained from speaking. He had come to the island expecting some form of 'meet and greet' with some variety of an 'alien'. He had expected something he could tell his family and friends about. He had not expected what he was getting at this meeting.

"Perhaps the question is ambiguous," Plato said. "So let me make it clearer. "The idiot twenty something year old Supreme Leader was not responsible. You don't charge the mentally incompetent child who starts a fire with arson. Nor were the brow beaten and destitute people of North Korea responsible – they are the victims. So who is responsible?"

Pairs of eyes looked upwards, others downwards and others to the sides. A few looked expectantly back at Plato.

Plato began again. "As you look around you here, you will see some of the most influential people in the world, certainly in your country. More people like you will be coming to later meetings like this. Collectively you all influence to a substantial degree almost every major social and political activity and event. They too will see what you have seen. They too will be asked what I have just asked you."

Plato approached a tall balding man in a dark gray suit. "Mr. Washburn, you are CEO of a Communications empire, is it fair for me to say that you and the other people here and others like you, have the power to influence almost everything that occurs through political action?"

Jack Washburn looked back at Plato. Known for his take charge manner, he was not cowed. "Though it is true that we all together have great influence, the truth is that for the most part we cancel each other out. There is disagreement on every issue. So our influence is much less than you might think." He then looked to the room, confident in his response.

"Oh, I see," said Plato. "Mr. Washburn here believes that some of you here actually thought that the idiot Supreme Leader should have had the power to start a nuclear war. Now which of you actually believed that? Please don't be shy."

Davis Strohan, the self-help guru who had a million followers spoke up to say, "I'm sure none of us believed that."

Plato shot back, "And by extension would you say that none of the other influencers who will come to later meetings would have believed that either?"

"I'm sure they too would not have believed that the Supreme Leader as you call him should have had that power."

"So Mr. Strohan, on this issue, you would disagree with Mr. Washburn. All of you influencers would not have cancelled each other out on the issue of the Supreme Leader having nuclear weapons for toys. Is that correct?"

"Yes I suppose so."

"Mr. Washburn do you think your views would have been cancelled out on this issue."

"I suspect we would all agree on this one."

Plato looked around the room again. "So let's come back to the issue of responsibility. Who is responsible for the death of millions of people in the land of Korea?"

Then from the President of an Ivy League university, "No man is an island unto himself but each a part of the continent...ask not for whom the bell tolls, the bell tolls for thee."

"Thank you Ms. Latham," said Plato. Then he added, "Is there anyone here who thinks they do not share some responsibility?"

A young man who was the hottest young country music singer spoke up, "I guess I could have done somethin' but that was our government's job to figure out what to do. Not mine."

"A fair point. Now Mr. Reynolds. Do you generally have confidence in your government?"

"Not particularly." Several people in the room laughed.

Plato smiled too. "Now we are getting to it. So Mr. Reynolds, who is the government in this case?"

"The President and his guys."

"And who elected them?"

"The People did."

"And who influenced the people?"

Rusty Reynolds saw where Plato was going and didn't back away from it. "I guess we all here and the others coming did that. That's your point, isn't it? We chose the government; the government screwed up on Korea, Korea blows the shit up. So that makes us here responsible. That's it, isn't it?"

Plato turned back to Washburn, "Is this where all you influencers had to cancel each other out?"

Washburn shook his head, "My news commentators said this President's Korea policies were stupid."

"You don't support this President do you?"

"No sir I don't."

"But you did support the last one?"

"Yes we did."

"But they both had the same policy on Korea, didn't they?"

Washburn just nodded and closed his eyes.

Plato looked into the faces of those in the room. "The difference between what happened to Earth #278 and what happened to the land of Korea is just a matter of degree – both are horrible. But Korea here is a forewarning; Earth #278 is a fatal finality. This Earth is on a pathway that leads to where that Earth ended.

"It is in your power, your collective power, to determine Earth's fate."

Then he suggested everyone take a fifteen minute break.

During the break, Plato was approached by the university president Margaret Latham. She said, "Plato, I presume you know the histories of many Earths, is our moment in time right now common among them?"

Plato nodded, "Though the histories that get them to this point are varied, a moment in time when the world is at a tipping point is not unusual."

"Are you optimistic for us?"

"It depends on how people like those of you here accept responsibility."

"In these other worlds does America provide good leadership?"

Plato shook his head, "In most Earth worlds the United States as you know it does not exist. Historically a continent spanning new nation is an anomaly. Also, your 18th Century revolution often fails. Or the South wins the Civil War – which by the way has devastating consequences for the world where that occurs."

"How so?" Howard Kosar, a hedge fund titan who was listening in to the conversation asked.

"First the United States splits in two. A few years later a major slave rebellion tears apart the South which had been weakened by the War. Texas pulls away and resumes its independence and California follows suit. There is no United States to save Europe in World War I and Germany wins. Germany gets the atom bomb first. There is no United States to restrain Japan in the East, so Germany and Japan in their most militant moments conquer over every other nation, then destroy each other and take the planet down with them."

Ms. Latham looked sadly at Plato, "What you are showing us is that as our world develops, what happens politically affects not only our individual lives, it affects our planet's destiny. It is so interdependent and fragile."

Plato called the group together to resume.

"Government matters!" Plato stated to start the session. "Yet here you treat it as of only occasional interest and put immense power in the hands of inexperienced, ill-informed and arrogant second-raters. Both major parties are equally guilty. You claim to appreciate wisdom and honor, but put forth candidates who have neither. You claim to seek moderation and community but fan the flames of partisanship.

"And it is you and those like you who are the influencers who are responsible for this!"

Plato regarded the room. "And unfortunately you do not cancel each other out; rather you help build monolithic blocks incapable of compromise. Who here would say otherwise?"

"You can't compromise with people whose views would ruin our great country!" a hugely popular talk show host responded.

"Thank you Mr. Lewis for speaking up and saying what so many of you obviously think. And you Mr. Winthrop," Plato said to a famous actor, winner of several Academy Awards, who spouted his political views at every opportunity, "You think Mr. Lewis is completely wrong in his views and believe he should be taken out and shot somewhere – that is something you have been quoted as saying, isn't that correct?"

George Winthrop cleared his throat and said, "I was exaggerating. I wouldn't want him shot..." then relying on his charm and dashing smile, he said, "But a good dog muzzle could be useful."

No one laughed.

Plato continued, "I take no pleasure in this. I am just trying to make you see the consequences of your actions. You have another Presidential election coming up. Are you going to do better than you have in the past?"

After looking around the room again, Plato changed the discussion. "I have something I'd like you to do now. You are highly intelligent people – you have answers to the problems your country and your world face. So let me ask you to call out solutions that you know are correct and really should be acceptable to the other side. Please, what should your next president do?"

"Fix education. Our kids are being left behind."

"Invest in infrastructure. Infrastructure fuels productivity growth. Productivity growth fuels job creation."

"Maintain our military – the world is a dangerous place."

"Fix income inequality with more and better jobs!"

Plato smiled, "You see you do agree. Each of those objectives will require compromise, but if four years from now this country has made no progress on those issues, and others like them, then you are betraying your country and will be contributing to the disaster that follows."

Plato was about to move on to his next issue when Catherine Ozawa came in to the lobby and motioned to Plato.

"You need to come outside and see what has appeared in the sky."

Plato and many of the others there in the room went outside to look.

There slowly creeping across the sky was a cylinder shaped object that everyone looking guessed correctly was not from this Earth.

David sought out Plato to find out what he knew about the new object in the sky. The news media would be hungry for even a shred of information and Plato's comments on it would go worldwide. David wanted to be on the front end of the story. And he thought Plato would want to set the tone too.

When he saw David approaching him, he waved David over.

"Do you know who they are?" David asked.

"Yes. I was expecting them."

"Are they trouble?"

"Most definitely."

"So what should we say about their arrival -- the world will want to hear from you."

"Now is not the time for speeches. Just quote me as saying 'now is the time to act wisely'."

"That's pretty cryptic."

Plato smiled, "All the better."

Later that day he sat next to Catherine Ozawa on a low barrier wall separating the beach from the retreat grounds. Looking westward, they saw the sun sliding into the horizon, its job for that day done.

"I have seen a sun set on a hundred worlds. It is always perfect." Plato said.

"It knows what it is to do." Catherine responded.

"I hope I do. Things are going to start getting bad now. I had hoped I would have more time before others arrived. I am afraid for this world. I fear losing this one the way I lost the other just before I came here. My ten years there accomplished nothing and millions of people died because of my failure. That world was so similar to this one. I could not bear that again. I would have to stop my Don Quixote wanderings and return to my own world."

Catherine Ozawa saw the pain still so fresh in his face. She reached out and took his hand and held it against her thigh. "Put down that baggage. You have learned from your experience on that other world so now put that other world away. Live in this one."

The horizon was painted in a broad-brushed flowing rose; even as the sky darkened, its rosy glow lingered, unwilling to surrender until the last moment.

"You see that sky there," Catherine pointed to the horizon. "Well I was here yesterday at this same time and the sunset was a feeble, unremarkable one. Yet our celestial painter once more took out his brush today undeterred by yesterday's failure."

Plato turned away from the horizon to look into the face of the woman next to him. Without saying anything he lifted their entwined hands and kissed the back of hers. Then he turned his gaze back to the quiet ocean.

# PART TWO

## Time: Three weeks later

*"Dr. Einstein, Why is it that when the mind of man has stretched so far as to discover the structure of the atom, we have been unable to devise the political means to keep the atom from destroying us?"*

*"That is simple my friend. It is because politics is more difficult than physics."*

Albert Einstein

# CHAPTER TEN

*"Once you make a decision, the universe conspires to make it happen."*

Ralph Waldo Emerson

It was with more than a little trepidation that David mounted the steps to what he could only describe as a shuttle craft that looked like it belonged in a Star Trek movie. He had been directed to an out of the way field in northern New Jersey to catch his ride up to the second Object that had suddenly appeared over the world's skies three weeks ago. He now knew the name of this Object was The Freya. The craft to take him to The Freya had arrived almost immediately after he had parked his car along the side of the infrequently used road.

A soldier in a tight fitting, dark grey uniform had come out of the door of the craft and beckoned for him to come forward. David approached and said hello. Without any response to his greeting, the soldier patted David down and David was directed to hand over his backpack and the soldier looked through it. There wasn't much in it – just his laptop, a pad of paper, some pens, a Kindle and some bottled water. Then the soldier gestured for him to take a seat with a harness. He placed his backpack between his feet and strapped in, the door was closed and the shuttle launched upwards. Not a word had been said by the soldier. That did not make David feel more comfortable.

Two days earlier while sitting at his desk in his New York apartment writing an article for The Washington Post about the importance of philosophy in Plato's homeworld, he had received an email telling him he had been granted an interview with the Captain of The Freya. David was stunned since he had not asked for an interview and thus far there had been only a video message when the new Object first arrived. In that video message, which had been picked up world-wide, the Captain had been stern and succinct: he and his crew had come to observe this new Earth and would meet with this earth's leaders in due course. There was no reason for alarm.

In the email David had been told where to go and when to be there. He had been told to come alone. It said he had been granted this exclusive interview because he seemed to be the leading journalist on the subject of 'Many Earths.' That was all the email said. Its tone was more of a command then an invitation.

Gabriela came in to the apartment soon after he had read the email. She tossed her backpack into the corner of the couch and plopped down next to it. She kicked off her shoes and asked him what was new.

David looked over at her and considered whether to mention the prospective interview. He knew she'd be concerned – she saw risks where he didn't and even he could see there were risks here. Just sitting there on the couch with her black hair pulled back in a ponytail and only a trace of make-up, he still found her irresistible and he wanted to share this new development with her.

He read her the email. "So what do you think?"

"Have you told Plato?" she asked.

"No. I haven't decided whether I should or not."

"Why wouldn't you?"

"My instincts tell me to keep things simple. If I tell Plato, it will add a degree of complexity. From what Plato has said in the past, these other Earths have their own interests and agendas, interests sometimes hostile to Plato's."

Gabriela did not like hearing any of this. "But he might tell you that going to them is dangerous!"

"Probably would."

"David, you are a science writer – not some kind of wartime correspondent. You are not the dashing, danger-seeking type."

"Nice to know you think I'm a wuss."

"That's not what I mean. I've been very proud of all that you've been doing. Your writing is published all over the world; people everywhere look to you to understand how things will change, whether they should be afraid or not, what they should believe.

You have taken the lead in explaining to the world one of the greatest stories of all time."

David ignored the tightening feeling in his stomach. In the last months he had found it best to not think too much about his particular role in what was going on. He was not some important player on the world stage; he was just writing about the goings-on. His job was to be a chronicler not a participant. He was more determined than he had ever been in his life to do what he was doing as well as he could do it. "And that's why I have to go ... you know that, right?"

Gabriela regarded David with a look of both concern and respect. She had always thought David blessed with a wonderful mind that was mostly wasted through a rudder-less ambition. He wanted to do great things but could never pick which one. Now he had his mind and ambition focused on the same thing – but it was something that was huge, complex and dangerous. And now she feared for him whenever he was out of her sight. "Can I go too?"

"Hell no! ... I mean the email said I have to come alone." Actually he wished someone else would be going with him – just not his girlfriend.

*****

The inside of The Freya left no doubt that it was a military vessel. What he could see was all very utilitarian and cramped. There was no decoration. David had once been on a new nuclear submarine and this spaceship reminded him of that – though it was larger than the sub. The people he saw, both men and women, all wore the form fitted dark grey uniform, all walked or stood with ramrod posture, all went about their business with precision and discipline and no idle chatter.

Upon arrival at the ship David had been met by a tall reddish haired and bearded man who introduced himself as Lieutenant Benson, the communications officer.

Benson told David that it was he who would first answer David's questions, and then David would be introduced to the Captain for any questions that Benson needed to defer to the Captain. David was led to a small room with a table and two chairs and pointed to the one David was to sit at. David took the seat and pulled out a small pad of paper to take notes even though he planned to record. Also he pulled out one of the two small water bottles he carried. As he sat across from David, Benson said to record the conversation if he wished. David did.

"Lieutenant, if we could start with your telling me about the Earth you come from and then why you are here? Then I'll follow up with questions I might have."

"Excellent. First, I should say that though we have been studying your Earth since we arrived six weeks ago --"

"I'm sorry," interrupted David, "I thought you arrived three weeks ago?"

"Six weeks is correct – we only made our presence known three weeks ago."

"I see."

"As I was about to say, "Our understanding of your Earth is still quite limited. For example on my world, your country, the United States, does not exist. In fact I come from a city that is where you now live – the City you call New York is New Narvik in my Earth and is part of a country you think of as Scandinavia. As I think you now know, our Earths multiply through a physics you call 'Many Worlds'. I believe my Earth and your Earth shared a common history until about the 11th Century. In your history, the Vikings came to North America and settled in Greenland but did not settle permanently in North America. In our history, Vikings roamed further south and set up a permanent settlement in what you call Massachusetts. From there our hunters and farmers established towns and cities. Our Scandinavia covers now a large part of Europe and the eastern coast of what you call the United States and Canada."

"A very different history from that point forward, I'm sure. " David's mind spun as he considered the differences.

"Yes. We are a Viking culture."

"So why are you here now?" David asked.

"We are here because it is the nature of Vikings to go to all new lands. But do not worry, we no longer rape and pillage. Though our traditions are honored, we have long ago learned the importance of peaceful co-existence. Besides, as I think you know, the physical laws that separate our worlds only allow for limited and focused interaction."

"So I've been told. But why is that?"

"I am a warrior not a scientist, but my understanding is that since we move across the dimensional boundaries that separate us based on 'mentalization' as you call it, only those who can sustain that mentalization within the community of travelers can transport themselves and their limited equipment. As the size of the group of people to transport together increases, the spillage of distracted mindsets causes disruption in the transportation. As the number of people increases, so does the spillage, with disastrous consequences – so no armies can cross the dimensions."

"I see. Yet a moment ago you called yourself a 'warrior'?"

"Ah, a language slip-up. We all call ourselves warriors in Scandinavia. But I am a statesman. Perhaps now is a good time for you to briefly meet our Captain."

Lieutenant Benson led David to a different part of the ship which resembled a lounge area. There were tables and chairs for about twenty people but only a few were occupied. The people there seemed to be drinking what looked like coffee out of ceramic mugs. It all looked so ordinary that if a Starbucks logo had been on one of the mugs it almost would have seemed natural. But nothing about this was natural and David wondered if it had all been staged for his benefit. "See, nothing to worry about" was the implied message.

There David was introduced to a tall, slender man with short cropped dark hair, a thin angular face and a pale complexion. His uniform was also form fitting but seemed a darker shade of grey than the others. The only insignia on the uniform was a small golden replica of a 13th Century Viking longship on his shoulder. David recognized him as the Captain who had spoken in the initial video transmission when The Freya had arrived.

The Captain held out his hand to shake, "Mr. Randall, I am Captain Hans Ragnar, thank you for coming to us. I have been following all your stories. It seems you are now the thought leader for your country, perhaps the world."

David shook his head, "There is no such person. I just have been lucky in being at the right place when first things started to happen."

"You took action before others did. In my world that is highly valued."

"From what your Lieutenant Benson was telling me, your Earth is quite different from this one."

The Captain nodded, "Yes, our histories departed time-lines over a thousand years ago. I find the developmental histories of the different Earths that I encounter very interesting. Your Earth in particular is interesting."

"Why is that?"

Captain Ragnar held up his index finger and then pointed it downward as if aiming at the planet he now orbited. "Here the most powerful country is your United States of America. But in almost all Earths that is not the case. Rarely has such a large continent spanning country with such developed political systems come into existence and then flourish so late in the historical cycle. In the other Earths, your North American continent has split into five to ten different countries and there is no unification of power. Your country is quite the historical exception."

"I am still getting used to the idea that this is not the only Earth. That they will all be different culturally and historically is somewhat mind numbing."

"The worlds are not as different as you might think at first. The biological, sociological and political imperatives that drive history forward are the same everywhere. Your DNA and mine are the same. Our goals and ambitions are the same. Though our worlds separate as a result of a major clash of conscious wills, major battles or wars, for example, from there our histories are just the results of random and accidental variances multiplied by changed cause and effect consequences."

As he listened, David studied the man in front of him. It was hard to know whether his instincts in assessing people would be reliable indicators or not. Things like trustworthiness, generosity and honesty, morality in general, were culturally driven. One of David's mantras was 'you are what you do.' It was too soon to know what this Captain Ragnar would do. But at least he could ask.

"So Captain, why are you here? What is your objective?"

"Good, let's get to business. I want to answer that question. You may be surprised by the directness of my answer, but we have found through experience that it is best to be direct. You will find to your peril that others who come are not so forthright as we are. They will lie and dissemble. We will not.

"We have come to build alliances with the powerful countries here. Our goal is to open up trade in intellectual property. In our developed worlds –worlds ahead of where you are, but your development will accelerate now –we have found that intellectual property is the only resource that matters. The power of the mind, of minds, is the only real power in the universe. The more the minds are harnessed and linked together, the more that can be accomplished."

"Is that what the others that will come here will also want from us?"

"Of course. The power of mind is the only power that transcends across dimensions."

"I guess I don't really know what that means," David admitted.

Captain Ragnar considered how best to respond. He was coming to believe that this particular Earth offered huge potential for him to finally accomplish what he had been looking for. It was much like the last Earth he had just been visiting but things there had deteriorated too far and he had lost control of it. He needed to more carefully calibrate the results of the action he would take. Even this interview was a part of his plan and he needed to manage these early communications with a clear vision of how things should proceed.

"David, I think your world will quickly come to understand that mental energy is the true source of all power. But mankind has evolved for thousands of years without ever truly understanding that. On every Earth that is true. But once that veil of ignorance is lifted, change comes quite rapidly. And in that time of change there is great opportunity to bring prosperity to all peoples. The universe can be very bountiful. That is why we are here." He did not add that his objective and that of his crew was to steal as much of that prosperity as possible.

David still didn't really understand why The Freya had come, but he realized that Captain Ragnar was not going to tell him.

The Captain looked at David and saw David still did not understand. He wasn't surprised. He knew his answer was impossibly vague; but it was quite adequate for his purpose. He had no intention of telling the world what his true intentions were. He also knew that the description of their world that Lieutenant Benson had just given David, though true in its historical beginnings, told nothing about their world's actual present state. It was now a world that people wanted to leave. Like the early Vikings who left their cold, dark brutal country for richer lands, the crew of The Freya was looking for a better place to live. A place of their own that they could control. And Captain Ragnar liked the quaint old idea of being a king.

As David left The Freya on the shuttle and returned to his car to go back to the city, his mind kept turning over what the Captain had said. It sounded reasonable. But David had trouble with the juxtaposition of the trade of intellectual property with the rigorous militaristic discipline he had seen on The Freya. And there was also Lieutenant Benson's comment that all of his people were warriors. In retrospect, David thought the Captain had told him the truth – just not all of it. And the part that was left out was the important part. He also had to admit he was glad to get off The Freya.

While driving home David listened to the news. Turmoil in the Middle East seemed to be increasing. Iran now that everyone knew it had nuclear weapons, was promoting its support of terrorism more openly. China and Japan were tussling over some islands of disputed sovereignty in the South China Sea. Russia was bullying smaller countries that used to be part of The Soviet Union. There was a new civil war in a central African country where prisoners' hands were being chopped off and their women were raped. Radioactive winds from the Korea disaster were blowing over Asian farmlands threatening mass famine for a generation. Then the news stopped for a moment its usual litany of global alarm and issued an emergency bulletin. A third Object had just been observed in the Sky.

*****

Kahlil stayed seated at the outdoor café in the Beirut suburb after his visitor had arisen from the table and left. It had been their second meeting and Khalil's mind was spinning no less this time than it had after the first meeting. An opportunity to do something momentous was strangely coming to him, an opportunity so important to his cause, to his religion, and to his people that it both thrilled him and scared him.

Senior leaders of his cause had passed the word to be prepared to take advantage of the new circumstances created by these visitors from other Earths – a concept so strange that it had at first shaken his beliefs. Was Islam even a part of these other worlds? Was The Prophet Mohammad The Prophet there too? And it had not occurred to him that he would be the one to be involved with any of these visitors. Though it was true that he had risen to be a group leader because of things he had accomplished. He personally had orchestrated suicide bombings that had killed more than 150 people and several were dramatic enough to gain world-wide press coverage. And he and his group had done bombings across all the borders, even within the hated Israel. Among those who knew such things, he was a man to be taken seriously.

At the first meeting with the strange visitor it had been as if his prayers had been answered – and the faith that had been shaken by the arrival of the Objects in the sky, had been fully restored. The truth was more glorious than he had imagined! That meeting had seemed to be an accident, which Kahlil soon realized had been planned. He had bumped into the Visitor who identified himself just as Hasan on a street corner. Hasan had apologized and he had called Khalil by his full name. And then he said he was to be called Hasan and that he needed to speak to him. Khalil had looked him over but had seen nothing unusual. He was dressed as everyone dressed; he was average height and looked like he was a son of the desert, as they all did. His Arabic had a strange accent but that was all that distinguished him.

He was of course reluctant to meet with him but then Hasan had said he was from one of the Objects in the sky and all he suggested was that they talk at a little café there on the street. So Khalil went with him to the café but there he said he wanted some proof that Hasan was from where he said. And that was when Khalil's faith was so restored! Hasan's proof was majestic.

After they had ordered their coffee, Hasan brought out of his briefcase what looked at first like an iPad that was a little larger than usual. But Hasan showed how it could do things no iPad could do. Hasan showed images of what he said was a different Earth and these images were in 3D and holographic, so realistic that they were like a miniaturized reality. And he showed cities with mosques everywhere and people everywhere praying to Mecca. In this world Hasan told him, Islam ruled. There was no Israel. Europe was Muslim. There were no powerful Christian countries. Khalil was astounded. How could that be, he questioned?

Hasan's answer was the answer Khalil had always feared would be true. Hasan said that he was from that Earth and he had been shocked to see how weak Islam was here. Weak because Muslims here had been afraid to fight for their faith, to die for their faith. When Khalil tried to argue that he was a fighter and that people he knew had died for their faith, Hasan had pointed around the café and said simply, "Where is the evidence of jihad? You have a puny faith here!" Hasan had made Khalil feel ashamed. The Earth Hasan came from was the proof of what Hasan said.

That had been the first meeting. Then Hasan had arranged the second meeting which had just concluded. Sitting there at the café, Khalil's hands shook a little as he contemplated a different future than he could have imagined just a few days ago. Hasan had promised him a gift that would be a killing blow against both Israel and the Americans.

Khalil contemplated how to use this new technology weapon that Hasan had promised him. A weapon no larger than a big rifle that could shoot a missile that could destroy a fortified compound. Hasan had suggested it should be deployed against the U.S. Embassy in Tel Aviv. What a dramatic moment in history that would be for his cause! And he would survive it for he could shoot the weapon from blocks away. Though he told himself he would be a martyr if it was necessary, he preferred that others make that sacrifice.

Hasan had shown him again the wonder of the other Earth where Islam ruled all. Hasan had never felt his faith welling so strong within him. Here was a destiny to fight for. For this he had lived his life and suffered its ignominies. And Hasan had said this weapon would be his soon, but that it must be used quickly. It would be dangerous for them all if this weapon was known by too many people to exist. There were spies and traitors everywhere.

It needed to be a surprise to everyone. Hasan had made Khalil swear to keep it secret from even his superiors. Afterward he could tell all.

*****

**Illusions or Reality**
By David Randall

*Like everyone, I am stunned by recent events. The aliens of The Object turn out to be humans from another Earth. Their Leader Plato warned us that more Other Earthers would be coming. And now two other spaceships have arrived. One of them we still know nothing of while the other new arrival comes from an Earth with a Viking culture. The United States does not even exist on that Earth. I've met the captain of the Viking spaceship and he seems to be like us. At least I want to think so. But his cultural history has to be very different from ours. So are he and his crew really like us? Should we think of these humans from Other Earths as cosmic cousins or are they really aliens who happen to look like us? What actually makes an alien an alien?*

*So are we to be the Indians of the New World greeting Columbus in 1492? Plato says his Earth has a different history than ours and has a technological lead on us of hundreds of years. What does that even mean? Actually Columbus and the explorers and settlers that followed had that kind of advantage over the Indians – and how did that work out for the Indians?*

*Now I'm not suggesting that Plato is a modern day Cortes or that these Other Earths mean us harm, but it needs to be remembered that these Other Earthers coming are men and women just like us, they have our same DNA. On every Earth it seems that Man always rises to the top of the food chain. We are voracious survivors who seek to dominate our environment. And these new visitors to our Earth have power we can't imagine. Historically – whether ours or theirs, I'll bet, – mankind is unkind to those of his neighbors who have less power than they do. With good intentions or not, things tend to go badly for those who are without power. That's just how man is.*

*Coincidentally (or not, more on that later), we are now learning thanks to Ben Planck and his work, that our understanding of the laws of the universe needs some amending. Something called 'Consciousness' is the foundation of the Universe and what we call reality is a consequence of that consciousness – and is malleable to it. I think that means we are what we think we are. The Universe appears as we want it to appear. It works the way we want it to work. That's pretty cool. But then I wonder, 'who is WE?' Whose consciousness is it? And where did it come from? And when? Is my consciousness part of it? Is yours? If so, how big a part? Is it human consciousness aggregated together? (Which now I guess includes the consciousness of all those Other Earthers.) And what about animals and trees? What about rocks? Does a rock have consciousness – even if only just a scintilla?*

*Now this sort of speculation may seem pretty sophomoric, but when Planck tells us that theoretically a single human being can alter the physical reality of an object, then it seems to me that what was once the discussion topic for physics majors having coffee at Starbucks is now an important subject for all of us. It means that we all have far more power than we ever imagined! And Plato tells us that some of the visitors from Other Earths understand how to use this power. For instance, Plato does. So it seems to me, we better figure out how to use it too!*

*****

General Greene sat at a poolside table at Planck's Retreat and watched a very pretty young woman with short dark brown hair wearing a competitive swimmer's bathing suit dive into the pool and start doing freestyle laps. Her strokes were long and fluid and her somersault turns effortless. His daughters had both been competitive swimmers and he had watched them at many of their high school swim meets. Though obviously older, this girl reminded him of them. But General Greene knew there was a huge difference between the young woman he was now watching and his daughters. This woman had grown up on a different world. A world that was somehow Earth, but not this Earth. Then he laughed as he said to himself, "It makes my head swim."

Plato then came up and sat down across from him. As usual Plato was the picture of health with his Greek god good looks, yet his eyes looked even older than their usual hundred years.

Greene greeted him and then said, "I've been meaning to ask, how is it that all of your people and you yourself are all so good looking?"

Plato laughed, "Because we choose to be – it is a simple transformation. From childhood we learn how to think ourselves to good health. And if one or another of our genetically endowed features is not quite what we'd like, we envision what it should be like and that look comes to be. One's mind can always control one's own body."

"I need to learn how to do that." He thought about how much harder it was to stay in shape now that he was in his fifties. Yet he doubted that he would try to rethink his body. He would just work harder in the gym.

"You will."

"Well anyway...thank you for agreeing to meet with me again. Things are coming to pass as you said. We now have other Objects circling above. The Freya seems to have arrived first and now one that identifies itself as The Lucky Dragon. Do you know of them?"

"I know of them both...or rather I should say, I know the worlds from whence they came."

"So should we be concerned?"

"They are quite different. The Freya is the shark sensing the blood in the water and now circling its target. The Lucky Dragon comes from a proud Earth dominated by a Japanese empire. Their goal is to extend their empire across other Earths. They are very formidable."

"But you say The Freya is a shark? How will it attack?"

Plato considered for a moment, and then held up his hand. "Perhaps a shark is the wrong metaphor. A shark just moves in and attacks. It has no subtlety. Though the Captain of The Freya will claim that they are straightforward and honest, they are in fact tactical opportunists that allow for their machinations to evolve over time."

Plato paused there but then had an additional thought, "I have noticed something about your United States - and it seems to be true about how your government is run and how your businesses run and how your people live their lives."

General Greene looked back at Plato quizzically, "Oh, OK, and what is it?"

"Your whole country is consumed with the here and now. It is as if the future is meaningless - and may never occur. Everything is for the short term. No one plans for longer than the next day and a half."

"Are we the exception in this? Aren't other cultures on other Earths just like that? Isn't that a natural human trait?"

Plato shook his head, "Not on Earths that survive. On my Earth we have a saying, 'the long term and the short term are the same thing.' People who do not know that squander their resources and lose to those who think strategically. And as I said, the people on The Freya think very strategically. They like to set dangerous forces in motion and then from a safe distance watch what happens. "

"So what will be there goal?"

"First they will try to create chaos here. Then they will find a way to take advantage of that chaos. They know that if the world stays stable, then there is little they can gain."

"What will they want from us - from out of the rubble they will create?"

"They will try to make your Earth, once sufficiently weakened, to be a carcass they can chew on; they are homeless predators looking for places where they can settle for a while and then move on after having taken what they wanted."

"Do you want that too?" General Greene asked.

"No, my friend. They want control over a poor and weak Earth. We would rather have the friendship of a strong and prosperous Earth."

*****

Reverend Teddy loosened his tie as he walked toward the front of the retreat building on Pirate's Cay. Though accustomed to Houston's hot and humid summer, he was also used to having air-conditioning everywhere. At 6'3" and 300 pounds, his body did not do well under a sweltering tropical sun. Even though his beige suit was a summer weight, he still now wished he had opted to wear slacks and a polo shirt.

It didn't help that he was nervous at the thought of meeting with Plato and Benjamin Planck. Events were moving so fast that he could only pray that he could keep up. It was only a few weeks since he had given the sermon about Plato coming to Earth as God's emissary and that Planck's theory was also not coincidentally God given. In those weeks his words had gone viral and the video of his sermon had become a You Tube sensation. Now his congregation had grown by the millions and was still growing.

Now he was here on Planck's island to speak to Plato and Planck and he didn't know how he should speak to them. How does one speak to someone sent from the Almighty? He was in awe too that they had summoned him to meet with them. And now here he was on an island that in the future he knew would be viewed as a holy site. He was a sincere and passionate believer and it was all he could do not to kneel down and kiss the sands of the island.

Then coming up to him were Plato and Planck and Reverend Teddy was struck by how beautiful the two of them were and it proved to him again how favored they were by God. There greeting to him was so natural that he responded in kind. They exchanged smiles and greetings and shook hands.

"Reverend Teddy, we are so glad you could come and meet with us," Plato stated.

"Yes, welcome to Pirate's Cay," added Planck. He noticed how hot the reverend appeared in his suit. "How about we go inside to an alcove off the lobby, there's no air-conditioning there but the circulating fans keep it cooler?"

"Yes, I'd appreciate that – and perhaps I'll take off this jacket and roll my sleeves up," said Reverend Teddy. He saw that both Planck and Plato were casually dressed in shorts and golf shirts. They walked to the side of the lobby area and sat down at a wicker and glass table with matching big cushioned chairs. The red hibiscus pattern on the cushions on the chairs was faded and the wicker of the chairs a little frayed. Reverend Teddy noticed this and approved; he was not a believer in ostentation. He knew the retreat had once been a resort hotel and he surmised the furniture was a holdover from those days.

Reverend Teddy looked at the two of them and began by saying, "I was so surprised to receive your invitation – I have no understanding of why I'm here. But I am glad that I am. Is there some way I can help you?"

Plato responded, "Reverend, you are here because you now have millions of followers – and the number is growing with every new sermon you give. Sermons that are about how Planck and I are here to save this Earth – and that somehow we are here because your God wants us to be here. That places us in an uncomfortable position."

"It was not my intention to do anything that would make you uncomfortable. But yes, I do believe you are here as God's emissaries – and thank God for that, you are dearly needed." The Reverend Teddy returned their gaze on him with a steadfast and firm demeanor. "That you might not know that does not surprise me, God works his wonders in His own way."

When Plato did not immediately respond, Planck spoke up, "The problem for me personally is that I believe in much of what you are preaching. I believe that the Universe comes to us from a benign and all powerful creative force that does interact with us in our personal lives. I believe that force is God. And somehow I am now in a position to understand just a little more of the ways of God and his creation. But I am certain that I am no Emissary from God. I'm just an ordinary person who happens to be a scientist."

Reverend Teddy smiled. "Ben Planck, you are certainly not ordinary. And how do you know how it is that your theory came to you? How would you know what God has in store for you? The consciousness of the universe seems to speak directly to you. Is that not so?"

Planck looked back at the reverend and said nothing. Then Reverend Teddy continued, "Now I am not the brilliant physicist here or a visitor from another world, but as I understand what you two have been saying, the universe is founded and guided by consciousness. This consciousness is open to us and wants to give us what we need and want; we are the children of that consciousness. And it is you Plato and you Planck who are teaching us about this Universe and about this consciousness. If as I believe, consciousness is an emanation of God, then why is it not also true that consciousness, that God, has brought you both here to this island for His greater purpose?"

Plato smiled at Reverend Teddy. "I wondered what manner of man you were. Now I see why millions follow you and millions more will do so. I would very much like you to be my friend. I would very much like your assistance in what we are to do. What we must do."

Reverend Teddy was overwhelmed. He could only stammer, "I will do everything I can."

Plato rose up and held his hand out to Reverend Teddy, " I have to leave now but I have very much enjoyed our talk." Then he turned to Planck and said, "Perhaps you could help Reverend Teddy understand how through the focusing of the mind sickness can be defeated and health restored."

Reverend Teddy interrupted, "You mean you can make the lame walk and the blind see?"

"Something like that," Plato said as he walked away.

Planck looked back at Reverend Teddy, "He should not joke like that. It is sacrilegious."

"Then he was joking? You can't do that?" responded the reverend.

"No, actually we can do that. Well, actually it depends a little on what is causing the physical problem. Perhaps I should explain....But first, I have a question for you. As you see, I live on a small out of the way island. I really don't understand what is driving the growth of your church. And how could I be perceived as some sort of ... of ...disciple?"

Reverend Teddy regarded the handsome young man before him, seeing not just the features of a blond, blue eyed and tanned beach boy but also the brilliance of a deep and searching mind unfettered by egotism or arrogance. Reverend Teddy reasoned that Planck's clarity of thought might well be the result of an innocent disregard for his own being.

Reverend Teddy smiled at Planck, "I am myself amazed at what is happening to my following. But I believe I understand. The events of our present time are so confounding and alarming that people are hungry for explanation and security. You and Plato offer both. But more importantly, your message is one of connectedness. The more we sit and think together, the more we can influence events around us. We are not islands of self. We are meant to come together, think together. The Universe is ours, it serves us. It is God's gift to us. And it connects us to each other even as it grants each of us a tiny piece of that consciousness, which though tiny is still real and matters to us individually. It is the best of all worlds."

Planck nodded. "I think it is God."

Reverend Teddy held up his hand and waved it at Planck, "I think it becomes a matter of semantics as to whether the Consciousness that guides the Universe is God or a gift of God's. And though I know religious wars have been fought over semantical differences, I fight no such wars. My church is not so doctrinal. We are open to interpretations. So as people find us, they can bring their own interpretations, but they still stay within the basic tenets – and they want that structure.

"So what is my role in all this?" Planck asked.

"You bring an intellectual depth to it. With the strength and provability of your theory, you dash the concept that we live in a random mechanistic world. Atheism makes no sense if Consciousness is the foundation of the Universe."

Planck leaned back in his chair and looked out of the lobby area through to the sea. He had never seriously discussed his religious views with anyone. He thought himself to be a scientist trying to unlock the Universe's secrets. He knew that most of his peers were atheistic or at least agnostic, but as Planck evolved his theory of consciousness, he found no foundation for atheism. This Universe seemed created for intelligent life; the extremely fine-tuned laws of physics -from the very weak size of the gravitational force to the exquisite balancing of the strong and weak nuclear forces - were too precisely calibrated. Though Super-string theorists explained that away as a random result of there being almost an infinite number of universes, that to Planck seemed too much of a stretch. For that reason he had gone in search of a different explanation – and that led him to explore the Observer requirement in Quantum Physics, and that led to Consciousness.

Reverend Teddy did not interrupt Planck in his contemplation. He sat quietly and waited for Planck to resume the conversation.

After more moments, Planck looked back at the reverend. "Plato suggested that I tell you about how we deal with sickness here. Recently one of our colleagues was diagnosed with an inoperable brain tumor. We on the island gathered together to help cure him. The brain tumor has now disappeared. Would you like me to explain that?"

Reverend Teddy looked at Planck with an expression not of surprise and doubt but of joy and conviction. "Yes, please tell me." That was all he could say.

Planck explained how his group would meditate together and how consciousness could be applied to changing the physical state of molecules –or cancer cells. When Planck had finished, Reverend Teddy had only one request. "Planck, would you be willing to come and speak to my congregation? Perhaps this coming Sunday?"

Planck nodded before he had really considered what that would mean.

*****

As Hank Scarpetti ushered Captain Ragnar of The Freya into the Oval Office to meet President Morningstar he noted that though both men were about the same height and both looked physically fit, and both had dark hair, whatever resemblance they shared was superficial. Though Scarpetti had never really noticed it before, the President had no real physical dominance. His was a congenial, photography model presence. Captain Ragnar was different; with a hawkish intensity he controlled the space he occupied. On a battlefield he would be the one the men would follow.

As he shook the President's hand, the Captain smiled broadly, "Mr. President it is an honor for me to meet you! In my time here I have been learning of how well you are leading this great country and indeed the whole world. I can only imagine what it feels like to be the most powerful person on the whole of the planet."

The President's smile broadened as he gave his two handed hearty greeting – his 'A' greeting reserved for the most important people. "I'm just an elected official. You give me too much credit. I am fortunate to be at the head of this great country."

"It is the country's good fortune and a demonstration of its good sense to put you in power."

"Well, please let's sit and be comfortable. I am eager to learn of your Earth and your country there. And of course I want to begin on what I hope will be a beneficial and lasting mutual relationship."

"That is our wish too!"

President Morningstar sat straighter in his chair, unconsciously matching the Captain's posture. He had been apprehensive about this meeting, but now saw he had worried needlessly. He was sure he and Captain Ragnar were much alike and could work well together. And besides he was the President of the most powerful country and the Captain was, when all was considered, just a military officer. He was used to dealing with the military as their Commander in Chief.

"So Captain, please tell me about your Earth. As I understand it, your predominant culture is a Scandinavian one – a Viking culture. Many of our citizens here trace their ancestors to Sweden and Norway."

"So I understand. Yet there are many differences because our worlds parted a thousand years ago." The Captain went on to describe his world where The United Scandinavian States was very much the counterpart to the United States. There too they had a long history of democratic government. They too had brought an enlightened political system to other countries. Those countries had prospered and his world was a place where people of all races and creeds got along well together with equality of justice and opportunity.

As Captain Ragnar described the homeworld he came from, a world coincidentally very much like the world President Morningstar had described as his vision in his first Inaugural Address, the Captain found himself almost wishing that what he was saying was in fact true. As before, he marveled at how real a lie could be. Just saying it would make it so – at least until it was disproven, and sometimes even the discovered truth could not undo it. Then it occurred to him that he probably would find such a world too boring. The actual world he came from offered a far more competitive and brutal existence.

While the Captain and the President were talking, Hank Scarpetti was doing what he did best, he was watching. He quickly noticed how the President had relaxed and was enjoying the conversation. He noticed too how the President had switched into his more authoritative tone of voice. The President was feeling in charge of the situation.

Scarpetti saw that the Captain was playing to the President. That didn't bother Scarpetti particularly; it was to be expected. Most people who came into the Oval Office played up to the President, even some of those who had not intended to. He thought the President could usually see through that, but not always. He thought the President was too easily succumbing to the Captain's praise. The power of the Oval Office was strong. But when the Captain had twice used a turn of phrase that came out of President Morningstar speeches, Scarpetti's cynical mind cranked up. Scarpetti decided he needed to push matters forward a little.

During a pause in their conversation, Scarpetti asked the Captain about the other Earths that had arrived in the skies. He mentioned Plato and The Bucephalus.

The Captain's smile hardened, "I know of that Earth. In fact I have seen the effects on a world like yours of the visit of this particular man who calls himself Plato – quite an affectation, I think. The effects are not good. He presents a false sense of benign friendship. He is not to be trusted."

"And what about The Lucky Dragon?" Scarpetti asked.

The Captain just brushed the Earth of The Lucky Dragon away with a dismissive hand motion. "You should not concern yourselves with them." His past dealings with the empire behind The Lucky Dragon did not go well. He did not want them involved in his plans here.

"They have yet to reach out to me to meet."

"I'm not surprised. They like to first reflect on and analyze what they find. Also, their focus is usually on the geopolitical struggle between Japan and China. They have a narrow view of what is worth pursuing. I have not paid much attention to them in the past. I do not believe in getting too involved in the affairs of others." The lies came easily to him.

The President shook the index finger of his left hand but softened his objection with a smile, "Perhaps I don't agree with you on that, Captain. I believe in internationalism. The world is a better place when nations work together and all are equal. No one country should dominate."

"I would say that too if I was the leader of the most powerful country. But I would not surrender any of my power. And in my world you only have the power that others can see. If others don't know you have the power, they will test you. And even when you win the struggle, you have less than when you started. Acting as an equal only weakens the stronger country. Better to show overwhelming strength, then no one will test you."

The President shook his head. 'I don't believe that. Our twentieth Century was based on that kind of thinking and we had two World Wars to show for it. My foreign policy is based on mutual respect and friendship."

"And yet your world is fraught with instability and terrorism. My world is more stable than yours."

*****

General Carl Greene took another sip from his glass of scotch as he looked across the kitchen table at his friend Hank Scarpetti. Hank had invited him to drop by to catch up on things and had just finished telling Greene about the Captain of The Freya's meeting with the President two days earlier.

"So I gather the President liked Captain Ragnar?" the General said.

"Absolutely. He thinks my doubts are unwarranted, just my being cynical."

"But you don't trust him?"

"No. In fact I think he was accusing Plato of sins that he is guilty of. You trust Plato, don't you?"

"You don't become a general in this man's army while having a strong sense of trust in people –but yes, for the most part I find myself trusting Plato."

Scarpetti lifted his glass and swished the amber liquid around. "I don't know if you get the same reports I do, but we are picking up some indications of an upsurge in trouble in the Middle East."

The general nodded, "Our intelligence officers are reporting that too."

"In the President's briefing today I heard something for the first time. I heard that there are whisperings among certain terrorist groups that on one of these 'many Earths' Islam is the dominant religion and Muslims rule that world. It is being said that the reason they are not dominant here is because there they were willing to sacrifice for their religion but not here."

"Oh great! Believing that would only cause them to increase their level of fanaticism."

Hank Scarpetti pushed the point further, "I suppose that rumor could just be some terrorist leader's idea to energize his troops. But what if one of our visitors from these other Earths is putting that story out? And if I understand how the histories evolve with these many Earths, it probably is true on some of them."

General Greene thought about that. "Actually, some military historians believe that if the Turks had won the battle of Lepanto in the late 16th Century then the Ottoman Empire would have pushed further into Europe and we might all be Muslims now."

Scarpetti laughed, "OK Mr. historian – that wasn't the point. What if Plato or the Freya Captain or whoever is the leader of The Lucky Dragon is the one putting these stories out?"

"If that is true, then we have a big problem."

"That's what I was thinking. I suggested to the President that perhaps we should raise the alert level at our Embassies and

Consulates in the areas that are real hotspots – of course that would be most of them in the Middle East right now."

"How high of an alert?"

"Increase security forces. Send non-essentials home."

"What did the President say? What about the State Department?"

"He thinks it will blow over. State agreed with him. Of course our dear Secretary of State is still mad at me because I didn't invite him to the meeting with the Captain of The Freya – who had requested that the meeting be kept private and confidential. And nothing that includes the State Department ever stays private or confidential!"

"I love your internal rivalries – it makes what goes on in the military seem almost genteel."

"Maybe. But the bottom line is no increase in the alert status for now."

# CHAPTER ELEVEN

*"The release of atomic energy has not created a new problem. It has merely made more urgent the necessity of solving an existing one."*

Albert Einstein

Khalil stared at the cube-like block of a building with the American flag raised above it. From the window of the hotel room he was in it was several blocks away; and he could see that it was dwarfed by several high-rise buildings around it. Yet to him it still manifested the power of The United States of America. The Embassy in Tel Aviv was a hated symbol in the midst of a hated city.

He had seen it many times before. Its impregnability always had struck him like a blow to his stomach. He knew that others like him had wanted to target it, to destroy it. The attempts were not sufficient to the task. Now the task before him seemed so simple.

Khalil had seen the ruins of crusader castles in the desert. Structures once viewed as impenetrable fortresses were now dust-blown skeletons of minor historic interest. In their time they might have seemed monstrous and everlasting to their foes but time moved past them with its withering indifference.

Khalil saw that the powerful block of a building now targeted by this amazing new weapon he had been given was no different than those old crusader castles. Invaders had come to these lands confident and imperious and had built structures they thought would last a thousand years and protect them behind their walls. Such walls could never be built high enough or strong enough, not here where their religion did not belong. Here was the true God who served and guided his followers and instructed them how to deal with such infidels.

Inside that not so impregnable building Khalil knew were hundreds of people, some of whom...many of whom he knew were innocents, Muslims like himself. They had to die today with all the others. It was necessary, Khalil believed. In the past days he had come to truly understand what was necessary for Islam here to rule the way Islam ruled in that other Earth that Hasan had showed him. The vision in Hasan's iPad-like device was now the vision that Khalil carried in his mind. No sacrifice was too great to establish that vision here on this Earth. Khalil admitted to himself that even he had never imagined such a complete victory, but now that was all he could see.

He had listened as hard as he could when Hasan tried to explain to him this idea of other Earths. Nothing in his limited schooling prepared him for it. What was important he decided was that Allah was there. It was like looking up at the star filled night-time sky when out in the desert and knowing that Allah was everywhere out there. So that there were many Earths did not change anything. He knew on this Earth there was a country or a continent or an island, he wasn't sure which, that was called Australia. It was very far away and he would never go there but he knew it existed. Other Earths were like Australia to him.

He thought of Hasan the same way. He was not from Iran or Syria or Lebanon or any other country that Khalil had ever heard of. But he was a Muslim and an Arab, one look told him that. That Khalil actually knew very little about Hasan did not bother Khalil. They shared what was most important. And Hasan wanted to help Khalil do what Khalil had prayed for help to do. His beliefs were Hasan's beliefs. More than just beliefs, Hasan shared his anger, his resentment and his cry for vengeance. And now Hasan had shared his weapon, an unbelievably powerful weapon. Khalil had hungered to use it ever since Hasan had first mentioned it.

Khalil had held guns and rifles in his hands since he was a young boy. He had killed his first enemy when he was ten years old. He knew the killing power of weapons; he had watched his older brother die in a street and his father die in a bomb blast. He knew it was just fate that he was still alive and they were dead. He had prayed many times for Allah to give him the strength and the opportunity to avenge their deaths and to serve Allah. Now his prayers were to be answered.

The weapon in his hands was like a larger rifle but not a rifle, more like a Stinger missile, but more streamlined. Its fabrication was a mystery to Khalil, not a plastic nor a metal but something with the characteristics of each. It had a scope which Hassan had said would target the missile. Line up the target in the crosshairs of the scope and the weapon would do the rest. Distance did not matter. Weather conditions would be adjusted for.

Hassan had told Khalil the weapon could be used only once. He had been told that after firing it, he should put it down on the ground or the floor and step away. The weapon would then self-destruct. It would melt down so as to be unrecognizable as a weapon.

Khalil had also been told of its power. The explosion would be concentrated, not a nuclear weapon but similar in destructive force, though limited in scope. It would destroy the targeted building, but not much beyond it. Khalil knew enough of weapons that what he now held in his hands was beyond anything from his Earth. It was from an Earth with advanced technology. It was a gift from Allah to answer his prayers.

Khalil knew he should not be delaying like he was. This moment was so large. His life was about to change and he had to be ready for that. And he was ready now. First he uttered a quiet prayer. Then he opened the window facing the US Embassy. Now his actions were steady and deliberate. Smoothly he raised the weapon and targeted it on the middle floor at the center of the building. He fired.

The noise was like the clap of two hands and the recoil was insignificant. In the first moment he thought the weapon had misfired. Then the US Embassy exploded. Khalil put the weapon on the floor and watched it seem to vaporize as he left the room.

Out on the street he saw the building collapsing in on itself, like pictures of purposefully demolished old buildings, only more smoke and fire, and a towering blue-tinged cloud above it with a vague mushroom shape. Not quite like the famous mushroom shaped cloud of a nuclear bomb but similar.

Khalil hurried away.

*****

Like millions of others, President Morningstar was watching the cable news footage of the US Embassy explosion and its aftermath. Hundreds of people were reported dead and hundreds more were severely wounded. He was in the Situation Room with his closest advisors. He would allow no one else to see him until he was composed and knew what to say to the media. He remembered that right after 9/11 President Bush was on camera at that Kindergarten or nursery school, or something like that, he couldn't quite remember, but everything that Bush had said, every expression on his face had been exhaustively, endlessly replayed and analyzed. Now it would be the same for him.

He knew he had to be firm and resolute and commanding. He had to show sympathy and concern for the victims, but more importantly he needed the country to know that he would ensure that justice was done. The perpetrators would be captured and punished. His thoughts were interrupted by his chief political advisor, Barbara Wilcox. She handed him the text of a speech she and her team had been rushing to prepare.

"We've got to do this in fifteen minutes. Are you ready to go on camera?"

He looked around at the others in the room and then back to her. "I'm...I'm ready. Of course, I'm ready. I have to do this."

"Yes, same as always. You'll be great. Don't worry."

"But what about questions afterwards? I have to take a few questions, don't I?"

"Yes, but just say we don't know enough yet to comment. Don't guess or speculate."

The President's manner seemed shaky to those in the room, but they were scarcely calmer themselves and no one said anything.

"But what if they ask me about the explosion? Anyone can see on their TV set that that explosion looks different. And that damn cloud above it is a nightmare all by itself!"

Hank Scarpetti spoke up then, "Again don't speculate. Confirm that it was not a nuclear explosion. But obviously powerful explosives were used. And it was via some sort of a missile. When we know more, we'll tell them more."

The President nodded, "OK that's what I'll do. But just between us in this room, what the hell was it? And where did it come from?

What terrorist group can get their hands on a weapon like that? And are there more of them out there?"

Those were the same questions Scarpetti had been thinking about for the last hour, ever since the reports of the embassy explosion started coming in. He was afraid of the answer that he came up with. He excused himself by saying he had to get back to his office to start handling this crisis. He knew no one in the Situation Room had a clue what to do.

Three hours later General Carl Greene was sitting across from Scarpetti in his White House office. Scarpetti had summoned Greene because he thought the general would be the one best able to discuss what Scarpetti feared most. The general had just sat down when Scarpetti asked, "Where do you think the bomb or whatever it was came from?"

Greene's answer was immediate, "We don't have anything that would match the profile of what happened at the embassy."

"Would anyone else have anything like that?"

"No."

"And that's the problem, isn't it?" Scarpetti looked back at his long-time friend not expecting an answer. "All right, until I say otherwise, everything we are about to talk about is just between you and me. Not really because I know anything, but the subject itself is dangerous – if it gets out to the public, it will be mass panic and riots in the street again."

General Greene nodded, "I agree. So do you want me to say it first? But you should know, people at The Pentagon are already on to this."

Scarpetti nodded, "Go ahead…say it."

"The weapon had to have come from The Bucephalus, The Freya or The Lucky Dragon, but I have no idea which one."

Scarpetti nodded again, "Plato warned us that bad things were coming. But maybe that was all a cover. He told us not to trust the Captain of The Freya. And Captain Ragnar told us not to trust Plato. Both seemed to think The Lucky Dragon could be formidable but would not act precipitously. So let's put them aside for the moment – and I haven't met them yet anyway."

General Greene smiled ruefully, "This is like that old puzzle, you come across two tribes, one tells the truth all the time and one lies all the time, how do you tell which is which?"

"I never could figure that one out. Besides, in this case they both could be lying. And we don't really know anything about either of them other than what they tell us."

General Greene shook his head, "That's not entirely true. They both told us that their ability to wage war here is very limited because of the crossing dimensions issue. I think they are telling the truth about that. And there's something else. I've spent a fair amount of time with Plato and I think I trust him. You spent a little time with the Captain of The Freya and you did not trust him. That's something to consider anyway."

"I'm not betting the future of this world on that."

Greene shrugged, "Nor would I. But it is a place to start."

"If you are going to talk to Plato, I'm going too."

*****

Up on The Freya, Captain Ragnar was meeting with the man Khalil called Hasan. "You were right about choosing Khalil. He did everything as instructed."

Hasan, whose real name was Erickson, accepted his Captain's compliment with pride. The Captain was spare with his praise. "He's a good soldier. Also he has a lot of hate in him. Our researchers were right in suggesting him. Once I met with him the first time, I knew he was the right one. Now what would you like me to do with him?"

Captain Ragnar considered what should come next. "Now we wait and see what we have stirred up. If we chose the correct target, other terrorists will take heart and become more aggressive and deadly. Have you begun to spread the story of how on other Earths Islam is dominant?"

"Yes...that story is being told everywhere. That was a brilliant idea." Erickson knew the idea had been the Captain's.

"Then the first stage of our plan is well begun. The next stage will begin soon. We are fortunate to find on this world such a politically turbulent region as the Middle East here. It is perfect for our purposes. Hatred is the best tool of those who seek destruction. For us, chaos is our friend and destruction is a child of chaos."

Erickson was grateful to be serving on The Freya headed by a Captain like Ragnar. Their homeworld was not rich and opportunities were rare. The planet itself was overpopulated with its ten billion people and its natural resources and ecosystem were literally drying up. What a blessing it had been to discover other Earths both richer and more vulnerable. Better to serve on this pirate ship – officially sanctioned by their government of course -- than to be home with nothing. And it was in his nature to scavenge for leftovers – he had been doing it for far less reward since he was a child. In chaos he had learned was opportunity – opportunity for those who could think clearly and act quickly while all others were still numb and lamenting.

"So what should I work on now?" Erickson asked.

"Go back down and spread the idea that Iran was behind the attack in Tel Aviv against the American embassy. Hint at other targets inside Israel. Our goal is to push Israel to attack Iran or vice-versa. I don't care which. Perhaps we can even get them to use their nuclear weapons. That would be excellent."

"What should I do about Khalil? He is Palestinian not Iranian." Erickson said.

"Do nothing. Let him claim that he destroyed the Embassy. He has no proof and it will increase confusion – which is better for us to hide our tracks. I think he will act more aggressively in the future."

"Won't it be obvious that the weapon Hasan used is too technologically advanced? Isn't that a problem for us?"

Captain Ragnar was pleased with the question. He liked the intricacy of his plan and wanted to tell Erickson who he knew would then share the plan's brilliance with the rest of the crew. That was the best way to gain a crew's admiration.

"Only the leaders of the technologically advanced countries with strong militaries will know – and they won't tell the others. But they won't know whether the weapon came from us or The Bucephalus or The Lucky Dragon or even some other Earth hiding in the sky. And they won't know how many more such weapons are available to be used. Or what other targets there might be. Also, we have just posted on this world's internet how to substantially increase the destructive power of homemade bombs using available materials. That should prove interesting to observe. I think the terror community will spur each other on – even though their issues and hatreds may be different. There will come a tipping point where counter-terrorism resources are overwhelmed."

Captain Ragnar considered the outcome he was promoting. His prior actions on prior Earths were not so bold but they had been instructive. Democratic political systems assumed a certain cultural stability and rational behavior. They were structurally ill-equipped to deal with random and rampant rabid dog attacks. The more disorganized and unrelated the attacks were, the harder they were to combat. He considered his plan to be both simple and devastating: arm the crazies and show them success. Among the few who understood such things, the success of The Freya in plundering this Earth would be legendary.

The Captain regarded Erickson to make sure he understood what he was saying. Erickson's ability to inflame the passions and ambitions of these terrorists while still chameleon-like operating secretly in plain sight was important to the plan. He was the best of Ragnar's team of what he called his 'rabble rousers.' The others had not yet accomplished anything as dramatic as blowing up the U.S. Embassy in Tel Aviv.

On other worlds, Erickson had proven himself to be very capable, but he worked best when he saw the bigger picture. The Captain was satisfied that Erickson understood, so he went on, "So everyone will be on edge. They will be wary and afraid. We will push them harder. We are also working to take advantage of the historical enmity between China and Japan. Our role there must be more subtle and less apparent – but I have a plan for there too. And India and Pakistan hate each other and both have nuclear weapons. We will spread terrorist actions of increasing magnitude across the globe. Then one of these superpowers will do something stupid. They will attack someone else. This Earth is made of gunpowder. Our reclamation teams will soon be at work here. The spoils of war will be ours without us ever actually firing a single weapon."

"As I said, a brilliant plan!" exclaimed Erickson, proud to be voyaging with such a Captain.

When Erickson left, the Captain watched him go with satisfaction. Erickson was doing what needed to be done, confident that he was in on the plan. The Captain smiled to himself as he thought about how the plan was evolving. Already his financial team had started to take advantage of the capital markets. With the gold they had created through mentalization they had made major investments in the world's stock markets. As they had anticipated, the destruction of the U.S. Embassy in Tel Aviv had sent the market into a temporary fall. They had bet on the fall and the climb back and now had earned over a hundred million dollars. The capital markets had not yet figured out that when one can change the state of molecules with mentalization, that gold would lose all its value. It was the alchemists dream through the ages – turning ordinary metals into gold and silver. His financial team could literally mint money. But his gold needed to be invested quickly.

He knew what he wanted to buy. Throughout time and dimensions the best commodity to own was land. And the best time to acquire it was when times were uncertain and economies in depression. He knew now what land he wanted. He had gotten the idea from following the actions of Plato and his crew on Planck's island. He too wanted an island. But the one he wanted was much more spectacular than the little piece of sand that Planck had.

He marveled at how different each Earth could be. Where on others he could see no chance to get what he most wanted, here it seemed possible. His destiny had been to travel through light-years and dimensions seeking out the perfect world for him. In this he was just like his Viking ancestors. In their wooden boats they had sailed all the way to the Mediterranean Sea and taken what they wanted through force. They had set his world's culture – provided the model.

His task was much the same. They had done it, so could he. All he had to do was to destroy the economic and political integrity of one country. And he believed that country, the United States, could easily break into multiple pieces, the sum of which would be much weaker than the whole of it together.

The country had never even formed in many Earths; its political unity was too unlikely. And better yet, by disintegrating this one country, the world itself would go into an economic tailspin – perfect for his plan to work. His plan was bold, yes, but not too ambitious he thought. This world was so fragile. Just a few hammer blows at the right points and everything would shatter.

Then he would grab what he wanted and it wasn't so much; he just wanted to rule over one of the islands in what was called Hawaii. He thought Kauai would be perfect. It was beautiful with a limited population and could be self-sustaining during the economic shambles that would result. And it was far away from everywhere else. Perfect.

He had already had one of his lieutenants start buying up property on Kauai. He now owned already a huge beachside estate. Soon more and more of the island of Kauai would be his. Then in the chaos that would come he would split it away from its political ties with the United States.

He wouldn't really call himself the King, he thought. That was too blatant and attention getting. But with him and his crew, their technological superiority and their full understanding of how to take advantage of Participatory Physics, they would be able to claim and defend the island. He was delighted with his vision. It was for lesser men to find opportunity in chaos. It was the great man who would first create the chaos from which he would snatch all the opportunities.

*****

Hank Scarpetti and General Greene walked up the steps into the lobby of Planck's retreat on Pirate's Cay. Greene had tried to get Plato to come to Washington to meet with them but Plato had said he would only meet them there on the island. Plato did not say so but Greene and Scarpetti both thought that Plato felt more secure on the island. They didn't argue the point.

Plato met them in the lobby and they exchanged greetings as if nothing was particularly new or different since the last time they had met. Plato then directed them to a conference room where the three of them could meet privately. The charade of normalcy ended as soon as they took seats at the conference table.

"I am sorry about the loss of life at the embassy in Tel Aviv," Plato began.

Scarpetti regarded him with a grim resoluteness. "Almost a thousand people died there. And two of our embassies were attacked in Africa soon afterwards. But we think those were just spontaneous – no direct connection to Tel Aviv. The whole region is stirred up."

General Greene focused on Plato, "You know me well enough now to expect directness. So I have to ask, what do you know about Tel Aviv and the over-all situation? You had predicted that bad things were coming. Did you know about this specifically?"

Plato's look was as grim as that of the two men before him. "No, I did not know specifically what was going to happen. And I will tell you what you did not ask. Neither I nor anyone from The Bucephalus had anything to do with these terrorist activities. I believe the Captain of The Freya is responsible. I have seen how he and his people have operated on other worlds."

Scarpetti interrupted, "So you are saying that The Freya destroyed our embassy?"

"No I do not believe that. What I believe is that they furnished the weapon; that is not the same as saying that they fired it."

"So who fired it?" Greene asked.

"A Palestinian who goes by the name of Khalil Mohammed Azzis."

Scarpetti and Greene exchanged surprised looks. Neither had expected such a specific answer. "If you weren't involved, how do you know that?" Scarpetti asked.

Plato regarded them silently as he considered how much he should say. He had been considering multiple approaches but now opted for the most direct and complete.

"We have the capability to monitor with extreme exactitude all that occurs on this planet. What you can do with your AWACS, we can do on a much broader and more precise basis. When we saw the explosion of the embassy, we backtracked our data file and saw where the missile was fired from – a hotel room a couple of blocks away. We saw someone going into the building carrying what looked like it could be the weapon and then saw him leave immediately afterwards without what he had carried in. We then used facial recognition software against files that we have. As I said, a Palestinian named Khalil Azzis."

Scarpetti and Greene exchanged surprised looks again, but this time their looks contained shock and a bit of awe. They had never imagined the degree of global surveillance that Plato's words suggested. Scarpetti asked, "You have the whole world covered under your ... your ...cameras?"

Almost simultaneously with Scarpetti, General Greene asked, "Can we have access to all that?"

Plato did not respond to Scarpetti's question but to Greene he agreed, "To all that is relevant, yes."

"What was the weapon?" Greene wanted to know. "It didn't originate here, did it?"

"No, the technology is more advanced. But not by very much. You will develop something similar within twenty years."

"Could you have developed such a weapon if you had wanted?" Greene wanted to know.

Plato's smile was soft and fleeting, "From a technological standpoint, my Earth - and the technology just aboard the Bucephalus - is more than two hundred years ahead of yours at your present pace of development."

General Greene and Scarpetti looked over at each other; they shared the same blank look. Until that moment they had not clearly appreciated the vast gulf of knowledge that separated them from Plato.

General Greene's mind was spinning with the ramifications of what Plato was revealing, but he knew he needed to get answers to critical questions. "And what about the level of technology of The Freya? And The Lucky Dragon?"

"It is not as simple as putting a date on it. Technology develops unevenly. The Freya's war technology is perhaps thirty years ahead of yours but your engineering capability may be the same as theirs. However, they learned about the New Physics - Participatory Physics -- over thirty years ago. So they are ahead of you on that. And they have been crossing dimensions to other Earths for at least twenty years that I know of."

"And The Lucky Dragon?" Greene asked.

"More advanced than The Freya, but not by much. Their culture is less aggressive in the short run - though quite aggressive over time. Their goal is to empire build not plunder. Their danger to you will be in how they work with the Japan of this Earth. You can be sure Japan here will become more powerful."

"Are there Earths out there more advanced than yours?" Scarpetti asked.

Plato nodded, "Yes...a few."

"Will they come here too? Will they be dangerous?"

"I cannot say – I don't know. What I do know is that the more advanced the culture, the safer the universe becomes – once the culture survives the stage you are just beginning."

"And what stage is that?" Scarpetti asked.

"The stage where you first develop the technology to destroy yourself."

It was then that General Greene thought he understood the answer to the question that had been troubling him. "That's why you are here, isn't it? You're here to help us get past this stage. You are a missionary."

Plato nodded, "Not a term I would use. And no I do not regard you as ignorant savages in need of salvation."

"And what about The Freya?"

"Perhaps they are the savages," Plato responded.

General Greene considered what he was hearing, then said, "I'm guessing that you and The Bucephalus could destroy The Freya, if you wanted to. Your technology is way ahead of theirs. I do believe you want to help us. And I believe The Freya is a profound threat to us. So can you protect us from them? Can you destroy The Freya?"

"No General, that we will not do. The laws of my Earth are very pacifist. Our leaders do not like the idea of interfering with other Earths. My actions and those of my crew are scrutinized to ensure we do not actively engage unless directly provoked. Perhaps we might do something if The Freya were to attack you directly, but they will not. They are like Iago in Shakespeare's Othello. They will stir up trouble but not take direct action. The troubled environment was here before they arrived. They had nothing to do with the exchange of nuclear weapons in Korea. The hatred in the Middle East is not their doing. The Freya is a scavenger, that is all."

Scarpetti wasn't sure what he should believe, if anything. But he hoped Plato was telling the truth. "So have you done this before? Do you have a playbook for this?"

"There are things we can do. But under the new circumstances, I'm afraid we will need to employ a more aggressive approach."

"That doesn't sound good somehow," said Scarpetti.

To their surprise a few minutes later Scarpetti and General Greene were joined in the room by David Randall and Gabriela, by Dr. Wheeling and by Planck. Hank Scarpetti was introduced to Gabriela and Planck, whom he had not met before. Everyone sat down around the table.

"With due respect to the others, I had thought this would be a private meeting," Scarpetti said to Plato.

Plato turned back to him, "The only person in this room that I don't know that I can trust is you, Mr. Scarpetti. Your planet is at risk and there is much that has to be done to save it. And time is precious. When you and your President were first confronted with the appearance of The Bucephalus and the advent of Participatory Physics, your instinctive response was to imprison David and Dr. Wheeling. You sought to control what you didn't understand. You and your government's leaders fancy yourselves, to use your phrase, the 'best and the brightest.' In fact you are neither. Your country chooses its leaders by default, for the best and the brightest have no interest in pursuing political careers. Your country was blessed early in its history with truly exceptional leaders and except for a few rare exceptions like Lincoln and the Roosevelts, you have been squandering their political capital ever since.

"Now Mr. Scarpetti," Plato continued, "I am about to suggest a course of action that will profoundly change the future of this planet. It has its risks and rewards. These changes are going to occur whether you and your President...your government wants them to or not. But I assure you, these changes will not be subject to your control. Your assistance, however, could be very valuable."

Hank Scarpetti could not remember when anyone had dared to talk to him the way Plato just had. He wanted to attack back, every part of him wanted to threaten Plato and put him in his place. Didn't Plato know the power he wielded as Chief of Staff to the President of the United States! And Plato had insulted the President too! He looked over at his friend and three star general to see that Greene would support him. Greene returned his glance calmly and just shook his head, no.

Then Scarpetti remembered back to a few weeks ago sitting in his office alone and scared that the situation was becoming bigger than he was. He remembered thinking he didn't know anyone in the government who he would trust with making decisions that would affect the future of the planet. And he had known that he wasn't prepared for it either. His anger at Plato for telling what Scarpetti had to admit was the truth began to subside. Too much was at stake for politicians like him to be allowed ego tantrums.

Hank Scarpetti looked back at Plato and held his hands out in surrender, "All right, I'm listening."

"Good," Plato replied. Then he looked around the room at the others. "We are here together somewhat haphazardly... I went looking for Benjamin Planck because of his work on Participatory Physics. Then David you went looking for him and ultimately brought Dr. Wheeling and Gabriela with you. Each of you has important skills and connections that can be very useful in succeeding with the challenges we face.

"This Earth now is at the beginning of what will be three separate but interrelated revolutions. The first is a scientific revolution based on the combination of Participatory Physics with its mind over matter foundation and the introduction of new advanced technologies which will be brought to this Earth from other Earths, for both good intentions and bad. The second revolution will be political based on changing bases for power through the new scientific discoveries plus the new potential Earth/other Earth alliances. For example, The Lucky Dragon will build an alliance with Japan. The third revolution will be philosophical. The people of this Earth will have to re-orient themselves to a different universe with different laws of physics and different Earths with different histories. This will cause a fundamental psychological readjustment."

"What a thrilling moment in time to be alive," said Dr. Wheeling, not at all overwhelmed.

Plato smiled at the professor, "I wish everyone could face it with the confidence that you do."

Hank Scarpetti did not share Wheeling's excitement. "What you are saying Plato, is that we face decades of social and political turbulence while at the same time new and more dangerous technologies will be available to terrorists and rogue nations. That is a nightmare scenario that your coming here has brought to us."

"Yes it is a potentially nightmare scenario but it is not one that I brought to you. Participatory Physics was already discovered before I arrived – and not just by Planck here. The Chinese had also discovered its potential. So that Pandora's Box was already opened. But even without it, the pace of technological change here was already accelerating. Technological change drives societal change; there is no holding it back. The technology your world will have 30 years from now just based on the path you are on will overwhelm your current political structure." He looked at the faces around him and could see that though they wanted to understand, they did not.

"Let me give you a couple of examples," Plato said. "What happens to your economy when the average person has a lifespan of 120 years? What happens to your societal structure when the affluent can genetically improve their children – higher IQ's, healthier bodies, but the other half of the population cannot? Similarly terrorism is steadily increasing. And the threat of nuclear destruction was here already as well and it gets worse as more countries have nuclear arsenals. The threats to this Earth are of your own making."

"We thought we were handling it," Scarpetti said.

Plato rejected that. "You were self-satisfied in your ignorance with a false sense of security."

David had been listening but had not understood why he was there. What role could he play, he wondered? So he thought he would ask. "Plato, I think you have a plan. What do you want from us?'

"Yes, David, there is a plan. One should always remember that during revolutions you must gain control of the times and you must be able to influence the people to act productively not destructively. Your American Revolution is a great example of leadership producing a positive result. On the other hand, the French Revolution just a few years later led to destruction of the social order and guillotining thousands of people in the streets of Paris."

"So how do we lead productively?" Scarpetti asked.

Plato's answer was overwhelming to them all. "We give the people the best of what these revolutions can offer and thus gain their support for the struggle that is inevitable."

"So what do we have to give them?" David asked.

Plato held his arms out with his palms up. "We show them an open hand and we show them a closed fist. With the open hand we show how to reduce the cost of energy to almost zero. This will create a dramatic increase in productivity that will drive higher employment and profitability. We show how growth and productivity improvements can and must benefit the many not just the few. Economies around the world will grow stronger and poverty will be reduced. And we show those who would commit acts of terror that we will find them and kill them."

"Wow," said David. "We can do that?"

"You MUST do that – or you will not survive. And yes you can do that!" declared Plato.

# CHAPTER TWELVE

*"It turns out that an eerie type of chaos can lurk just behind a façade of order – and yet, deep inside the chaos lurks an even eerier type of order."*

Douglas Hofstadter
*Metemagical Themas:*
*Questing for the Essence of Mind and Pattern*

Hank Scarpetti frowned and stood up. "This is ridiculous. We can't do those things. The U.S. government can't do any of those things. You can't just create cheap and plentiful energy and make the world safe from terrorists. That's just not reality. No government can do that!"

"Yes, Mr. Scarpetti, I suspect you are right," said Plato. "No government can do that. I am not suggesting that any government can do that. But people can do it. For you see, not only can we bring them the benefits of Participatory Physics but I can also share the scientific knowledge of my homeworld – an Earth with technology more than 200 years ahead of yours. And I assure you, the technology and knowledge does exist to solve the energy problem. All you have to do is unleash the creative powers of your people aided by the information we can give them."

Gabriela spoke up then, with the conversation so serious and the tension in the room so electric she needed, and she felt the others needed, to lighten the moment. "You know Plato, I've noticed how great all your people look. If you really want to gain the support of the people, just show women how to clear up our skin and get rid of wrinkles and men how to cure baldness and you'll have everyone cheering for you."

Plato laughed, "Good point! We'll do that too!"

"Really?" Gabriela asked. "I thought I was joking."

"Your own science will soon be able to accomplish those things," Plato replied.

"So where do we start?" David asked.

"Planck and Gabriela will work with the scientific community to demonstrate how with Participatory Physics and new technology mankind can have limitless low cost energy. I'm going to ask Dr. Wheeling and David to make it their mission to explain to the world how to make it all work. And Mr. Scarpetti, I'm going to charge you with eliminating the regulatory roadblocks – note I said eliminate not buildup. And I know there will be resistance from both energy companies and countries who export oil. There will be a lot of resistance – this will take a while. But there can be immediate short term benefits."

"This all sounds great, though I think the energy industry will be far more resistant than we can imagine," Scarpetti said, though he didn't make it sound like he really thought it sounded great, "But that still leaves us with The Freya helping terrorists and The Lucky Dragon stirring up trouble with the Japanese. Iran will still have nuclear weapons and will continue to hate Israel. Nothing you are saying will help us now – what you propose will take years to put in effect. It seems to me we are still in just as much danger as we were before."

Plato regarded Hank Scarpetti with a patient stare. "We need to start by getting people to understand that the changes coming will be good for them. That will take time but the effort must be begun immediately. If we do not fight for the long term, we will never escape the short term; and in the short term we will lose. But you are right; we still must deal with The Freya and The Lucky Dragon."

General Greene spoke up, "I understand Plato's strategy. We have to win 'hearts and minds.' But that even includes our own people. Everyone is going to be scared. So we show them how they will benefit. But we also do not tolerate acts of terror. And if we have access to the global surveillance capability that Plato described earlier, then we really can strike back at the terrorists."

David interrupted, "I don't think we should say anything about global surveillance capability. That will freak out a lot of people concerned about privacy rights."

"Privacy rights are essential to an enlightened society," Plato stated. "For a society under attack they are a very expensive privilege."

*****

Reverend Teddy Wentworth's church was much bigger than Planck had imagined. He'd seen big corporations with smaller office facilities. And it didn't look much like any church that Planck had ever been at. The grounds looked more like those of a small college campus and the main church was more like a modern auditorium although it did have a dramatic arched roofline that was vaguely modernized gothic. And this Sunday, the auditorium /church was as crowded as if there was to be an NBA play-off game. There were thousands of people there, packed to overflowing. But unlike a sporting event, the crowd was quiet, though an expectant buzz of what sounded like thousands of people whispering filled the hall.

There were more people than could be seated, so many were standing at the back and in the aisles. Many had brought their children and there were mothers and fathers holding babies in their arms. Like the parents, the children were dressed in their Sunday church clothes and were running around less than they would have wanted.

As the service was about to begin, Planck moved from a side room where he had been anxiously watching the filling up of the auditorium to take a seat at the front which had been saved for him. Reverend Teddy had explained how he would introduce Planck and have him talk during the time he normally would be giving his sermon. So first there would be the singing of hymns, followed by a prayer and then more hymn singing. As the service began, Planck was surprised to see a band and featured singers who obviously were professional. And he had to admit he had never heard any of the songs before, though it seemed that most of the people in the huge room did not need the words on the screens in front of them to sing along. He was surprised also to see many in the hall to be rhythmically waving their upraised arms in pace with the music.

Sitting there, Planck's hands were shaking and he could barely breath there was such a weight in his chest. Even with the chilly air-conditioning he felt hot in his dark blue suit. He fiddled with his tie which he knew was a pretty poor attempt at a Windsor knot. He had not imagined any of this. He was not a churchgoer and the wedding services he had attended were at the traditional protestant and catholic churches that hadn't changed in a hundred years.

He could not understand what he had been thinking of when he had agreed. It had just seemed important at the time. Now there were thousands of people here to listen to him and so many more at their homes watching on the cable channel that carried Reverend Teddy's weekly Sunday service.

He believed that somehow Plato had set him up for this. He didn't know how, but Plato was obviously happy that Planck was doing this. And somehow Plato had talked him out of preparing a short message which he could just read. Instead Plato had told him to just have a few notes and then just talk to the crowd of people. Now Planck was very afraid that his moment would come and he would be literally speechless. As it was, as the service began and the hymns were sung, Planck just sat there with an empty mind – or should he say a dazed mind, which he realized wasn't a good thing at that moment.

Then he reconsidered. An empty mind was exactly what he needed. He should do what he knew Catherine Ozawa would counsel. He sought a still mind. He focused on breathing and put the crowd and the TV cameras and his fear outside of himself. He just breathed. And he let his body relax. Then he let his mind slip lightly onto his ideas of consciousness. Moments passed and he then heard Reverend Teddy introducing him. He went to the podium on the stage.

Standing there at the podium, he didn't know what to expect. All eyes were on him, quietly observing him, not really knowing what to expect either. For a long moment he just looked back at them. He saw they were eager to hear him, eager to learn more about how strange the universe might be, eager to discover there were miracles. He feared he could only fail them. But he found he wanted to try not to.

"I'm here because Reverend Teddy asked me to come speak to you – and he is a hard man to say 'no' to.... After I had agreed and after I had recovered from the shock of what it was I had agreed to do, I thought about what I should say. The easy thing for me to tell you about would be about my work in physics and in particular Quantum Physics.... But then I realized that before I was half done everyone would be asleep or confused." A few people laughed and that helped him go forward. "So instead I'm going to try and tell you what it actually means – and anyone who wants to pursue the physics behind what I'm going to tell you can go online and read the paper I will soon publish." Planck paused then and just looked at all the faces staring at him from the audience. His words had come out in a rush. He needed to slow down and just talk to them. He took a deep breath and let it out slowly.

"Now what I am going to tell you is just what I believe. And I think it is pretty miraculous. In fact I think it is the biggest miracle of all. You have already heard that I believe that consciousness is the foundation of the Universe. It is the basis for how the Universe was created. Without consciousness the universe is just an infinite potentiality – we physicists would call it a probability wave. It is formless, structure-less. It is lifeless. Consciousness is what transforms potentiality to reality. It is the basis for how everything in the Universe is created. It is in me and it is in you. It is in everything.

"Now I am not the only scientist who believes this. Many brilliant thinkers before me have believed this too. Perhaps I have gone a step or two further – not theoretically, but more as an engineer. I have figured out how to tap into this universal consciousness to somehow put it to work. I believe it can help us feed everyone on this planet. I believe it can help us stay healthy. It can give us what we want."

Planck paused again and smiled at the crowd. "Just as an example – and this is by no means an important one, but when Plato came down to my island and he brought some of his crew along, they were all noticeably young and very good looking. In fact many were quite old in years. But through focused meditation that channels into consciousness, they change their bodies and keep their youthful appearance. So no wrinkles, no baldness, no imperfections – just the glow of health. Not that any of you would care about such superficial benefits."

The crowd laughed at that. With their laughter, Planck relaxed and turned serious.

"One of the things that led my scientific inquiry into consciousness is something I think many of you do every day. That is prayer. When I was a child, one of the few things my parents agreed on when it came to religion was the importance of prayer. My father was Jewish, my mother Catholic and one of my Grandparents was Lutheran. So they didn't agree about a lot of things, but they all wanted me to say my prayers. I remember kneeling by my bed at night and saying my prayers aloud.

"As I got older, I wondered how God could hear my prayers. My future as a physicist started then. How could God hear me? What was the physical process? Then I was told about silent prayers – I didn't even have to say my prayers out loud – I just had to say them in my mind! How could that work? Even as a young child I knew that made no sense. Think about that." Planck paused then to let the people before him think about what he was about to say.

"I believe in prayer. You believe in prayer – even silent prayer. And you know, as I know, that the more people that pray for you, the better. And like me, you probably have wondered how that works. Well...what I think is – what my theory explains is that our prayers are accessing the universal consciousness that I think is God – or actually God's mind.

"Meditation is just another way of praying. In meditation one quiets his or her mind in order to connect to something much greater. Group meditation is stronger just the way many people praying for the same thing is stronger than one person praying for that thing."

Planck stopped then to gather his own thoughts. He knew there was more he wanted to say.

"When I talk to other physicists about how the Universe is the way it is, most of them struggle to explain why the Universe seems to be so perfect for us – the children of God. And they really struggle with the idea that an 'Observer' is necessary at the quantum level for potentiality to turn into reality. But their experiments keep showing the importance of that Observer. They hate that 'Consciousness' seems to be built into the fabric of the Universe. They hate that how our consciousness developed is unknown – they have no legitimate theory. But they love their own consciousness – it is what distinguishes us. It is us. It is how we are different from a rock or a tree." Planck smiled again.

"Now I could go into how the brain emits distinct electromagnetic waves for each thought of a person. And we could talk about how fundamental to the Universe electromagnetic waves are – but I promised no hard physics. Just know that there are ways to explain how consciousness works. The engineer in me has focused on the utilization of those electromagnetic waves – that is part of my theory.

"So I will leave you with just a few simple thoughts. First, prayer and meditation are how we can access the great all-powerful force that is the consciousness of the Universe. That consciousness is benevolent and loving and wants us to share in its power. It wants to answer our prayers. That consciousness is fundamental to the Universe. I think it is the mind of God.

"Lastly, none of this is new. Consciousness has been at our service since the first single cell organism began the long evolutionary march to becoming us. What is new today is that in our evolutionary development we are now learning how to utilize the benefits of consciousness so as to build a better future. This is just the next stage of existence for mankind. And it comes at a time when we really need it. I don't think that is an accident."

"Thank you for listening. Please keep me in your prayers. You will be in mine."

The audience seemed in a stunned silence. They wanted to react but the decorum of the church silenced them. Then one person somewhere in the middle of the room started to clap. Then another joined in and then more and more. Then voices were raised in shouts of glee and exclamation. And then the shouts turned to a chant and the chant was 'no accident! No accident! No accident. And there were many 'Hallelujahs!' thrown in."

Reverend Teddy came up to Planck and put him in a bear hug. "Thank you Planck! That is what they needed to hear from you! Thank you!"

As Planck exited the church through a side door he looked for Reverend Teddy who had promised him he would arrange for someone to drive him to the airport. As he looked around he saw a young woman who could have been a Miss Texas in a beauty pageant come toward him. She was a brunette with 'big hair' Texas style and big blue eyes that were trained on him. She smiled and he smiled back. "I hear you need a ride to the airport. Reverend Teddy asked me to take you."

"I like Reverend Teddy's taste in drivers," Planck responded.

She smiled again, "I'm Megan Baxter." She held out her hand and they shook hands. Planck noticed it was a firm business like grip but she held on just a fraction of a moment longer than necessary, "I'm supposed to do more than just drive you. He wants us to talk about social media on the way."

"Really? Why?"

"Reverend Teddy has millions of followers. He's very active on Facebook and Twitter. And now, after what you just did in the service, there will be millions more."

"Really?" Planck repeated, feeling sort of stupid in front of this beautiful young woman. "What did I do? Was it something dumb that will be on YouTube?"

Megan realized Planck didn't understand the effect he had just had on the crowd – and would have on all the Cable TV viewers. "You will be accessed on YouTube, but people won't be laughing. If I'm right, and I've been in the social media business for ten years now and I'm pretty good at this... you're about to become huge."

All Planck could say was "Really?" again.

She nodded, "Of course, Reverend Teddy wants me to help make that happen."

"Reverend Teddy does?"

"Reverend Teddy prays to God for help. But he doesn't wait for it. Reverend Teddy has his own plans. And he is usually a step or two ahead of everyone else."

Planck was beginning to see. "So it's not an accident that he asked you to drive me to the airport."

Megan grinned, "Reverend Teddy can see around corners."

Just then a man and a woman holding the hands of a small girl came up to them. The couple looked at Planck with hopeful smiles and the man asked if Planck had a moment. The little girl looked about five years old. She had blond hair in two pigtails tied with red ribbons and she wore a blue and white striped dress. She was pale and thin. Planck stopped and said "Sure."

The man appeared about thirty years old and was tall and lean with the look of someone who worked outside all day. He also looked shy about saying anything. His pretty wife spoke up. "Mr. Planck we loved what you just said. It's hard to believe but well…we need to believe. Our daughter here… Heather, say Hi to Mr. Planck."

The little girl tugged away from her Mom's hand and looked away and then back at Planck and mumbled hello.

The young woman then said, "Well Heather is sick. She has a bad heart. But the Doctors say she isn't a good candidate for a heart transplant. They are wonderful doctors but they say there isn't much they can do. We were wondering if you…if you could do something?"

Planck looked back at the little girl and her parents. He didn't know how to answer. He was most comfortable in an impersonal, theoretical world. Megan Baxter came to his rescue – sort of. "How is it you think Dr. Planck can help?"

The young father spoke then, "We hoped he would pray for Heather. Help make her well. Help her get a healthy heart."

Planck realized he had to try. It was time for him to leave his island. "I will pray for Heather. But Heather needs your help more than mine. I'm sure you pray for her already, but I'd like you to try a different approach. Gather your friends and family all together. Have as many people there as possible. Have them sit and be still. Then ask each of them simultaneously to have but a single thought in their head. Have them all see in their minds a healthy heart beating in Heather's chest. Just that thought, nothing else. Have them hold that thought in their minds for at least fifteen minutes. All together…all with that same thought. A healthy heart beating in Heather's chest. Do you understand? Can you do that?"

The young couple looked back at Planck with hope and gratitude and fear shining in their faces. They nodded their heads as they looked at their little girl and said they would do that. Then Megan Baxter took out a paper and pen from her purse and wrote down their names and phone number then gave them her business card and asked them to stay in touch with her and to tell her if they needed help from the church.

When the couple and their child had walked away, Megan turned back to Planck. "Do you think she'll get better?"

"I don't know."

"I think they'll do what you told them. And I think that little child will get better. And then I am going to post that in the social media channels and I can't even imagine what will happen after that!"

Megan gave him a smile that weakened his knees as she took his hand. "Come on, my car's over here....By the way, I noticed you're not on LinkedIn or Twitter – not even Facebook."

Planck just shook his head, "Until all this started I was hiding out on a remote island – pretty much off the grid as people say now."

"Yea, I get that – well that is all going to change."

Holding her hand, Planck just let her lead on.

*****

David glanced out the window of his flat in New York City with a thousand yard stare. The sentence he wanted to write wouldn't quite formulate itself into the paragraph he was writing. The article was to be about how Plato's sessions with the influence leaders in the country was taking root in the current presidential election cycle. The political debates seemed more substantive and less gladiatorial. The candidates were pushed by their peers and by the media to address the serious issues of the world with clarity and understanding. And the public was paying attention. The blogging universe seemed to be making sure of that. Already a formerly front-running candidate from each of the Republicans and the Democrats had washed out in the polls because their total lack of intellectual depth was exposed to all.

In the two months since the attack on the U.S. Embassy in Tel Aviv, David had been busier than he had ever been in his life – and happier too. During the two months he had written countless articles on how new technological advances shared by the crew of the Bucephalus plus the benefits of Participatory Physics could help raise the standard of living for everyone on Earth. The potential was so extraordinary that people found it hard to believe. But they wanted to believe and of course they were impatient to have it immediately. That was David's biggest problem as a writer. How does one make what is coming in the future make a difference in the present?

And Plato kept warning them that the current peacefulness was not to last; though using the word 'peacefulness' was somewhat a misnomer. There were still bombs going off every day in Baghdad and Cairo and Beirut. Civil war was still killing effortlessly in Syria. Iran was fomenting violence everywhere. Still that passed for quiet and peaceful.

Every day that could be used to bring the future benefits closer to fruition was valuable. David already missed the early days on Pirates Cay when he and Gabriela and Dr. Wheeling were talking physics with Planck and Ozawa and then he and Gabriela would go walking down the beach hand in hand, and sometimes spotting Plato and Catherine Ozawa walking together as well.

Now he rarely saw Dr. Wheeling or even Gabriela. Both were consumed by their work in showing how Plato's tech advances and Participatory Physics could be put to work. Dr. Wheeling had been enormously effective already in focusing the physics community on finding solutions. His talks had taken him to the major universities of the world where his lectures had packed the auditoriums.

Plank's island had become the locus point for discussions about Participatory Physics. Also all meetings with Plato were held there. The Bahamian government had been very helpful in isolating Pirate's Cay from unwanted visitors - which meant almost everyone except the invited few. The US Coast Guard and Air Force were also policing the area with the permission of the Bahamian Government.

In Washington D.C. Hank Scarpetti and General Greene were leading a different type of team. They were preparing for a more active terrorist environment. The Embassy explosion had both horrified and excited the Potomac community. It wasn't as big an event as 9/11 but it was big. And the film coverage was exhaustive. The accumulation of body bags and ambulances held the media's attention for hours. Construction and demolition experts gave clinical dissections of how the missile had caused the building to implode.

The intelligence community was exhorted to greater effort and determination. Homeland Security raised the Alert status at government facilities and airports. The country's political leaders were in constant sessions talking about what needed to be done and more importantly, who was to blame and to show it wasn't their fault. As General Greene said to Scarpetti disgustedly, they were practicing on their fiddles while waiting for Rome to start burning.

David thought about these things and stared at the blank Word Document he had opened on his laptop. He had started with the idea of writing an optimistic piece about how the new technology could work to the benefit of everyone. Yet he really wasn't feeling very optimistic just then. Rather the opposite. He thought events were going to get worse before they could possibly get better.

*****

**When is Progress not Progress**
By David Randall

*I've always had an optimistic view of the future. Looking back over the last 12,000 years of "civilized" mankind it seemed to me that things kept getting better and better. We stopped our ceaseless wanderings and settled down and created villages. We learned how to grow more food, build stronger shelters, live longer lives and understand more about how things worked. Life seemed to get better. The trend lines for those 12,000 years all pointed toward better living conditions and better lives. The future is a wonderful place to get to.*

*When we look back at those years – that great expanse of time – we sacrifice the details in order to see the overarching direction. What blurs is the very uneven and circuitous path the real storyline of those 12,000 years took to get us to where we are. Depending on where you were, in Europe, in Asia, in the Americas, or in Africa, your actual experience of all those "future" years would have varied greatly. What would come in the future would be better in the long term, but sometimes it would be worse for a while. Sometimes much worse.*

*There were decades and even centuries when living conditions for the average person did not change at all – or life even worsened. The future is not by its nature benevolent; rather it is amoral. It gives you what you earn. "As ye sow, so shall ye reap."*

*I think we should keep that in mind.*

*****

The week that forever after would be called "Hell Week" began on a busy Tuesday morning at Paris' Charles De Gaulle Airport just as the transatlantic flights were landing with their load of tourists and business travelers. Four men wearing full body armor and armed with machineguns and hand grenades jumped out of a car that pulled up near the waiting taxi line outside of the arrivals area and ran into the baggage claim area through its unguarded exit. There were over a thousand people crowded around the huge room waiting for their bags to be unloaded and placed on the conveyer belts. Shouting unintelligibly about Allah the four men started firing randomly at the travelers all bunched together and threw their hand grenades.

In seconds the baggage claim area was total bedlam. Running and screaming people trampled over each other in a dash for safety that did not exist in the confines of the area. Bodies accumulated in heaps on a floor slippery with blood. The weapons fire was continuous and mind-numbing.

When security forces began arriving, the terrorists staged the second part of their plan -- a running firefight into the immigration area that bordered Baggage Claim where hundreds of international airline passengers who had been queued up waiting at Passport Control would be caught in the crossfire. The terrorists with their plan clearly in mind, then reversed back toward the baggage claim area where all was chaotic and tried to flee through the baggage claim exit. So far no more than five minutes had gone by.

One of the terrorists had died in the immigration area but the other three were still running and shooting at the policemen. They made it back outside to the taxi line where their car was waiting. Their plan failed there as the driving lanes were all backed up and their car had nowhere to go. The airport security killed them with a barrage of bullets as they were stalled in their vehicle, stuck in the traffic jam their actions had created but they had not anticipated.

*****

That same Tuesday at 5:15PM EDT Jack was stalled in rush hour traffic on Broadway just a few yards away from the Tickets facility in the middle of Times Square. The air conditioner in the ten year old Ford Taurus didn't work and he was sweating in the afternoon heat. He knew he was sweating because he was nervous but he blamed the air conditioner. He should have stolen a newer car. There was that new Mercedes he could have taken but he knew he wouldn't have felt right in it. Besides it wouldn't matter for much longer. For once he didn't mind being stuck in traffic. And he didn't mind that the crowds of pedestrians on the sidewalks were cutting between the cars in their hurry to get to wherever they were going.

He saw a street peddler on a side street with his pile of knock-off purses and wallets trying to get passers-by to stop and buy something. A couple of years ago he had been just like that guy. Only he liked the corner of 5th Avenue and 37th Street; people there were more eager for a deal, they didn't care if it was a knock-off as long as the Gucci or Louis Vuitton logo was visible and the quality wasn't total shit. At first he rather liked selling on the street, but over time he came to hate how everybody treated him like he was nothing. They just saw him as some Middle Eastern immigrant that somehow had got into their country. He would tell people he was Pakistani and their countries were allies but they didn't care.

A friend had told him that he should pick an American name because people would treat you better. So he picked 'Jack', what could be more American than that? He even worked on his accent. His English wasn't so bad, he was good with languages, but his pronunciation was a problem. Even after being in the U.S. for eight years, people had trouble understanding him. So he stuck pretty close to other Pakistanis, guys who were even more recent into the country than he was.

But they liked him. And like him they were passionate in their beliefs. Like him they thought people from India were horrible people and that Pakistan should be treated with more respect because Pakistan had developed nuclear weapons. And they worshipped Islam like he did. And more and more they talked about how that was the center of a man's life. At first, they were more fervid than he was, but being around them really made things clear for him. He was meant to be a servant of Allah and he would be rewarded for his service. He was not meant to sell fake purses on dirty New York Streets to people who treated him like he didn't belong there.

Then just six weeks ago the man who said he should be called Hasan had come into their group. Jack didn't know exactly how that had happened but Hasan was a man who knew how to do things. And Hasan knew what needed to be done and he made them all realize that it was no longer acceptable to just talk about things they should do. Soon his friends were arguing about who would be the first to really strike a blow. Then somehow he was the one to say he would do it and they all looked at him with more respect. And Hasan explained how to do what was needed and the last few weeks were the most exciting weeks of his life.

Jack started to feel too nervous sitting in the traffic jam in the middle of Times Square. He thought he saw a policeman looking at him. Then that policeman turned to another policeman standing near him and said something. Then the two policemen looked over in his direction. The plan was to position the car as close to the big Marriott Hotel as possible and then to set the timer on the bomb for one minute and leave the car and walk away quickly but not too fast to draw attention. But everyone had told him that he had to explode the bomb no matter what. He could not fail – not like the fool a couple of years earlier who failed to explode the bomb right about a block away from where he was sitting there in traffic.

Then he saw the two policemen start to walk in his direction. Jack reached for the device that would trigger the bomb. His hands shook a little bit. The two policemen kept coming closer to his car. And Jack pressed the button. Jack never saw the beautiful blonde girl walking across the street behind him who the policemen were coming closer to get a better look at.

The blast was huge. Nearby cars hurtled into the air, storefronts were demolished, shattered glass from windows of the overlooking skyscrapers cascaded down like a waterfall onto the streets, and bodies and parts of bodies were shot away from the blast center like grisly missiles. Death and destruction littered the streets. Soon the wailing sirens of police cars and fire trucks and emergency vehicles descended on that iconic center of New York City and there would be no Broadway shows that night.

*****

Two days later at the Munich Germany train station, Hans Mueller, a tall, thin 23 year-old with blond hair cut short and with a Nazi swastika tattooed on his right forearm took off his knapsack and dropped it into a trashcan at the front of the platform that hundreds of passengers de-boarding the 6 PM express train from Frankfurt had to pass by in just a few moments. He started to walk away when two plain clothed security guards who had spotted him earlier seized him from behind and pinned his arms behind him and snapped on handcuffs. They searched him quickly and found the cell phone they thought would detonate the bomb they suspected to be in the knapsack.

Recklessly one of the guards pulled the top off the trash can and checked the knapsack. The bomb was there. Other security personnel cordoned off the area around the trashcan and maneuvered the people coming off the Frankfurt train to enter the station through a different entryway that entwined them in the crowd of passengers coming off the express train from Berlin. Dieter Strauss, a pimply mousy haired teenager wearing jeans and a black tee shirt with a fake Iron Cross medal hanging around his neck inside his tee shirt watched Hans being detained. He looked around and observed that no one seemed to have noticed him. He wondered if he could do anything to help Hans and then put that thought aside. He didn't really like Hans anyway. Hans talked too much and picked on him because of his skin blotches. And Hans was not very smart either.

Dieter made up his mind quickly. He would explode both bombs. Han's bomb would now not be very effective but the bomb that Dieter had positioned to target the passengers from Berlin was now perfect to get the Frankfurt passengers too. He watched the police ushering Hans in the direction of the station building, close to where Dieter's bomb was. He saw Hans look desperately at Dieter as he realized how close he was coming to the trashcan where Dieter's bomb had been placed. Hans started violently shaking his head and shouting "No!"

Dieter pressed the key on his cell phone and the trashcan in the middle of the crowd of people coming off the Frankfurt and Berlin trains exploded. Dieter turned away and ran off in the middle of a crowd of people who were fleeing.

*****

The sun was setting over The Great Hall of the People on the western edge of Tiananmen Square. The meeting place of the National People's Congress was crowded that evening with high-level Communist Party participants celebrating the 80th birthday of one of their most respected ministers. Security was as always very tight, but that evening particularly so because the General Secretary himself was supposed to arrive within the hour. He was running a little late but had promised to come for a few minutes.

When the General Secretary was just a block away from The Great Hall, the blast of an explosion rocked his car. The bomb blast centered on the East Gate at the center of the huge building and toppled the columns there and engulfed that part of the building in flames. Most of the people in the area where the bomb was set off escaped through the rubble and fire. But not all escaped; the minister whose birthday it was did not survive and several other senior ministers perished with him. In all, over fifty people died there that evening.

Later there was discovered on an undamaged outside wall of The Great Hall a spray painted statement, 'A typhoon's wind blows in both directions.'

*****

Joan Smithson and her ten year-old daughter Meagan stood in a line; a queue she thought to herself was what the English called it, at Trafalgar Square in London waiting for a double decker bus. They had just seen the towering statue of Lord Nelson at the center of the square and now were headed back to their hotel to meet up with her husband Don. He had just called them and said his meeting was over. Now he was free to join them and play tourist.

A hesitant sun was now struggling through the morning clouds and promised a sunny afternoon. The first two days of their trip had been rainy and now the idea of riding on the top level of the bus seemed perfect. Meagan had been eager to do it and now Joan liked the idea too. Such a London thing to do. Sure it was a little stereotypical, but who cared; it would be fun. And with the sun coming out it seemed to prove going on this trip had been the right thing to do. They had almost cancelled the trip when they saw on television the news reporting about the massacre at the Paris Airport and then just as they were leaving from JFK details about the bomb at Time Square were coming out. Their apartment was only a few blocks away!

She had also heard something yesterday about a bomb exploding at some train station in Germany. She hadn't really followed what happened there; she and Don had been too wrapped up in watching the Times Square news footage. As a New Yorker it reminded her of when the planes hit the twin towers of the World Trade Center on 9/11. Only now it seemed worse somehow. She knew more people had died there but now the terrorists seemed to be hitting everywhere.

Joan found herself fretting about these terrorist acts as she stood there in the line holding Meagan's hand. It wasn't like her to be feeling apprehensive. Her husband was a very successful lawyer at one of the top New York firms. Meagan liked her school and was doing well there and she was busy with the work she did at their church and at the food bank. And she did love the shopping and Don seemed to like that her secret fashionista tendencies were coming out now that they had some money. She had dressed like a mouse when she was working to put him through law school at NYU. So why the anxious feeling?

She looked at the crowds of people standing around this historic square honoring Britain's most famous naval hero. Her sense of anxiety increased as she thought about the terrorism. This was the kind of place where terrorists would strike. She shuddered.

There were about ten people in front of them in the bus queue and she hoped the next bus wasn't too full, but a lot of people would probably get off there too. Suddenly she just wanted to get back to their hotel and away from the crowds of people. Then she saw the bus pulling up; it was very full. When it pulled to a stop about a dozen people started getting off and Joan figured they would be fine, they'd be able to board the bus. Then she noticed the sun had gone back behind a cloud and the world looked a little greyer. The line started to move forward to get on the bus.

Joan couldn't shake the dark feeling coming over her and she gave into it. She tugged Meagan's hand to pull her out of the line and told her all of a sudden she wanted to walk. The hotel wasn't that far. Meagan resisted but Joan felt she had to walk. She hustled Meagan away and almost found herself running; then when they were about thirty yards from the bus stop, the bomb that had just been left behind under a seat on the bus exploded. The blast knocked both Joan and Meagan to the ground, breaking Meagan's arm and giving Joan a concussion. They were among the lucky ones.

*****

Khalil sat by himself at the same outdoor café in Beirut where he had first talked to the man who called himself Hasan. Khalil had been trying to reach Hasan by calling the cell phone number Hasan had given him and he had left numerous messages but Hasan had never called him back. He didn't really expect Hasan to just show up at this café but Khalil had been going there every afternoon for the last two weeks anyway.

Khalil was consumed by the big idea he had. He hungered to regain the sense of joy that he had felt in the first few hours after destroying the U.S. Embassy in Tel Aviv. But when he started to tell people that he was the one who did it, very few believed him! And then there were the rumors that some secret cell of Iranians had done it. Looking back now he realized he had not handled that well. He had lost his temper and had screamed at people he should not have screamed at. Quite reasonably they thought he was deranged. He was claiming credit for the greatest act against both Israel and the Americans and he had no proof. And he had not told anyone ahead of time. So no one gave him any recognition or credit. But he knew he had been the one!

He knew and it gave him confidence that he could do it again. And the act would be even bigger! But he knew he needed the help of Hasan. He needed the special missile that was so powerful and left that strange blue-tinged mushroom-like cloud of smoke. And he needed other help as well, but he believed Hasan could help him do it. He had thought a lot about Hasan in the last two months and believed that he understood what Hasan was doing. Though Khalil didn't know how, he suspected that Hasan might have been involved with the acts of terrorism in New York and Paris and London. Khalil had to admit he was jealous of those acts. How he wished he had been part of that!

Khalil figured that Hasan had been very busy recently. Hasan wanted all these acts of terrorism to happen. It bothered Khalil that he did not know why. Hasan had told him he was helping to do the work of the Great Prophet because that was his beliefs too. Maybe so, but Hasan's Earth was not Khalil's Earth, so Khalil feared trusting him too much. But he could ask for Hasan's help without trusting him too much. The target was worth taking many risks! To strike inside America at one of its mightiest landmarks would stun the world. Khalil's reward in both this life and the next would be great – and this time he would make sure that there would be no doubts that he was the one.

Khalil ordered another cup of espresso and watched the people going by. At times he envied those people who led normal lives. He would have liked a wife and sons. Looking back he wasn't sure when his path had been chosen. He didn't think he had ever made the decision. Perhaps it was like they said: a man's life was written in the sands of time before he was ever born. His fate was unavoidable. He could believe that. And he would not seek to change it. His destiny was to do great things. When he had done them, then he could have a wife and strong sons.

A man came from behind Khalil and slid into the seat next to him at the small table.

"Hello Khalil, you wish to talk to me?" Hasan asked.

*****

David looked up from his desk where he was reading the latest news stories on his laptop and studied Gabriela as she was reading a physics paper while lying on their couch. She wasn't going to like what he was thinking. She saw him looking over at her and put down her iPad.

"I think I need to try to get another interview with Captain Ragnar. And I think I need to try to meet with the Captain of The Lucky Dragon too."

Gabriela looked at him like he was crazy, "No you don't. You really don't. Things are too dangerous now. This isn't about science anymore. The massacre at the Paris airport wasn't about science. The bombing at Times Square wasn't about science. And whatever it was that happened in Beijing, that wasn't about science either!"

Gabriela straightened up to a sitting position on the couch, "David, I'm scared. And you should be too. What's going on now isn't like anything we had before. The cable news stations can't even keep up with it all. Last week was horrible. I love New York, but I'm afraid to walk down the street."

David rose up from the desk and came to sit in the armchair close to Gabriela. "Now that's crazy. The odds are far against anything happening to you. Or to me. You know that."

"Sure I know that. But I don't feel that. I feel like suddenly the world is a much more dangerous place!"

"It was always dangerous. We just didn't focus on that."

"Exactly. It wasn't happening here. Well now it is happening to us. And I can't ignore it now."

David looked at this woman whom he loved and didn't really have anything to tell her that would make her feel any better.

Instead he was offering something that would scare her more. "I know. I feel it too. It is happening to us now. But I do think it is connected to the arrival of these other Earths – if only because the timing can't be coincidental. And I feel I have to do everything I can do to help. And if I can meet with Captain Ragnar and whoever is the boss on The Lucky Dragon, then I need to do it."

"But they aren't going to tell you anything."

"I won't know that until I ask."

"Why can't you just go talk to Plato? What does he think about all this?"

"I think this is what he was warning us about. But you're right; I should talk to him too." David breathed out slowly as he thought about what he knew he had to do. He felt like he had no choice. Somewhere earlier he had started down a path that led him now to meetings with these leaders from other Earths and he knew he just had to stay on the path. Even as he knew the path was getting more treacherous, he had to stay on it.

"Good. Then we can go to Planck's island."

"Yes, but not until after I go up to The Freya and The Lucky Dragon."

Gabriela could see he was not going to change his mind. "But after that we can go to the island, right?"

"What is this 'we can go' thing?" David teased.

"Don't even pretend to think you can go without me!"

*****

The same shuttle came to pick David up at the same place as the last time. The same soldier was on board and once again gave him a quick security check. The soldier seemed as bored with his task as any airport security guard. The only real difference was there was no x-ray machine and he was allowed to keep his small bottles of water.

David sat at the same table in The Freya's lounge as he had the last time he had interviewed the Captain. This time he had more time to look around as Captain Ragnar had not yet arrived. He was struck how similar this lounge looked to that of the U.S. Navy ship lounges he had been on when he was researching an article on an advanced model of a Destroyer class ship. There was even what looked like a big refrigerator and next to it a microwave oven. The few tables and chairs looked made out of aluminum and plastic. It certainly did not look particularly space age.

It also struck him this time that the ship was probably not that large. The lounge looked like it could only accommodate about twenty people at a time and he thought he recognized a couple of people from the last time he was there. He wondered if there was some minimum number of people required to meditate together to move the ship through the dimensions necessary to transport the Freya from its world to this Earth. He made a note to talk to Plato about that.

He also started noticing that the people he had seen walking in the hallways or sitting in the lounge seemed to fall into two groups. Though all wore the same uniform, some looked much more militaristic in them than others. The ones who looked like they didn't belong in a uniform had a more calm and slow moving way of being. David noticed too that the two groups didn't mix. The non-militants seemed to be there at the sufferance of the real soldiers. To David's perception they seemed a recent adjunct to the crew.

After a five minute wait, the Captain arrived. He greeted David with a handshake and a quick and limited smile and took a seat. Captain Ragnar looked across the table at David Randall. He had quickly agreed to be interviewed this second time by David because he preferred putting his message across in the press rather than the TV media. With the press, messages could be more carefully crafted and one could always claim to have been misquoted or not understood. Visual media was too immediate and too subject to impressions. And he knew that he did not come across sufficiently amiable and friendly. He liked the indirectness of the print media.

He liked the timing of this interview as well as the fact that the interviewer was the foremost science writer and not a writer who wrote the usual front page news. Though very satisfied with the onslaught of recent terrorism, he did not want to be closely tied to it. He very much wanted to appear to be above it all. And he knew he needed to make that point.

David started by asking some warm up questions about how he was finding this Earth to be different from his Earth. As he had before, his answers made it appear that the two Earths were pretty similar. And he shared how he missed his wife and two children and looked forward to seeing them soon. He found he like talking about his non-existent family.

He was waiting for David to bring up the issue of the upsurge in terrorism and soon David did.

"So Captain, as you probably know a lot of people think that this recent wave of terrorism is somehow the result of your arrival and that of the other two ships from other Earths. What do you have to say about that?"

The Captain gave David his most concerned and sincere look. "The recent events are horrible to be sure. And I cannot really say what actions might have been taken by The Lucky Dragon or by The Bucephalus, but I can assure you we had no direct hand in any of it. But that is not to say that the increase in terrorist activity is unrelated to our arrival and the arrival of the others."

"And how is that?" David asked.

"The political situation on your planet is very unstable. With the arrival of what your people think of as three ships from outer space, tensions and anxieties and uncertainty is certain to increase. Plus there is the very strangeness of the Participatory Physics that they are learning about. These raise very unsettling issues and concerns. One's very worldview is shown to have been wrong at a fundamental level. Put all that together with religious extremists and long simmering nationalistic rivalries and it is like lighting a match in a fireworks factory. There are bound to be explosions. Our arrival is the incendiary factor – even though we took no provocative actions. When we have arrived in similar circumstances on other Earths where the local governments are more in control, there has not been any sudden increase in violence."

David considered the response, and then said, "So you think that we are essentially responsible for these recent acts of terror?"

"You must admit the problems preceded our arrival."

David nodded, "That is certainly true. But there are rumors of heightened provocations by unknown participants."

"I don't know of such rumors," the Captain said.

"For instance, "David persisted, "It seems that there is circulating through the Islamist extremist community the idea that on other Earths, Islam is much more powerful and that the Muslims here are somehow deficient in their commitment to Allah."

"Again, I'm sorry I don't know of that. But it is true that Islam is far more powerful on other Earths."

David decided he needed to change directions. "So Captain, what are your plans here now that you've been here a while?"

"Well we are still learning about your Earth. But I will tell you confidentially that we are in discussions with companies here over the sharing of intellectual capital. Our scientists have gone down different paths and I believe we have much to trade."

"Could you give some examples of that?"

The Captain waved the subject off. "That would be premature for now. But we are quite satisfied with how things are progressing."

David thought about the Captain's assessment. Even allowing for cultural differences, the Captain seemed rather smug in his final comment.

Looking around at The Freya's military austerity and the uniforms and demeanor of the crew who passed through the lounge, David couldn't quite reconcile what he saw with the Captain's statements that their mission was to find trading partners for intellectual property.

The Captain watched David leave with one of the men he had ordered to escort David back to his car. He was pleased with the interview and wondered how much more media he should do. He didn't like the attention and he didn't like dealing with the media. Though necessary, he thought nothing good could come of it. Still, he had needed to be public in his denials. As things continued to worsen, it would be increasingly important to have his denials on record. And as he knew better than anyone, events were going to get much worse. So he would place blame on everyone but himself. In fact he needed to think more on how to do that best. People would believe what they read in the newspaper.

# CHAPTER THIRTEEN

*"The unleashed power of the atom has changed everything save our modes of thinking and thus we drift toward unparalleled catastrophe."*

Albert Einstein

Hank Scarpetti sunk down into the corner of the sofa across from where the President was sitting in a facing sofa in the Oval Office. Though only the middle of the afternoon, he was bone deep tired. Still, he thought he looked and felt better than the President. The last ten days had been brutal and it showed on the President's face. He looked like he had aged ten years in just the ten days. He was slumped down, his face pale and slack and his eyes seemed to just randomly stare at things without any real comprehension of what he was looking at. Scarpetti realized he probably looked the same way. Right then both men had centered their gaze into the unlit fireplace at the north end of the room.

They had both just come out of another emergency meeting in the Situation Room. The meeting had accomplished nothing. Thoughtless recommendations had been tossed around by the cabinet members desperate to act as if they knew what to do. But they didn't. All they really accomplished was to share with each other all the real and imagined security threats that seemed to be popping up everywhere now. The intelligence briefings were jammed with fact-less rumors of devastating events and fearful 'what-ifs' that showcased real vulnerabilities. And then there were the things that were certainly true. And they were horrible as well.

After a few long silent moments the President turned his gaze from the formless depths of the fireplace to the haggard face of his Chief of Staff. "We need to do something!" President Morningstar declared. "There's got to be something we can do."

"We don't have enough information," Scarpetti responded. "I want to hit something but I don't know what to swing at."

"I know I can't just keep sitting here in the Oval Office doing nothing. I know a lot of Americans died in Paris....including Arthur Glass, a friend of mine dating back to law school. And his wife and son too. Five Americans died in that bombing in Munich. In London more Americans died. And Times Square was just terrible. The people are looking to me to do something! And you just say we don't know enough."

Scarpetti shared the President's anger and frustration. So he just said what they all knew already, "Each incident seems different – with different players. And who knows what went on in China? That is the most bizarre of all...and perhaps the most dangerous. That's the one that scares me."

The President nodded. "I agree. But let's come back to that one. And let's set aside the Munich train station bombing. I think that was a sort of copycat thing. They wanted to get in on the action. But London, Paris and Times Square seem related – and are probably tied some way to the Tel Aviv bombing of our Embassy. And since we think that the missile that destroyed the embassy didn't come from this world then by implication one of our visitors from other Earths may have had something to do with them too."

"OK. But which visitor? Plato and his guys? The Freya? The Lucky Dragon?"

"That's the problem isn't it?" The President tried looking up at the ceiling, but found no answers there either. He knew from his reading of history that great Presidents made the tough decisions that were proven by events to have been correct. Looking backwards over the decades and centuries those decisions had seemed easy enough to him. Now he was thinking that maybe they had not been so obvious back then.

"Yes Mr. President. But you know, General Greene said something interesting at the last meeting. He reminded us that at least according to Plato, they do not all have the same level of technology. So they are not all equally powerful."

"What are you getting at Hank?"

"Well...we know that shooting missiles at Plato's ship didn't work. But maybe The Freya or The Lucky Dragon can't do what The Bucephalus can do. Maybe we are not as powerless against them as we think."

The President thought about it. "You think we should try to find out?"

"I think we should at least develop plans. And I think we have to find out what each of them is up to. I think the guys at Langley should be told to do whatever it takes to find out whatever we can. Because I'll bet there is more coming at us. And it will get worse each time. I don't know that we are even safe here in the White House."

The President nodded glumly. "I've thought about that. But I have to stay here and be visible. The symbol matters. But I've ordered the Vice President to stay away from me until the situation normalizes."

Scarpetti gave a grim laugh, "Well, at least some good is coming out of this."

The President shook his head, "Don't get me started."

Scarpetti shuddered. "I don't want to think about him running the country!"

The President grimaced. "It's not my favorite thought either." He looked around the room and then returned his gaze to his Chief of Staff. "OK...now tell me about China. How bad is that situation?"

Scarpetti took a deep breath before turning to that. "We are picking up some strange intel that maybe the Japanese were behind it as some sort of retaliation for something China did to them. But again, I don't see how it could have happened. The security there around Tiananmen Square and The Great Hall is incredible. So it makes me think that one of the other Earths could be involved. But again we have the question as to which one?"

"It seems there has to be some way for us to learn who and what we are dealing with. Have we heard anything back yet as to meeting with The Lucky Dragon?"

Scarpetti shook his head, "Not yet. But we know that the Chinese have met with them. But we don't know what was said there. And we suspect but cannot get confirmation that the Japanese Prime Minister has had a meeting with them."

"That's not good enough! Tokyo has to keep me informed. I want to know everything that's going on. All of a sudden, everything going on over there seems to be in crisis mode and no one is telling us anything."

"Imagine if the General Secretary had not been running late. If he had died in the blast who knows what would have resulted!"

The President sat up straighter on the couch as he sought to lift up both his body and his spirit. "We have to learn more! What could have provoked the bombing there? If someone in Japan's government is behind that, we could be looking at World War III."

*****

As David and Gabriela looked out the window of the charter airplane as it came in to land on Pirate's Cay, it struck David that the pretty little island was like the quiet center of a turbulent hurricane. The gentle waves of the turquoise waters of the Caribbean lapping against the island's sandy shore foretold nothing of the political dramas playing out in the world's capital cities. The sunshine streaming onto the island belied the storm clouds gathering worldwide.

Once the small plane had landed and come to a stop near the little shed that served as the island's airport, David and Gabriela grabbed their bags and as they exited the plane were glad to see Planck waiting for them next to his Landrover. Next to him was a very pretty woman holding his hand. Planck introduced her, "This is Megan Baxter. She has been helping me with social media stuff." They all exchanged handshakes and Gabriela hugged Planck.

"It's great to see you, it's been a while!" Planck said. David and Gabriela both echoed the sentiment. They were now clearly comrades in arms and wanted to share their recent battle stories.

Gabriela grinned at Megan, "Now I understand how it is that Planck has become such a media sensation – it would have taken a lot to get him out of his island mentality!"

David gave Planck a friendly punch on the shoulder, "Apparently not so much – just the determination of a beautiful – and I'm sure talented woman."

"Planck has told me a lot about the two of you. And of course, David, I follow your articles and your blog posts. I'm looking forward to knowing you both better." Megan responded.

"Definitely," said Gabriela, "You'll find it is a very small island."

"Guess what?" Planck continued, "Dr. Wheeling is here – with a lady friend I might add – and he and I want to bring you up to date on what we've been figuring out the last two months. And then I think you are supposed to meet with Plato. He's here a lot now...but very busy. A lot of people keep coming here to meet with him. It's a real list of the movers and the shakers. Most of who seem to have their own airplanes – though not all."

"I can't wait, let's do it!" declared Gabriela, dashing David's idea of first taking a swim in the ocean.

They met in one of the conference rooms in the main building. The room seemed to have been converted into a classroom with desks arranged in a half-circle and whiteboards in the front and on the side walls. When David and Gabriela entered the room, the professor was there with Planck and Catherine Ozawa was there as well. David noticed immediately that Catherine somehow looked different and then realized that she looked ten years younger than when he had seen her last which he figured was about two months earlier. He saw that Gabriela had noticed the change too.

After the greetings were done, Dr. Wheeling stepped to the front and turned to focus particularly on David and Gabriela. It seemed Planck and Ozawa were already in the know.

"In the last few weeks we have really come to understand more of the basics of Participatory Physics," he began. "We have pretty much had to figure things out from first principles as Plato's people seem prohibited from sharing too much. Still, in science it is always much easier to reverse engineer a theory once you know the result. And they have helped us understand the potentialities that are the product of a Participatory universe."

Planck interrupted, "It's so cool! The Professor has taken the work I had done and saw how to extend it. He even figured out the beginnings of an equation that can be used to show the energy requirements to transform the states and molecular structure of matter to effect the desired changes. It's remarkable – some changes require relatively little energistic expenditure and others quite a lot. But for the equation to work we had to come up with a new constant."

The professor took back control. "Yes we think there is a necessary constant. And Plato's people seem to confirm its necessity. And despite my young friend's exuberance for it, we are not going to call it 'the other Planck constant.' That would go too far." David and Gabriela laughed, all sharing a joke that only other physicists would think was funny.

"So where does the energy come from?" Gabriela asked.

"It's all around us!" Planck exclaimed. "And it's the most abundant and cheapest energy in the universe."

"Dark energy," both David and Gabriela said simultaneously.

"Precisely," stated Dr. Wheeling.

"And how do you tap into it?" asked David.

"Through the mind of course. But that is where the challenge lies. It all occurs at the electromagnetic level. And because the pulses are so tiny there are quantum fluctuations that must be accounted for. And that is what we have been focusing on for the last few weeks. And I should say that Dr. Ozawa has been invaluable in this area."

Catherine Ozawa shook her head, "These guys are way over my head. I just help with the meditation aspects that prove the theory. You see we are learning that not all people have equal abilities to do the mentalization. And the variance among people seems to exist both because of training differentials but also genetic differences. Some people seem naturally pre-wired so to speak, while others seem to have no wiring for it at all."

Gabriela quickly saw the sociological implications, "So mankind will once again be split into the haves and the have nots. And I presume the variability among individuals lies along a spectrum, with some with a very high potentiality, some in the middle and some at the low end."

Catherine nodded, "Yes, we think so, but it is too early to tell how that spectrum will map parabolically."

David then spoke up, "Did I understand correctly that you said that there is variability in the degree of difficulty – or perhaps I should say the energistic requirements -- to mentalize certain changes?"

"Precisely" Dr. Wheeling answered. "The more energy required to turn X into Y or the more energy required to move X from A to B, the greater the amount of mentalization is required – that's where our equation is put to work with the new mathematical constant."

Planck then added, "And we were correct here in believing that mentalization powers can be synergistically linked together through a highly focused group meditation – particularly among those trained in meditation. And we were correct about the enhancement capabilities of our amplifier – though I have to admit that Plato's people could not keep from laughing at how primitive my amplifier is. Which obviously means that there is a lot of room for improving output and efficiency."

"Are you determining the limits as to what can and cannot be accomplished through mentalization?" David asked.

Planck nodded, "We're developing parameters. For instance, we can recombine and alter molecular structures, but we can't affect whether the Cowboys beat the Redskins in a football game – too many moving parts and too many variables. Though let me take that back ...I suppose that if we mentalized the weakening of a knee joint for instance of a key player, if that player then blew out his knee that might affect the outcome of the game."

David grimaced, "Put that power into the hands of the gamblers in Las Vegas and betting on sports would change forever."

Dr. Wheeling chastised them, "Let's focus on the physics, please. What we are discovering is that as we would have hoped, once again our understanding of how the universe works does comport with a mathematical system that can be used to predict outcomes which can then be proven empirically."

Gabriela laughed, obviously delighted with how this was proceeding. "What I love about Physics is that Physics provides an understanding of how to describe what the universe does while the universe itself remains such a mystery to us. We now know that consciousness is absolutely at the heart of all existence while still not understanding what consciousness is or where it comes from."

Dr. Wheeling seemed almost insulted by Gabriela's outburst. "Gabriela, the day will come when we better understand the nature of existence; but for now we face a very immediate existential threat created by our own political ineptitude and the arrival of these other Earths. Our work here may help us survive these perilous times."

Planck then further added to the professor's concerns, "I still fear what happens when people everywhere find they have what would just a few months ago have seemed like super powers reserved for Marvel comic book heroes and villains."

Catherine Ozawa had been quiet until then, but now offered a different view. "Personally, I'm very excited at the potentiality offered to us by our Participatory universe. Excuse the pun but keep in mind that the doorway to mentalization is meditation. Meditation by its nature requires calm and quiet and balance. A world filled with people who practice meditation will be a very different world than the one we have today. I think it will be a very much better world. And those who cannot achieve a calm and serene state of mind – a peaceful state of mind – will find they are the victims, not the aggressors. Our leaders in such a world might well more closely resemble the philosopher king ideal found in Plato's Republic." Then it was Catherine's time to laugh and she might have blushed as well. "Of course that's the Plato of our own Greek history, not our new friend – who also espouses that ideal."

*****

Later David sought out Plato for their pre-arranged meeting. When David found Plato in a room that Plato had set up as his office, he was surprised to see that General Carl Greene was there too. The general and David shook hands and Plato greeted him with what was now his customary locked forearms – a practice from his home Earth.

"David, I asked the general to join us because I think it will save us time – and time could be very important to us."

"It's fine with me."

"Good," General Greene stated. "But as I have been telling Plato, I'm not really the right representative of the U.S. Government to be working with you guys here. There are others whose jobs are more closely tied to protecting our national security against terrorism. And in inviting me here, that is what Plato tells me this meeting is about."

"But as I keep telling the general," Plato interrupted, "he is the only one I am willing to work with. I know him; I do not know the phalanx of others who would want to meet with me."

"Then maybe I'm the one who shouldn't be here," David said. "I don't know there is anything I can do about this wave of terrorism that is occurring right now."

"In that respect I think you are wrong." Plato responded. "You see David, I believe you are uniquely able to be of assistance. As General Greene can tell you, the United States believes that either The Freya, The Lucky Dragon or The Bucephalus is actually a major instigator of terrorism and is behind the recent attacks and may even now be setting up future attacks."

"OK. But how does that link to me?"

"It links to you because I believe you can tell us which one of the visitors from other Earths is the guilty one."

"I can do that?"

"Yes I think so. But first I need to clarify something. The charter that I operate under as I go to the many Earths is a limited one. The limits are imposed on me by my government and they have proven over time and many experiences to be wise limitations. The most important limit is that my crew and I are never to be direct actors – we can take no direct action. Nor are we to take sides politically that might favor one local government or political faction over another. We have learned that the chain of cause and effect is too unpredictable and random for us to know what is best for the future of any Earth. However, that is not to say that I am prohibited from providing guidance and counsel, nor are we prohibited from facilitating technological development. In fact that is what my true role is. But the participants from each Earth get to decide for themselves what they should do. So here, your future is in your hands, not mine."

"Sounds like the Prime Directive from Star Trek. And I always thought it was stupid." David interjected.

General Greene spoke up, "We'll take whatever help we can get. I'm not concerned about philosophical nuances. Plato, just by coming here you have altered the flow of our future. Whatever our future trajectory would have been, it now will be different.

Maybe that will prove to be a good thing, maybe not. As you say, the chain of cause and effect is beyond all understanding. Our cultural, political, scientific and religious foundations are now all in flux. We may not have been all that stable before, but we are on the edge of disaster now. So what can you do?"

"I believe I can help David give you the answer to the biggest question you have right now." Plato replied.

"I know the answer? I don't even know the question!" David responded. Greene's look at David showed he was as doubtful as David was.

Plato nodded at both of them. "David, you may not know this, but you are the only person from your Earth who has actually been on The Freya. And you have been on it twice. And I believe you will also soon go to The Lucky Dragon."

"I did seek a meeting with the Captain of The Lucky Dragon last week and was told yes, we could meet. But the date they gave was for next week."

"Really?" General Greene exclaimed. "They have been ignoring us so far."

Plato explained, "David now has a global following. And his ability to explain to everyone what is occurring has made him a valuable presenter of the points of view of the other Earths. David limits his expression of personal judgment and his urge to pontificate – though he does cross that line occasionally."

"The President will love hearing this. He thinks he's the leader of the free world." The general wouldn't admit to it but he found David's position compared to the President's somewhat ironical given this particular president's intellectual pretensions. And he liked David and didn't particularly like the President.

"In any case," Plato continued, "David can help us here. General, you will recall no doubt that I showed you some surveillance video that directly linked a Palestinian named Khalil to the destruction of your Tel Aviv Embassy with a weapon not from this Earth."

"Yes, you gave us that video. We have been looking for that man but have not yet found him. We almost got him a couple of times. We have learned that he has claimed to be the one to fire the rocket though he hasn't really been able to prove it within the community. I don't suppose you could tell us where to find him?"

"No I cannot to that. But I can show you more of his actions." First Plato replayed the video material of Khalil going into the hotel in Tel Aviv with the weapon used to destroy the embassy and then leaving without it. The video included a visual of the rocket firing from the hotel window. Plato reconfirmed that it was Khalil who fired the missile. Then Plato stated that The Bucephalus had been continuing to monitor the movements of Khalil. He then showed a meeting that Khalil had very recently in a café in Beirut with a man whose back was to the surveillance equipment. As the meeting concluded, that man stood up and turned so that his face could be seen.

"I recognize that man!" David exclaimed. "I saw him on The Freya when I was there a few days ago. He was sitting at a table just a few feet away from me when I was interviewing Captain Ragnar."

"Are you sure?" General Greene asked.

"I'm positive. Almost all the other people I saw on The Freya were blond or light haired. The Captain and this guy were the only ones with black hair. But better yet, I used my smart phone to take pictures. And he's in at least one of them." David took out his device and scrolled his pictures to find what he was looking for. "That's him, isn't it?" he said when he found the right one.

"Yes," Plato and Greene said as they were looking at Hasan.

Greene studied the picture and then wanted to see again the whole of the meeting between Hasan and Khalil. "Plato, you say this meeting was only a couple of days ago?"

"Yes."

General Greene was immediately concerned. "I can't imagine why this guy from The Freya would meet with Khalil again unless they are planning something again. And we have some sources telling us that a guy who claims to have been responsible for the embassy bombing is now bragging that he has something even bigger being planned. Something that would hit the U.S. inside the country."

"My counsel to you is to take that as being true."

"That's your counsel, is it? Your counsel that the guy who blew up our embassy with the help of The Freya is now about to hit us inside the U.S. probably again with the help of this guy Hasan who David shows us is a crew member of the Freya?"

"Yes," Plato said sadly.

"That's your counsel and that is all you can tell us?" Greene repeated. His agitation showed as he leaned forward in his chair with his hands balled up into fists. The warrior in him wanted to strike out, but his experience kept him seated. "I don't suppose you could counsel us on how to find this guy Khalil before he blows something up and kill even more Americans, could you?"

"Yes, I probably can give you counsel there," stated Plato, to Greene's surprise. "But perhaps I can give you better counsel than that. Khalil and others like him – of which there are too many to keep track of – are not your main problem. Your problem is to stop the activities of Captain Ragnar and his crew which are further destabilizing your planet."

"And how do we do that?" Greene asked, his distemper showing with no attempt by him to hide it.

Plato looked back at Greene, stern and resolute, "Why you kill them, of course."

*****

David looked around at the paintings on the walls of the Oval Office. He'd read that the President could have his pick of artwork on loan from museums so he looked to see what he could learn about this President from the art on his walls. The picture of George Washington over the mantel of the fireplace was the traditional choice. It certainly set the tone. The other paintings maintained the American history motif. To the side of the fireplace was a bronze bust of Abraham Lincoln. Lincoln was David's pick of best president of all time, so it was easy to agree with Honest Abe looking over the goings on in the room.

David was reasonably confident that his meeting this time would not end the way his last meeting in the Oval Office had ended. He had no interest in another unwanted stay locked in a bedroom in the bowels of the Pentagon. This meeting certainly had started better. He had been overnighted at the historic and beautifully restored Willard Hotel and then walked the few blocks to The White House for his 11 AM meeting on a lovely warm and sunny day. Then when he arrived, the President had been very cordial and welcoming; though he made no mention or apology for locking him up last time.

Also sitting on the couches in the center of the office were Hank Scarpetti and General Greene. The President had chosen to sit on a chair on the perimeter of the couches. General Greene had just finished summarizing the meeting he and David had with Plato. David was pretty sure that at least Scarpetti and probably the President had already heard it all.

The President turned his focus on to him. "David, the reason I asked you to join us for this meeting is that it seems I have to decide whether Captain Ragnar and his crew are the ones behind the recent upsurge in terrorism. You have been aboard The Freya and interviewed Captain Ragnar twice. And you ID'd the man called Hasan as a member of the crew of The Freya and Plato has shown us video of Hasan meeting with the man who allegedly bombed our embassy in Tel Aviv. That's right isn't it?"

"Yes sir," David replied.

The President went on, "You also have spent a lot of time with Plato and members of his team, too. Correct? And you have first-hand experience in observing that the level of technology possessed by Plato is well beyond our capabilities. Correct again?"

"Yes sir, to both questions."

"David, is it correct for me to say that you now believe that Captain Ragnar and The Freya are the instigators of this wave of terror and that Plato is trying to help us?"

David felt like he was being cross-examined. The President early in his career had been the lead prosecutor in a major organized crime case, the case that started his rise in politics, and David now felt like he was a defendant. Still, he just had to say what he thought and he figured he'd put it very simply. "Yes, I believe Captain Ragnar is our enemy and that Plato is our friend."

The President held up his hand. "And now we are at the heart of the issue. You see we don't have any real corroboration that Captain Ragnar is behind the bombing of our embassy. We don't know that the man we call Khalil is the one who did it with Ragnar's help. We know that even among many of his peers, Khalil is not credited with doing it. All we really have is video given to us from Plato. If you believe the videos, then it is easy to see that Captain Ragnar is the instigator. But if the video is just a fiction created by Plato to point blame away from himself, then Ragnar is probably innocent and it is Plato who is the villain here. And wouldn't you say that Plato with all his advanced technology could fool us with false videos if he wanted to?"

David felt trapped. He knew Plato was on their side - at least as much as he could be. And his perception of Captain Ragnar was that he was not to be trusted. So he said all that to the President. He shared his appreciation and respect that he had for Plato and how well his crew always comported themselves. And he shared how Dr. Wheeling's and Planck's research was being aided by Plato's science team, though that aid was as much guidance as instruction - but still invaluable. He finished with a definitive statement of his conviction that Plato could be trusted and that the U.S. needed to trust him.

The President listened carefully without interrupting.

When David had finished, he looked to General Greene for support but the general remained silent. And the President then said, "So on the basis of all that, I am supposed to try and blow The Freya out of the sky - assuming that we even could? For Plato's advice to us is that we need quote 'to kill them.' That is what he said, isn't it?"

David saw how things were going, but he knew he had to go all in, "That's right. Plato said that. And I believe him. I think that is what we should do."

"What I think is that he may be manipulating us. I think to try and kill Captain Ragnar and his crew on so little evidence - evidence that could be fictitious - is a very questionable proposition."

David looked back at General Greene. "You agree with me, don't you?"

The President answered for him. "Yes, the general does agree with you. But he admits he doesn't have much to go on, it is just his judgment. And though I highly respect the general, it is my judgment that counts, not his. And I don't have enough reliable facts to make a decision as consequential as trying to execute the Captain and his crew for acts that at best are indirect - if they occurred at all."

The President leaned over to reach for a glass of water on a side table. David thought he seemed pleased with how he had conducted the conversation. David looked over at Hank Scarpetti who just looked away.

The President then shifted the subject. "David, I would like to get your views on something I know you are actually an expert on, tell me what you think the societal effects are going to be from the Participatory Physics. The more my experts describe to me the new insights and developments, the more I perceive how momentous the changes can be. What do you think?"

David forced himself to ignore the President's somewhat belittling tone of voice – the question was too important. Also he saw a way to buttress his case for Plato. "When Planck first explained his introductory work on Participatory Physics it was fascinating but we thought it would take years to put into practice. But with Plato's guidance we are moving much faster than we ever thought possible. We will be able to put it to use in important ways soon. It can be used to improve the yield of our crops. It can be used to improve healthcare. It can be used to increase energy output. However the social and economic adjustments are going to be huge. The healthcare industry and the energy industry are going to be hammered by Wall Street."

"And what about weaponizing what you are learning? Are the scientists you are talking to giving that any thought?"

David considered the question, then he looked to General Greene whose face remained impassive. "I have not heard yet of any new weapons that can be created, though I don't doubt that they will come. What I have heard being considered is whether Participatory Physics will make it easier to develop nuclear weapons through changing ordinary uranium into the uranium variants necessary for a bomb."

"Is that right, General?" the President asked.

"Yes, that is our conclusion too."

Scarpetti sighed and rested his head back against the couch. "God save us. What a world we are creating!"

"Yes, on that note," the President interrupted, "David, as I'm sure you know, your friend Dr. Planck now seems to be a media sensation. Ever since the social media picked up the story of how that little girl down in Houston with the fatal heart condition has been cured – how her heart is now healthy. That church and

Planck seemed to be leading a religious revival. What's that minister's name, Hank?"

Scarpetti answered, "Wentworth but everyone calls him Reverend Teddy."

"Yes, that's the one," the President said. "David, is that all for real? That little girl was really cured based on the advice Planck gave them? Is that Participatory Physics or just prayer?"

David had been as surprised as anyone that his once reclusive friend was now a leading figure in the growth of a religious movement that tens of millions of people were joining. But David did not believe he should speak to what Planck was doing to the President. "I think you need to ask Planck that. Or Reverend Teddy."

The President nodded, "Yes....David, and thank you. I am going to have to think about all this. Rest assured I take this all very seriously - and I appreciate hearing your point of view. The United States will do what it must. We will lead our nation and the people of the world through this period. The future once we get to it will be so bright." The President stood up and David saw the meeting was over.

The President had Hank Scarpetti and General Greene remain behind after David had been escorted out. "General, you still don't agree with me about not trusting Plato, do you?"

If possible, Greene sat up even straighter in his chair, "No sir, I don't."

"And what about you, Hank?"

Scarpetti had kept his own counsel so far. He knew that the President would want him to agree with his view. Only he didn't agree, but he knew he could only go so far. "I think that it might be riskier to not trust Plato then to trust him. If Plato is right and acting as our friend, we really do have to destroy The Freya. If The Freya keeps doing what he accuses them of doing, our whole world could end up in flames before we ever get to that rosy future. On the other hand, if Plato is playing us as you suspect, we don't appear to lose much by attacking The Freya - we aren't getting anything from them. They are doing some exchanges of intellectual property so far, but to a pretty limited extent. It's not really clear why they are here."

The President shook his head, "I hear you Hank, but I just don't trust Plato. You know he is meeting on that damn island the most influential people in our country? They are flocking to him like he's some damn pied piper. And he's preaching an idyllic political creed that would have them far more involved in politics than they ever were before – like a Roman Senate of the rich and famous. And boy!... are they swallowing it all! It plays to their ego that they really do know what needs to be done. I've talked to a number of people who have gone to hear Plato – and you should see the look in their eyes. All of a sudden they think they are responsible for our government! Not me. The last thing we want is more involvement by business and social leaders. What do they know? It would be anarchy! They need to leave government to those of us here in Washington. We are the professionals! I'm the one the people elected. I know what's best."

The President looked to the two men for agreement. "General, what do you think? You've been on that island. You've spent time with Plato and seen these alleged leaders there."

Greene wasn't interested in voicing his private view. "I'm in the military. I don't have an opinion about political matters."

"Good for you, but Hank, you can't say that. What do you think?"

"I think I would rather have Plato as my friend than my enemy."

"And what about this Reverend Teddy? Do we need to pay attention to him?" the President asked.

"Absolutely!" Scarpetti answered immediately. "His followers are becoming true believers and it's a short step from religion to politics these days. And for some there's no difference at all."

"That's what I was thinking," responded the President as he ran his hand nervously through his dark hair. "And I don't think it bodes well for us – Reverend Teddy could create some real problems for us in the future."

# CHAPTER FOURTEEN

*"Those ages which seem most peaceful were least in search of peace. Those whose quest for it seems unending appear least able to achieve tranquility. Whenever peace – conceived as the avoidance of war – has been the primary objective ... the international system has been at the mercy of its most ruthless member."*

Dr. Henry Kissinger,
*former United States Secretary of State*

It had taken David longer to get the interview with the Captain of The Lucky Dragon than he had expected. But now that it was happening, David found himself excited to be doing it. Things were different. The Lucky Dragon was bigger than The Freya but smaller than The Bucephalus. Its furnishing was spare and less militaristic than that on The Freya and more artfully crafted. It seemed elegant and timeless. Rather than meeting in a lounge area, David had been led to a large conference room with a table and chairs made out of what looked like dark rosewood. The wall decorations signaled a dominant culture that David recognized: a culture foreign, ancient and familiar. The exquisitely mounted Katana and Wakizashi swords were ample evidence but the full suit of Samurai armor in the corner of the room left no doubt.

The man in the close fitting white tunic who had greeted David on the ground and brought him up to the ship saw David admiring the sword. "It dates back to the late 16th century. You could take it off the wall right now and easily cut off the head of an adversary. And that short sword there, the Wakizashi, has been used even in recent times by officers who failed in their mission and were permitted to perform seppuku."

David looked back at the man who had introduced himself as Lieutenant Uesugi Maeda. He was young, tall, with black straight hair and could walk any street in Tokyo and fit right in. "Should I assume the dominant culture on your Earth is Japanese based?" David asked.

"That is correct. From the research we have done since we arrived, it appears our worlds split apart at the time of the Battle of Sekigahara – that would be the year 1600. It was perhaps the most important battle in Japanese history. Over 160,000 warriors fought there that day. In your world that battle was won by the forces of Tokugawa Ieyasu. In our world the forces of Ishida Mitsunari were victorious and Ieyasu was slain on the battlefield."

From behind them a man who had just entered the conference room interrupted Maeda's account. David turned back to look at him. The man spoke in a strong confident voice. "We were very surprised and disheartened to learn how the victory here by Ieyasu would lead to such a weakened Japan. As shoguns he and his successors pacified the country to such an extent that they never expanded their territory over the next two centuries and then were too weak to withstand the growing power of the West in the early twentieth century. It is always enlightening to me to see how delicately balanced the flows of history are. A world is far more interdependent and susceptible to a change in the prevailing winds of chance than one would think possible.

"My home Earth is dominated by two great historical sets of foes: the Germans oppose the Russians and we Japanese oppose the Chinese. We and the Germans are allies as are the Russians and the Chinese. But we are the greatest among them. Our world speaks Japanese not German or Russian. And what a surprise it was to find your country, the United States is the most powerful here. In our world your continent has eight separate countries and none of them significant. They are like your Europe here."

"This is Captain Ukita Terumoto," Lieutenant Maeda said to David. As he had come to expect of all other Earthers, the Captain was tall and fit looking, but nonetheless broad shouldered and heavy framed. He was clean shaven with dark bushy eyebrows over dark eyes and his facial features were so dominant they could have been chiseled out of stone. Something about him suggested he could easily wield the katana in battle and few would stand up against him in individual combat.

David went to shake his hand and introduced himself, then said, "It must be quite a shock to see how different your country's history can be."

"On other Earths, Japan has been powerful, not always dominant but still worthy to join our empire. This Japan is different. Wars can be won or lost. Honor can be maintained in both circumstances. The situation here is unforgivable. Its loss in what you call World War II has led the Japanese leaders to bring ridicule to the Emperor and to accept demilitarization. Their very constitution prohibiting war is an embarrassment. They can barely defend themselves. They are dependent on your country to defend them against the rising power of China. There is no honor in that. This cannot be tolerated."

David saw in the Captain no attempt to be politically correct or to speak guardedly. Looking at the man, he was not surprised. The Captain stood ramrod straight and his uniform was starched and glaringly white. His eyes were deep set and intense and his mouth had yet to smile.

"Well, Captain let me start by thanking you for letting me come aboard and interview you. I have interviewed – "

"Yes I know. That is why I agreed to this. You have a reputation of not filtering or altering information. I do not wish my statements to be reduced or reconstructed. My words are my own. A Samurai does not dissemble or chatter like children on a playground."

"So let's start with that," David said. "You view yourself as a Samurai? Are your crew Samurai as well?"

The look on the captain's face bordered on contemptuous, but then softened. "Forgive me. You could not know. Yes, of course we are all Samurai. What else could we be?" he paused then and considered. "The Japan here is the exception. It has surrendered its heritage. On my world and the other worlds I know of, Japan is still an Empire led by shoguns. The Code of the Samurai is to us what your Constitution is to you."

David was puzzled, "Our Constitution is a political document not a moral code."

"All political organizations are but the shadows cast by moral codes. The stronger the moral code the less the political organization is required. The Samurai Code is self-enforcing and societally rigorous. A big and powerful government is an indication of a people with a weak moral structure."

"I'll have to think about that," said David. "But back to the point. Why are you here? What brings you to come from your Earth to ours?"

Captain Terumoto paused a moment before speaking. Then he spoke slowly so that his words would be reported correctly. "We are here because my government wishes to ally with all of the Japans throughout the universe. As you can see just by looking at us, we are a people apart. Our islands are precious to us. Our language and culture and writing are all original to us. What other country can say that? Perhaps only Egypt – and Egypt has been meaningless for millennia."

"There's China," David proposed.

"Here there is China, yes. But on other Earths, China is but our reflection, China is ours. Throughout its history, China was always invaded by others, led by others. China endures, it is true. It has its own beating heart. But it has no head of its own."

David felt he was close to something important about The Lucky Dragon and its Captain, "China is more dominant here. Some think China will soon surpass the United States in power and influence. Will that affect your mission here?"

Captain Terumoto didn't hesitate. "My mission is to restore pride and honor to this Japan. Then and only then can we invite it to join the Empire that exists throughout this universe and its many dimensions."

"Is that what you want me to write?"

"That was the purpose for inviting you here."

"I have heard that you have already met with Japan's Prime Minister. How are those discussions going?"

The Captain paused for a moment to frame his response. "We have much to learn about each other. These things cannot be rushed. Clearly there is dissension among the Japanese people and their leaders as to the proper path to take for their return to prominence. But I have confidence in the will of the people; they will not tolerate for much longer to remain a weakling in world affairs."

"So how will things change?" David asked.

"A country can only be as strong as the Code that it lives by. Where there is no code, there is no honor. Where there is no honor, there is no strength. A country without strength dissipates until it is just dust under the feet of future civilizations."

"I guess I don't understand. So what is it you are going to do here?"

"We are going to help this Japan recover its soul. We will restore the Code of the Samurai."

As he left on the shuttle provided by Captain Terumoto to return him to where he left his car, David leaned forward in his seat and held his forehead in the palms of his hands. He had come to The Lucky Dragon directly after his meeting in the White House and he was feeling mentally drained. He still wasn't sure how he had come to be where he was. He found himself in the front row center seat of a world in crisis and somehow he was supposed to explain things to the rest of the audience sitting in distant seats who weren't close enough to see and hear for themselves. Worse yet, increasingly he found himself crossing the boundary between audience and actors. He was starting to fear that he had a role to play.

Then he remembered all the nights he had dreams about being in a play and not knowing his lines. They weren't quite nightmares, yet he was always anxious to awake from them. He explained away those dreams as his subconscious getting even with him for all the years in school where he didn't study or do his homework. Years later his psyche still hadn't forgiven him.

He had other recurring dreams like being chased and having to run or being naked in a crowd of people; why he had those recurring dreams he still had no idea, though a psychologist friend of his said that everyone had them. But the dreams about not being prepared for a big test or being in a play or movie and not having learned the lines, those dreams he still had and they were really annoying. The other dreams he could wake up out of, but the dreams of being unprepared lasted long. Now he was awake, he was sure of it, but he was living that dream. He was not prepared for this role he was now playing. And it scared him.

*****

Hank Scarpetti looked over his glass of scotch at his friend General Carl Greene sitting across his kitchen table sipping his own drink. These late evening sessions were happening more often than ever before. They were on their second round and Hank still had not raised the real subject that he wanted to discuss with Greene. He had known he needed to talk to Greene ever since he had heard the intelligence briefing earlier that day. Greene was the only person in Washington who Hank could both trust with his real un-politicized thoughts and whose opinion would be worth listening to. Greene's security clearance was high enough and his information sources broad and deep enough that Hank didn't have to do much explaining or revealing. Greene already understood the mess the world was in.

Scarpetti decided to get to the point. It was too easy to just keep sitting there drinking great scotch while ignoring the crisis around them. "In today's briefing the CIA reported that there is a lot of chatter among the extreme Islamists that a high profile target in the U.S. is going to get hit soon. I know we have heard that kind of thing before. But the chatter we're hearing now has an additional continuing refrain – that one of the other Earths is part of the plot. That the weapon itself may come from off this world. We have even heard the name Hasan associated to it."

The general nodded, "I'm hearing that too. But we don't know the target or the details."

Scarpetti continued, "But a consistent theme in what we are picking up is that the flames are being fanned by stories of the glorious success of Islam on the other Earths. The result is that the drumbeat of jihad is pounding louder and faster. Iran keeps screaming about the destruction of Israel. When countries with nuclear weapons start screaming, you better take it seriously. Market bombings in Cairo, Baghdad and Kabul are happening so often now CNN doesn't bother mentioning them. Christian churches throughout the Middle East are starting to take security measures once reserved for foreign embassies. And the government of the United States is not doing anything. We have no plan, no foreign policy worth a damn."

General Greene looked over at his friend. One of the most powerful people on the planet was dispiritedly sipping at his drink and feeling like he couldn't do anything. Greene remembered talking once to a CEO friend of his whose Fortune 500 company was losing billions of dollars. The CEO said that when he sat at his desk he had phones and computers, secretaries and assistants and vice presidents, all there to put his every decision and order into effect. And he wondered why nothing good ever seemed to happen. Then the CEO said that one day he tried to leave the office for a minute and he discovered that he was actually in a giant bubble and nothing he said or did ever reached outside of the bubble. The phones and computers weren't connected to anything. The secretaries and assistants were actors on a staged set. The CEO realized he was in an episode of The Twilight Zone.

It had taken Greene a little while through the CEO's comments to realize his friend was sort of joking. But he also realized that the CEO was serious too. It was easier to believe that it all was an episode from the Twilight Zone then that the company he had built and loved could be doing so badly. And now Scarpetti probably wished he was in a Twilight Zone episode too. The world couldn't really be in the huge mess it seemed to be in, could it?

"I presume the President is not yet ready to change his position on doing something about Captain Ragnar and The Freya?" the general asked.

"No, he's not. He thinks Plato is the problem."

"That's nonsense. Plato is our best hope....I think the problem is that Plato doesn't have much confidence in the ability of our government, or any government for that matter, to actually deal with the situation. One way or another, I've spent a lot of time talking to Plato. One thing I've learned from him is that he always tries to simplify things. He doesn't believe you can untangle complicated webs. You just have to cut through them."

The general paused to remember what Plato had said. "He likes the story of Alexander the Great and the Gordian knot. Supposedly there was a prophesy that whoever could untie this hugely complicated knotted rope would become the ruler of Asia.

Alexander took out his sword and cut the knot off. That solved the problem. That's the way Plato thinks things need to be done."

Scarpetti nodded, "If you see a snake, you cut its head off. Plato says that Captain Ragnar is the snake. So we have to cut its head off. I suspect he also thinks if you can't tell the difference between your friend and a snake, then that's a whole other problem."

General Greene sat there in the quiet of Scarpetti's kitchen with a bone deep hunger to take action. As a soldier he wanted to fight something. With every terrorist event where Americans died, he felt more and more a need to strike back. "So, Hank, what are we going to do? We can't just do nothing! If The Freya really is helping some terrorists to blow up something here, then we are in really big trouble. We saw what happened to our embassy in Tel Aviv. And we had no clue that was going to happen. Imagine shooting a missile like that one at The White House or the Empire State building – or worse, one of the new towers standing on the site of the World Trade Center. If The Freya is helping, I don't know that we could stop it."

Scarpetti's glum expression told the story, "I know. I know. I'll keep working on the President. But I don't know what advice he'll listen to."

"Tell him to listen to Plato."

"He doesn't like that Plato acts like he knows more than he does."

"Plato does know more than he does."

"Yea, that's the problem."

*****

In his small office on The Freya Captain Ragnar looked over at the man even he was starting to call Hasan. Hasan/Erickson had just confirmed that Khalil wanted to strike at the Americans soon. Now Ragnar had to make a big decision. Should he give all the help this man Khalil would need to strike hard. In truth for what was required, Khalil could at best just be the man who aimed and pulled the trigger on the weapon. The weapon itself and overcoming the transportation obstacles would all require the assistance of The Freya. That assistance would be very active and direct.

If the role of The Freya was discovered, the United States would have no choice but to attack his ship. He might be able to evade the attack initially but he would be forced to leave this Earth immediately. Still if that was all that was lost, the reward would be worth that risk. There were other Earths that he could target. Still this one was so ripe for his plans.

He knew he would only get one opportunity to strike the cataclysmic blow that would ignite the disintegration process. The old adage, "when you strike at a king, make sure you kill him" was to be remembered. His target was not a paper tiger; just a divided and weakly led and confused one. But a tiger nonetheless.

His instincts told him he needed to be more cautious. He was getting ahead of himself. He needed to be more patient. Much as he wanted Khalil to go forward with the attack on American soil, he wasn't certain the blow Khalil planned would be enough. There still needed to be more de-stabilizing events. For what he wanted, a nuclear bomb exploding over Washington or New York City would probably be required. That would take longer to arrange.

But he would find a way to help Khalil. It would be an important link in the chain of events he foresaw. Then it occurred to him how it should be done. He could take advantage of the uncertainty that existed as to which of the Other Earths could be trusted. He needed to help Khalil destroy his target but make it look like Plato and the crew of The Bucephalus were behind it. Ragnar smiled; that plan would accomplish several goals at once!

He turned his attention back to Erickson who had been sitting still while his Captain thought through the plan. "So here is what I want you to do," Ragnar said and proceeded to tell him.

*****

Plato listened to David as he described his meeting with President Morningstar. It did not surprise him that the American President was not going to take any action against The Freya – or anyone else. Plato was not even surprised that the President continued to distrust him. Plato's version of the unfolding of the future did not match with what the President wanted it to be. Plato knew too well that the challenge of leadership was in dealing with unpleasant realities. Leadership would be so much easier if the future would only behave.

Plato was not unsympathetic to this President. His successors had squandered the resources and the warrior spirit of the United States on wars in Iraq and Afghanistan that could not be won given the political and cultural environments there. The goal of punishing terrorism and eliminating destabilizing despots had morphed into nation building – an impossibility where no underlying nation existed, just disparate religious sexts banded together by accidents of geography.

Yet past geopolitical mistakes could not excuse geopolitical weakness in the present. The costs to be paid in the future would be too great. The engulfing fires of terrorism unchecked would keep burning until the planet itself was consumed. Plato had seen that happen before.

David looked around the room where they were meeting. Out the sliding glass doors of the ground level room he could see the beach and then the Caribbean Sea. A steady rain cast a gloom over the island and kept everyone indoors or back on The Bucephalus. "So what do we do next?" he asked Plato.

"I'm not sure that I know," Plato replied. "If you wait and do nothing, the acts of terror will increase – and there will be a strike at a major target inside the U.S. As devastating as that will be, maybe it will be what is required to channel the energies and resources of your country to attack the central problems."

"But even if that is the case, I don't know that we would know who to attack." David interrupted. "The Freya may be the enabler and we could go after it, but the underlying problems would remain. And if we suffer another tragedy like losing the World Trade Center towers, I don't know that our people will feel sufficiently revenged just by destroying The Freya – even assuming we can."

"I understand that."

"So I think we have to do something." David looked down at his fist pounding the table in surprise. He wasn't one who normally pounded tables.

"Which 'we' is that?"

David just shook his head, knowing he was out of his depth. "I don't know. I wish it would be the government. But if it is not them, then us, I guess. If I have to do something to stop what is happening, I will. I know that The Freya and Captain Ragnar are stirring things up. And I know the embassy in Tel Aviv was destroyed with their help. The weapon used there came from them. So now we think that some minor terrorist with their help could attack and kill Americans in Washington or New York. If I can help stop that, then I have to try."

Plato looked at David both fondly and with respect. Over the months he had dealt with him he had watched David take more and more responsibility. But these were dangerous times and he hoped he could help David stay safe. David was treading close to what could become a killing zone.

David was right. A major strike now against the Americans could only make the world more unstable. It would encourage other countries like Iran to be more aggressive against Israel and it would encourage al-Qaeda and other terrorist groups to increase their efforts. They would sense victory coming close. The path to a nuclear attack would be easier. Plato had seen it happen.

Every generation of global leaders had to learn their own lessons about the use of power. Somehow they thought the lessons of history would not apply to them. They assumed that because they were rational and caring and well intentioned, that everyone else would be too. Yet every century for thousands of years had its share of major wars. The only way to maintain geopolitical balance was to match will with will, force with force. The ruthless and aggressive nations and peoples needed to know for certain that their every attack would be met by greater force and will. They could not be allowed to win even small battles.

Plato looked to David, "I'm afraid you are right. We have to stop an attack facilitated by The Freya. If that succeeds, the U.S. will be weakened and the forces that fill the void will make the world much more dangerous."

"So how vulnerable is The Freya? Does it have the technology to make missiles disappear like you did?... How did you do that anyway?" David realized he had never asked Plato that before.

Plato smiled. "I was actually quite pleased when those missiles were shot at us. It allowed me to show our capability while still being peaceful. Those missiles were redirected to a dimension of space where they could do no harm. As to The Freya...I do not know for sure but I think missiles would not work against them. Though missiles might chase them away. They can be destroyed, if they stayed, by a coordinated attack."

"I guess that is helpful to know," David responded. "Only there is no one to mount one. The Freya is being allowed to create havoc and destruction and no one stands against them."

*****

Captain Ukita Terumoto went to the head of the conference table and took his seat. Four of his officers were sitting there already awaiting his arrival which was as always precisely on time. He felt energized from the exercise session he had just finished. He had just engaged the fitness master in a spirited sword fight with the wooden katana practice weapons. He had been bested but had pushed his old teacher to use his most advanced moves. Throughout the fight, even during the most energetic attacks, Terumoto had maintained his inner calm. He had been drilled to match the yin of mental stillness with the yang of aggressive physical movement. Now as he faced his officers, he wanted to bring that same balance to the challenge they faced in restoring this Japan to its rightful honor.

"Kagekatsu, how are you progressing on your task to repeal the obnoxious anti-war provisions of the Japanese Constitution? Until that is changed, all our efforts will be for naught." The Captain asked his chief political officer.

"Indeed sir. I believe that momentum is building both within the government and among the people to repeal those provisions. As you had predicted, the destruction of the Koreas by nuclear weapons has strengthened our case – it showed everyone that there is no hiding from nuclear weapons. Only by matching strength against strength can Japan survive into the next century. It is plain that its army can never match the million man army of China, so it must use advanced weapons to fight off any invasion.

"Also, the Prime Minister is convinced that Japan cannot rely on some nuclear umbrella provided by the Americans. Should China rush onto the beaches of Japan's islands, there is no one in the government who is certain that the Americans will commit their soldiers to defend Japan's shores."

The Captain nodded his approval. "It amazes me that Japan could have waited so long to start standing on its own feet. For them to think that America would fight China to save Japan is ludicrous. And to think that China would hesitate a moment to attack Japan once it has risen to its full power is to ignore centuries of animosity between China and Japan. Two alpha male tigers do not sleep quietly next to each other."

The Captain looked at his other senior officers. "Yamoto, how are you proceeding with weaponry technology?"

"I have been in contact, secretly of course, with key members of the military – the one's most embarrassed at their country's pacification. As you know, Japan has all the technology know-how and the industrial base to quickly develop nuclear weapons and delivery systems. I am showing them how to both speed up the process and how to increase the destructive power of the bombs. The power of the military can be increased substantially almost immediately if the will is there."

"That is a great point, Yamoto," the Captain responded. "The will must be there. We all should surreptitiously work at reaffirming Japan's samurai heritage. I cannot stress enough how important that is. For centuries Japan had been ruled by warriors. Clan fought clan for primacy and losers were exiled and killed. We were strong because life depended on it. But also because it was part of our culture – how we defined ourselves. We must return this Japan to that which is in fact their natural way of being."

Yamoto signaled that he had a point to make. "Captain, I think you will be pleased to know of the very positive though only whispered excitement that the bombing of the Great Hall of the People in Tiananmen Square has produced among the next generation of military and industrial leaders in Tokyo. They know that it was a blow by Japan against some insult by China, but they do not know how they know that. Everywhere in quiet conversations they wonder who among them is responsible. They grapple with the ambiguity of the graffiti statement on the wall, 'A typhoon's wind blows in both directions'. It is now grown to mythic proportions. Some believe it to be true while others doubt it –but all discuss it. All wonder of its significance. Yet they smile when contemplating it."

"Good. Thank you Yamoto, it is important to remember the power of icons. Now, Munenori, tell me about the monasteries. Are the Zen Masters promoting mentalization among their students and monks?"

Munenori was the oldest among the senior leaders and unlike the others he was more thoughtful and dispassionate. The Captain had given him the task of gaining the trust of the monks who practiced meditation. Then once trusted, he was to lead them to take responsibility for Japan's use of mentalization to strengthen Japan.

Munenori maintained his quiet demeanor even as he was eager to update his captain. The history of warrior monks in earlier ages had made his task easier than expected. The monks were eager to use their long years of training in meditation to accomplish what they considered magical transformations. And they too were eager to embrace a return of Japan's might and influence in Asia.

"Captain, on this we are ahead of schedule. And as with our other efforts, we are acting in the shadows of government. I have handpicked certain monasteries for special attention and their powers are already a force to be reckoned with. Their elders are particularly honored in this. Their years of training in meditation has prepared and strengthened their minds like no others. For a group who were so proud of their bare minimum living conditions, they are strangely exuberant in turning common metals into gold. They take delight in managing weather conditions. They move boulders about as if they were Hercules."

"And are they willing to be active in restoring the honor and traditions of their homeland? Or have their years in the monasteries made them passive and weak?"

Munenori did not respond immediately; the Captain had voiced his greatest concern. "Sir, it would be a mistake to think that they will all act of one accord. Some will hold back - either from temerity or as a natural result of their disciplines. But many will rise to our banners. They will take pride in serving their country. It will be up to us to identify who should take the lead among them. I am certain of this - they will provide surprising mental power to our cause."

"Well done! Yours is the most important of our work. Restoring Japan's honor and destiny is impossible without controlling the territory of the mind. With such warriors, we will have no fear of losing in the war that will inevitably come. China will discover to its peril that what they see as a weak and timorous dog called Japan is really a lion waking up out of a bad dream."

# CHAPTER FIFTEEN

*"To be, or not to be: that is the question:*
*Whether 'tis nobler in the mind to suffer*
*The slings and arrows of outrageous fortune,*
*Or to take arms against a sea of troubles,*
*And by opposing, end them?..."*

William Shakespeare
*Hamlet*_Act III

Sitting at the outdoor table of the Beirut café while waiting for Hasan to appear, Khalil thought about America. He knew it well, he believed. He had never been there but he had seen movies and TV shows and his English was good enough to understand what was happening on screen. His favorites were the action movies that featured heroes like Ironman and Batman and even though he cheered for them to beat their evil foes he liked seeing all the destruction of the cities in the climactic scenes. And he liked seeing all the beautiful women in their sexy clothes. Truly America was the devil's playground.

He liked thinking of himself as a powerful warrior of Allah. Pure and devout when no action was required, but indomitable when heeding the call to do Allah's will. Had he not single-handedly knocked down the fortress that had been the American Embassy in Tel Aviv? And now was he not preparing an even greater blow against the most powerful infidel? He was the real Ironman.

In truth, he realized, he didn't understand why the great Allah would allow for Americans to be so rich while His people were so poor. The Saudi princes were fabulously rich but they were just a few and they were not true to their faith. They left their homeland on their private jets with their bejeweled whores to play and gamble in places like Monte Carlo and Las Vegas. They thought that warriors like him did not know of this but he was not such a fool! Their punishment would come too! Why would Allah allow the Saudi princes to so flaunt their wealth? It was very confusing to him. And now he was hearing that these strange Other Earths were giving even ordinary people strange powers to manipulate things with their minds. Some said that even oil would become so plentiful that everything would change in the Middle East. Khalil wondered if that meant the Americans would go away and leave the people of the desert to return to their deserts the way it was before oil became important. Khalil wasn't so sure that would be such a good thing – even though he and his friends all prayed for America to leave their lands.

He hated America, he reminded himself. It was godless and evil and it was the Americans' fault that his brother and father were killed in the streets and that he had no wife or sons. As he sat there, Khalil wondered what it would be like to go home to a family, his family, every night. How would it be if his father and brother had never died – if they could all be together? What would it be like to have a wife who made his meals and shared his bed? A wife who would always respect him and follow his lead – do as he instructed? He blamed America. It was America's fault that he had no family.

Hasan quietly took the seat opposite Khalil at the small table. "So, my friend, how are things?" Khalil looked up surprised. Hasan always moved as if he was more shadow than person.

"I am well but I am impatient. I hunger to strike another blow against the Americans." Khalil regarded Hasan. He had planned to say those words to show his intention and resolve. He hoped it would encourage Hasan to move forward both quickly and boldly.

"I am glad to hear that, for we too are eager to move forward. However, we are concerned about your ability to be effective in what you plan. We cannot afford for there to be mistakes or for things to go wrong because of things you do not anticipate."

Khalil could not believe what he was hearing, how could they doubt him? "Did I not perform precisely as planned against the embassy? Why would you doubt me?"

Hasan held up his open palms to Khalil. "Do not feel so concerned. We are only trying to ensure that things do not go wrong because of your lack of familiarity with the people and customs in the United States. You have never been there, correct?"

"Does that matter? You said before that you can put me into the city there without detection. Once there, a city is a city. My English is not so bad. I can take a taxi as well there as here. In Washington D.C. they are used to foreigners. I will not stand out."

"Perhaps that is so," responded Hasan. "But great endeavors such as this should never trust that events will transpire as planned. One must always provide for surprises."

Khalil saw now that his mission was not going to be cancelled. Relief flooded through him, yet he knew Hasan had something else in mind. "So how should I prepare for such surprises? What would you have me do? I will do whatever it takes."

"Khalil that is why I like you! You see already that we are on the same side. Yes, you are right, we do want to alter the plan – but in a way I think you will like. You see my boss, the Captain of our ship, thinks that the action you will take is very important to our cause. It is so important that he insists on being personally involved. In fact he wants to accompany you when you go into Washington. He is very familiar with that city and if he is with you, the success of your mission will be assured."

Khalil was now concerned again. He wanted no confusion this time over his central role in striking this titanic blow against America. This would be to his glory not someone else's. "So then it would be your Captain who would lead this? What need would there be for me? But this is my dream not his."

Hasan knew Khalil well enough to know what Khalil's worry was. "We do not doubt you on this. This will be your accomplishment. The Captain will not want any credit. He just wants to be sure it goes as planned. It will be you holding the weapon – you pulling the trigger."

Khalil was still concerned; he wanted no repeat of the embassy bombing where his peers doubted his central role. "So can I meet your Captain? I would like to hear from him that this will still be my mission. When can I meet him?"

Hasan smiled back at Khalil, "Why you can meet him right now. Here he is."

A very tall fair skinned man wearing a baseball cap and a large pair of sunglasses took one of the two remaining seats at the small table. "Hello Khalil," he said. "Just call me Captain, if you like."

Khalil looked at the man closely. His face seemed to look familiar, but with the hat and sunglasses, he couldn't quite place him. But one thing was clear and it was a surprise. "You are not an Arab! Hasan, I thought you came from a world where Muslims ruled. Yet your Captain –"

Hasan interrupted, "My Captain is obviously not an Arab – he is a Muslim."

Khalil looked again at the man who had just sat down with him. "Yes, Khalil," the man said and as he did so, he took off his sunglasses so as to better look at Khalil eye to eye. "I am a devout Muslim."

Then Khalil knew the man he was looking at, "You are the one they call Plato – are you not?"

The man quickly put the sunglasses back on, "Please, do not call me that here!"

"But I have read about you," Khalil said. "I never read you were Muslim."

"There are many things you have not read about me – but surely you know that to succeed one cannot tell all of one's secrets. Isn't it enough that we are all believers in Allah and are dedicated to his cause? Will you distrust me because of my skin color? On my Earth Islam has taken over all of Europe. Islam is not just for the Arab in the desert. Are there not Muslims here who are not Arabs?"

"Yes, of course. But still it takes getting used to seeing you here," replied

Khalil.

"Do not be concerned," said the crewmember from The Freya who had had his appearance altered to closely resemble Plato. "I will help you in your great service to Allah! We together will strike such a blow against Satan's lackeys. The Americans will fall from their high mountain of pride and arrogance. You Khalil will be a hero to your people. Your praises will be sung."

Khalil could not quite believe his good fortune. This was better than he had hoped! "And will we do this soon?" he asked.

The false Plato nodded, "Yes, very soon. Very soon you will fire the missile that will destroy the mighty dome of The Capitol which rises so haughtily above the skyline of Washington. Your missile will send to Hell the leaders of America's government! And by killing their leaders we will cripple their country. They will pull their soldiers back home and hide under their beds like children afraid of the night. Have no doubts, Khalil! It will happen! You will see the crumbling of the dome and the engulfing flames with your own eyes."

*****

Hand in hand Gabriela and David walked down the beach of Pirate's Cay as the sun kissed against the horizon. They had found that walking together along the beach following a long meditation session was a perfect way to re-open their minds to the breadth of existence while stretching their legs as well. They had spent time meditating every day for the past two months, whether they were on the island or back home at their apartment in New York. Part of each session was focused on mentalization and they both were beginning to show progress. Planck had promised to build them each their own amplifier as soon as they were ready.

*****

They had been walking in silence for a while, each enjoying the gentle breeze and the squish of the wet sand beneath their bare feet. David also enjoyed just looking at Gabriela with her olive-tinged Bahama tanned skin contrasting her short white shorts and pink halter top barely covering her slim and lanky form. She might not be the most brilliant physicist – though she could hold her own -- but she was definitely the best looking one he had ever seen. Though he should probably tell her that more often, he realized. But he didn't seem to have the time. And as he walked he realized how lame that was. And then he started thinking about the times they were in. And the now-ness of walking hand in hand on a beautiful beach with the beautiful woman he was going to marry started sliding away from him.

David's mind had lost its meditation induced calm and now anxiously gnawed at his consciousness with the fears associated with the scary present. "You know," he said, breaking the silence, "the part I struggle with is the idea the future could be so great with the benefits of Participatory Physics but to get there we have to entrust an immature and hate-ridden world with powers of frightful magnitude. How do we survive the short term to get to the long term?"

Gabriela squeezed his hand, "I know coming from me, this will surprise you, but I think you just have to believe we will. I guess that is what we have to put out to the universe. You have to have faith."

"Faith?"

"Yes faith. Believe David! You have to believe."

"That's strange talk coming from a physicist," David responded.

Gabriela stopped their walking to turn toward him. She looked at him with a gentle smile flickering on her face. "I'm a physicist who has now learned that the universe is founded on consciousness. Physicists have actually known that that elephant has been hiding in the kitchen for quite a while, but we didn't like the implications and couldn't do any math that supported it. So we ignored it. I did too. But now I know it is true and I wouldn't be much of a physicist if I wasn't willing to go where our data and experience takes us. So consciousness matters. The mind matters. So belief matters."

David thought it through as he stared out over the turquoise waters. "So if I fear the catastrophe, I am helping to bring it on. I have to believe we will survive this?"

"Yes, but it wouldn't hurt for us to do everything we can to beat back the terrorism and whatever it is that The Freya is up to."

"Good point. But don't forget about The Lucky Dragon. Trust me, those guys are really scary! They make Captain Ragnar look no worse than a street punk in a bad neighborhood."

When David and Gabriela finished their walk, they returned to the main building and saw Plato sitting at an umbrella covered table near the pool with Catherine Ozawa. Plato waved David and Gabriela over to join them and they took the two remaining seats – Gabriela took the one not shaded and David was happy with the one remaining seat still under cover of the umbrella.

"There are things that must be done soon," Plato said immediately. "Events are moving faster than I thought they would."

"What is it that we have to deal with?" David asked.

"Another terrorist attack facilitated by Captain Ragnar – which I think will be a major strike within the United States." Plato responded.

"How do we know this?" asked Gabriela.

Plato looked at them with a gleam in his eye that made him look more fierce than his usual wise and calm demeanor. "There is good and bad to this. The bad is that I believe The Freya is again working with the terrorist who blew up the American Embassy in Tel Aviv with a weapon put in his hands by The Freya. And judging The Freya from past experience, I think they are seeking a more dramatic and destabilizing strike than the one against the Embassy."

Gabriela's eyes widened at the thought, "That was horrible enough!"

"Yes, but the next will be worse."

"So what's the good part?" David asked.

"The good part is that they are going to try and blame it on me!" Plato said with a smile belonging to a cat that just ate the goldfish.

David and Gabriela looked at each other in confusion. Catherine Ozawa asked the question they each had in their mind. "And why is that a good thing, Plato?"

Still smiling, Plato answered, "I have told you that I am severely limited in the degree that I can become involved in activities on this world. The limitations imposed on me by my homeworld are not absolute or without qualification. One of the enabling exceptions to the prohibitions applies to circumstances when as a result of actions taken by other parties, my role as advisor is compromised and it is made to appear that I am actively engaged in support of a particular faction. When my reputation or character is under attack, I can take such actions as are necessary to protect myself and ensure that such actions by others do not continue."

David shook his head as if to bring his gaze into focus. "And that means what?"

"It means that since Captain Ragnar is trying to make it look like I am in support of these terrorist actions, I can take whatever actions are necessary to prevent him from succeeding."

"And who decides what the limits are to your actions?" Ozawa asked.

"Why I do, of course," Plato replied.

David felt more relieved than he had in weeks. "So this means you can help us stop whatever The Freya is trying to do? Is that right?"

"Yes, that is correct. I can do whatever I deem necessary to stop them - including taking such action as will be quite permanent in effect. I still have limitations as to the extent of my actions here, but they are far looser now."

Ozawa, David and Gabriela exchanged looks as each considered the possible meaning of the word 'permanent' as Plato had just used it. No one said anything. After moments had passed, Gabriela asked, "One thing I don't understand, how do you know, Plato, that Captain Ragnar is planning to blame a terrorist action in the U.S. on you?"

Plato leaned back in his chair so that he could turn his attention onto all three of them. "Well, remember that I told you that my home Earth's technology is quite ahead of yours because our civilization traces back to a continuous development from the glory days of ancient Greece without the thousand years of knowledge atrophy you call the Middle Ages here?"

David nodded, "You said that your technology is like 200 years ahead of ours."

"Approximately, yes. And though Captain Ragnar is not aware of it, we are just about as far ahead of him."

"So what does that mean for us?" Ozawa asked.

"It means that I can keep track of things that go on here – on this planet -- at a level that would probably amaze you. For instance, our surveillance capability of the six billion people on this planet is almost 100%. We can focus our cameras on anyone and everyone at any time and follow them wherever they may go.

We can access any data recording, any digitized surveillance video of anyone or anyplace. In other words, if one of our cameras sees something – and we have a lot of cameras – or anyone else's cameras see something, we will have it stored in our data libraries."

David had to think about the amount of raw data that meant was stored somewhere and mentally gulped. But then his doubtful mind was triggered. "But that isn't much use is it really? Because it's just raw data."

Plato shook his head, "David, to get that raw data, isn't much of an accomplishment. Even your Earth is only a few years away from being able to do that. As I said, our technology is considerably more advanced than yours and our data storage is literally managed in a different dimension. No it is not just raw data. We can access the data in a myriad of ways. I can call up instantly a video stream of everything you have done when you were either outside or being reviewed by any security camera anywhere since The Bucephalus arrived. And I can do that on anyone of the other six billion people here."

David's smile was one of wonder not disbelief. "Really, you can call up anything?"

Plato returned David's smile. 'Shall I give an example? You and Gabriela were just before walking on the beach, correct?" David nodded.

"Then see for yourself." In that moment there appeared a hologram right beside the table they were sitting at. In the hologram were David and Gabriela walking along the beach holding hands, wearing what they now were wearing. Then Plato said out loud, "Show all the times on a fast forward basis Gabriela and David walked along the beach." Now the hologram raced through a number of such walks – including one walk where David and Gabriela were passionately connecting on what they thought was an unobserved deserted beach. When Plato noticed that particular hologram, he shut it down.

"Wow!" David responded. "And you can do that to basically everyone in the world?"

"Yes," replied Plato.

"OK," Gabriela persisted. "So how do you know about Ragnar's plans?"

Plato's look turned serious. "We have tracked every one of his team every time they left The Freya. Neither he nor any of his men have gone anywhere or met with anyone we are not aware of. So it was quite the surprise to see the man he refers to as Hasan when on this Earth meet with the individual who we determined was the one who shot a Freya missile at the Tel Aviv embassy and then see someone who very much looked like me show up at the table in Beirut."

"So let me get this straight," David said. "Because you saw someone who appeared to be you with one of The Freya's men meet with a known terrorist, you determined they are going to frame you – which now enables you to help us, if you so choose."

"Correct," said Plato.

David continued, "If that had not happened you would not be now telling us about this awesome surveillance capability and you would not help us stop The Freya from doing whatever it is they are planning. Am I right?"

"Yes again."

"So what are they planning to do?" Gabriela asked when David took a moment to think it all through.

Plato looked back at them expressionlessly and said, "They are going to try to blow up The Capitol in Washington."

"Oh shit!" said David. "Well somebody has to stop them! You can stop them right, Plato?"

"Yes someone has to stop them – but not me. The action needs to be done by someone from this Earth"

"And why is that, Plato?" Ozawa asked.

"If I do it, what is learned?"

*****

David arranged to meet with General Greene the next day. Immediately after talking to Plato on Pirate's Cay he had called the General saying that he had something urgent to tell him. When pressed David said it dealt with a major terrorist strike within the United States. They set up a late afternoon meeting and the general arranged for transportation for David from the island to Washington D.C. General Greene had him met at a designated Pentagon entrance and ushered through the vast complex until

David found himself at Greene's office where Hank Scarpetti was also waiting for him.

The general was in his dress uniform but his jacket was off. Hank Scarpetti was wearing a blue pinstriped suit with a blue and white striped shirt and a red and blue striped tie. Too many stripes, David thought. And even though the suit was expensive, Scarpetti could have used a better tailor. Like Scarpetti himself, it looked tired and stressed.

They said their hellos and Greene explained that he had invited Scarpetti to the meeting because it was probably best to save time. That was fine with David. Greene returned to sit behind his uncluttered desk and Scarpetti and David took the seats across from him.

"So what about this terrorist attack? What can you tell us?" Greene asked David.

The general and Scarpetti listened carefully as David repeated the basics of his conversation the day before with Plato. They asked questions just to clarify what David had said. Both asked about the extent of Plato's surveillance capability and considered what that meant about the technology requirements to do what Plato said they could do. When asked about data mining and manipulation technology operating out of another dimension the best David could answer was a guess about quantum computing which theoretical physicists had speculated about.

Then David explained about the meeting in Beirut with the terrorists identified as Hasan and Khalil and how they were joined by someone who looked like Plato. And then David said how that freed Plato up to help more aggressively. Scarpetti and Greene asked a lot of questions about that too. Finally, David finished the way Plato had – by saying that Plato believed the target was going to be The Capitol, specifically to blow up the dome of The Capitol.

"God help us!" Scarpetti responded, his face whitening.

"When is this supposed to happen?" General Greene asked.

"Plato doesn't know – only that it will be soon."

"And how does Plato know what the target will be?"

David shook his head, "I don't know for sure. I suspect that their surveillance capability could include listening technology if it happens in real time. Plato never tells all his secrets."

"So is he going to stop it from happening?" Scarpetti asked.

David shook his head again, "No. He'll help us but he said we have to actually take the action to save ourselves. He said otherwise we don't learn anything."

Greene turned to look from David to Scarpetti, "Is this enough to change the President's mind? Do you think he'll let us go after The Freya?"

Scarpetti looked away from the general and ignored the question. Instead he asked, "David, did you see the video of the meeting with Hasan, Khalil and the false Plato?"

"No, I didn't see it. Plato told me about it. But I'm sure it exists."

Scarpetti just shook his head slowly while looking at General Greene. Then he said, "I guess if Plato says it exists, one way or another it will exist. My problem is, now even if we through our antiquated surveillance methods find that such a meeting did exist – and if we even observed that someone looking like Plato was there, now Plato is telling us, it wasn't him. So now, not only is Plato telling us again that we have to trust him and that Captain Ragnar is the villain, but we shouldn't even believe our own eyes if we were to see these terrorists with Plato. That's pretty much it, isn't it, David?"

David just stared back at Scarpetti knowing there was nothing he could say. Finally he conceded, "Yea, that's about right."

Scarpetti turned back to face General Greene, "What do I do with this, Carl? I can't go to the President with this."

Greene looked back at Scarpetti and then turned to regard David, "Hold on Hank, let me ask a couple of questions. "David, assume for the moment that everything that Plato is telling you is the truth and that The Freya is going to help this terrorist to blow up the Capitol. What kind of help could they give? Obviously they could give them the same weapon that blew up our Tel Aviv embassy. But how would they get the terrorist and the weapon into the US?"

David realized then that the general was probably on his side on this. "Plato and I talked about this. And unfortunately the answer is that getting the terrorist and the weapon into the country is pretty simple....You know that I have twice already interviewed Captain Ragnar?"

Greene nodded.

"And do you know that I conducted the interview on The Freya?"

Greene nodded again, "Yes...I guess I knew that."

"Well, did you ever wonder how I got on The Freya?"

Greene looked back at Scarpetti and neither man liked what all of a sudden they were thinking. "No, but I guess I should have," the general said.

"They picked me up with their shuttle. They had me drive to an open field where a small shuttle craft came and picked me up. And that's where they dropped me off later. Do you remember General, when you first met Plato on Pirate's Cay and he showed you what his shuttle could do?"

Greene nodded.

"Well, it was like that. And think about it, have you ever heard anything from the FAA or the Air Force or anyone else about all the shuttle flights that have taken place in the last few months? I know you haven't because I checked. Near as I can tell both Plato's shuttles and The Freya shuttles do not show up on any of our radar or other sensing devices. Even when you look at them, they are hard to see. If they don't want you to see or detect them, you won't."

Greene turned to Scarpetti, "This is bad Hank, real bad." Then he focused on David again, "So The Freya could pick up the terrorists anywhere in the Middle East, fly them in The Freya – or maybe even a shuttle – who knows what their range is – and drop them off somewhere in the DC area with the weapon. The terrorists shoot the missile at The Capitol, the shuttle picks them up somewhere previously designated and flies them back to wherever they picked them up....and while this shuttle is flying over our heads, we won't even be able to see it. That's right, isn't it?"

"Yes, General, I think that is exactly right," said David.

"Hank, how are we supposed to stop something like that?" the general asked his friend.

Scarpetti's eyes traveled all around the room searching for an answer and finding none. No one said anything. Greene unconsciously was staring up and to his right hoping for something to occur to him. David just stared at the two men. Finally Scarpetti said what all three were thinking, "If we do nothing and Plato is telling us the truth, then sometime soon someone is going to blow up The Capitol and probably kill half of our legislative branch or worse."

General Greene found he could no longer sit still. He rose out of his chair and walked around his desk to stand in front of Scarpetti. "Or we can choose to believe Plato and with whatever help he can give us, we fight and keep that disaster from happening – or at least we god damn well tried!"

Scarpetti stood up too. "Then what?" he almost shouted. "Just because some alien – and I don't care what his DNA says he is – he is an alien. Because he says we should attack another alien – we go and do it? Just because he says so? With no evidence at all!"

Greene didn't back up an inch. "We have evidence! We have Americans dying all over the planet. We have our embassy destroyed with hundreds of our best dead and more injured. We are bordering on chaos and our citizens all over the country are scared and looking to us for leadership – and we are doing nothing! Nothing!"

Scarpetti's face was red and his hands were balled into fists. "How do we know Plato isn't behind all of that? He could be playing us! Don't you see that? What do I tell the President? We should trust David here? What the hell does he know? He's a damn writer – nobody elected him to anything. Maybe the President's instincts on this are right! You ever think about that?"

General Carl Greene then calmed himself down. Now was not the time to lose control. But now was not the time to back off and play politics either. He walked away from Scarpetti to reduce the physical aggression. Then he said, "Hank, the President is over his head here. He can't wait for some kind of divine sign as to what to do. It is what battlefield generals have to learn: in the chaotic cloud of battle you have to use your best judgment and do what needs to be done. There is no certainty. But there is no doing nothing either!

"He knows that if he goes along with believing in Plato, he has to take action – he has to initiate that action, not just wait for somebody to do something that is incontrovertible. And I think he is afraid to do the wrong thing. So it paralyzes him and he thinks he should just wait. He wants to wait and see. I wish we could, but we can't. We don't live in that world anymore. We have to hit first and hit hard or really bad things will happen."

Scarpetti too tried to calm down. He hadn't lost his sense of control like that in years and years. Looking at his friend, he saw the combat general that Carl Greene once had been. He saw the general who had won a Silver Star for heroism. He saw a man ready and even eager to fight.

"Carl, I'll go to the President with all this," Scarpetti said. "But frankly, I don't think he'll change his mind. Honestly, I'm not going to try to change his mind. I don't agree that we have to act when we don't even really know who the bad guy is. We just don't know."

David had listened to it all. He desperately wanted the general to succeed in his argument with Scarpetti. But it was clear that he had lost. David felt like he had just been punched in the stomach by the Heavyweight Champion of the world.

# Chapter Sixteen

*"Victorious warriors win first and then go to war, while defeated warriors go to war first and then seek to win."*

Sun Tzu
*The Art of War*

Captain Terumoto looked across the conference room table in The Lucky Dragon at the leader of Japan's New Nationalist Party, Akira Watanabe. The two of them had been meeting for over two hours and so far the Captain approved of the man. He liked that he sat up straight at the table, not slouching over like a half-filled bag of rice. More importantly, Watanabe showed he had vigor and tenacity and perhaps even a true warrior's spirit. The New Nationalist Party was not in the majority but under Watanabe's leadership it had been growing and now represented a proud and vocal minority in Japan's government.

The New Nationalists made no apology for Japan's World War II actions. They revered the soldiers and leaders of that war just as they did for those of any other war going back to the warring centuries when samurai fought samurai. Their mandate was to rebuild Japan to once again be an empire expanding nation – to once again be the dominant tiger of Asia. And Watanabe saw China as the greatest threat to that vision.

Captain Terumoto took a sip from the Coke he had on a coaster by his note pad, a drink that he found was one of the best things about this particular Earth. He now rarely had tea in the afternoon. He noticed Watanabe's eyes focusing on the Coke and he said, "One must always be open to blending the best of the new ways with the best of the old ways. Just because something was done by our ancestors does not mean it was necessary, just as all things new are not always cheap and superficial."

Watanabe agreed, "The sword loses to the gun, the gun loses to the bomb."

Terumoto held up his index finger to add to the point just made, "But the bomb has no discrimination and it tends to invite other bombs. In worlds where mutual annihilation is possible, the precision of a sword stroke may have advantages."

Watanabe nodded his head as if he understood, but Terumoto saw that he did not. "For example, though the strike against The Great Hall in Tiananmen Square recently took advantage of a bomb, it was actually a very precise sword stroke, a ninja-like attack, deadly and silent and anonymous."

This time when he nodded, Terumoto could see that Watanabe understood. Watanabe then said, "Thank you for the lesson. I will not forget it. Now is the time for quiet daring and strategic moves. Before a tsunami can roar across the land it must first build its strength by crossing a thousand miles of ocean."

Terumoto was pleased, "Perhaps that is a particularly apt metaphor. But keep in mind that China does not sit idly by. It is growing its military might year over year at more than ten percent. Sooner or later it will use that power. No man or country can have great power and for long resist the urge to use it. By then China will have convinced the Americans that Asia belongs to them. Make no mistake: the Americans will not fight China to protect Japan. That treaty is meaningless. Only Japan can protect Japan."

"Captain, I believe that too! My countrymen who long for peace do not understand there is no peace for the weak – only servitude. They ignore the lessons of history."

"Watanabe, my friend, I feel better knowing you know that. So I will share something with you: the history you refer to is true not just for this world but all the others too. All peoples are tribal at heart. Our tribe must grow strong to defend us against other tribes. Men always fight to gain domination over others. It is in our genes. Through our million years of Darwinian evolution, the warrior gene is continued. Were it not so, our species would have lost out to the saber-toothed tiger and the grizzly bear. Warfare is an evolutionary inevitability. And that is just the truth."

Terumoto paused if for no other reason than to enjoy the effect his words were having on Akira Watanabe. Clearly this young and ambitious man shared the same views. There was much they could do together!

"One more thing is true," the Captain added, "On all worlds Japan and China are historical adversaries. The countries of the West come and go, but ultimately they always go. Asia is not for them, we are trading partners, nothing more. That is always true."

Watanabe saw that now was the time to press forward on his agenda for meeting with the Captain of The Lucky Dragon. "I came today to meet with you to discuss how best to move forward. I was hoping you would help my Party to gain more prominence and to soon take on more responsibility for guiding Japan's future. Your guidance and support is very necessary. Will you help me?"

"Be aware my friend that what you ask for is no little thing. To go down the path you suggest will take you to places perhaps you will not want to go. It is not an easy or a safe path."

"The path does not scare me. I fear the greater danger is to not go down the path."

"Then take up your sword, Akira Watanabe. And I mean that quite literally. Those of Japan's leaders who are afraid to pick up their swords must die by swords. And China must quickly learn that Japan is no paper tiger."

*****

To David's surprise, General Greene accompanied him back to Pirate's Cay. The general said that he had arranged to meet with Plato there. David was glad to hear it. Upon landing on the island, David went to find Gabriela who was then meeting with Professor Wheeling. Greene went immediately to find Plato.

Greene found Plato in the room that Plato had turned into his office. Though it was an office that seemed to have no equipment or desk in it, it did have chairs and a table and walls that turned into screens whenever Plato wished it. Plato rose out of the chair and greeted the general with his clasped forearms greeting. As usually happened, Greene was struck by the sheer size and physical presence of Plato, standing just a few inches short of seven feet tall but with an Olympic swimmers hard trim body. Greene noticed his skin was now more tanned than when he had first appeared on the island.

After the greeting, Greene wasted no time on conversational politeness, "David tells me he has already briefed you about our meeting with Hank Scarpetti. Since then, Hank did talk to the President and got the response he expected."

"I am saddened by that but not surprised."

"I want you to know that I do not agree with the President. If it was up to me, I'd be shooting everything we have at The Freya."

"That is what needs to be done," Plato replied.

General Greene held up his hands in resignation. "I really don't blame the President. I've talked to my counterparts in London and Paris and Berlin and their leaders have all taken the same position. Everyone wants to wait and see. They are hesitant to take action. Only Israel is ready to fight, but they won't go alone. They really can't."

Plato nodded, "I know, I have spoken to all the world's leaders. Not one of them seems able to change their world view. They judge the future in terms of their experience of the past. The future is now changing too fast for them. Part of what one must learn from the past is that with each new technological age, new dynamics come into play which require new paradigms and new strategies. And the time to adjust gets shorter and shorter."

"Plato, you probably don't know this but the reason I was put in charge originally of the Armed Forces response to the arrival of your ship in our skies is because my responsibilities for the Army was to understand the effects and consequences of new technologies. What I found out over the last few years was that it was almost impossible for me and my team to keep up with the changes. New important technologies kept surfacing faster and faster. And I look into just a few years of the future and the pace of change keeps accelerating. Like I said, I don't really blame our political leaders; new technologies are changing the world faster than they can keep up."

Plato rejected that, "Leadership is critical now. Your world depends on it. When Leaders make mistakes now, millions of lives can be lost. Your very world can be lost. That point must be pressed upon them!"

Greene just shrugged his shoulders in defeat, "How can we do that? They don't want to hear what you have to tell them. They want to believe that things will stay normal long enough for them to retire from the stage."

"General, there is one more thing I can do that I hope will convince them. I have had my team preparing it. It is the most brutal of lessons with far reaching consequences."

The general interrupted, "Is it dangerous? Are people going to be hurt? Killed?"

"Not in the way you think. Think of it as a violent movie." Then Plato smiled though his ancient eyes showed no real amusement, "Years ago on this Earth there was a movie called 'Jaws' about a Great White shark that attacked a seaside community. The movie was very popular and scary and I am told that for years afterward some people were afraid to swim out in the ocean. What I have in mind is like that."

Now it was the general's turn to smile. "I saw that movie. I used to love swimming in the ocean and after I saw it I had to screw up all my courage just to take a three minute swim."

General Greene could not imagine one more disaster movie could make much of a difference. "So what am I going to do about the terrorist plot you mention to destroy The Capitol? I believe you, but I don't know what I can do to stop it – and that would be a lesson I really want to spare my country."

Plato agreed, "The bombing of your Capitol would be highly destabilizing. You fought wars in Iraq and Afghanistan because of the destruction on 9/11 of the World Trade Center towers. So we must find a way to prevent that from happening. But you General Greene are going to have to take action. However, I have examined the command structure within which you operate and I believe that it will be within your power, if not your authority, to do what needs to be done. There is an expression here, 'act first, and seek forgiveness later'."

General Greene didn't hesitate, "I will take whatever action is necessary if there is any chance at all that I can save The Capitol from destruction."

"I thought that would be your response, General." Plato then told the general what he would need to do and how Plato would help him.

After the general had left, Plato asked David to come see him. A few minutes later David was sitting at the front of his desk. Over his many years, Plato had learned that one could never predict which individuals would rise to the challenges of their times. In part that was because history has a way of choosing its own heroes and villains but also there was the dormant force of character that only awoke for some individuals when confronted with extreme circumstances. Plato believed that David was one of those.

"David, I think I have for you what will be the most important writing assignment of your life. What you write I will see is spread all across the internet. I know other commentators and pundits will use all media outlets to expound upon what I am about to do, but I want your communication to act as a foundational structure for all other commentary – and the world will read what you write."

David regarded Plato wide-eyed and doubtful; he couldn't imagine what Plato wanted him to write. Also, he was very aware that though he now had a global following for his various forms of communication, that there could be no foundational writing for anything: there were simply too many points of view and too many wannabe pundits and experts – real or just in their own minds – and the world audience was not particularly attentive or discriminating.

Plato laughed, "I see David you are doubtful. You think no one has the power I suggest that you will have. But I am going to give you a big advantage over everyone else: I am going to show you what I am going to do before anyone else sees it. You will have time to prepare your communication so that it can be submitted immediately – while everyone else is still reeling mentally. And I personally will help you in what you are to do. No one else will have that advantage either.

At that moment, Gabriela, Planck, Ozawa and Dr. Wheeling arrived together. Plato smiled at them all. "Welcome, please take seats. You might want to face that wall there. I have something to show you all. I think you will find it very interesting – though I confess that you will find it enjoyable only if you like extreme horror movies."

They pulled seats up as they all looked at each other quizzically and quickly realized that each of them was equally unaware of what was to be seen. They made themselves comfortable and Dr. Wheeling, to everyone's surprise, asked whether anyone had brought popcorn. A sense of humor was something no one expected from the professor. He was happy in his work on the island and it showed. Any thought of popcorn and an amusing movie experience left their minds almost immediately upon the beginning of Plato's screening. What they watched over the next two hours left them in shock and in tears.

Like before when he had shown a documentary relating to Earth #278 to his audience of world influencers, he showed them what was at its essence a silent documentary of an Earth destroying itself in a nuclear war. Yet this one was different; instead of showing an Earth that had an identifiably different cultural and historical timeline, this new Earth looked just like their Earth. When asked about that, Plato told them that the Earth they were watching was a new clone - the result of the violent clash of opinion world-wide in early 2003 over the United States decision to invade Iraq based on the claim that Saddam Hussein had weapons of mass destruction which he intended to use against Israel and the United States. On this Earth which Plato labeled #309, the United States threatened to invade and Hussein backed down and allowed investigators into his country who showed conclusively that he did not possess the WMD's and war was averted.

Gabriela asked if her Earth had a number. Plato had smiled and said it was #310.

"So we are actually the clone of that one?" She asked.

"No, you both are the same - like identical twins at birth," answered Plato.

Plato then continued his silent collection of pictures and film. As it progressed through the years from 2003, a question filled David's mind which he really did not want to ask. Plato answered it for him anyway. With Plato directing what appeared on the screen, panoramic shots showing large scale events were inter-spliced with video projections of individuals such as the President and other world leaders - leaders who David recognized as leaders of his own Earth. David saw they were alive on both

Earths simultaneously. Then he saw a video of Dr. Wheeling giving his Nobel Prize acceptance speech - which David had attended, though he couldn't tell whether he was there or not. Then that existential question was answered. Plato followed certain prompts that led to a view of Earth #309 where David saw a video of himself walking into the New York Public Library. Plato then used the documentary menu to search for Planck and found him on his island and Ozawa there with him. Manipulating the interactive features of the documentary footage almost faster than they could follow, Plato then found a brief video of Gabriela and David walking hand in hand past a bank and when they came closer to what was obviously the bank's surveillance cameras, she pushed her hair away from her left ear.

"I've got a wedding ring on," Gabriela exclaimed.

"As you see, the historical timeline has already started changing," said Plato. "Here you are engaged, there you married earlier."

Then the documentary continued with more of a focus on political events. It showed the election of President Morningstar and in one portion of video there was Hank Scarpetti standing next to him. It showed rising clashes and terrorism in the Middle East. Then there was footage of Hussein acquiring two nuclear weapons from North Korea and Iran building nuclear weapons of their own. Nuclear weapons from old Russian stockpiles ended up in the hands of al-Qaeda.

A view of the sky showed circling high above was The Bucephalus and then also The Freya.

Catherine Ozawa turned to face Plato, "So this was the Earth you were at before you came here? When you told me that you had failed in your previous mission - it was your mission to this Earth, Earth #309, that failed? That is why you came here - to rectify the mistakes you believe you made there?"

Plato nodded sadly, "I felt I had to try."

The screening continued. Video showed crewmembers off The Freya meeting with al-Qaeda leaders. Those same leaders were shown to deliver a nuclear device into Washington D.C. with the help of The Freya. Then there was a high altitude picture of an explosion destroying the center of the city and a mushroom shaped cloud taking shape over the Potomac River.

Then within hours a chain reaction of nuclear destruction took place: US nuclear missiles destroyed Tehran as Iran bombed Saudi Arabia. Then North and South Korea bombed each other, Iraq set off a nuclear device in Tel Aviv and Israel retaliated against Bagdad. Then nothing happened for 24 hours and then China launched nuclear missiles against Tokyo. That was the end of it.

The silent documentary then showed the results and the victims. Fifty million people died directly from nuclear explosions, hundreds of millions of people were exposed to radioactive fall-out. The oil fields of the Middle East pumped no oil. Economic turmoil and world-wide Depression buffeted everyone.

The documentary showed how to make it interactive and how all individuals could use Google-like search queries to access menu options to see what happened to them; if there was a video record anywhere it could be accessed both by individual and by date. Then all in the room with Plato wanted to search where they were when the nuclear explosions started. David followed the suggestions on the screen and discovered he had been visiting a friend in Chicago and was fine. Then it was Gabriela's turn. There were pictures of her walking through Reagan National Airport on the date the nuclear device was exploded in Washington and then checking into the downtown Washington D.C. Hyatt. Then you saw her in a crowd of people there for a conference. She sought out later images but nothing showed up. The counter at the top of the screen showing the date crept forward day after day but there was nothing more of her. Then she tried a different search query and there appeared a video of David speaking at a funeral and her family and friends were in the church pews. Dr. Wheeling was there.

Her friends in the room looked at her and could see in her expression that she had just lost something very important.

Planck considered not searching for his counterpart but then shrugged his shoulders and sought himself out. He found himself on Pirate's Cay. Further searches suggested he had not yet made any important discovery. The Retreat grounds were unoccupied. Most of their followers had left the island to return to their families. Catherine Ozawa looked first at Plato and considered seeking out more about her alternate life. She decided not to know more. "My *qi* is here with me. I do not need to know more – it would only be a distraction."

Dr. Wheeling just said that he would look later.

The documentary returned to the larger picture of events. They saw the US President and his White House Staff and more than half of the members of Congress were all gone. The man who had been the Secretary of State was now President; he had been out of the country on a visit to Brazil.

With a puzzled look, Gabriela said, "I'm dead on that Earth. I was alive but now I'm dead."

David had tears in his eyes, "Somehow I feel it. I spoke at your funeral. We were married."

Dr. Wheeling had stared silently at the screen for long moments, not wanting to believe what he had just seen. "What happened, Plato? I guess I understand that al-Qaeda with the help of The Freya set off a nuclear device in D.C. – but why everything else that followed?"

Plato looked around at the people in the room; all eyes were on him, all trying to understand. "One should never forget how ruthless man can be. Why do soldiers sack a city and rape and pillage? Why can leaders like Hitler and Stalin do what they did? The answer is that when given the power, man takes all that he can. When the United States was critically injured with the detonating of a nuclear device in its capital city, with its President dead along with most of its leadership, in that moment all constraints were removed at the geopolitical level – there was no sheriff in town. The United States was severely wounded. If you had a nuclear weapon at your disposal and longtime enemies, that was your moment to strike. Israel was suddenly exposed to those who sought its extinction – why should it surprise you when the destruction of Israel is what the Mullahs of Iran preach to their children at prayer? China has hated Japan for centuries. When it saw that the United States was momentarily paralyzed, it knew it would never have a better chance. And its analysis was correct. The United States could do nothing right then. And later, it would be too late; a new world order would have evolved."

Dr. Wheeling was still trying to understand. "Plato, I was against the US invading Iraq in 2003 but now it seems that was the right answer. On that Earth, Hussein was one of the reasons the nuclear destruction occurred."

"No Dr. Wheeling, that is not how to look at it," Plato responded. "It is not so simple. Attacking Iraq in 2003 is one of the reasons this Earth is in such peril. To have gone into Iraq after Hussein or not to do so, that is not the correct discussion. That is thinking about the issues with your mind locked into a Twentieth Century paradigm. Historically, armies invaded countries for territorial gains not ideological ones. Hitler invaded countries to get the land and the resources and the populations. George Bush invaded Iraq to stop Hussein. He attacked Afghanistan to stop the Taliban. But when he looked up, he was occupying two countries where he didn't belong trying to change ideologies that could not be changed by soldiers with guns - no matter how many soldiers or how many guns."

"So we shouldn't have done anything?" David asked.

"It's very simple," Plato replied, "If you don't like an ideology or believe certain leaders are dangerous - kill the leaders."

"But then they will try and kill our leaders," Dr. Wheeling said.

"Better that than sending tens of thousands of young men and women into battles that can't be won." Plato responded. Then added, "You would be surprised how reasonable world leaders become when they learn that if they act ruthlessly or promote actions that are anti-societal that the other powers in the world kill them and their families and destroy their palaces and take their billions of dollars out of their Swiss bank accounts. When you want to stop a snake, just cut off its head!"

"And is that the lesson that you want people to learn from this documentary, Plato?" David asked."

"Yes, David, that is one of them."

"What else?" Catherine Ozawa asked.

"The world - both its leaders and its billions of citizens - need to understand how delicately balanced world security really is. Cataclysmic events start chain reactions of greater and greater calamity. This Earth #310 is at the cusp of dramatic technological advance that will be the equivalent of giving loaded machine guns to six year olds to play with in a crowded mall. Over its next thirty years weapons of mass destruction will be available to any ruthless nation or major terrorist organization; who will vouchsafe the safety of the planet? How do you stop the first triggering event?"

David thought about how he would write about what he had just seen. There were so many story lines that needed to be pursued; so many fascinating tangents that cried out to be explored. But what was the central issue that needed to be explained? Right then he had no idea what was needed – actually, that wasn't right, he had too many ideas. "How much time do I have to come up with a communication plan?"

Plato answered, "Two or three days at most?"

Catherine Ozawa was as stunned as the others. She had used the documentary controls and found that several of her family members in Tokyo had died in the Chinese attack on Earth #309. "Plato, is this going to work?"

"Many of your Earth's world leaders will discover that their other selves died on Earth #309. The effect of first learning of one's alternate existence and then seeing one's death is not an inconsiderable existential shock." Plato responded.

Gabriela looked at David, "It's like all of a sudden I lost a part of me that I didn't know I had – but I feel the loss."

"I can't believe I am still there but now without you," David sighed.

In the silence that followed each of them searched inside themselves for echoes of their other selves. Then Dr. Wheeling voiced his internal thoughts, "It is one thing for physicists to embrace the 'Many Worlds' theory or to have ideas of Parallel Worlds, it is quite another thing to witness their reality."

Planck added, "I can't even begin to come up with a definition of reality."

Ozawa looked at her friends, "the reality is that the sun is now setting and we should all go out on the beach and watch it."

"Fair enough," replied David. "But even that is too much reality for me. I need a beer. Anyone else want one?"

They all did.

# CHAPTER SEVENTEEN

*"Even if it seems certain you will lose, retaliate. Neither wisdom nor technique has a place in this. A real man does not think of victory or defeat. He plunges recklessly towards an irrational death. By doing this, you will awaken from your dreams."*

Yamamoto Tsunetomo
*The Hagekure: The Book of the Samurai*

**Too Many Worlds**
By David Randall

*The fate of Earth #309 which Plato has shown us challenges all of our perceptions and understanding. Individual existence is multiplied by two and perhaps by many more. We exist here and there and perhaps elsewhere. For some of us, our lives followed almost identical paths; for others the departures were greater: but in all cases, we were there. When we were unaware of these twinned existences we can be forgiven for mistakes we made multiple times on multiple Earths – our lack of connection excused our lack of learning. But now thanks to Plato we have peered into our alternate existence – a horrifying existence – and now it is up to us to see what we must learn. Repeating the mistakes of Earth #309 would be too horrible to contemplate.*

*So what must we learn from the destruction of Earth #309? The first thing to learn, it seems to me, is that Man can and has destroyed Earth. And if Plato is to be believed, we have done it multiple times. Leaders of the world are dangerously short-sighted, self-absorbed, immoral and supremely arrogant and, too often, megalomaniacal. Their pretensions are based on too little learning and too little worldly experience. And sometimes they are just plain stupid. The wise and benevolent leader is as much a myth as Unicorns and tooth fairies. Men and women with wisdom and experience and caring hearts don't enter politics; they live quiet lives and write books which no one reads.*

*If that sounds too harsh a condemnation, just look around at the condition our world is in. It is a very dangerous place and with each new technological advance it becomes more so. Our leaders are not up to the task ahead of them.*

*I offer no immediate solution to this leadership problem. But I do know that recognizing and admitting to a problem is the first step to solving it. Our lives and those of our future generations all depend on us managing our Earth and its geopolitics much better than we are.*

*The second thing to learn is that life itself, for every one of us, is a far more expansive and mysterious reality than we ever imagined. Our existence is not insignificant; each of us is multiplied across the universe. Our Consciousness – together and individually – rules across time and space. Reality is our creation.*

*What that says to me is that we must challenge ourselves to take individual responsibility and voyage forth into a future of unknown potentiality. Now is not the time for timidity and shallow visions. Be bold. The Universe embraces us.*

*So yes, we can and must master the new technology that is coming. We can and must master the gifts of consciousness. We can and must find leaders that will move us forward into the light and not threaten us with darkness. All that is within our power.*

*This all may seem like a new challenge, but it is not. Mankind has faced this challenge before many times. And wiser minds and better words than mine have illuminated the path. I'll end with a few lines from the 19th Century poet, Alfred, Lord Tennyson's Ulysses:*

*"Yet all experience is an arch where through gleams that untraveled world whose margin fades forever and forever when I move. How dull it is to pause, to make an end, to rust unburnished and not to shine in use! As though to breathe were life."*

*****

Khalil searched the night-time sky for the shuttle he was told would come for him. As directed he had driven his old Volkswagen to the deserted edge of the city, near to where the desert started. The only light came from the stars and a crescent moon. The heat of the day was already dissipating off the barren rocky landscape as it was absorbed by the infinity of stars above on this cloudless night. Khalil thought it the kind of night for the doing of great things.

Impatiently he smoked a cigarette and glanced around to ensure no one else was watching him and then again he looked skyward. He ran through his mind all that he had done in preparation for what was to happen. Truthfully, he admitted it wasn't much. Hasan was making his task quite easy. Yet it was his resolve and vision that had led to this moment. Hasan would furnish the weapon and the transportation. Hasan would get him to the streets of Washington, D.C. and then with the man Hasan was calling Plato, they would take the weapon to a place where they would have an unobstructed view of The Capitol and he, Khalil, would aim the weapon and pull the trigger. That act was to be his alone! They could be as much as two miles away, it would not matter. Then he and Plato would return to where the shuttle had left them and he would be returned to the exact spot where he was standing now.

This time he assured himself there would be no doubt that he would get the credit. Without giving details he had told others whom he trusted what he was about to do. He did not tell them how it would happen, so few believed him. That did not matter, afterwards they would remember.

He thanked the Prophet that he was being given this chance. That such a blessing would come to him was almost beyond imagining. And the manner of it was also almost beyond imagining. His friends could not have envisioned such a thing. Yet he would do it. His devotion and courage were great. Not without fear he admitted to himself. To go with these strange people from another Earth to fly to America - that land of blasphemous infidels - in a spacecraft he could see hovering in the sky like some huge bird - that should scare anyone. He was OK with his fear - it only sharpened his senses. Yet alongside his fear was also great excitement! What a thing for him to do! His fame would go even beyond that of those servants of Allah who had knocked down the Twin Towers of greed and corruption.

While staring into the sky, he sensed more than saw that a vehicle was approaching. It was something he could almost hear and almost see, he could not explain how that could be, but it was so. And there it was all of a sudden...landed, so close, not more than thirty feet away. He saw Hasan open the door and wave for him to come. He boarded the craft and almost instantly it was airborne, he barely had a chance to take a seat. Hasan smiled at him and said everything was good. Khalil heard him easily even though Hasan was several feet away. This craft was so silent Hasan could have whispered and Khalil would have heard. And what seemed like just a moment later, Hasan led him off the shuttle onboard what was The Freya.

Onboard The Freya he was led to where he was to sit and wait. He was offered coffee. Mostly he was ignored by the crewmembers except for when Hasan came to him to review exactly what was to be done. Hasan spoke slowly and clearly, as if he was giving difficult instructions to a child. Kahlil burned inside from the insulting tone but said nothing. Now he just must wait patiently. When Hasan left, Kahlil prayed that he would do well.

He tried to relax but he admitted to himself that he was very nervous. He tried to not let it show.

Four hours later he was back on the shuttle; this time with the tall blond man they wanted him to call Plato but whom he had heard someone call Lars. It didn't matter to him that they wanted to call this man Plato. The people of The Freya had their own interests to serve. Either way, they were serving Allah, for in Khalil's arms was now a weapon like the one he had used to destroy the American Embassy in Tel Aviv. And like there, he knew how to use it.

From the shuttle windows he could see the lights spreading countless miles in every direction that was Washington, D.C. The night here was clear as well, not as bright and clear as on the desert he had left just hours ago, but still clear. He saw a wide river which from his study of the city he knew was the Potomac. He could not help but smile; he saw it! First what they called the Washington Monument and then the great dome of the Capitol! Such an arrogant display of wealth and power! Such architectural wonder should be exclusively for mosques proclaiming the wonder of Allah!

He knew they were to land at a park on the Virginia side of the river not far from the site they had chosen as the best place from which to fire the weapon. People in this country where everyone was so rich were afraid to be in their own parks after sunset and now it was midnight. Only rapists and thieves would be out this late in the park. Khalil laughed at the irony of that. It was all the advantage he needed.

When the craft landed, he and the one they called Plato went out the door. Plato was carrying what looked like an ordinary Kalashnikov and Khalil had in his arms the missile weapon – he had no other name for it. Both weapons were hidden under the raincoats they were wearing. The night air was a little warm to be wearing the coats but that could not be helped. Hasan stayed on the shuttle and promised all would go well and that they would be waiting for them to return.

The park was a perfect place to land except that it was not quite close enough to the target and there was no clear line of site to the Capitol. They had to walk about a mile along the river to the Memorial Bridge. Though the target would still be a ways away he had been assured that distance was well in the range of his weapon. A clean unobstructed line of site was what was important. If through the viewfinder he could line up on the target, the weapon would do the rest from there.

They left the shuttle and walked toward the river where they found the jogging path they had scouted. No one was in sight and wordlessly the two of them set off walking. Hasan had been very clear about exactly where they were to set up and fire the weapon. He was told to waste no time; that once they arrived at the designated spot, Khalil should fire immediately.

As a cloud drifted in front of the moon the night darkened. Kahlil hoped the cloud would remain there; he felt safer in the dark. Now he felt the momentousness of what he was doing. This city was a city of great power and he was just a poor minor soldier of Allah, a man of no power or great gifts. Yet he was going to strike at its most powerful symbol. He was fearful that he was striving for something too much beyond him.

He reminded himself that he was a trained soldier. Many times he had aimed a weapon and fired it. He had killed many opponents. He knew how to do that. That was all he needed to do now. Allah would take care of the rest.

As the site came into view, Khalil now understood why. Though deserted now, the designated spot, so close to the bridge and to the Lincoln Memorial certainly would have surveillance cameras. Hasan wanted them to show up on the cameras later – that was why Lars had been made to look like Plato. Since that was the price of their assistance, Khalil would go along. As long as he succeeded in blowing up the Capitol, what happened afterwards did not matter so much. Though of course it would be better if he survived, he thought to himself. Still, when he had strapped on the bomb to his chest before being picked up by The Freya, he had accepted that he might soon be a martyr to Allah.

The bomb he carried was his own idea, not Hasan's. In fact he had not told Hasan about it. Kahlil wore it because he was afraid that things would go wrong with the plan. If something got in the way, he could always find another target in this city. He resolved that he would accomplish something – even if it meant his own life would be sacrificed. He would be a willing martyr.

As he and the Plato person walked, Khalil forced himself to breathe deeply and with a steady rhythm. He emptied his mind of all doubts and stray thoughts and just concentrated on reaching the designated spot, now just a few hundred yards away. The Capitol was already clearly in view.

*****

Captain Nick Hoyle and his team of three other Delta Force members were rapidly closing in on the two men approaching the bridge from the jogging path on the Virginia side of the river. Like other teams spread out across the city for the last two days, he and his team had been hoping they would be the ones needed. Their instructions had been to just stay ready to move very quickly. They had also been told that under no circumstances were they to allow the target individuals to fire any weapon that looked like it might resemble a Stinger missile. Capturing the terrorists would be a good thing, but stopping them was essential.

Nick and his team had been on combat missions before but never on one that was inside the U.S. That made this different. There was no politically abstruse issue of fighting for democracy or defending the victims of geopolitical power struggles. This was no village in the mountains of Afghanistan where everyone spoke a language he had never even heard before and had been fighting each other for a thousand years and would probably keep doing that for another thousand years. This was his city. He was here to protect his home – he had been brought up just a few miles away in Fairfax Virginia. He'd gone on grade school field trips to the Lincoln Memorial and the White House and The Capitol. Now some terrorists wanted to blow places up here. Not going to happen! Not if he could help it!

Two days ago when his and the other teams had been deployed around Washington and told to be ready to move on a moment's notice and all rules of engagement could be ignored as necessary, all his senses went on red alert. They had been told to dress in civilian clothes and try not to be noticeable. They didn't need to be told that this was totally off the grid and don't say anything to anyone. Of course they were told anyway. They had been told to expect some form of stinger missile like device that was going to target The Capitol but other targets were possible. They didn't know from which direction the terrorists would come in from. And the missile could be shot from as much as two or even three miles away. That left a pretty large area to cover. And minutes mattered. Seconds mattered.

Ten minutes ago Nick had received the call from Lieutenant General Carl Greene that the terrorists had just landed and Nick received the coordinates and their direction of travel. Even as he and his team started moving, Nick wondered first how any vehicle could land where they had been told it just landed and secondly how could the intel about it be so good? It was like someone on the other end of his radio was watching from up above exactly what was happening.

Nick and his team did not lose a moment thinking about those questions. They had jumped in their SUV and driven as directed until they had eyes on two individuals who the radio in his ear identified as the targets. They were up ahead of him and walking quickly with their backs to the SUV on a path along the river. He drove closer to them on the road and then he jumped the curb and drove onto the jogging path and was just three hundred yards behind. Then he cut the engine and coasted to where the distance was less than two hundred yards. Neither of the two suspected terrorists had yet to turn around. Nick and his team jumped out of their vehicle and Pete Sagan, the best shooter of the four of them stayed at the vehicle and took a comfortable position and lined up his rifle on the taller of the two suspects. If either moved in any way deemed hostile, they would be dead before they could complete what they were trying to do.

That was when Khalil thought something was wrong. Some sound was wrong. He looked again at the designated spot where he was to fire the missile and it was just fifty yards away. He paused for a moment and tapped Lars-Plato on the shoulder. He paused too and looked at Kahlil. Then both of them looked around, then looked behind. Now everything was wrong! How could it be so? Allah, please help me now. Let me just do this thing and then take me away. I accept dying on this cursed land.

Three men running toward him all with guns. Lars-Plato now saw it too and turned around and he brought his Kalashnikov out from under his raincoat and tried to shoot at the men coming from behind. Khalil heard the crash of rifle fire and saw Lars fall to the ground as the Kalashnikov fired. But only a few rounds were scattered into the sky before the gun went silent.

Khalil had only one thought, get his missile weapon out from under his coat and fire at the Capitol. He had practiced this and he had opened his coat earlier. Quickly he started to raise the weapon in order to aim it. The dome of The Capitol was before his eyes. It was huge and gleaming before him – the symbol of all he hated! Now all he had to do was bring the view of the dome into the cross hatches of the scope of the weapon. Just like he had done at the Tel Aviv Embassy. Then he had time. He had savored that moment. But now he was rushing and his hands were shaking. He needed an extra moment to get the weapon lined up. Just one more moment, then pull the trigger.

All four of the Delta Force team saw Khalil raise the weapon. All four fired at him and one of their bullets hit the bomb strapped to his chest and Khalil exploded in front of them. The concussive force knocked all but Pete, fifty yards further back, off their feet. They were lucky not to be closer.

Nick still on the ground looked around and saw no other threat. He called out to his team and they called back they were OK.

As soon as he was able, Nick called in what had just happened. Again he talked to General Greene and said the threat was ended. He wasn't sure since his head was still buzzing but he thought he heard the general say "Thank you Plato!" What a Greek philosopher had to do with this mission was beyond Captain Nick Hoyle.

*****

Within minutes Captain Ragnar up on The Freya was told by his observers about the failure of the mission. He turned to Hasan who had just arrived back on the shuttle and was now standing across from him. He glared at Hasan as he fought down the urge to take out his pistol and shoot him for the failure. Hasan stood soldier straight; his fear showing only in the pallor of his face. He has seen others killed for smaller failures.

"What went wrong?" Ragnar asked, his eyes boring into Hasan. "Were we just unlucky? Did a stray patrol happen to spot us?" The Captain's right hand settled against his right hip, just inches from the butt of the pistol he had in his black leather holster.

Hasan considered agreeing to that conclusion. Yet his Captain too often had said that he did not believe in luck or fate. He believed only in execution. Finally, reluctantly, Hasan said, "No Captain, I do not believe it was a random patrol. I think somehow they knew we were coming and where. How they knew that I do not know. But that patrol was looking for us. And they knew about where to look."

The Captain moved his hand away from his pistol. If Hasan had said it was just bad luck, Ragnar would have shot him. He agreed with Hasan; somehow the Americans were expecting them and knew where to look for them. Before he would attack them again, he needed to know how that had happened. He had his suspicions. If he was right, then it meant that somehow the Americans had tracked the movements of The Freya and its shuttle. He still doubted that this Earth had the technology to do that, but that was the most likely answer. His instincts said that had been what happened. He could not blame Hasan if that was it. Then he thought some more. And he knew. His mind told him to follow the technology. Without question there was one party who had such technology – better technology than he could even imagine. For The Bucephalus it would be as easy as an adult reading a book for kindergarten students.

Captain Ragnar made his mind up then. For the next attack against America, he would be very careful. He would not use idiots like Khalil. He would anticipate that Plato was now actively involved. But he would succeed – he would set off a nuclear device in Washington, D.C. After all, he had done it before with The Bucephalus circling above.

*****

When General Greene entered Hank Scarpetti's office at The White House, his friend told him that the congratulatory meeting with the President would have to be postponed. The President had something else more important come up. As he sat down on the couch in Scarpetti's office he thought he knew what had caused his meeting to be postponed.

Plato's 'Documentary' about Earth #309 had been released that morning. Though its long term effect was not yet known; in the short term its worldwide viewership made the Super Bowl media audience look like that of a high school football game. Not only was the audience for it huge, but its interactive capabilities were fully utilized. People spent hours on the site. Once again, Greene marveled at the necessary computing power to deliver the interactive documentary to so many with no glitches or outages.

Scarpetti took the chair across from the general. "Did you survive?" he asked, not needing to explain the question further.

"Yes, I was at a meeting in London."

"I didn't. I was here." Scarpetti said.

"I'm sorry."

"Bizarre isn't it? It feels so real."

"It is real, Hank. Don't you get it? Everything there really happened."

Scarpetti looked over at his friend of thirty years; a man who he knew was as level headed and intelligent as they come. If Greene believed it, it was real. "I guess I know that. I think more than anything, I don't want it to be real. On #309, I was Chief of Staff. This President was in the White House. That means that whatever happened there was in part our fault – my fault. And fifty million people died and that world is so fucked!"

The general was sympathetic to his friend but only to a point. "So make sure it doesn't happen here!"

Scarpetti just stared out his window. What could he say when the best he could do might not be good enough – and the world itself was at stake?

The President's secretary walked into Scarpetti's office. "He wants to see you. General you should go in too."

The two men looked at each other and stood up and followed her into the Oval Office. The President stood up from his desk when they came in and pointed them to one of the couches and took a seat near the fireplace. Scarpetti saw immediately that the President lacked his usual bounce to his step and easy access smile.

"Congratulations, General. Thank you for what you did in stopping the attack on the Capitol. Hank tells me that Plato helped us. I guess I was wrong about him."

"Yes sir," said the general. "His surveillance capabilities made it all possible. The Bucephalus has been tracking every move of The Freya and its shuttles for days. They gave us their positions in real time."

"Our surveillance technology couldn't do that?"

"No sir. The Freya and its shuttles don't show up on our radar and we can't see them from our AWACs."

"But you had already lined up Delta Force. That was the right move." The President gave him a thumbs up.

"Delta Force did a great job. They should be commended."

"I'll see to it," Scarpetti said.

"So the question now is, what do we do about Captain Ragnar and The Freya?" the President said. "We still really don't know what their military capability is, do we General?"

General Greene shook his head, "No we don't sir."

"I don't suppose your friend Plato could handle this for us?" His tone was resigned; clearly he knew the weight on his back couldn't be shifted to anywhere else.

The general shook his head again, "Plato has his own rules as to what he does and doesn't do. He has said that The Freya's technology isn't that far ahead of ours. He seems to think we can handle this ourselves."

The President nodded to the general. "I think this is something we have to take care of ourselves. My highest priority is to protect my country and its citizens. And I want to protect the peoples of the world. We are not the only nation feeling the effects of The Freya's actions. I'm setting up emergency discussions with my counterparts in London, Paris and Berlin to set up a plan of attack. And I need to talk to Beijing and Moscow. Then we'll determine who else needs to be brought into this. Our world needs to take a united stand."

"What about us taking unilateral action?" General Greene asked.

The President regarded the general with both a determined and sympathetic gaze, "Believe me, I'd like to just order a missile attack against them, but I just don't think that is wise. This isn't just about us and I don't think we should go into this alone. I'm confident that I can get them to join us. This needs to be an international effort. We can all do this together. That's how it should be done."

"What about the Chinese and Russians? Do you think they'll join us too?"

The President nodded, "I think they will. It won't be easy. The Russians haven't really been affected by The Freya. And we don't know why that is. And the Chinese did have that bombing of The Great Hall which has never been explained."

Scarpetti added, "And there's the matter of The Lucky Dragon. No one seems to know what they want or what kind of risk they pose. They might have some sort of relationship to The Freya, for all we know."

General Greene discovered he just didn't want to stay silent. Politically correct or not, he had to say what he thought. "Sir, what you are suggesting is going to take time. Too much time. We don't need any help. We can launch a much better attack if we don't have to coordinate anything with anyone. And if by chance The Freya can take us on, then we better find that out too. Sometimes, you just have to attack – then deal with what follows."

The President met the gaze of General Greene with a steady resoluteness, "I really do wish we could do just that. But it wouldn't be wise. We need to take the time to do this right. The Freya may be the first of the ships from other Earths to threaten us this way, but they won't be the last. What we do will set a precedent. We need to establish a protocol for this and we need to have allies with this. Don't worry General, we will take action – and it will be the right action and it will be definitive."

On one level General Greene understood that what the President wanted to do probably seemed the right course of action. Still he knew it was the wrong thing to do. The President was correct about one thing; more threats would come from other Earths. And that was why his proposed course of action was wrong. They had to learn the United States was a fighter. You hit us; we'll hit you back – as hard as we can. We won't wait and talk about it. We'll strike. But the general knew he couldn't argue further.

The President saw that the general would say no more. He knew the Pentagon would be frustrated by his seeking the support of the international community. That was their problem. He would do what he knew was right. Still he appreciated that Greene had been right about Plato and had done what needed to be done. He valued Greene and what he could do. He had to think about whether he should push to get Greene another star – it would be good to have a 4 Star General owe him.

"So General, how did you do on 309? I think you know that I bit the dust there." The President was trying to make light of it – he didn't feel good about any of it, though. Somewhere deep inside him he knew it had happened. Since he had seen Plato's documentary and spent time with its interactive capability he had felt sick to his stomach. He really had died there. And worse, now he knew that what had happened on 309 could happen here and it would be his fault. And he didn't know how to make sure it didn't. It would be his fault. His fault.

General Greene replied, "I survived the blasts. Maybe the lucky ones didn't. Life there is going to be very hard for a while. All the radioactivity – it's got to be a nightmare."

After General Greene had left, the President looked over at Scarpetti who had remained behind. "What do you think, Hank? How do we manage the fallout of 309? Don't I need to get in front of the people and tell them something? Something reassuring?"

"What would you want to tell them? It raises way too many questions and doesn't give any answers. My advice is don't say anything right away. Give everyone a chance to just breathe. Create a gold plated, non-partisan commission to study 309. Get recommendations from this commission to ensure events there don't replicate here. Then create a second commission with lots of brilliant academics to consider the scientific and religious implications of 309. We probably should have done that before anyway. Let the media get all excited about who gets appointed and what their missions are. What we don't want right now is you answering questions about what went wrong there."

The President thought about that advice, then he nodded – it matched his political instincts. "Hank, that's a great idea. Two special commissions: one to address the geopolitical issues and the other to address the scientific and cultural ramifications. The media will love it! But let's make sure we have people we can trust on it. We want those commissions to come up with the right answers."

"Absolutely. We'll get the right people selected. But let's not be too obvious about that. Let's make it look non-partisan."

"Sure – we'll do it that way." The President liked this approach. He felt relieved. "Hank, it wasn't our fault, was it? ... You know, I've felt sick ever since I saw Plato's documentary.... You don't suppose it might be something he created – you know like it didn't really happen."

"How could it have been our fault? It's not even our world!" Hank said what he knew his President needed to hear. But it had been years since he had last wanted so much to just go out to a bar and not stop drinking until the world went blank.

*****

After General Greene had called him and shared the information that the President was reaching out to other world leaders to determine what to do about The Freya, Plato asked David to come meet with him. They were both on Plank's island where David had set up shop to do all the writing. His articles on Earth #309 had been on the front pages of newspapers around the world and his on-line posts had tens of millions of viewers. Plato had fed him facts and details that no other journalists, reporters or pundits had access to. To the world, David was the doorway to all things Other Earth, he was the reporter, the teacher, the philosopher and the guru, all rolled into one. He was also exhausted.

When David took a seat across from him, Plato asked, "How's Gabriela?"

David tried for a smile that came off a little weak. "She's ok. She always had a tendency to see the world through a darkened window. This doesn't help. She says she now knows what death feels like. I don't really know what that means but....anyway, I think she's dealing with something we all have to deal with now. As soon as I have a chance, I'm looking forward to going into a deep philosophical funk for at least a week or two."

Plato looked out the sliding glass doors to the patio outside his room. He understood David's comment even more than David would know. Once he had been in that mental malaise that bled the joy out of everything. He had been like that for almost a year. From that dark time he had learned to just be the best he could be, moment to moment, and accept what follows.

"David, you'll have to wait on going into that funk. There is more we have to do. We have to find a way to stop The Freya from creating more havoc and chaos." Plato then went on to share with David the attempt to destroy the Capitol and the President's determination to gather international support before he would take any action against The Freya. He finished by saying that the President's course of action, though reasonable on its face, would take too much time - time that The Freya would use to create more destruction - since Captain Ragnar would quickly learn of the attempt to build an international coalition against him.

Tired as he was, David's mind was clear. "He has to be stopped. If he isn't stopped, everything continues to escalate. That's what happened on #309, isn't it? Things kept escalating. Then mankind's self-destructive tendencies come to the fore. The most ruthless leaders' paranoia sets in and they strike against perceived enemies before they are struck at themselves. A chain reaction of devastation."

Plato just nodded.

"So what do we do?" David asked.

Plato knew the answer but couldn't be the one to give it, at least not all of it. "The Freya has to be destroyed as soon as possible."

"And our military isn't going to do it, is it?"

"Much as General Greene would like to - and he said that he argued with the President - the military will not be given the green light. We cannot look there for an answer."

David saw what needed to be done but wasn't ready to say it. Instead he said, "But how do you destroy The Freya when it never comes down to land? It's always fifty thousand feet in the air."

"Yes, it is," replied Plato patiently.

"So theoretically, if it won't come down here, whoever is going to destroy it has to go up there."

"Theoretically, yes."

David sat there silently for a moment, just staring back into Plato's ancient eyes. "Still thinking theoretically, if someone went there to destroy it, wouldn't they be destroyed with it? That sort of would be a negative."

"It would be if there was no alternative. But I believe there is a quite safe way to accomplish the goal – if someone was invited up onto The Freya for a seemingly legitimate reason."

At that point David was too tired to play the theoretical game any further. "Plato, we both know that I am the only one who we know can get invited up there. Are you saying that there is a way that I could blow up The Freya and live to tell the tale to my grandkids? By the way, did I mention that Gabriela is pregnant?" David was sort of sorry he blurted the last comment out. He hadn't intended to but he didn't like any of this.

Plato just regarded David and said nothing. Then after a moment, with a wise and benign look on his face, he said "First, congratulations to you and Gabriela. And yes, you will live to tell the tale."

Telling Gabriela was the hard part. Before he said a word, he knew his sanity would be questioned. Sitting on the bed in their room at the retreat, Gabriela's comment when she first heard what he intended to do was simply, "Are you nuts? No! No! No! You are going to be a father, you idiot!"

In various combinations of words, David kept repeating that The Freya needed to be stopped and he was the only one who could get himself invited up to The Freya. Then he would add that Plato had a plan to do it safely.

Then Gabriela would repeat, hell no and tell Plato to do it himself.

Halfway into the conversation, they both knew he was going to do it. The best argument he had was that their child needed to grow up in a better world than this one.

*****

Setting up the interview with Captain Ragnar aboard The Freya had been easy. Through his usual contact with Lieutenant Benson David had said he needed to get his Captain's views on what had happened at Earth #309. Captain Ragnar had agreed and moreover wanted to do it soon.

David had been confident he would get the interview. What concerned him was how he was to smuggle a bomb onboard The Freya and blow it up when he wasn't there. That was the part Plato was confident about. When Plato showed him the bomb, David had to admit that getting it onboard was probably going to be easy, though not without its stressful moments. When Plato told him how he was to detonate the bomb, David became much more doubtful. He wasn't at all sure he could do it. He had never done anything like it before.

The interview on The Freya was set up for the next day. The shuttle pickup was to be at their usual spot in a deserted field in New Jersey not far from the George Washington Bridge. David and Gabriela had returned the night before to their apartment in New York City. To his surprise, Gabriela no longer tried to talk him out of going forward with their plan. She said that Plato had assured her that David would be all right. Plato said that he would be right there with David monitoring everything – not physically of course. David thought that whatever Plato's powers of monitoring might be, it wasn't the same as being there and holding his hand.

Before David had left Pirate's Cay, David had practiced detonating the bomb. The first few attempts failed. He couldn't seem to set his mind to it. Then just as they were running out of time, David got it right. The bomb exploded. Well, a version of the bomb, a much less powerful one, but Plato said the principle was the same.

As David drove up to the designated spot where The Freya shuttle was to pick him up, he wanted to turn the car around and leave. What had been hypothetical until now had just turned real and imminent. He asked himself again why it had to be him but the same answers came up. He tried to just concentrate on the interview questions he had for the Captain. The interview had to be for real. He had to handle himself just as he had the previous two times he had interviewed Captain Ragnar on The Freya.

As David stepped out of his car, he checked his watch and saw he was still a few minutes early. The sky was clouding over and he felt a stiff wind blowing his hair. Using his fingers as a comb he tried to straighten it but the wind was insistent. He stared at the spot in the field where he expected the shuttle to land and then looked up into the sky to search for it. As he waited he felt his hands tensing and balling up into fists. He told himself to relax, which didn't work. He continued to stare at the field and then up into the cloudy sky. He wished the wind would stop blowing.

Then as it was just a few hundred feet above the ground, David saw the shuttle. As before, it could only be seen when it was quite close. Its coloring always seemed blended to the background sky. David watched it touch down as smoothly and softly as a hawk touching down onto a tree branch.

David walked over to it and the same soldier as before ushered him onboard, patted him down for weapons and went through his backpack. David tried to act normally as the soldier searched the backpack and took his laptop, Kindle, water bottles and pad of paper out and then put them back in. Though the routine was no different than before, David thought the soldier was more serious, more diligent. By then, David had no idea what acting normal was, he felt sure his face must have looked like a deer's caught in headlights.

He knew that as the soldier put the two bottles of water back in his backpack he had been holding his breath. For now one of the two seemingly identical bottles of water was something very different. The two plastic bottles with the liquid that looked like water had been given to him by Plato. One was just distilled water but the other, though it looked just like the water bottle David had sipped from during the interviews with Captain Ragnar in the past was chemically something else entirely. In fact, Plato had told him that if necessary he could even drink the liquid in the second bottle, though it would taste somewhat salty and metallic. In its current state it was harmless.

Plato said that with just a slight rearrangement of its molecular structure, the liquid in that little 16.9 oz. plastic bottle became an explosive that could level a ten story apartment building. Carefully, David kept that thought out of his mind.

When the soldier-flight attendant was through with his search he returned to his seat up front next to the pilot. David took out his iPhone and pretended to look for messages but his mind saw little of what his eyes were looking at. Several times David ran his fingers through his wind tossed hair trying to restore his longish hair to normalcy. The rest of the five minute trip David spent thinking about how he would leave the bottle-bomb behind on The Freya – where could he place it?

Once the shuttle entered The Freya's cargo doors, David exited and was escorted to the lounge area where they had conducted the interviews previously. Captain Ragnar was already seated there waiting for him. Even seated, his back was straight and his uniform was tucked in and unwrinkled and his dark hair was cut short and combed. As he walked to the table David glanced around the deck area hoping to see where he could put the water bottle. Now that he was looking closely he noticed how bare the crew area was. There was no place to dispose of trash and leftovers, just a seemingly voracious garbage disposal unit that looked like it doubled as a paper shredder. For all David knew it could reduce all waste to recyclable molecules. His idea of leaving the bottle in a trash can was not possible.

The Captain stood up to shake David's hand. His grip was strong and David found himself squeezing his grip more firmly than he would normally. The Captain's smile was brief. David took the seat left for him and took out of his bag his pad of paper and a bottle of water – twice making sure he was taking the right bottle. His mouth was so dry he wasn't sure he could speak without drinking something.

"Thank you Captain for agreeing to this interview. I suspect you know that the whole world has now watched the 'documentary' for lack of a better word that The Bucephalus has shown online which presents the destruction at Earth #309?"

Captain Ragnar presented his usual unsmiling and resolute expression. "Yes, David, I know of it. I thought it a little melodramatic but I suspect Plato was pleased with its effect."

David now found that he could just follow through with his questions as he had countless times before. Each breath was now coming naturally, not the product of a reminder to 'just breathe'.

"Well, Captain, from the video it was clear that The Freya was there just before the nuclear weapons started going off. My readers will want to know what you believe set everything off. And what advice do you have for us to ensure that what happened there does not repeat itself here?"

Captain Ragnar could not help himself from showing a small ironic smile. This was exactly the question he had been asking himself ever since the destruction of #309. Things there had advanced too quickly and too far to meet his purposes. Too many nuclear devices had gone off and that Earth was too far destroyed to be useful to him. He had not anticipated the chain reaction of attacks that had followed the bomb blast in Washington, D.C. That was why he was taking things slower here. Chaos could outrun opportunity if the chaos left radioactive particles all over the planet.

Of course that wasn't the answer he gave David.

So David asked his questions about #309 and Ragnar gave his answers: answers which showed he had tried to help the planet but had not succeeded, answers that pointed at Plato as a potential instigator, answers that showed how sorry he was at the great loss of life and how this Earth #310 – an Earth so like #309 – needed to learn from #309's mistakes, answers that showed what a powerful assistance The Freya could provide in the interests of world peace.

David recorded everything and dutifully asked the logical follow-ups and made the appropriate commentary. All the while, in the back part of his brain he marveled at the power of 'the big lie.' He found himself wanting to believe Captain Ragnar; if he believed him, he wouldn't have to try and kill him – and kill all of his crew there onboard. Only he knew better. He didn't believe Ragnar. He found deep inside himself, he blamed Ragnar for killing Gabriela on #309 and taking her away from him there. His mind had opened up a new portal which he could pass through and find the feelings of loss that the death of Gabriela on #309 produced.

After what seemed like just moments, David checked the time and found the hour set for the interview had passed and he checked his notes and found he had asked all his questions. The interview was apparently over and David still had no idea where to place the bottle. The Captain stood up and shook David's hand and said he looked forward to reading David's article. He said he appreciated that David's past articles had seemed fair and balanced. David gathered up his things and slung his backpack over his right shoulder.

Then the Captain turned back to him. "You know David, I've never asked you. What do you really think? Do you fear for your world? Do you trust those of us from other Earths?" Perhaps the Captain's demeanor was no more intimidating than usual; but to David's heightened sensitivities it seemed more aggressive and suspicious. The Captain's dark eyes were focused on David as if he sensed a new danger.

Standing there, David felt trapped. He knew he should not answer with what he believed to be true. And his mind was still desperately thinking about what to do about the bomb. But he found the truth was welling out of him. "Captain, my world changed the day we learned there were other Earths. The history of my Earth has taught me that no one from other Earths should be trusted. I believe to you we are the natives of a backward land and you are colonialists. You are here to take things from us and give to us trinkets and beads."

Captain Ragnar's expression hardened. He stared back at David and seemed about to say something, then turned and walked away. David stared at his back and then once more looked around for a place to stash the bottle. But there was nowhere. And then as he went to pick up his backpack which still contained the bottle bomb, one of the crew members came over to him to usher him back to the cargo area where the shuttle was awaiting him. The crew member picked up David's backpack to carry it for him. Half-heartedly David tried to wrest it back but the soldier just smiled and started walking with it to the shuttle. Both relieved and frustrated, David followed him.

Once on the shuttle, the shuttle pilot closed the shuttle door and saw that David was harnessed into a seat, and then went to sit upfront as David had seen him do each time before. The soldier flight attendant seemed to be looking at his personal digital device from the co-pilot seat and never looked up. As the shuttle was pulling away from The Freya, David saw that the pilot and the soldier about fifteen feet in front had their faces turned from him and were looking out through the front view screen. And then it was obvious what he should do. Quickly David took the second unopened bottle of water and placed it in a leather seat pocket designed for the seat next to him.

Then David closed his eyes and tried to envision the details of the shuttle, where he was sitting in it and particularly the location of the seat pocket where he had put the bottle of water. Only now he didn't think of it as a bottle of water – which it never had been.

The rest of the five minute trip David spent memorizing the interior of the shuttle, where he was sitting and the look of the seat pocket of the seat next to him. Then he would envision the plastic bottle lying on its side in the seat pocket exactly as he had placed it. He had been told by Plato that being able to visualize the exact location of the bottle was essential.

The shuttle landed exactly where it had come to rest a little over an hour ago when it had come to pick him up. David unhooked his harness and stood. He tried to just move the way he normally moved. He snuck a look at the soldier who had stood up and opened the door for David. The usual boredom was all that David saw on his face. David stepped down onto the grass of the field and almost immediately the soldier had closed the shuttle door. David walked back to where his car was parked and watched the shuttle take off and quickly disappear from sight.

Then a tall figure stepped out from behind a tree and David nearly jumped out of his skin. He had not been expecting anyone. But as soon as he saw who it was, he felt relieved.

"So David, do you have it all envisioned?" Plato asked.

"What are you doing here? I thought I was doing this alone."

"I brought you something. It will help." Plato handed David a tiny device that David recognized as one of Plank's mentalization amplifiers. David was struck once more by its innocuous look – yet its enabling power was still immeasurable.

David took the amplifier and inserted it into his ear as he had seen Planck do. "How come you didn't give me this before? If I had it when I was practicing yesterday I'm sure I would have done better."

"Probably, but you might not have worked so hard. Now you will be more confident and have no doubt you can do it. As you know, doubts destroy mental clarity." Then Plato shifted his glance away from David as he seemed to be listening to something elsewhere.

Plato turned back to face David, "The shuttle is just now docking at The Freya. Now before anything changes further is the time. David, are you ready? You are sure you should do what you are about to do?"

David had already prepared himself. He knew he had to do it. "Yes."

"All right, sit with me on the grass here." They both sat down. "Now empty your mind of everything and just focus on breathing in and out, in and out, in and out." David focused on his breathing even as he let his mind relax into the soft comfortable space filled by Plato's voice. He found that same meditative trance that he had learned how to access in the months of practice at Planck's retreat.

"Now do what you know how to do," Plato said and then said no more.

David envisioned the shuttle parked inside the cargo bay. He saw it there. Then he moved his mind inside the shuttle until he saw the seat where he had been sitting. Then he envisioned the seat next to him with the seat pocket and the plastic bottle wedged into the bottom of it. His mind took hold of that bottle and he held it there just as if he held it in his hands.

Then he saw the liquid in the bottle but this time he saw it as a powerful explosive, a very powerful explosive that once shaken roughly would explode. He stayed with that thought until it was absolutely clear in his mind, nothing else existed in his mind but that thought. Then he shook the bottle violently and he saw in his mind a huge explosion. He held that thought for what seemed endless time.

Then he opened his eyes and looked upward where he knew The Freya had been. There was a streak of far off light and the dim sound like a distant peel of thunder.

With a mental clarity new to him, he looked over at Plato. He didn't need to ask. He knew The Freya was gone. He had destroyed it almost down to its constituent atoms.

Plato just nodded. His eyes just looked even older then before – and sadder.

# CHAPTER EIGHTEEN

*"Now this is not the end. It is not even the beginning of the end. But it is, perhaps, the end of the beginning."*

Winston Churchill

General Carl Greene knocked on the door of David and Gabriela's apartment in New York. They had been told by Plato to expect him but didn't know why he was coming. In the week since the destruction of The Freya, David and Gabriela had kept mostly to themselves. David had just wanted to go about doing what he used to do: write at his desk, eat out at their local restaurants and sleep in his own bed. Really sleep with no dreams. In his dreams he kept watching The Freya blow up, with details that he had never actually seen.

David went to the door and welcomed the general into their apartment. Gabriela went and gave him a hug and the three of them took seats in the small living room. The general unlike his usual practice didn't seem to know how to begin. He asked what they had been doing. When would they go back to the island? How was Gabriela's research on participatory physics going?

They answered while wondering what he was trying to get to. They had come to genuinely like the general.

Finally, General Greene said what he had come to say. "David, you did a great service to your country and to the people of the world. Before you deny anything, I have talked to Plato and I do know exactly what happened. I convinced Plato that someone like me needed to know if only to be able to assess future risks."

David regarded the general solemnly, "It is not something I want known. The fewer people that know, the better. If it gets out,

I'll be a hero to some, a villain to others and a target for everyone – good and bad. And I probably committed a crime as well – I could be tried for murder."

Greene nodded, "Well, you are a hero to me – and to some very senior officers at the Pentagon. And they are not going to forget you. You did what absolutely needed to be done."

Gabriela interrupted, "Well then why couldn't somebody from the military have done it? David should never have had to be the one!" Her bitterness and fear still showed.

General Greene looked down at his spotlessly shined shoes. "I very much wish we could have."

David saw that Greene was embarrassed. He could tell that the military man in front of him would have given his life to do what David had done. He felt sorry for him. "You know, our country was founded by citizen soldiers. Maybe this isn't such a bad thing."

"I just wish I could have been that citizen." Greene replied.

"Does the President know?" Gabriela asked.

"No, as I said, just a handful of very closed mouthed generals. I'll tell the President if you want me to."

David was quick to say, "No...So what is the explanation?"

"We aren't giving one. We are saying it was some kind of internal explosion. Obviously there were no missiles fired at it or bombs dropped on it. And at the time it was up at about 50,000 feet. Also, there was no record of the shuttle picking up anyone or taking anyone down off the ship. As far as any records or data show, you were never there."

David nodded, "Good! I have destroyed any proof that I was there. There was no interview as far as I'm concerned."

"That's how it will be then," General Greene declared. Then he looked over at Gabriela and smiled, "I'm told I should congratulate you, too. Or I should say congratulations to the two of you – soon to be three."

Gabriela gave her first real smile since he had arrived, "Thank you General, but first there has to be a wedding! Which by the way, we would love it if you could come."

"I'd be honored," General Greene replied.

# EPILOGUE

## One year later

It would be nice to say that Earth #310 took a pause and breathed deeply and found a better geopolitical balance point where peoples everywhere could go about their lives in greater security, peace and prosperity. And to some degree that was true for a short period of time. The message of what had happened on Earth #309 was not lost on world leaders. Iran limited its sanctioning of terrorism and was less vocal in its condemnation of Israel. Russia didn't launch any new invasions of its old Soviet Union territory. No foreign embassies were bombed.

Other geopolitical activities were not so benign. China continued to increase its military expenditures. Japan's New Nationalist Party took political control and the first thing Akira Watanabe did was to change Japan's Constitution so that it was no longer limited in its war making capabilities. In truth, all the major powers added to their war making capabilities by authorizing extensive research and development of advanced weaponry using Participatory Physics.

The United States not only led in that effort but also took the lead in planning an expedition to Other Earths. General Carl Greene was awarded his 4th Star and was put in charge of that effort. He recruited Brigadier Mark Randall to join his team and Randall put off his retirement.

David and Gabriela were married and after a very easy pregnancy, Gabriela gave birth to a beautiful 9 pound baby boy. David's articles were in very high demand and he was working on a book. The three of them spent a lot of time on Pirate's Cay where they continued with their meditation exercises, talked Physics with Planck and his team and visited with Plato and Catherine Ozawa who were living together.

Planck and Catherine Ozawa patented their Mentalization Amplifier. Planck and Megan Baxter were still dating with Megan pushing to get married while Planck had commitment issues. Planck did his best to hide-out from his global celebrity while Megan worked to increase it.

People everywhere were trying to figure out what Participatory Physics could do for them. The Captain and crew of The Lucky Dragon fully understood Participatory Physics and used the ability to continue with their mission. They did so quietly and relentlessly.

As it happens, during the whole of the year not a single hurricane or typhoon caused any extensive damage as a result of hitting any large populated area.

But nothing had changed really.

NOT THE END

CPSIA information can be obtained
at www.ICGtesting.com
Printed in the USA
BVHW030535180223
658665BV00001B/137